PRAISE FOR J. LINCOLN

DEAD SOULS

"Darkly entertaining. Perfectly written. Fans of Chuck Palahniuk, meet your new favorite author."

—**Ania Ahlborn, bestselling author of** *Brother*

"Wickedly entertaining."

—*The New York Times*

"Whether you call it grisly horror or macabre fiction, this book is one of the scariest and best to come down the pike in ages. The characters are difficult but compelling, and the writing is seamless. The narrative twists and turns are reminiscent of Dean Koontz or Stephen King at their finest."

—*Publishers Weekly* (starred review)

"An uninhibited thriller with a dash of social commentary where the devil is in the details . . . A wild, well-written novel that fuels suspicions about what might be going on in our oh-so-unbalanced world."

—*Kirkus Reviews*

"Brilliantly written. Gritty horror, heart-wrenching suspense, and impactful prose."

—*Cemetery Dance*

POE

"A delightful, bravura piece of gothic pop . . . there's a literate edge to the pyrotechnics that makes for an unlikely and welcome marriage between the spook story and literature of altogether less ectoplasmic substance."

—*Publishers Weekly*

"Hitting the high notes of multiple genres, [Fenn's] talent is wicked raw and proudly untamed. [We] can't wait to see what comes next."

—**Bloody-Disgusting.com**

"J. Lincoln Fenn's *Poe* is a shining display of humorous morbid entertainment. With a thrilling mystery, Fenn takes dark themes and gives us a witty novel with ties to history and magic. Suspense and intrigue are the name of the game."

—**Literary Escapism**

"Bowled over by *Poe* . . . The novel jumps into my own top five of my best novels of [the year] and is nipping at the heels of number one. I highly recommend this to anyone who likes great, well-paced fiction."

—**The Novel Pursuit**

THE
NIGHTMARCHERS

Also available from
J. LINCOLN FENN

Dead Souls

Poe

THE
NIGHTMARCHERS

A NOVEL

J. LINCOLN FENN

G

GALLERY BOOKS

NEW YORK LONDON TORONTO SYDNEY NEW DELHI

G

Gallery Books
An Imprint of Simon & Schuster, LLC
1230 Avenue of the Americas
New York, NY 10020

First Gallery Books trade paperback edition October 2024

GALLERY BOOKS and colophon are registered trademarks of
Simon & Schuster, LLC

Simon & Schuster: Celebrating 100 Years of Publishing in 2024

For information about special discounts for bulk purchases, please contact
Simon & Schuster Special Sales at 1-866-506-1949 or
business@simonandschuster.com.

The Simon & Schuster Speakers Bureau can bring authors to your live event. For
more information or to book an event, contact the Simon & Schuster Speakers
Bureau at 1-866-248-3049 or visit our website at www.simonspeakers.com.

Interior design by Erika R. Genova

Manufactured in the United States of America

1   3   5   7   9   10   8   6   4   2

Library of Congress Cataloging-in-Publication Data is available

ISBN 978-1-5011-1095-5
ISBN 978-1-5011-1096-2 (ebook)

For the little girl who used to play in the woods.

There is no coming to consciousness without pain.
—*Carl Jung*

Show me your garden and I shall tell you what you are.
—*Alfred Austin*

PROLOGUE

THE LETTERS

April 3, 1939

It was a longer journey than I'd expected (I did not, as you'd rightly predicted, Liddy, find my sea legs), and you can imagine with what trepidation I boarded the prop plane for the final leg, but after a few heart-pounding bumps I made the decision that if it was my destiny to perish over an anonymous bit of Pacific, then so be it. At least I would be with Charles and Lila. I know my thoughts are not supposed to bend that way, but they do.

You will be happy to know that my destiny proved otherwise. The small plane managed to land on a long stretch of cleared sugarcane, the dirt runway rutted by prior takeoffs. As promised, I was met by Reverend Palmer, a pale, reedy man with thinning blond hair, and a doe-eyed girl of ten or twelve who I assumed was his daughter. Quite an odd-looking creature, with green eyes so light as to be almost gray, and white-blond hair, a strange contrast to her deeply bronzed skin. She said nothing and simply stared. While the Reverend is mildly pleasant, I don't expect much from him in the way of scintillating conversation either. But then, the companionship of an intellectual equal was not what I came here for.

It is quiet. Do you remember those early mornings in Devon? I have never found so much peace in my life as during those predawn walks through our stolid British woods, nothing stirring, just the silent company of the birch, the maples, the alder, and the elms. I think there is something about the combination of sea, wind, and palm trees that may prove to be a balm for my troubled soul. At the very least, I can absorb myself in my work. The good Reverend had a very quaint plantation cottage readied for me, complete with gingham curtains, and it took some time for me to explain to his satisfaction that I had no intention of living "in town," that for my studies I needed to be immersed in the natural environment. Thank you, Liddy, for shipping my tent; the timing was, of course, spot-on.

I will write more when I am settled in.

April 14, 1939

I have a feeling I am legendary in the annals of ignorant foreigners, at least among the local people. After much labor and what appeared to be dissuasive and heated commentary in a language I am ignorant of, I was led to a spot in the rain forest close to a natural waterfall, yet still within walking distance of the settlement. Your concern that I would be surrounded by lepers is quite amusing. I have it on the authority of none other than the Reverend himself that they are all settled on the distant isle of Molokai, and in fact I have never encountered a healthier community. All here almost glow with it. Kapu's fresh air, sun, and food, no doubt.

The entire time they were setting up my tent and readying my camp stove, etc., my fingers were simply itching to start sketching. Already on the brief hike I have spotted *Touchardia latifolia, Pipturus albidus,* and *Asplenium nidus,* but there is also a dizzying array of species that I suspect have never been documented. No doubt I could easily fill three sketchbooks within the first month.

Your specimen jars arrived intact, save for two that were cracked and beyond saving. I can already hear you fretting I will be so distracted by the variety of flora that I will forget my fauna obligations. Fear not—I have it on good authority that the centipedes in this part of the world are as long as your hand and easy to find. I plan to keep you and your microscope busy for the next year.

I have more than enough canned goods to last a month, but the Reverend has promised to send fresh fruit, meat, and fish once a week (although I fear that this is based more on old-fashioned nosiness than on Christian charity). I reluctantly agreed. One brief, weekly visit is a small price for any woman to pay for solitude.

I have been duly warned by the Reverend about the dangers of flash floods. The patch of blue sky above can be completely sunny and bright, but at the higher altitudes of the volcano peak, clouds can drop immense quantities of rain in a very short period of time. More than a few foreigners (or **haoles,** as we're called by the locals) have met their death this way. It is not an easy, or welcome, task to find their bodies.

The doe-eyed little girl appeared as if she had something to say on the subject when the Reverend peremptorily cut her off. Even in Eden, it appears Eve must learn her place.

No, I did not open the letter from Father. I used it as kindling for a small fire to warm a can of beans. At least it served a purpose. You can tell him what you will.

April 21, 1939

Oh Liddy, why does my mind perseverate on that which it can never alter? It is night now. Night in the rain forest is a very different thing than night in Devon—the darkness is as thick as mud, and every sound triggers a question.

What's that buzzing? What's that snuffling? What's that scratching? When a coconut falls to the ground, there's a loud crash as it falls through the foliage before it lands with a dull thud in the dirt, and some of the palms are so large that when a frond drops, it sounds like a tree being felled. There are two geckos right now clinging to the fabric ceiling of my tent, watching for insects, and they are loud companions, chirping to each other some kind of unintelligible news. I would chase them out, but when they're startled, their tails fall off and wriggle on the ground for a good minute after. It's a sight that is nauseating, unnerving, and yet strangely captivating. Of course I've saved one in a jar for you; it sits on the table as I write this, literally burning the midnight oil.

I find it almost impossible to sleep.

I had a visit this afternoon from the doe-eyed girl, who, it turns out, is very curious about my presence and quite capable of speech. I highly doubt she had permission, which of course gained her my immediate respect. Her name is Agnes. There is something wild about her, untamed. She wears her cotton dress indifferently, as if it's just there to humor propriety but serves no real purpose, and I was surprised to see that she had hiked through the jungle barefoot.

She told me that geckos are considered sacred by the natives, revered for their ability to change colors and regenerate their tails. According to legend, they house the spirits of the recently deceased, and are guardians of their still-living family members.

Are these geckos really Charles and little Lila, then, watching out for me? It's a laughable idea in the daytime, but at night, shadows seem pregnant with other meanings.

———————

May 1, 1939

Two weeks with no trade winds have made me a cranky girl, although my work, frankly, has never been finer. Half a sketchbook is already completely penciled in, and I have occasionally run across an unfamiliar plant that simply takes my breath away. The *Capparis sandwichiana*, called *maiapilo* in the native tongue, looks like an orchid with wild, protruding stamen, calling to mind the tendrils of something oceanic, a jellyfish perhaps. And yesterday I was nearly startled out of my skin when I saw what appeared to be a twig start crawling toward me, a ferocious cousin of the Phasmida family—with a nasty bite, I unfortunately discovered, after claiming it for your specimen jar.

I am even becoming somewhat proficient in the use of a machete (you are laughing now, I know). But it truly is almost impossible to walk five feet without clearing vegetation, and the going is even harder when it rains—the mud sucks at your feet as if it can, and will, pull you into Hades itself.

And I now have an assistant of sorts. Agnes has become a regular visitor. Her unannounced appearances were at first a grating distraction (I have come all this way, after all, to lose myself in research), but she has proven to be a useful guide and doesn't have that intolerable, attention-seeking yet demure behavior exhibited by most "city" girls her age. Better still, she's genuinely inquisitive and doesn't mind long stretches of silence when I am particularly absorbed.

Her story, though, is also a sad one. She is apparently an orphan (I did not pry), marooned in the care of Reverend Palmer, whose primary interest has been the state of her soul and not her education. Tutors are peripatetic and often find paradise not to their liking once they discover it requires pumping one's water and rough, outdoor latrines.

She has a remarkable knowledge of the local flora and, if I provide a rough sketch, can usually lead me right to a living example. Agnes tells me that she often trails along with the natives during their foraging expeditions, and has learned of medicinal properties that I have found in no book. The leaves of the *Adenostemma lavenia* are commonly used to reduce fever. The buds of hibiscus flowers are crushed to treat cuts and injuries. I am taking copious notes. Of course nothing is ever free, even here in paradise, but the price she's exacting is simply that I tell her about England, or a fairy tale, or recite some poetry. If this child was close to a library I wonder if she'd ever set foot outside again—her appetite for the world beyond the island is that voracious. "Hansel and Gretel" is a particular favorite.

I have shared some of my own story with her, but not all. I daresay she has more than enough material for nightmares without it, but I wonder if somehow this isn't some kind of island for lost souls, a tropical purgatory. There are times, Liddy, when I'm alone in the middle of the jungle yet I sense I'm being watched, as if the leaves are eyes and the trees mark my progress. That some kind of judgment will soon be rendered.

Silly, I know. I'm sure a good night's sleep will put all to right.

May 3, 1939

For two days, I have not been able to keep food down. Not uncommon in the tropics, but it makes one feel like a detective in one of those mystery novels you always detested. Who, or what, is the culprit? It could be an insect bite, or perhaps there was some unseen mold on the pineapple Agnes brought from the village, or I might have brushed a hand against something mildly poisonous and then wiped my mouth with it. I am surrounded by suspects, none with a good alibi.

Agnes has been a dear. She promised to hide my condition from the Reverend, because we are both quite certain he would insist on my return to the cottage, which would greatly limit both our freedoms. Apparently he believed her story that I am schooling her until the next tutor arrives—not exactly a truth but not exactly a lie either. A pleasant, ambiguous middle ground.

In spite of my intestinal revolt, yesterday I managed to forge deeper into the jungle than I ever have before, thanks in part to the discovery of a low wall made of lava rocks that served as a passable road. The wall was marked by two crossed staffs, each capped with a white ball—a typical marker of an area deemed *pahu kapu:* sacred, or forbidden, Agnes tells me. Entering this remote area was like walking back in time and seeing what might have happened if evolution had taken a different route. Flora looks like fauna, fauna looks like flora, and encountering the fantastical is becoming commonplace. I happened upon a stretch of forest floor that appeared to be *breathing,* and thought perhaps I'd stumbled across a sleeping giant, but on closer inspection I found that the roots of an old stump had detached from their moorings, and the wind was lifting the root system, which was entwined with a strange, gossamer kind of white fungus. Each exhale sent out a fine white mist of pollen, or spores, I'm not sure.

Farther on, I found a line of weaver ants trudging through the undergrowth and I thought they might lead me to an interesting nest, but instead they were keen on their own destruction, dutifully following a trail that led to the lip of a large purple pitcher plant. I watched them perish, one after another after another. Utterly fascinating. Kapu could easily keep a battalion of scientists busy for the next decade. Send more jars as soon as you can.

I admit I am starting to be a little concerned about my general state of sleeplessness. The moist, tropical heat clings to me like a second skin, and the long, dark nights creep into the farthest corners of my mind. I turn this way on my cot, that way, and I can't help but think, what if, what if, what if?

There is no use in such thoughts, but that doesn't deter them in the slightest.

May 4, 1939

Alas, I long to return to my explorations, but today a fierce headache has been added to my list of woes, so I am relenting and trying to rest (oh, to have come so far to be deterred by a microorganism). Agnes has been trying to distract me with the stories and local superstitions, which remain tightly rooted in the island culture despite the best ministrations of the Reverend and his threats of eternal damnation.

My favorite is the tale that explains the curious appearance of scaevola, or naupaka, a small white flower that looks like it was torn in half. Apparently, star-crossed lovers are popular the world over, and the shape of the flower is the result of a thwarted love between a beautiful princess and Kaui, a commoner. Of course, they were unable to marry due to their respective stations in life, so when they parted for the last time, the princess tore the flower in half and it has grown that way ever since.

I teasingly asked Agnes about the nightmarchers then, but at that she became strangely quiet. The pilot of the plane had joked about it before our departure—*Beware the nightmarchers*, he'd said in a theatrical tone—and I was surprised that this superstition seemed to hold weight with my ordinarily very practical young assistant.

After a reluctant moment, she told me that the nightmarchers are reputedly the ghosts of ancient ancestor warriors, the "Spirit Ranks," and that on moonless nights they rise from their burial sites before sunrise or sunset, marching to sacred places. If you stumble across their path and look upon them, you're condemned to join the ranks too, marching with them for all eternity. Instead, you should throw yourself on the ground and close your eyes until they pass.

"My goodness," I said, trying to lighten the mood. "Just the other day I followed a mysterious trail and thought the worst that could happen was getting gored by a boar. I had no idea the true peril I was in."

I was amazed to see actual tears bead in Agnes's eyes and apologized if I had offended her in some way, thinking that perhaps she was like a child after all, believing in the confabulations of leprechauns, bogeymen, and Santa Claus.

But then she explained why this story disturbed her so. One moonless night, her little brother (the first time she'd mentioned him) had complained to her about a noise. He'd been woken up by the sound of a conch shell blowing and what he thought was an army passing by, chanting. Agnes didn't believe him, of course, told him that he was being a baby and imagining things. But the next night Agnes heard it too. Her brother woke her father up and together they went outside.

They've never been seen again. Their footprints were found in the mud, walking into the jungle, joined by other, unknown footprints.

A chilling tale indeed, and one that struck particularly close to home, the sudden, tragic loss of a man, a child. A part of me understands her conviction. Calamity requires an explanation, no matter how bizarre, if we are to live with ourselves. Perhaps that's why I can't sleep. I have no such measure for what I've done.

May 4, 1939

You will think a fever has taken hold of me, but I tell you, Liddy, in all seriousness, tonight I heard Lila laughing.

May 5, 1939

The obligatory visit from the kind Reverend today nearly ended in disaster. "You look pale," he said, "and thin. I don't know if this isolation agrees with you. The jungle can do tricky things to the Western mind that lacks spiritual protection. I have seen it before and have no wish to see it again."

I replied with more cheer than I possessed that I was fine, better than fine, I was completely fulfilled by my work and eating more than I ever had in my life. The long, healthy walks explained my thinner frame, and my pallor was the result of the lack of sunlight that made its way to the rain forest floor.

"My mother always admonished me that I spent far too much time in the sun. So horrible for one's complexion," I said in the simpering tone expected of women.

Agnes had to suppress a giggle with a faked sneeze.

She helped me pull the visit off, too, jumping up to pour the tea so my trembling hands wouldn't be noticeable, and she even slipped some extra honey into my cup, which gave me a slight energetic boost. The Reverend didn't look completely convinced as he departed, but the important part is that he *departed*, with only a mild chastisement that a short hike down to the chapel on Sundays was a small price to pay for one's immortal soul.

As if I had one to lose anymore.

I expect to feel much better tomorrow. Agnes informed me that there is nothing more diabolical than a stomach flu passing through the inhabitants, picked up by one of the natives when he traveled to the far side of the island to purchase dry goods. She left me with a tincture, which she said should calm my stomach and nerves.

She is a perceptive one, that Agnes. I had no idea she knew my nerves were on edge.

May 6, 1939

Fecund. It's a word I find myself perseverating on. So much *life* here, pressing and reaching into every nook and cranny with a curious intent.

The air is pregnant with the scent of plumeria, with water that drips down the sides of my tent, with salt from the ocean that rusts my eyeglasses. Vegetation creeps up, around, and through the bamboo tent platform, mildew encroaches on the good English muslin of the tent, and today, when I picked up my pencil, I found a tiny jelly fungus sprouting from its tip. I sometimes wonder, when I do manage a fitful sleep, if I'll end up entombed by nettles, like Sleeping Beauty.

This morning, I wiped the sweat from my brow with a cold rag and forced myself to drink a sludge of thick coffee with an indecent amount of sugar, determined to venture even deeper into the island's sunless, interior country, flu be damned. You would not have approved, but then you are so very, very far away and I am left to my own devices.

While I've acclimated to the sense of being watched, I'd swear on my life that the leaves whisper rhymes—*clink, rink, slink*—and sometimes I play at a response—*shrink, mink, wink*—just to help pass the time. I managed to make it all the way to the sleeping giant and then through an eerie, dark bamboo forest where the whispering leaves gave way to the soft clicks of bamboo stalks hitting bamboo stalks, when I found a steep path down to a small cove. The oddest-looking banyan trees rose up the steep slope above it, with red flowers sprouting from their supple limbs. These blooms smelled like rotting corpses. Of course I had to collect one, and I did.

A few moments after I'd placed it in a jar, I was struck motionless; like Lot's wife, I was frozen stiff, rooted in place. A panic started to rise, but for some reason it didn't concern me; it was as though the panic was being experienced by someone, *something* else. Time passed. Shadows lengthened. Thoughts tumbled through my mind, but they weren't *my* thoughts exactly. I was on a ship, I was in a church, I was diving underwater with a spear in my hand. I was a mother, father, sister, brother. I had names, I was nameless. It was almost like those walks in Devon, when the burden of self seemed to lift off like dew evaporating in the morning sun.

I must have lost consciousness, because the next thing I knew, I was lying on the rocky earth and Agnes was cradling my head, some kind of bitter plant compote in my mouth. I spat it out, along with coffee-flavored vomit, and with her help managed to waveringly get back on my feet.

She impulsively grabbed me around the waist and clung with more emotion I'd thought her capable of. "Never leave, never leave, never leave," she said.

Which is funny, and not. Because it was one of the things I thought I'd heard the leaves whispering too.

———————————

MAY 9, 1939

I should have burned with them, Charles and Lila. Maybe that's why I'm burning now, the nerves beneath my skin itching like at any moment maggots will burst forth, having begun to eat me from the inside out. I would welcome that now, Liddy, I really would. My mind races, incessantly rhyming words in a form of madness—die, lie, my; rose, toes, nose—like each word is a key that's being tried in a lock that will open all the castle's secrets.

Was it our sin, or Father's? Annabelle was smart to run as soon as she could. I know you think it vulgar to speak of such things, but I am ill, and free of your dour consternation. Mother chose to lose her mind, a neat escape. I wonder if perhaps God is punishing me, punishing us all. I can tell you quite honestly that in the face of death, the bright light of science is no match for a religious mythos of good and evil, right and wrong. Suddenly one feels the desperate need for there to be a heaven, for there to be an after. Which of course means there's a hell, too.

Something marvelously bizarre happened to the gecko tail in the specimen jar. I'm afraid to write it down, lest you think I have gone mad.

Was Agnes here today? No, she was, I remember her wiping my brow and pouring some tea. Tea is all I can stomach these days, and I am weak now, so weak that I'm not certain I could make it to the settlement even if I wanted to (which I still don't—I think freedom is denied women because we would enjoy it too much). But my condition must be terrible, because it has alarmed even Agnes. Thankfully there is a doctor in town, paying his annual visit, and she will return with him tomorrow. I must cling to that word, *tomorrow.*

I want to die, but I don't. Isn't that a strange thing? The will to live has an ornery mind of its own; I can feel its tentacles pulling me into this second, the next second, the second after. The corporeal body has no desire to join the moldering dirt, but it is such a burden, our physical form, that it's a wonder we procreate and perpetuate the suffering.

Lila. I heard her laughing again not too long ago. I managed to pull myself up and lurch outside the tent, and for the briefest moment I thought I saw them, Lila holding her father's hand, standing just beyond the sphere of light cast by my oil lamp and watching me from within the protection of dense foliage. I wanted so much to call out to her, to *them,* to invite them in and tell them *I'm sorry, I'm sorry, I'm sorry,* but all I could do was bend over and purge the little that was in my stomach. Then they were gone, and I could viscerally feel it again . . . *that* moment.

Oh Liddy, what kind of insane impulse was it to wake to a rampant fire licking the walls, the ceiling, and run from the house, leaving one's child and husband behind? I didn't even realize I was outside until I'd reached the oak tree, but by then the door was engulfed in flames. Where was that protective instinct mothers are so famous for? You know they found Charles with Lila, cradling her small body in his arms? I didn't have the heart to separate them in death, and now they share the same coffin, although there are two stones to mark their passing. *Four years.* For four years I was a mother. Until I wasn't.

One of the investigators asked if I heard screams, an answer I will take to my grave.

I am going to finish up the rest of Agnes's tincture, and try to settle myself down. That is what my ornery "will to live" compels me to do, but I blame it, I blame it fiercely.

———————

[ILLEGIBLE], 1939

Do not be sad for me, my dear sister. Do not weep. Today I am happy. Today I am free. I *heard* it, Liddy, I heard the conch shell and the sound of the nightmarchers. I stumbled out of my tent and through the thick brush until I got to the gulch where the waterfall drops into a deep pool. They were there, a line of warriors tramping along the river's edge, thousands strong, and then I saw *them*, my Charles and my Lila, she was riding along on Charles's back as she loved to do, and then Lila gave me a loving wave as they disappeared into the forest. I am leaving now to join them; I will spend eternity marching in their ranks because I have looked, Liddy, I have finally **looked**, and my ornery will to live has finally been vanquished. It is gone. I leave you this brief note to compel your heart not to grieve. Tell Father I don't blame him anymore, that it isn't madness we suffer from. It's liberation.

And our deaths, our deaths are not the end of anything.

———————

MAY 31, 1939

Dear Miss Greer,

Enclosed are the letters we discovered in your late sister's encampment. I hope you find them a source of comfort, not distress, in what must be a difficult time for you and your family. I feel it is my Christian duty to perhaps offer some context for their troubling content.

My ward, Agnes, did visit Irene on a few occasions, but certainly not with the frequency described herein, and to my knowledge, Agnes has no memory of her kin. We discovered Agnes here, practically feral, but through our dedicated ministrations she has evolved into a dutiful daughter and a good Christian. I can't fathom why she would make up such a tale about a brother and father, and suspect this was part of your sister's deteriorating state of mental health. When I last saw her, I became so concerned that I sent for a doctor to come and pay her a visit. Sadly, he arrived too late to save her life.

I hope you don't mind, but I showed him the letters to see if we could determine what could have caused such a delusion. After examining the samples of flora your sister had collected, he noted a specimen of a fungus commonly known here as the corpse flower, the spores of which can cause psychosis, paranoid delusions, and hallucinations. To the untrained eye it simply looks like a harmless orchid, though it has a revolting stench. This is what we presume occurred. There indeed was a procession that passed by her camp near sunset—we had just baptized our newest member in the waterfall and were returning to the village; in her confused state of mind, she took the members of our group to be "the nightmarchers" and her own dearly departed husband and daughter. It was agreed by all that she was not in her right mind when she fell from the cliff, and she has been given a proper Christian burial in our small cemetery. Enclosed is a brooch Agnes made with Irene's hair. She thought you might take some comfort from a memorial keepsake.

I wish I could say that such tragedies are rare, but two years ago I lost my own beloved wife. She'd been missing for three days when we found her body washed up on shore, the apparent victim of a flash flood. We have suffered the loss of two tutors as well, the first a young woman of promise who sadly did take her own life after suffering from some kind of strange fugue, and then a very sensible woman from Fiji with exceptional references who became catatonic before disappearing entirely one morning, never to be seen again. There is no paradise without its serpent, although, with true faith, death has no sting, since we are simply reunited with our brethren in the holy land of Heaven.

I understand and admire your desire to come and personally collect your sister's remains, but the good doctor is concerned about the possible spread of contagion. In addition to the fever your sister described, there were strange lesions on her skin, and we recently discovered that some of the natives had smuggled relatives from the leper colony on Molokai. They earnestly believe that the spirit of this island can heal any disease, even one as vile and incurable as Hansen's. Thus we are in a state of quarantine until our officials decide how to proceed next.

I fear not the future. God's love for us is great. I feel it here on this island more strongly than I ever felt it in the paved and genteel streets of England. It is embedded in every leaf, every root, every tree limb that reaches for the sky. Know your sister rests well in it.

Praise be to God,
Reverend Waldo Palmer
Church of Eternal Light

#NDC DEV ORG HUB

01:12:01	<isir528>	is lilith primed?
01:12:05	<bai908>	yes and no. there's a hitch. exhibit is gone.
01:12:16	<isir528>	the fuck? gone? explain gone.
01:12:24	<bai908>	gone as in someone leaked something they shouldn't have, and it was stolen.
01:12:43	<isir528>	leak? what leak?
01:12:47	<bai908>	you tell me.
01:12:51	<isir528>	you're not laying that blame here, are you? cause that would be some chickenshit excuse.
01:13:13	<bai908>	transference will have to be in theater.
01:13:23	<isir528>	jesus h. christ, we did not sign up for that.
01:13:34	<bai908>	we'll send a specialist.
01:13:40	<isir528>	that was not the deal.
01:13:46	<bai908>	you'll need to close loose ends after.
01:13:56	<isir528>	not. the. deal.
01:14:01	<bai908>	extra 400k in your account first thing a.m.
01:14:13	<isir528>	goddammit. this fucking sucks.
01:14:22	<bai908>	pleasure doing business with you too.
01:14:33		--> **bai908** has quit

ONE

SHE DOESN'T NOTICE THE letter at first. Buried in the pile of mail threatening to become a paper avalanche, it takes her a good minute to pull all of it out of her mailbox, which resists her mightily, like there's something on the other side trying to pull her in.

And these days it takes a good two glasses of cheap wine—from a box with a spout, all she can afford—for Julia to even work up the nerve to place that tiny mailbox key in the tiny metal lock. Letters are enemies. Letters are black ravens, harbingers of bad news, and if she doesn't look at the mail she can pretend it isn't there. Not the bills stamped red and URGENT, not the letters from her husband's—her *ex-husband's*—attorney, not the blocky envelopes from the IRS marked CERTIFIED DELIVERY, TIME-SENSITIVE. She would have put it off for another day, maybe two, but the electricity in her claustrophobic studio apartment has been cut off, the temperature's over a hundred, and she's too ashamed to call for the minimum balance.

You reap what you sow. Something her mother always said that never really made sense to Julia. Like her father leaving them, for instance. Had her mother sown that seed? Was it really her mother's fault that he'd packed a bag after that explosive fight and then vanished for the rest of their lives?

Was it her fault Ethan had deserted her? *Desertion.* A perfect word—she pictures a WWII soldier abandoning a post under fire, running to save himself while the rest of his troop is slaughtered. The film of sweat above his lip, his boots sinking into a French bog.

A barking dog startles her. It's inside one of the ground-floor apartments, wet nose pressed against the mosquito screen of the window. She quickly wraps the mail in a Kmart flyer, tucks it all under her arm, and begins the long climb to the fifth floor—cement steps held aloft by a rusting metal frame that shivers when a freight truck passes by. There are cracks in the stucco walls. Occasional splatters of graffiti. Red scrawls that look like letters, the meaning incomprehensible.

She should get out more. *It's not good to be alone all the time.* That's what her therapist said when she could still afford the co-pay to see him. *Your divorce isn't the end of your life. You need to go on. For Evie.*

But it *was* the end of her life, and if there's another one out here for her, damn if she can find it. All she feels is suspended—between the past and the present, between the future that she wanted and the one she's living.

Maybe she'll end up like 216. John, she thinks his name was. Or Dan? Only met him once when she was moving in—thin and broken, with bloodshot eyes, a limp handshake and a softly spoken offer to take anything she didn't need off her hands. After that, his door was perpetually shut. After that, there was a piece of plywood nailed over the window.

After that, there'd been a smell.

She'd thought it was a dead rat in the walls, or maybe even a whole nest of them, because the smell had grown stronger, so bad she had to leave the windows open even with the air-conditioning on. Calls to the landlord went unanswered. Just as she was thinking about reporting a code violation, she came home one day from a fruitless job interview only to find a dumpster rolled up in the parking lot, men in hazmat-type suits and gas masks carting out junk from 216, a van marked BIO-KLEEN in the courtyard, some kind of pump with a hose connecting to the apartment's window.

Hoarder, one neighbor said.

Found him when they were spraying, said another. *Body just went and exploded when they tried to wheel him out.*

It took a while for the cleanup. Everything had to be replaced. And things that had been tossed in the dumpster, some of it made its way back into the complex. She'd watched one woman pull a floor lamp out of the detritus, a few splotches of God-knows-what on the lampshade. John/Dan's car—a clunky, rusting Oldsmobile with a year's worth of dried leaves stuck under the windshield wipers—eventually lost its tires. Then the hood, and most of the engine. Someone bashed the windshield, even cut out the leather from the seats before it was eventually towed away. A family moved into 216 not long after the fresh paint had dried. Probably thought they were getting a steal with all new appliances, countertops, and closet doors.

Finally she reaches her apartment and pulls out her key to unlock the security door. Ignores the scratches where attempts to force it open have failed.

Not that there's anything here worth stealing. Slim pickings. If she died alone in the apartment, they could probably just roll her up in a rug and rent it out the next day.

She steps inside. The smell of cigarette smoke and cat piss greets her, worked so deep into the brown carpet by the previous tenant that it still lingers one year later.

No, her place is just a dreary, small box with a view of a Del

Taco parking lot and a stretch of the southbound Los Angeles 405 freeway. Furniture so scarce as to be practically nonexistent. Blankets on the floor where her air mattress popped—can't afford a new one. Folding chair and TV-dinner tray for a table. An ugly gnome for a doorstop; it had been abandoned along with the folding chair by a neighbor who was moving out of state. Stack of library books in the corner, novels she picks up and then puts down again, realizing she hasn't read a word.

A Christmas tree ornament with Evie's picture hangs from the overhead fan blades. Something Evie made for her. The only thing Julia has left from her life before.

Her life before. A rambling Victorian in Palo Alto she'd bought with Ethan and spent years lovingly renovating.

Don't go there, Julia. Don't go there.

But where the hell else is she supposed to go? She closes her eyes, tries to concentrate on the sounds around her, the *here and now*, her therapist would say; she tries not to think how naively happy she was, bringing the Victorian back to life, or the layers of paint, stain, and grime she scraped and buffed out of the mahogany staircase. She tries not to think how much he probably got for it.

But then she does. *Another cool million at least. Enough for a year's worth of motions. Not that he was short of cash in the first place.*

Did he feel *anything* when he toured the realtor through the house, pointing out the vaulted ceilings she'd painted, the crystal chandelier she'd picked out, the oak floors she'd refurbished? Or was it by then just another object among all his other objects, an acquisition that had outlived its purpose, bereft of meaning?

It had been astonishing how cold he became, and how quickly. Like the person she thought she'd married was just a mask, a performance, until the real Ethan seeped through.

A baby cries. She tries to hold onto that sound, tries to land herself in the present. It's hot inside. God it's so un-fucking-believably hot inside. An oven. A furnace. A pyre.

Of course she'd signed the prenup. Of course she'd thought it'd last forever. *Idiot, idiot, idiot.* He'd had two divorces, but the exes weren't like her, he'd said. She was special, he'd said. *Unique.* Words never used to describe Julia Greer, not even remotely. *They were so superficial. Boring. Not like you. You're so smart, and funny, and clever.* At the time, a part of her—a huge part—had wanted to laugh it off, and maybe she would have if she hadn't just been spectacularly dumped from a five-year relationship. In her secret, wounded heart, it felt like some kind of vindication, this love from a man who was rich, and charming, and handsome. Everyone told her how lucky she was—they were incredulous, in fact, that she'd landed him.

Now, not so much.

Did I lock the door? Christ, no, she hadn't. What was she thinking? Someone could have followed her, someone could have . . .

Julia takes a breath, opens her eyes, and locks the door behind her—*dead bolt*, check, *chain*, check.

Next. Just think about next. She heads for the kitchen, where the refrigerator's hum is sadly absent, pink liquid oozing from the freezer—*goddamn, the ice cream*—then it's time for a quick bill sort on the kitchen counter, ordered by post date with the most recent on top. Ads and junk straight into the trash, letters from DOUGLAS CLARK, ATTORNEY AT LAW dropped into a drawer, which is quietly, ominously, filling with other, unopened envelopes. So many she can hardly close it.

Without thinking, she flips a light switch. Nothing, of course.

This is my life now. I can't believe this is my life now.

And it's true, she simply can't. Getting work again was harder than she'd expected—she'd let too many years slip, content to be the stay-at-home wife and mother, or that's what she'd told herself when Ethan had frowned on her particular beat. *Do you have to do investigative pieces? I* know *some of these people. It could make Christmas parties embarrassing.* The truth was probably—no, the truth *was*—that the entire experience had turned her head. She'd tossed aside her pragmatic, doggedly inquisitive self for the very things she'd always poked fun at. Playdates. Decoupage parties. Evenings at the opera while the requisite Stanford chemical engineering student/babysitter read stories to Evie in French. It was another strata, this world, a completely different atmosphere. She'd spent so many gritty years taking cracks at it, trying to find her way in through the air vent, talk her way past the doorman, to expose the concealed, ugly downside, that to suddenly be invited in through the front door, to watch the careful machinations of celebrities, politicians, CEOs, see true power move . . . well, it was breathtaking. So alluring to become, tangentially, a part of it.

And then the clock struck twelve. The carriage turned back into a pumpkin. And she was abruptly dumped back into her old life. Actually, far worse than her old life. Because now no one wanted real reporting anymore, just headlines to be outraged about, with as little substance as possible. All the editors she'd used to know had either wisely shifted to public relations firms or had just been laid off, working in whole other industries altogether. So now she pushes out pitches the way a castaway tosses bottles into the ocean, with about the same level of expectation. Maybe one day she won't have to cobble together freelance blog gigs, barely eking out an existence from week to week—"Thigh

Gaps to Die For," "The Puppy That's Besties with a Bear," "Worst Celebrity Selfies." Maybe one day she'll be able to afford an attorney to look through that drawer, to respond to the motions she subconsciously knows are being passed by the judge in her absence, building an impenetrable wall, brick by brick, between her and her daughter. Maybe one day she'll see Evie again.

But she doubts it. Not without a miracle, and she's not the miracle-believing kind. She couldn't even afford the plane ticket.

Is she thinking of me right now?

She remembers the last time she saw Evie, the funny, floppy wave she gave Julia with her six-year-old hand, trying to cheer *her* up; she remembers the moment Evie turned her back—small shoulders hunched and sad—then walked across the parking lot to Ethan's silver Mercedes. Somehow Julia managed to hold it together as Evie got in the car; she managed to stay upright, crack a smile, wave, even though her heart threatened to erupt from her chest. There was the purr of the engine, a soft fog of exhaust, and then the car slipped away, merged into traffic, disappeared. *Gone.* Gone on an airplane, gone five thousand miles away. Had Evie ever spent a night without her? Maybe a handful.

She'd seen news footage of women keening after a bomb exploded on their family homes in some distant country, faces twisted in anguish. She'd done the same in the parking lot after Evie was gone. A vocal register she never knew she was capable of. Her legs had given way. Arms had gone numb. Eventually someone called an ambulance. She doesn't remember much after, and lost time—a few days at least—before her fractured mind started to bind itself together again. Functional, but never the same. She doesn't think it would take much to send all the pieces careening off in different directions. At least she's poor enough to be on Medicaid, so the prescriptions are free.

Black spots threaten the corners of Julia's eyes, the kind that
warn of an impending migraine. She needs to unwind somehow.
The boxed wine in the fridge will be warm and it's practically
empty, but she might be able to get half a glass. *When taking this
medication, do not consume alcoholic beverages,* her yellow pill bottles say. It gives her a small sense of satisfaction to disobey them,
these little missives from the pharmaceutical companies, with
their little strike-out symbol over a martini glass. *Use caution
when operating a vehicle.*

As if that could be the worst of her problems, getting into a
car accident. What pill can she take to get her daughter back?

And that's when she sees it. A strange, pale blue envelope
dropped on the floor like it was wisely trying to escape. At first
she thinks it must have been put in her mailbox by mistake—the
paper's too nice—but it's her name and address written in shaky
blue cursive on the front (the sorters at the US Postal Service
can still read cursive?). A neat return address label in the corner,
the kind you can buy with your personal checks. DR. LYDIA
GREER.

God, Aunt Liddy? She's still alive? The woman must be ancient by now; the only time they'd met was well over twenty years
ago. Julia remembers a large, Spanish-style house in the Pasadena
hills, a wide grove of orange trees just beyond a Victorian greenhouse, and crystal bowls filled with candy in just about every
room. Her mother had instructed her not to play in the basement, which of course made it just too tempting. After venturing
down the creaky wooden stairs, she discovered rough-hewn
shelves filled with dusty jars, holding dead and dried insects,
strange, marvelous, and threatening. A range of faded moths
pinned on a velvet board, a thick bug the size of her hand curled
into a ball under a microscope, small stuffed birds with mean

glass eyes and molting feathers. Creatures that made appearances in her nightmares for years to come.

And something else, a bizarre shape under the stairs. What was it? It'd almost made her lose her mind; she remembers bolting up the stairs in a near panic. A sheet . . . there was a sheet, and the sound of something digging. She'd pictured it chasing her, snatching at her heels as she ran back up the stairs into the kitchen.

Don't let your imagination get the best of you. Something else her mother would say, frequently.

It wasn't her imagination, though, that had gotten the best of her in the end. Rather the lack of it. Because she'd never imagined being the third ex-wife.

For a moment, Julia hesitates before opening the letter. Wonders what new disaster looms on the horizon. But she tears it open anyway, a dare to the universe, or God, or whoever.

TWO

My dearest Julia,

I fear you won't remember me, since it has been so long since we last met—
you were still a young child then, but I remember your curious nature and
gifted you a black widow (your mother, I believe, frowned at the idea, but
a dead spider is a harmless spider, and girls are too frequently immersed in
dolls and dresses and other meaningless pursuits). I am your great-aunt,
sister to Annabelle, your mother's mother, and I have a proposition of sorts
that, I believe, merits your serious consideration.

Although it would be very American for me to just outright state my
intentions, I was raised in a time, and a country, when it was gauche to do
so, so instead I choose to defer to my more indirect upbringing. Would you
be so kind as to join me for tea? The orange blossoms are lovely, and I still
have enough land for beekeeping, so our honey is infused with their
flavor.

Ah, this is the problem with writing by hand. How ridiculous that
last sentence seems to me now, how easy it would be to backspace over it
on a computer and pretend it never existed. Who gives a damn about
honey? Pens force a commitment to all one's thoughts, no matter how
ridiculous, and my hands are too arthritic to throw my previous effort
away. Let me try again.

I apologize for our estrangement, because that's what it is. You
must have wondered why you visited so rarely (two or three times

maybe, all told), and I doubt your mother ever spoke much about her family. We pass on, generationally, not only our physical traits—color of eyes, etc.—but the sorrows of familial conflict. I was sorry to hear of her passing, and found out too late to properly express my condolences.

You see, when Annabelle married, she did so without my father's permission, and she was subsequently cut off from the family: shunned, so to speak. We had pretensions of nobility (although the money was gone, the crest remained), but I suspect it wasn't so much her elopement as the fact that she'd eloped with a Jew. Father, you see, was an advocate of eugenics and a good friend of Ernst Rüdin, and Annabelle was a free and open spirit, with more heart and compassion than the rest of us combined. My older sister, Irene, and I hoped he would eventually get over it, but he never did, and by the time we reached out to Annabelle, she was so hurt by our silence that she refused all our letters. Nothing poisons quite so well as rejection.

When your father left, I reached out to your mother, hoping to rekindle our relationship, and I was encouraged when she chose to revert to Annabelle's maiden name, Greer (that crest is so very alluring). Which is how you ended up in my house so long ago (I saw you, little sly one, creep past the door into the basement). But the damage was too great, the grudges too deeply set. And to be honest, the nurturing of emotions is not my strong suit. I inherited my father's fascination with genetics, and am much more comfortable developing a culture in a petri dish than developing a relationship. One reason why I am old, and alone. I was one of the first scientists to substantiate endosymbiotic theory, but unlike my single-cell friends, long-term interaction with any species is beyond my ken.

That said, there is nothing like the whisper of death to alter one's perspective. The things we bury have a way of digging their way out— they creep and clutch and bloom in our dark, shadowy places. I find myself haunted by things left unsaid, undone, by ghosts looking for a place to finally rest. I will explain more should you decide to come.

Perhaps it's too late, and, like your mother, you want nothing to do with a decrepit old woman teetering on the brink of annihilation. So now, because I'm desperate, I will be gauche. I understand you are facing dire financial challenges, while I am sitting on a nice fortune, with no heir in sight. Money is one of those things that have little value when you're too old to enjoy them. It's just numbers on a computer screen, it's ash in the mouth. You, however, could put it to good use.

I do hope you'll come for a visit. You are my last of last resorts.

Sincerely,

Dr. Lydia Greer

It's hard to know what to make of the letter. Mysteries hinted at, a jumble of scientific jargon and family history, and an endnote her great-aunt must have surely known would strike a chord—a fortune in play. Just the thought of it makes her heart beat a little faster, makes it hard to sift through the rest.

First things first. She remembers an epic fight between her parents before the visit to Aunt Liddy, something about braces, what they cost, how her father was doing the best he could, but *money doesn't grow on trees*. Of course somewhere simmering below that was the opinion her father, and many in her school and neighborhood, shared. Julia would never be a great beauty. Not with her crooked nose, somber gray eyes, and wild, curly brown hair that seemed to have a will of its own. Straight teeth would be a poor investment.

You're so clever, they would say. *You're so smart*.

Never *You're so pretty*.

Which was liberating, in a certain way. While girls her age experimented with different shades of blush, she experimented with different genres in the library, immersing herself in distant planets, alien cultures, swords waiting in stones for the right king to lay hands on them. She never tried to tame her frizzy, curly, rebellious brown hair, something that always made her Palo Alto hairdresser suck her teeth whenever Julia turned down the suggestion to straighten it. She never felt the need to look ten years younger, like the women in Ethan's circle. Over the years, she watched them voluntarily get cut and stretched and plumped into strange, mutant beings, until they barely resembled themselves, or women at all. *Frankenfemmes*, she'd whisper to Ethan at parties, and he'd laugh into his napkin.

No, it was her mother who had tried to fight reality, who'd ironed a dress (a dress!) and trundled her off to her great-aunt for inspection. Shortly afterward, Julia had gotten the braces, not that they'd done much good because her teeth had started to drift again in her twenties.

I love your crooked teeth, Ethan would say. Until he didn't.

What harm could there be in tea? In hearing Aunt Liddy out?

Still, something about it makes her uneasy. Other memories surface. Her mother's stiffness as they entered the mansion, the forced smile when Aunt Liddy extended a clawlike hand, something glazed and hard in her eyes. The foyer was massive—the size of their entire two-bedroom apartment—with gleaming marble floors covered by a soft Oriental carpet. A palace straight out of *Grimm's Fairy Tales*. Aunt Liddy told her to run along and explore, so she did, ditching her patent leather Mary Janes as soon as her mother and Aunt Liddy disappeared into the library, closing the oak doors behind them.

She found the vanilla cake in the kitchen first, cooling on the counter, and scooped a handful out with her fingers. Then she found the billiard room and dropped crumbs on the table as she rolled the balls around, trying to see how hard she could hit them. Then she found a small study with a desk and red carpeting, records stacked on shelving and an old turntable. Individually wrapped caramels in a crystal bowl; she filled her pockets with them. Some kind of servant checked in on her, asked if she'd like some lemonade. Julia felt a small amount of shame, since her mouth was covered with stolen crumbs, her pockets near bursting with candy. So she said no, although she would have loved a glass. When the servant headed in the direction of the library, Julia slipped back into the kitchen to see if she could get the lemonade for herself.

That's when she saw the basement door. Remembered her mother's warning. But she was angry at her mother—she didn't want thick metal covering her teeth; braces would only make her look even more awkward. And she'd always had that curious streak. She imagined herself a great explorer about to descend into an Egyptian tomb, took a broom with her to fight off the mummies.

So she opened the door. Felt the thrill of breaking a rule that could have no real consequence. Because, deep down, she knew there was no such thing as monsters.

Afterward, her mother chastised her for breaking the broom, which she doesn't remember doing. She doesn't remember going back to her great-aunt's again either, although the letter in her hand says she did.

But then, her parents' families were always a mystery. Once she'd overheard her mother on the phone, something about Annabelle—a divorce, a stint in a mental hospital, a suicide. Her father's side of the family wasn't much clearer. There were occasional references to cousins in New Jersey, and when her father was killed in a car accident—drunk driving, and oh, used to such great effect against her in court: *Your Honor, there's a family history*—none of his relatives showed up for his funeral.

At the time she hadn't understood why her mother had changed their names back to Greer—it felt somehow adulterous, like she was cheating on her father's memory. But after her divorce from Ethan, Julia understood. Just the name alone, spoken daily, was self-flagellation.

God, her mother's face that day at Aunt Liddy's, pale and tight when she left the library, as if she'd just been slapped. She'd said goodbye in a clipped, pained tone, hands shaking as she opened her purse for the car keys, and instantly Julia had felt defensive on her mother's behalf. So when Aunt Liddy extended an arm in some attempt at a hug, Julia slipped away and skipped to the entry, kicking the door with her bare feet, leaving dusty prints. She knew damn well how to be loud and annoying.

Julia drops the letter on the kitchen counter. That was all so long ago. Another lifetime, another person. Why stir up old ghosts?

Money, of course.

I am sitting on a nice fortune, with no heir in sight.

You, however, could put it to good use.

The allure of it quenches parched, hopeless places in her mind. Money for lawyers, money for appeals, money to relocate closer to Evie, bridge the vast distance that separates them. She has visitation rights. She could see her on the weekends. Maybe she could even get a fair divorce settlement, one that wasn't written by a pack of experts who knew she wouldn't be able to defend herself against any of the salacious allegations in court, not if she couldn't afford a lawyer, which they made damn sure she couldn't. *Alcoholic*, they submitted to the court. *Mentally unstable.* She'd believed in the justice system until then, foolishly thought that truth had a place there.

You are terminally naive, Ethan had texted back when she complained he'd committed perjury.

She pulls out the electric bill marked URGENT with a red stamp. Slices the envelope open with her finger. Pulls out the statement, scans for the total due, and the total overdue, and the late charges accrued. Overwhelming, of course. Impossible.

Or maybe not.

It's just tea.

THREE

THE ORANGE GROVES JULIA REMEMBERS are long gone, of course, replaced by strip malls with Laundromats, internet cafes, and Chinese markets—the standard, anonymous sprawl of Los Angeles concrete. The afternoon sun glares through a film of dust on the windshield. Julia hits it with a splash of wiper fluid, but there's not enough; the blades just smear the dust into half-moon circles. At least the sound drowns out the ping in the engine that's made her nervous for the past week. The airconditioning is on the way out, but it's working well enough to stave off the Santa Ana winds and keep the temperature an ambient eighty degrees.

It's strange to think that all this time she's been living within driving distance of her only living relative but never knew it. After the great unraveling of her life, Julia had headed back to Los Angeles with money from the sale of her engagement ring— that, at least, Ethan hadn't contested—thinking there would be more opportunities. And there were: in food service, anyway.

Her great-aunt's story is dodgy at best. No, there must be a trigger for this meeting, something important that Aunt Liddy wants. Probably at a hefty cost to Julia, although she can't imagine what it'll be.

That damn letter was so odd. Something disingenuous about it too, like every word was crafted to pique her interest.

You are my last of last resorts.

For a couple of days, she let it linger on her counter next to the bills—no need to become the patron saint of lost causes. But a Google search at the library revealed that Dr. Lydia Greer had indeed done quite well for herself—she'd sold the rights of a biological patent to one of the largest genetic and fertility research firms in the UK. Her six-bedroom house, according to Trulia, was worth more than eight million dollars.

Blue lights ahead, some kind of accident. A police officer waves for her to stop. She uses the time to glance at the crumpled city map she'd found buried in her closet—no GPS, since her cell phone was cut off that morning. Her great-aunt's estate is a ten-acre fortress plunked squarely in the middle of an ocean of townhomes. There had been an article about her unwillingness to sell, attributed to a kind of elderly kookiness since developers had offered mountains of money and a prime lot in Brentwood for relocation. Her new, middle-class neighbors complained that she was unfairly skewing the property taxes in their zip code. A request by the mayor to discuss the situation had been flatly refused.

I can always say no.

Can you? says Ethan between her ears. *You never say no when you should.*

She tries to mentally put him back in the imaginary closet, lock the door as her therapist advised. It's not his voice, really; he was never that cruel, or at least not until the end. *It's your own negativity speaking through him,* Dr. Stolz said, *using him as a cloak. Trying to hold you back, keep you from moving forward.*

Saying no to Aunt Liddy could be dangerous; maybe that's why Ethan's crept back into her mind. From her ex, she learned that the wealthy strike back when they don't get what they want—first through overwhelming force, sending you headfirst into an economic tailspin to soften you up, tenderize you for the feast to come, then a fat cash offer if you just sign X in order to absolve them and seal the lie. And then if you refuse, grinding you through systems weighted against the poor, then claiming victory, that justice has been done, that you are getting exactly what you deserve.

The thing is, she'd seen him do it before. He hadn't been shy about his techniques. There had been a fledgling start-up he'd gleefully run into the ground. She just never thought he'd apply that particular skill set to wife number three. And back then, Evie was just barely walking, and they had the house in Palo Alto with the view of the ocean, and he dazzled her with love, or maybe the affectation of love, and if she had any misgivings about the way he conducted his business, she banished them with the thought that this was the way the sausage was made.

At least, that's what she told herself at the time. She should have known better—no, she already *knew* better—it was just that she hadn't felt her own moral drift.

His lips, brushing the soft skin behind her ear. In spite of everything, even the memory of him is dazzling.

———————

She's buzzed in through wrought iron gates, which sweep open like curtains before an opening act. The Spanish-style house is larger than she remembers and impeccably kept up, a picture postcard of the kind of mansion a silent film star would own. The grass is so green, clipped and perfect, each shrub so meticulously trimmed, each redolent flower blooming as if on cue, that it unnerves her. The forced domination of nature, and in a desert at that. The grounds are protected by a twelve-foot-high wall covered in ivy, high enough to partially obscure the suburbs outside the realm.

The only thing out of place is Julia's battered Volvo, which seems unsure of the cobbled, circular drive—every turn of the wheel causes a minor shudder. There's a rectangular space near the front entrance that looks designated for guests, so that's where she parks. She half expects a butler in a tuxedo to greet her.

Just the kind of place where Ethan would shine. The thought causes a panicky roll at the base of her stomach. Maybe she should turn around. Leave. Go back to where she belongs— resume her uncontrolled free fall into poverty. But then she'd never know if she could have brought Evie back to her. She would always wonder.

And do I really have something better to do?

Not really.

The first time Ethan had taken her to one of his wealthy friend's estates—an actress, an after-party for a film premiere—he'd gripped her elbow and told her, *They're all sharks. Bored sharks. Pretend you don't notice and they'll find something else to eat.*

She opens the car door, ignoring its creak of protest, closes it behind her, and approaches the mansion's arched entrance. The scent of honeysuckle floats in the dry air. Before she has a chance to knock, a woman about her age—maybe a few years older— immediately opens it. She has bobbed blond hair and neat, white teeth. Whispers of cool air-conditioning escape, curl around Julia's ankles.

"You're Julia!" the woman exclaims, reaching out a hand. Manicured nails. "I'm Bailey, Dr. Greer's assistant."

Julia nods, offering her hand in exchange. They size each other up. Julia takes in the pressed khakis, the silk shirt distressed to look like cotton, navy blue Keds, and a chunky gold bracelet. In other words, Ethan's kind of people. She's sure her own thrift store jeans and the one decent black shirt she owns—bought with a Nordstrom gift card, a wedding present—barely passes muster. She can already feel sweat creating little half-moons under her armpits.

But then Bailey's the hired help. Ethan had a way of noticing but not noticing the help, a practiced aloofness. She decides to give it a shot.

"Come on in," says Bailey, and so Julia does. But she takes her time.

She steps into the entry, pauses. There's a quiet *shush* to the place, like a library or church. An elaborate, dark-stained mahogany staircase curls to the second-floor landing with a kind of feline grace, so ornate it makes the stairs in her old Victorian look like a poor cousin. White plaster walls unmarred by even a single hairline crack; gilt-framed Impressionist paintings tastefully arranged throughout; terra-cotta floors, darkened with patina, polished to a high shine. Her memory had served up marble floors, but the rest is pretty much as she recalls. A gigantic flower arrangement in a ceramic Art Deco vase settled on an antique, half-moon console table. That small crystal bowl filled with hard round candy.

"You've been here before?" Bailey takes a few leading steps in front of her, a prompt, *this way*.

Julia notices without noticing. She lets a hand drift to the flowers in the antique vase. Leans over to smell them. Lilacs and roses, asters and lilies. She reaches out for the cellophane-wrapped candies, picks up two, a cherry and an orange. Takes her damn sweet time.

"Yes," she finally says.

Now it's Bailey's turn to pause. She clasps her hands in front of her, a carefully arranged smile on her face. Waiting.

The order has been established. Julia feels a quiet thrill of victory, an emotion that's been woefully absent of late. She idly slips the candies in her pocket, gives Bailey a nod. Bailey returns it, beckons with an arm, and they move on.

———————

It's the kind of library that also seems pulled from a film set, the perfect setting for an Agatha Christie mystery—built-in walnut bookshelves, marble fireplace, a heavy oak desk and two matching antique pale blue silk settees with a low table between them. But the books themselves aren't right; they should be leather-bound with gilt titles but instead are academic textbooks, thin paperback journals, and hardcover books with sun-faded spines. *Structural Biochemistry, Evolutionary Pathways and Enigmatic Algae, Origin of Mitochondria and Hydrogenosomes*. Any leftover space is crammed with papers.

The first evidence that a real human being lives here.

"She'll be with you in a moment," says Bailey. "Please have a seat and make yourself comfortable. Could I get you some coffee? Tea?"

Julia's first instinct is to decline, but that would be so like her. "Coffee," she says instead. "Black."

"Would you like anything to eat? I just baked some scones this morning."

All Julia's eaten is cold spaghetti with a spoonful of peanut butter on the side. But she doesn't want to get too comfortable. *Every negotiation is an attempted robbery*, Ethan would say. *Keep your gun loaded at all times*. Hunger will give her a slightly irritated edge.

"No, thank you."

Bailey nods, her Keds barely making a sound as she leaves.

When she's gone, Julia lets out a sigh she didn't realize she'd been holding, and sits on the settee. It's as uncomfortable as it looks. Two tall French doors lead out to a brick patio, shaded by a lemon tree, ripe with fruit.

Another candy bowl, filled with saltwater taffy, sits on the coffee table. A small book beside it catches her attention, the cloth cover a faded red, the edges soft and fraying. She picks it up. *The Fall of Man, the Birth of Gods* in gilt lettering. *By Dr. Alfred Greer.* Her great-grandfather? She opens the cover and sees a faded inscription on the yellowing title page.

> *No wonder if the country's breed declines—*
> *Mixed metal, Kyrnos, that but dimly shines.*
> *—Father*

Her mother never mentioned Alfred Greer, and Julia's research at the library hadn't yielded much. He'd gotten his doctorate in chemistry at Cambridge University and was an amateur horticulturalist, an avid skier, a friend of Sir Francis Galton and Darwin, and an early proponent of eugenics. Probably why her mother never talked about that side of the family.

Suddenly she hears the *squeak, squeak* of wheels. She quickly places the book back on the table, like a child caught stealing.

Steady, Julia. Everything or nothing could be riding on the next hour.

"Ah, *there* she is," says a raspy voice. "I see your father's nose."

Briefly wondering if that's some kind of Jewish slight, Julia turns and finds an ancient woman confined to a wheelchair being pushed into the room by a servant or nurse. Her great-aunt has the bone structure of a desiccated bird—sharp cheekbones and a beaky chin, thin legs propped on the wheelchair's footplate at a neat right angle, elbows poking sharply from within a thin white cashmere sweater. A blanket on her lap. Her white hair is swept up into a French chignon, and she wears a Jackie Kennedy pearl choker. A waft of Chanel No. 5 drifts in with her. Another woman fighting reality.

Julia starts to stand.

"No need, my dear," her great-aunt says with a dismissive wave. "We might as well stay at eye level."

So Julia stays put. The nurse/servant pushes her great-aunt to a spot in front of the coffee table.

"Gracias, Guadalupe." Not so much a thanks as a dismissal. Guadalupe leaves without a word.

Her great-aunt then turns and regards her, faded blue eyes sparkling with a fierce intellect. "So. Please tell me Bailey's had the good sense to offer you something to drink."

"She's getting me coffee."

"Coffee? I would think a meeting of *this* importance would merit something stronger. Gin, at least."

There's an edge that makes Julia wonder if Aunt Liddy is being serious or sarcastic.

Maybe both.

"Coffee is fine."

"Ah, yes," replies Aunt Liddy. "Your father's side had those . . . issues. Forgive me."

Julia's face flushes just as Bailey enters with a tray. *Her father's side*—like her blood itself is partially tainted, like she's doomed to suffer the same fate. A quiet fury builds as Bailey places the cup and saucer—delicate bone china, gilt handles, decorated with pale roses—on the coffee table in front of her. *Your Honor, the family history suggests . . .*

"If I remember correctly, he wasn't a big supporter of the braces idea. You did get them, didn't you? I can't quite tell."

Another well-placed dig. *Parry, Julia.*

"Yes, not that it helped in the long run. Money can't solve every problem, apparently."

"Well," says Aunt Liddy, "that just proves nature has her own designs. Eventually we'll discover the gene that deals with tooth alignment and give her a run for her money."

Bailey has another cup on the tray, filled with tea the color of dishwater. This she places in front of Aunt Liddy.

"I remember a day when they blamed crooked teeth on different races mixing. And back then, different races meant Italians marrying Irish. Thank you, Bales."

"Would you like me to—"

Aunty Liddy cuts her off with a dismissive wave, and Bailey too leaves without another word.

"The problem with being very, very old and very, very rich," says Aunt Liddy, picking up her cup, "is that you never get a moment to yourself. When you die, you're alone. It's the one thing about it I am looking forward to."

There's a slight tremor in her great-aunt's hand, the skin so thin that it's nearly translucent, the white bones of her knuckles clearly visible. The tea in the cup quivers.

She doesn't think Aunt Liddy has that long to wait.

———————————

Julia reaches for her coffee so she won't have to say anything for a moment. Slowly takes a sip. It's strong, dark, and bitter. It was a mistake to show up without a strategy—Aunt Liddy may look frail, but her mind is sharp as the proverbial tack, and two insults in less than a minute is a definite attempt to throw Julia off-balance. Back in her reporting days, she would never have allowed herself to be so quickly ambushed. It's time to push back.

"And *your* father," Julia says. "Did you inherit his racist, anti-Semitic views?"

Aunt Liddy looks pleased. Like there was a test and Julia just passed it. "I *thought* I saw you looking at his book. I had Bailey go on a dig for it, to see if it's as bad as I remember."

Julia rests the coffee cup on her knee. "And is it?"

"Worse, I'm afraid," says Aunt Liddy with a rueful laugh. "Terrible thing for our family, landing on the wrong side of history. Genetics was all so new then, like peeking into God's toolbox; who can blame them for wanting to use the tools to become gods themselves? Remake the world?"

"I think there were six million Jews who could blame them."

"Touché, my dear. Believe me, I'm not trying to be an apologist for the Third Reich, or for the forced sterilization of the poor and minorities in America, which no one seems to remember or care about these days. Our greatest scientific achievements are always undermined by our baser fears. We think that by creating tribes, or religions, or ideologies we can somehow avoid the complete annihilation of death. But in the end, only the chromosomes survive. However, I like your spirit. I would say you get that from your mother, but I'm afraid that trait passed her entirely as well. No, you're much more like Annabelle."

Julia chooses to ignore the double-sided insult/compliment. It's better to draw her out. "I never knew my grandmother."

"Yes, I think you two would have gotten along very well. Until she went mad, of course. Like Mother." For a moment, Aunt Liddy seems to stare through Julia, lost in another time or place. "It runs in the family. That particular genetic inheritance seems to have skipped me, and hopefully you as well. And your . . . daughter, correct?"

She's trying to emotionally bait me. "Were you close to Annabelle?"

"Oh, she and Irene were very close, until the elopement. Irene was hurt that she didn't know beforehand."

"And you?"

"I was close to books, and data, and the numbers constantly swirling in my head. Half in this world and half in another. For me, Annabelle's departure was just a data point on a timeline. What I *did* inherit from my father is my clinical nature. Some consider it cold. I prefer to think of it as clarity. You need to have clarity if you're to fix nature's design flaws. Sentimentality is anathema in my field."

Sunlight stretches into the room, casting long, probing shadows. For a moment it's quiet, almost perfectly so, the distant traffic silenced by thick walls and carpeting. Dust motes float in a sunbeam. A faint scent of roses wilting in a glass vase. It strikes Julia that there's nothing electric in the room except for the overhead light fixture and a single floor lamp, and it feels like she's entered another time altogether. Sad and lonely, like she and the house and the things are marooned in a future they have no place in.

"Is mental illness a flaw?"

"Of course it is. And one day either pregnant women will be able to tell whether their fetus is carrying the gene for mental illness, and they'll chose to give birth, or not, or we'll be able to correct the gene in utero, thereby preventing the pain and devastation that follows. Which is eugenics, by the way. They'll give it a spiffier name, though, something along the line of 'designer babies,'" says Aunt Liddy, balancing the empty teacup on her lap.

"That sounds frightening."

"My dear, you, a test tube baby, shouldn't be so dramatic. Glass houses and stones, etc. There was quite an uproar just getting *that* through. The first IVF family was inundated with hate mail."

At first Julia thinks she misheard, but then realizes she didn't.

Her consternation must be visible, because her great-aunt says, "You didn't know?" She raises her cup and coolly sips from it. "Oh my goodness, I thought . . . Well, they tried for years, you know. They were desperate to have a child."

Julia can't help it; her mind spins off in different directions. Is it true? Why didn't her mother ever tell her? Or her father? Where was it done? Were there other fertilized eggs still out there, frozen, an embryonic sisterhood?

"And look at you now! Two arms, two legs, a robust intellect, and repairable teeth." There is the faintest hint of an evil twinkle in Aunt Liddy's eyes as she says this.

Oh, she's good, says Ethan. *She's very, very good.*

"But you didn't come all this way to hear an old woman prattle on," she continues, reaching over and patting Julia's leg. "We have business to discuss, do we not? Perhaps you wouldn't mind a bit of fresh air while we talk. You didn't get a chance to tour the greenhouse, did you? The last time you were here?"

Not a question, a directive, but best to make it look like a choice. Still reeling, Julia tries to keep her voice even. "If I remember correctly, that was off-limits too. But I'm always up to explore."

"Excellent. You won't be disappointed," Aunt Liddy says, placing her empty cup on the table. "You can see what mischief I get up to when I'm left to my own devices."

FOUR

JULIA OPENS THE FRENCH DOORS, letting in a wall of hot air that barely stirs the gauze curtains. She's grateful for the chance to refocus. Settle herself for a moment. Outside, there's a long, rectangular pool next to a gazebo shaded by ivy, several brick patio spaces separated by raised garden beds filled with tropical palms and flowers, classical balustrades. The orchard at the back of the property is still there, and the air does smell of orange blossoms. Ten degrees cooler, and it'd be paradise.

The wall is monstrous, though. The neighbors' roofs barely peek over the edge; something oppressive, like a prison, about it. *To keep something out, or to keep something in?*

An even, sloping cement walkway leads down to the Victorian greenhouse; sunlight glints off the glass panels, making it hard for Julia to look at the structure without squinting.

"The water bill is astonishing," says Aunt Liddy.

"I can imagine." Julia takes her assigned position behind the wheelchair and pushes her great-aunt carefully through the doors.

"Occasionally they try to restrict my usage, but generous campaign contributions usually settle things quickly." Aunt Liddy doesn't bother to hide the note of pride in her voice.

It's on the tip of Julia's tongue to say, *It must be nice to get away with corruption*, but she thinks better of it. Instead she closes the doors behind them and says, "It must be hard to keep it up."

"It is a *constant* battle. Los Angeles yearns to be a desert again, and perhaps one day we'll lose the war effort and all have to emigrate north. I hope to be dead by then. Unlike Irene, I never missed Devon. I enjoy the sun. The heat."

Julia pushes her great-aunt down the walkway toward the greenhouse. It's almost two stories high, supported by an ornate, ironwork frame. A cupola at the top, with a lazily rotating rooster weather vane.

"I didn't understand Irene's fascination with plants. They seemed so benign, so placid. Beauty often is. What do you think of my garden?"

"It's lovely." She wonders why Aunt Liddy doesn't have an electric wheelchair. *Probably does*. Everything has been thought through, carefully choreographed, even this walk. Something Julia can't afford to forget.

"Yes, lovely. A very forgettable word—I'd hoped you might come up with something more interesting. It's only lovely because it's tamed. But the truth is, every garden is a *war*. Every plant a soldier, trying to perpetuate itself, vanquish the enemy. People think we have to preserve nature, like it's a fragile blossom that won't survive without our divine intervention. What we have to save is ourselves. Every living creature is ruthless, and vicious, and self-preserving, without a whit of sympathy."

Julia wishes she would just get to the point. "Being a little overly anthropomorphic, don't you think?"

"I'm being as clear and calculating as the wild tobacco plant," Aunt Liddy says. "When it's attacked by the hawkmoth larva, the plant releases volatile compounds into the air, signals insects that enjoy munching on hawkmoth larva where to find it. The

enemy of my enemy is my friend. That's quite a strategic calcula-
tion for something regarded as barely more sentient than a rock.
The eucalyptus uses chemicals to inhibit the growth of competing plants."

"Are you saying it's thinking?"

"Define *thinking*. I bet you can't—no one can. Define *com-
munication*. That wonderful smell of freshly cut grass, do you
know what it really is?"

Play along, Julia. "No."

"It's the smell of grass *screaming*. A chemical distress signal.
Who needs cell phones when you have chemistry at your dis-
posal? In many ways, we are surprisingly less sophisticated than
weeds."

They finally reach the greenhouse. "Press the brake, there,"
says Aunt Liddy, pointing to a lever by the wheel.

Julia pushes it with her foot, grateful for something to do.
The door to the greenhouse is shaded by an arched ironwork
portico. She knows that somewhere inside will be the place and
the moment when Aunt Liddy tries to close the deal, probably
toward the end of the tour. A grand finale. *I just have to suffer
through the pitch.* The most important thing is to avoid looking
eager or desperate herself. Among the wealthy, desperation is
death.

"Irene sensed there was more to plants, their devious nature,
long before it was substantiated by science. I thought she'd
chosen a boring field. I couldn't have been more wrong."

Julia approaches the greenhouse. There's a copper plaque to
the right of the door, engraved. *Look like the innocent flower, but be
the serpent under't.* She can see Aunt Liddy's reflection behind
her in the glass—an intense expression, something like barely
contained triumph touched with fury. A strange mix.

"So maybe it's guilt," her great-aunt says, "that I've created this. A way to appease her ghost. And my conscience."

"Has it worked?"

"No, of course not. The dead never forgive. Or forget."

Julia reaches for the door handle—

"Wait, my dear. Lift the plaque, otherwise you'll set off the alarm."

Julie does, and finds a numeric keypad beneath with a red, blinking light. Security for a greenhouse?

"Six-four-eight-seven-nine-two-one-eight-four-three," says Aunt Liddy. "Be quick about it, this direct sun is trying."

Julia asks Aunt Liddy to repeat the numbers and then enters them—there's a beep, a click, and the light turns green. She cautiously opens the door wide, and finds another world.

Every inch inside is green: palms, ferns, and shrubs, tall trees covered with lichen, Spanish moss hanging from their branches, a pond with massive water lilies and purple lotus flowers, ivy creeping along and through the arching ironwork, a profusion of wildflowers, waist-high grasses, and colorful lilacs. Something wonderfully abandoned about it, like it all sprung up organically.

And then, for some unknown reason—was it a sound? A smell? Her entrance?—the air fills with green leaves. They flutter up toward the cupola—*up*—and collect like a flock of birds.

For a moment, it's hard for Julia to breathe. She was supposed to be impressed, and, against her better instincts, she is.

Aunt Liddy rolls up behind her. "Oh, that's not even the interesting part. Come, my dear, let's be quick and close the door before we introduce them into the environment. Some are endangered, quite a few are toxic, and I can just imagine the ruckus from my neighbors if their cats ate them and started dying en masse. I'd never hear the end of it from the mayor."

Julia steps aside and Aunt Liddy wheels herself in. Julia quickly shuts the greenhouse door behind her, hears a click and a beep. There's a wide, even pathway of concrete that curves, serpentine, to the right and left, enough of the vegetation cut back to allow them through. The leaves settle back into the dense foliage, although a few swirl in their general direction.

"I'm going to ask you to push me again," says Aunt Liddy, looking extraordinarily pleased at Julia's reaction. "I can manage short spurts, but my deteriorating muscle strength is problematic for longer distances. Let's go right."

Julia swallows the obvious question, *What are they?*, and gets behind her great-aunt's wheelchair, grateful for the privacy it will give her. One of the green leaves spirals down out of a nearby tree, lands on her shirt. It has eyes, six legs, antennae. Stares at her curiously.

"Katydids," says Julia. "They're just katydids."

"So much for my big reveal. You'll find other insects here, all invested deeply in camouflage. A very successful strategy for avoiding predators. The thing that hides itself in plain sight, that's always the thing you have to watch out for."

A meaning here she can't quite fathom, but Julia gets the sense it will have something to do with whatever it is her great-aunt wants from her. The katydid climbs up her sleeve, settles onto her shoulder as she pushes Aunt Liddy. Going along for the ride.

"So, great-grand-niece, how do you think this garden differs from the one outside?"

Julia pushes Aunt Liddy past a cluster of orchids. "It feels more organic. Less designed. But that probably means every inch of it's designed."

"In more ways than one. Very good, I'll add the two points back that I detracted when you called the outside landscape lovely. Every specimen you see here is perfect. Absolutely, utterly perfect, the best expression of its genome. Not a single chromosome flaw. Every plant here would win any horticulture contest. No question."

"Is that why there's an alarm?"

"Not entirely. Although this is a Garden of Eden even God himself would envy."

Another katydid trills from the cover of a fern, and the one on her shoulder jumps away.

"I see you don't struggle with self-doubt," says Julia.

"It's a futile exercise, my dear, best left to people under sixty."

Julia smiles, in spite of herself. She'll have to watch that, the other side of her great-aunt's blade. Charm. Something Ethan had no deficit of either. In fact, she imagines they'd get along well. She pushes Aunt Liddy around the next corner. A raised flower bed on their right, filled with tropical succulents, red blooms with needlelike petals.

"Oh, here's one of my favorites. Kahili flower," says Aunt Liddy. "A kind of protea. The flowers and seedpods contain hydrogen cyanide. A compound that's flammable *and* poisonous."

"Lovely."

"Now you're being funny. Two bonus points. But I will say don't touch anything without checking first."

There she goes, testing again. Julia senses Aunt Liddy listening closely, trying to gauge if this scares her. She decides the best approach is dark humor.

"I wish I'd known you before my divorce."

Aunt Liddy claps her hands. "Oh yes, we could have made *short* work of all that." They approach a shrub with bell-like flowers. "Like you, I understand loss all too well. I sent my sister to an island in the South Pacific and all I got back was a trunk. By then Annabelle was gone, Mother was in the institution, and Father . . . well, Father was Father. And poor Irene . . . she had been struggling for years to recover from a personal tragedy. A devastating fire. Her husband and baby girl perished. She'd suffered from survivor's guilt. I was so certain a change of scenery would do her good. I wish . . . Ah, it's too late for wishes. I thought, before she left, that I'd known pain. I'd barely tasted it."

Confiding invokes trust. A tactic Julia has used herself on more than one occasion, to get a source to reveal more than they were comfortable with. But inside the truth was always a subtle, manipulative idea, a push. Too late Julia had realized this worked on her as well. *I'm a great disappointment to my father,* Ethan had said the first time they met, at some kind of forgettable charity event she'd been pulled into at the last minute when the reporter assigned to cover it had gotten ill. Ethan had revealed a wound that night, one she'd eventually thought she could heal. It was a shock when, at their wedding reception, his father had offered a toast about how proud he'd always been of his son.

The path here twists again, revealing palms sprouting well over six feet, and the earthy smell of an old-growth forest.

"Irene was a fierce botanist," Aunt Liddy continues. "I say fierce because you had to be, at the time, if you were a woman with scientific aspirations. I'd run across some intriguing reports about an island that was still untouched by Western scientists, and began to have delusions of grandeur. Finding my own personal Galápagos, discovering some new, revolutionary organism. And Irene desperately needed something else to occupy herself. I thought a complete change of scenery might do her some good. Oh my dear, do watch the hogweed."

Julia pauses just inches from brushing against a flower she'd assumed was Queen Anne's lace.

"Hogweed was brought over in the eighteen hundreds as an ornamental plant, if you can believe that. Its sap burns the skin and can even cause blindness."

Something like a note of admiration in Aunt Liddy's tone.

"Why didn't you go with Irene?" Julia asks.

"Adventure is hard to come by when you're confined to a wheelchair."

Julia stops, surprised.

"Yes," Aunt Liddy says. "Most people assume it's the decrepitude of old age. I liked my horses on the spirited side when I was young, and paid a dear price for it. If the eugenics movement had taken off the way my father hoped, I probably would have been sent to a gas chamber myself."

Julia doesn't detect even the faintest hint of anger or resentment. "That's harsh, don't you think?"

Aunt Liddy shrugs. "I'm sure I was upset at the time, but now it's like something that happened to a character in a novel I read long ago. If I didn't have a few photos I don't think I'd even be able to remember Father's face. And when I die, it will all be gone anyway."

"I'm sure people will build off your research," Julia says.

"Thank you for your pity. It will be sad to me, if to no one else, when microbes eat all my ingenious chromosomes. Even this Eden here is destined for annihilation. The plants will die, or they'll reproduce with other, imperfect specimens, and ruin all my work."

The twists and turns have confused Julia's sense of direction, although judging by the cupola, she guesses they're almost halfway through.

"You could donate your research."

"And let someone else take the credit? I think *not*. Plus . . . an opportunity has presented itself. One that might link my name with a discovery that lives on forever. I'm starting to like that word more and more. Forever."

Julia smiles. "Isn't that just another way to avoid—how did you put it—the complete annihilation of death?"

"Oh, you do have a reporter's memory. I never said I'd overcome my *own* fears. Immortality has been, and always will be, the Holy Grail. Now stop here—there's something I want to show you. A couple of things, actually."

Julia does, next to a raised bed with a small, rather uninteresting flower that looks like a purple puffball with fernlike leaves. There's a rusting metal stool under the bed.

"Have a seat so I can see you."

And here we go. The ask will come soon.

Aunt Liddy pulls a battered, leather notebook out from underneath her blanket while Julia settles on the stool. "Here," she says. "Take this. It was Irene's. It's hard for me to look at."

Julia accepts the notebook. The cover is worn, the binding loose. A sheaf of letters in the front. She looks to Aunt Liddy for permission, which is granted with a nod. Gently, she opens it. *April 3, 1939. It was a longer journey than I'd expected. . . .* There's a very good illustration in the side margin, a prop plane descending through cloud cover, a sharp mountain peak in the background.

"How did she die?" Julia asks.

"That's what I'm hoping you will help me discover. You'll see her version of events inscribed there, and tucked away in the back is a letter with a different version. A backhanded accusation of suicide. It doesn't fit my sister. Something was . . . covered up."

Julia continues to turn the pages. Sketches of plants and flowers, each labeled in beautiful cursive script. The illustrations are very detailed, down to the root structure and fine veins on the leaves. A number of plants there are no names for, just a question mark beneath. Something primeval about them. They remind her of the images in her college paleontology textbook, the fossil on one side, the artist's rendering on the other. A lost world revealed.

"But if mental illness runs in the family . . . she really might have committed suicide."

"It runs in my *mother's* side of the family." She looks pointedly at Julia.

An awkward pause. "Oh . . . she was your *half* sister," says Julia.

"My father wasn't a huge believer in morality. He thought that it was simply a lesser vehicle for social construct through tribalism, war, and politics. The greater vehicle was through the pure rationality of science, free from dogma, superstition, or emotion."

Julia traces a finger along the edge of a page. "Doesn't sound like a warm family to grow up in."

"I didn't notice. I suppose I'm very much like him in that way."

Julia turns another page in the journal, trying to feign disinterest. There's a sketch of a very basic tent, just a bamboo pole with fabric tied to a slightly raised platform.

"Well, I don't know how I could possibly help," says Julia. "I'm just a journalist. *Was* a journalist."

"Exactly. You have a nose for when people aren't telling the truth."

"Maybe," says Julia with an ironic smile. "Not always."

"I did a little research on you myself. Your series on the use of toxic soil for park development in low-income neighborhoods was impressive. All I need is for you to connect with someone who is, mercifully, allowing me to disinter Irene and bury her in the family cemetery. Ask the right questions."

Sounds a little too easy. "You just want me to call this person?"

"No, I want you to go there. To the island, Kapu."

Julia almost starts to laugh, but she quickly realizes Aunt Liddy is serious. "*Go* there. This mysterious person doesn't have a phone?"

"He—the Reverend—leads a small, isolated Christian colony. No interest in the corrupt trappings of modernity and all that."

"Well, that's even better. So you want me to go to an island I've never heard of, where your sister died under mysterious circumstances, and by the way there's no phone service and a religious cult. Can't see why I'd turn that down."

"Don't be so dramatic—they're no more a cult than the Pennsylvania Dutch are. And to help support themselves, they run a small, and very exclusive, luxury eco-resort for those who can afford their outrageous prices and withstand a complete break from technology."

"And why would any tourist want that?"

"The romance of 'getting away from it all,' and all that nonsense."

Julia knows the type—in the days of Ethan, there were always one or two waifish women settled into a corner at a cocktail party, going on and on about their latest excursion to a place no one had heard of, where they earnestly gave up protein or gluten or electricity as some kind of purification rite, or tried their hand at coffee picking with locals, weaving baskets from palm fronds. Always within the thick, protective padding that wealth provided.

"I think I'd prefer the cult," Julia says.

Aunt Liddy smiles thinly. "Of course, we'll give you a satellite phone."

"That's really not my main issue. And . . . why me? Why not Bailey?"

"He won't release her remains to anyone except a family member, in person. It took more than seventy years to get even this concession, and I . . . well, I am obviously in no condition to travel."

"And I'm the only family you have left."

Aunt Liddy places both hands in her lap, one over the other. It's a prim, yet defensive gesture—she's trying to hide how important this is to her, and failing.

It gives Julia the confidence to press. "Isn't it sentimental to want to bury your sister? Didn't you say sentimentality was . . . anathema?"

Her great-aunt slaps the armrest on her wheelchair. "*Now* you're thinking like a Greer. Look through the journal until you find the red flower."

Julia arches an eyebrow, but does as she's told.

"She went to Paris, of course. Do you draw?"

"A little. Not well." Finally Julia finds the red bloom. It too is labeled with a question mark, *kupapa 'u flower* written underneath. The flower looks like a large orchid, with black dots leading into its center.

"She said this one smelled like a rotting corpse. That's what *kupapa 'u* means in Hawaiian, corpse. By the time the specimen arrived, it had no smell anymore, and had blackened into a thick pulp. But I planted it in the greenhouse anyway, thinking maybe the roots would sprout a new plant. They didn't. A scientist gets used to failure, so I didn't think much more about it."

"That's all very interesting," says Julia, closing the journal. "But I don't see what it has to do with Irene's death."

Aunt Liddy watches her for a moment. Appraising.

"Maybe nothing. Maybe everything. When they sent me Irene's things, they also sent me a funeral keepsake, a brooch made out of her hair. An old-fashioned idea, making jewelry out of hair, or teeth, or the bone of a loved one. I compared a few strands to a sample of hair from a brush Irene had left behind. They did seem to match, although that didn't prove much beyond the fact that she'd been there. So I carefully froze both samples. I was certain that one day we'd have processes that could reveal more than my primitive microscope."

There's no emotion as she says this, Julia notes. Not a single hint of sadness, or loss.

"As soon as we had the technology, I ran a genetic and chemical analysis of her hair, hoping to find what other factors were in play. There was a high level of neuromodulators in the sample taken from the brooch—puzzling, because they're usually only present when there's a neurological disorder. Which she didn't suffer from, at least not when she left for Kapu."

Julia knows she must listen very, very carefully to what Aunt Liddy says next, because everything else has been constructed to lead her to this moment.

"And then, not too long ago, six months, seven, I noticed a strange red bloom in the greenhouse. It gave off the smell of a rotting corpse. Excited, I found its match in Irene's notebook, and immediately took a sample. The center released pollen when I touched it. Then I ran some tests. It wasn't a flower at all—it was a fungus in disguise. The sample of Irene's hair from the brooch and the fungus contained an identical gene. I ran the tests on her hair from the brush, pre-visit. No such gene was present. It's possible there had been some kind of cross-contamination between the samples—it's not unheard of. I would have taken a fresh sample from the flower, but that very night there was a break-in."

Julia sits very, very still. She knows that every blink, every breath is being observed. "Someone took it."

Aunt Liddy nods.

Not just a sentimental mission, then, to collect the remains of a dearly departed sister. Julia wonders what her mother exchanged for those braces, because she senses there is not a single cell of compassion in her great-aunt's body. She is one hundred percent shark.

"Why is it so special?"

"I have theories only, and you're better off not knowing too much. But if it wasn't cross-contamination, well . . . let's just say it's the kind of discovery that could land one a Nobel Prize. And a much vaster fortune."

There she is again, dangling the carrot of the grand potential inheritance. Julia chooses to ignore it. "Any idea who broke in?"

"Again, theories. We conducted a thorough security investigation after it was stolen. Discovered surveillance bugs in the house, malware on the computers—even the cell phones had been hacked. Not the efforts of an amateur."

"So it's that dangerous?"

A slight pause. "I will, of course, compensate you very well."

Not an answer, a deflection.

"But if all you need is the flower, you could send someone with more expertise, a scientist at least. They could pretend to be a tourist."

"I need the body *and* the flower. There was precious little DNA in the few follicles I was able to preserve. I need more. Even a partial skeleton would be nice."

Even a partial skeleton would be nice. Julia can't imagine a world where she'd ever say that about someone she'd loved. Maybe the Greer side of the family isn't capable of love—maybe that's the real reason her great-grandmother severed all ties.

If she wasn't desperate, she would too.

Instead, Julia says nothing, trying to be completely inscrutable. She remembers Ethan in the car lot, after they'd gotten two grand off the sticker price of the Jaguar. *A strained silence is always your best negotiation tool.*

Her great-aunt rushes to fill it. "All the tourists have returned raving about how wonderful the unspoiled paradise is. But there may be some in the mix who, like you, are on a similar mission. How far they'd go is uncertain. You'd need to be careful. Discreet." The tremor in her hand develops into a shake. "And think what a *story* it would be. I know a very powerful literary agent who'd be perfect. I've already planted some seeds and she's intrigued, to say the least."

So. There it is. Money, a career-launching story, and danger. But for Julia, her own safety is of little concern. The first few weeks after Evie was gone, she'd walked to the beach at dawn every morning, having suffered sleepless night after sleepless night. Toyed with the urge to enter the water, fully clothed. She imagined her skin underwater, pale as the moon, the feel of the current lifting her hair, bubbles percolating from her mouth, eyes open. Would she have had the will to keep walking as her lungs burned? Maybe. Maybe not. She just wanted to be subsumed by something else. To not be trapped in the prison of what had happened to her.

Eventually she'd realized, though, that Evie would be truly lost then, and Ethan would truly win. Not much of a reason to live, but enough.

Is she willing to risk the only thing she has left, though: her life?

But her great-aunt has all that money, more than enough to finally put her on even footing with Ethan.

And the best part—the very, very best part—is the son of a bitch will never see it coming.

FIVE

IN THE DAYS THAT FOLLOW, Aunt Liddy proves true to her word, and Julia has to physically stop herself from checking her bank balance every few hours. It can't be real. It just *can't* be real. But it is. She packed up the few clothes that seemed halfway decent and checked into a hotel in Santa Monica with an ocean view, fully functional electricity, a television (with cable!), and unlimited toilet paper. That first night she stood for nearly a half hour in front of the air conditioner, enjoying cool air for the first time in weeks. She was finally able to pay off her cell phone bill, her car insurance that was again on the brink of cancellation, the remainder of her rent after she gave notice to her landlord.

And food. Now she's surrounded by food, and she can afford it, from the overpriced candy bars in the mini-fridge to the room service menu. Yes, she'll take a latte with that. No, please put the vinaigrette on the side. She's already on a first-name basis with the room service waiters, Don and Michelle; they smile and make a fuss about uncovering the dishes, with pleases and thank-yous and gratitude for the tips she hands them before they edge out the door. A part of her, though, still clocks the plates with food scraps in the hallway when she leaves for her morning run. Like it all might be taken away from her again.

It's frightening, the realization of how thin the razor edge of her life had become. Waiting in line at the food pantry for soft potatoes and pinto beans that had to be examined for mold. Curled up on the floor with a high fever, too scared to go to the emergency room because she'd never be able to afford the bill. Even a parking ticket was enough to potentially ruin her. No room for a single mistake, no buffer. Waking up every day to a new and immediate crisis—a lien on her checking account, a three-day pay-or-quit notice—which would only be followed by another crisis. Never an end in sight.

Things she'd taken for granted before the divorce now seem like small miracles. Orange juice. Clothes washed in a machine, not the bathtub. Toilet paper instead of napkins pilfered from Starbucks. Health insurance. It's like being reborn, becoming human again.

And there's progress on other fronts. Her newly retained lawyer—a referral from Aunt Liddy—is currently looking through all the unopened envelopes from Ethan's attorney. Just yesterday, her great-aunt cosigned a month-to-month lease for a small, two-bedroom house in Santa Monica within walking distance of the beach, which costs a heart-stopping nine thousand dollars a month, and to which Julia will move to after she returns. *It's important to live in a good neighborhood, with good schools,* her new lawyer said, *so we can prove Evie will have a decent quality of life here.* Even her initial call with the literary agent went well—it looks like proper representation might be in the works.

And yet.

Yeah. Standing in the hotel room, a glass of merlot in her hand—*real* merlot, forty-five dollars a bottle, a splurge, but she deserves it after the hell she's been through—with her boarding pass and itinerary for the morning flight printed, and her suitcase almost completely packed, she feels . . . dread. The same bottomless pit in her stomach she'd felt right before walking into court, alone and unrepresented.

It's all happened so fast. Maybe it's too much, too soon. Maybe she went from being terminally naive to being terminally skeptical.

Or maybe it's because she's starting to realize exactly what she signed on for. Like the suitcase with a false bottom—a special delivery. Julia hadn't exactly been thrilled with the smuggling part, but Aunt Liddy insisted. *We need to stay in touch, daily, and they collect cell phones on the flight over.* So along with her new clothes, she has a GPS device her great-aunt called a favor into DARPA for, which also works as a cell phone even without a nearby satellite tower. She had to sign a nondisclosure agreement to get it. It has waypoints programmed into the GPS where Irene's camp and the corpse flower might be, based on sketches from the notebook, and she can use the built-in camera to navigate the terrain, although she has a printed satellite map as backup. Also packed away are glass specimen jars with some kind of white gel, a knife, alcohol swabs (to sterilize the knife), a vial marked PLANT NUTRIENTS, and latex gloves. None of it on the "approved items to bring to Kapu" list of course. *Insect repellent is prohibited; eco-friendly biodegradable sunscreen and shampoo/soap only; no cameras of any kind; no electronics, computers, or tablets; no alcohol or medication not prescribed by a doctor; 100 percent organic snacks in biodegradable packaging allowed (5 max).*

Then there's a medication regimen she's to start as soon as she lands—small blue pills in an aluminum foil package with the Greer Enterprises slogan, *Bringing You Tomorrow, Today.* One pill in the morning, one at night—antibiotics, Bailey had said when she asked, a precaution against any number of nasty bacteria that might be lurking on the island. *Legionnaires' disease isn't uncommon in that part of the world, and you'll be trekking through some very biodiverse areas.*

Julia wasn't sure if she entirely believed her. A quick Google search hadn't turned up any pharmaceuticals made by Greer Enterprises—why would they be producing their own antibiotics? And there are so many other things she still doesn't know, gaps in the narrative.

Bailey made her a copy of Irene's notebook and the letters, nicely bound, thoughtful extra pages for her own notes. She's read through it from cover to cover, but can't shake the feeling she's missing something important.

Every ink drawing of the vegetation is so meticulous, as if each frond, stalk, or petal had been measured first. The work of a scientist, not an artist. Even Irene's penmanship is nearly perfect, the strokes carefully considered, with nearly identical loops and a consistent forward slant. Julia traces her finger over some of the names. *Aleurites moluccana. Hibiscus tiliaceus. Dicranopteris linearis.* A woman, like her, pouring herself into a project, to focus on something besides what a mess her life had become.

But how could a woman so meticulous forget her husband and daughter in a fire, leave them in a burning house? And how did the fire start? It wasn't too long after the tragedy that Irene, Liddy, Annabelle, and their father had moved to a ten-bedroom Victorian in Santa Barbara, funded by Charles's fortune. Online, Julia finds an article referencing an inquest into the fire that had gone nowhere, as far as she can tell.

And she's pretty sure some pages in the journal are missing. Why isn't there a sketch of Agnes, or the village, or the Reverend? Along with the ink sketch of Irene's camp, there's one of Liddy drawn from memory. A fantastic view from a cliff on Kapu. On closer examination, she found the faintest outlines of what looked like the edge of torn paper close to the spine, picked up by the copier's scanner. Her old, investigative instincts kicked in, firing up neurons that had atrophied.

She signed up for an online ancestry service, found some extra bits and pieces. A photo, black-and-white, *Liddy & Irene* written in ballpoint pen at the bottom. In the photo, Aunt Liddy is in a wheelchair, still thin and beaky, although her hair is thick, curling just above her shoulders. Irene stands tall in riding boots and jodhpurs, a necklace with a heart-shaped locket around her neck. She holds the reins of a palomino, and squints in the bright sunlight. There's a quiver with arrows slung over her shoulder. Something wild and Amazonian about the way she holds herself, like she could be mounted in a flash and charging through a forest, hunting.

Some digging at the historical society revealed more about the Church of Eternal Light, which had gotten its start in Texas and moved to San Bernardino before leaving for the island. She found a sepia-toned photo of Reverend Waldo Palmer and his congregation before they boarded the ship for Kapu, a stern and solemn tribe. Scattered references in academic journals—Palmer had much to say about the increasingly materialistic ambitions of the Protestants, felt that a true relationship with God could only be had in an unspoiled paradise. Bits and pieces of an apocalyptic vision, with only the pure, the chosen (his congregation, of course), surviving. He was fond of the Book of Ezekiel. *For I will take you from the nations, gather you from all the lands and bring you into your own land. . . . Moreover, I will give you a new heart and put a new spirit within you.*

The most interesting news about the church is recent. Reverend Abram Palmer, Waldo's grandson, pressed by the dwindling finances of the congregation and a lengthy court battle with the descendants of the natives wanting their land back, finally opens up Kapu for limited ecotourism. It quickly makes the "Best Of" magazine lists: *Best Secret Exotic Beach, Best Getaway for the Ultra-Rich, Best Place to Escape the Real World.* The church is characterized as a quaint holdout along the lines of the Amish or Pennsylvania Dutch, but no photos are allowed to be taken—in fact, the church has banned the use of any camera on the island, which only adds to the allure.

Then there's Kapu. The name itself means "forbidden," or "sacred." While no photography is allowed, there are pictures that people have taken over the years from their boats. A striking jagged peak rises from the center, the collapsed remains of an ancient volcano. It looks ethereal, unreal. Julia found one daring photo taken in a small cove of a redheaded young woman in a bikini posing on a small pebbled beach, some kind of cave or cavern behind her. A white flower is tucked behind her ear: the photo is captioned *Going Native.* Other than that, there are only a handful of pictures of the island's interior, taken in the late 1800s by a pair of Mormon missionaries. Palm-thatched huts with lava rock walls, bare-chested women wearing grass skirts weaving baskets, a boy holding up a fish half his size. The missionaries moved on though. No explanation. A few conspiracy websites say that Kapu was used by the US military to stage beach invasions prior to the Korean War, complete with bombing runs, and one site protesting the use of the island as a resort for only the very wealthy has an ongoing petition for an environmental impact study, with only twenty-eight signatures.

Costs a lot of money to leave the rest of the world behind. Although details about the eco-resort are kept pretty hush, she did find one thread that dropped the weekly rate. Ten thousand dollars. Not something that had to come out of her installment—thankfully, Aunt Liddy covered it directly.

Julia takes another long sip of her merlot. After the vinegar she's been drinking, it tastes like heaven.

There's one final mystery. A man not present in the story, but who could be at the heart of it. Dr. Alfred Greer. It took a good chunk of her first payment installment to locate and buy a copy of *The Fall of Man, the Birth of Gods*, but she felt it important to get under the skin of the family patriarch. A part of her wishes she hadn't.

It is our God-given duty to apply eugenically artificial selection for the betterment of man . . . he'd written. *Permitting degenerates, imbeciles, and low races to propagate will cause the decline and fall of Western civilization as we know it.* . . . *We must be indifferent to happiness and act with the cold precision of a surgeon bent on removing a decaying part to save the whole.* . . . *Nothing can ever be off-limits, true genius is the application of clarity against the dark mythos of religion, superstition, and societal norms.* . . . *We must remain open to the role technology may have in our perfection, and, if need be, tear the living secrets out of the breast of nature herself to form the ideal race.*

Nice. She's glad she's related to the woman who broke all ties. But she wonders if Aunt Liddy has truly rejected the philosophy, because her name appears on research papers online like "Human Heredity: The Application of Modern Genetics for a Better World"; "Modern Gene Therapy and Responses to Ethical Concerns"; "Future People: Myths, Marvels, and Medical Benefits." Anything directly referencing eugenics is carefully skirted with more oblique language—gene selection, genetic screening, preimplantation genetic diagnosis. Options at a high-tech genetic salad bar for parents who can afford it. But every once in a while, a different note creeps in. Phrases like "the evolution of rational design is a twenty-first-century necessity, particularly as classes become increasingly stratified," "reducing unwanted traits, like the predisposition toward psychopathy, violence, and other personality flaws could be the vanguard of a more peaceful society," and "with the advent of life-prolonging and potential age-reversing technologies, the question of population and resources must be addressed."

Not the same thing, but close for damn sure.

"What exactly are you up to, Aunt Liddy?" Julia says out loud.

She swirls the wine in her glass, puts the notebook on the bed, and walks over to the sliding glass doors of the balcony, takes in the ocean view, the night sky. Sees her own reflection staring pensively back at her.

The truth is, right now she feels like she's about to jump out of a plane, unsure whether the parachute will open.

SIX

THE MAUI AIRPORT IS TWENTY degrees cooler than Los Angeles, but it's still sweltering, just in a different way. No trade winds, apparently, so even though it's open in most parts, the air isn't moving, and there's a volcanic haze courtesy of the Big Island's Mauna Kea. The moisture makes Julia feel like she's trapped in a sauna, and the place is packed, too, a mosh pit of distracted tourists, pale, thick-waisted Midwesterners loading up in the gift shops, Japanese taking selfies, young lovers walking languidly, holding hands. A few professionals in business suits here and there, cutting through the tourists, focused on point A, point B, not even looking where they're going because they already know. It doesn't help that she got exactly zero sleep the night before; maybe an effect of the wine, her nerves, hard to say.

But the worst part is that the promised escort was a no-show—*Someone will be holding a sign with your name,* Bailey had told her—and even though it's a small airport, even though she's walked the length of the concourse at least three times, she can't seem to find the gate for the flight to Kapu, and no one she's asked seems to know anything either. She's directed to talk to a supervisor at her arrival gate, check Visitor Information, call the company that booked the trip (no office hours on Saturday) . . . has she tried searching online? Julia can't help but shake the feeling that she's being purposefully misdirected. There's something about the way eyes shift; they look down at the floor, over her left shoulder, at a piece of paper that's become suddenly interesting. Smiles grow still. Pensive.

For the fifth time, Julia flattens her inkjet copy of the itinerary on the desk at Visitor Information. "It's a charter flight. A private company. You've never heard of it?"

The woman behind the counter has long black hair and a plumeria flower behind her ear. A metal name tag, KALANI. She scans the itinerary as if it's the first time she's seen it (it's not).

"No, like I said, I don't know, but I'm new here. If you call the company you booked it through, I'm sure—"

"I tried, but it's Saturday and the office isn't open. Please, is there anyone you can ask . . . ?"

Sweat beads Julia's forehead, trickles down the curve of her spine. There's a family standing behind her; she feels the press of a toddler against her legs. She's holding up the line.

"You have my bag, right? I checked it at LAX. It must be somewhere." *Christ, if they lost my suitcase, I'm screwed.*

"I can try calling my manager again. . . ." The woman looks over Julia's shoulder at the people behind her. "I'll be with you folks in just a minute."

The toddler starts stomping; out of the corner of her eye Julia catches flashes of red light from the baby's sneakers.

"That's okay," says Julia, taking her paper. "I'll ask around some more. Hopefully my bag hasn't already taken off without me."

The agent gives her a courteous smile, barely able to hide her relief. Julia steps away from the desk, decides on taking another pass by the gates. Will they take off without her? What if they found the secret compartment in her suitcase? She gets a vision of a SWAT team pouring out of a navy van.

Don't psych yourself out, Julia. She pulls her cell phone out again—a burner she'd bought out of a vending machine—dials a number Bailey said was secure. She's already left two voice-mail messages—where the hell can she be? Maybe something more sinister is at play.

Maybe you should go to the bar, says Ethan. *Have a drink, wait in the air-conditioning until the Great White Witch calls you back.*

"Fuck you, Ethan," she whispers.

You have to forgive him before you can truly move forward, Dr. Stolz would say.

She wishes they'd all get the fuck out of her head. Christ, she needs to get a grip. She eyes the bathroom, thinks about going in, splashing some cool water on her face for a cogent moment, but just then an Asian-looking pilot strolls down the concourse with a small rolling suitcase, crowds of pasty-white tourists parting before him. His blue shirt remarkably crisp despite the humidity. He might know.

Julia raises a hand and approaches him. "Excuse me . . . can you tell me which gate is for private charter planes?"

He stops, and smiles broadly. "Can do. Where you going?"

"Kapu."

His smile falters. He looks away. *Here we go again.* For a moment, there seems to be some kind of an internal struggle, and just as she's sure she's going to get the runaround again, he seems to make a decision. He looks her in her eyes, dead serious.

"That's really where you're going . . . ?"

"Yes. Why, what's the problem?"

He hesitates again, then says, "Not a lot to do there. Just one beach, bad currents. Big bugs, too, the size of your fist. If I were you, I'd just stay here on Maui. Much nicer. Lots of great hotels, great food."

Julia feels a trickle of sweat drip down her forehead. "I'm not going there for . . . fun, exactly. And I really need to catch my flight. If you could just point me—"

"I heard one time, someone came back with rat lungworm disease. I have a cousin who treated him at Maui Memorial." He sounds genial, friendly, but there's a current underneath of things unsaid.

She doesn't have the time, or the energy, to figure out what. "Um . . . thanks," Julia says. "You know what, I'll ask the front desk—"

"It's not *for* you." The shift in tone is so abrupt she's momentarily shocked into silence.

"It's sacred," he continues, looking at her steadily. "Your people have no place there."

A relative, perhaps, of one of the dislocated natives? The world around them seems to retreat; for the first time she notices black lines of a tribal-looking tattoo peeking out from the edge of his shirtsleeve.

"My people. You mean *haoles*," says Julia. She'd seen the word in Irene's letters and looked up the meaning. A word for the strange Europeans who wouldn't lean in to mingle breath as a greeting, who instead gave salutations with handshakes, and smallpox, and musket balls. Not a slur, exactly, but close. Is that how he sees her?

But why wouldn't he? It's the money from the ecotourists that are supporting the church, and their legal fight to keep the land. Is that why she's been misdirected ever since she arrived?

"I don't mean to offend," he adds a little more kindly. "Kapu is not . . . It's just, there's a reason why its very name means 'forbidden.' When the sacred isn't respected, it can become dangerous."

Her head feels light all of a sudden, and she watches a group of teen girls trying on leis at the gift shop opposite them. They tease and pull and jostle each other. Aunt Liddy told her to trust no one, but with the pilot, she feels, only the truth will do. Or part of it.

"I know it's dangerous," Julia quietly says. She turns to face him. "My great-grandmother died there. I'm going to bring her body home, so we can bury her with our family."

He can't hide his surprise. A few seconds pass, a few more. "You know, the Hawaiian word for 'burying the dead' is the same as the word for 'planting.'"

He stares at her, waiting for some kind of acknowledgment, but she doesn't know exactly what he means, or what he's asking of her. It's a test she apparently fails, because he finally sighs, and looks away. She senses his mind floating to other priorities, his next flight maybe.

"You'd better hurry then," he says, still not looking at her. "There's a VIP lounge at the end of the terminal. They'll know what to do. Tell them to page Leanne if they give you any trouble."

"Thanks. Really . . . thanks."

He nods again—his fingers grip the handle of his suitcase tighter. Another internal struggle, like he's wondering if anything else he might say would be worth the effort. Finally he says, "Don't cross the wall." He looks up, his gaze piercing. "Stay on the makai, the ocean side of it."

Julia swallows. "Why?"

"You wouldn't understand."

With that he turns and walks away, the sound of his rolling suitcase wheels echoing off the concrete until it's lost among all the other sounds, until he disappears in the crowd, leaving her with the feeling that if she had any sense whatsoever, she'd never step foot on that island at all.

There's a heated discussion in the VIP lounge—a highly irritated service agent stands across from Julia, a phone receiver pressed into her ear, *They're already boarding and there's no Julia Greer on the list*—but at least the lounge has air-conditioning. Julia's warm sweat has chilled, making her even cooler. She tries to shake off what the pilot said. *Superstition,* she tells herself. *It's just superstition. Don't let your imagination get the best of you.*

She wishes she could take advantage of the light refreshments arranged on a long table—lemonade, iced tea, pineapple slices, and butter cookies shaped like pineapples. A little food in her stomach wouldn't be a bad thing. There'd been nothing about meeting in the VIP lounge on the itinerary; apparently that had been covered in a preflight package she never received because she was a late addition, and according to the brochure in front of her, she'd missed out on other perks too. *Indulge in a massage or spa treatment; enjoy lightning-speed free Wi-Fi; sample exotic island pupus in air-conditioned comfort.* Goddamn. She could have gotten a massage. But then, it had all been last-minute—Aunt Liddy had apparently paid off one of the tourists in order to get her the spot since the wait list was a year long. She could only imagine what it cost to bump the passenger.

"Fine," says the service agent in a clipped tone. She's savagely thin, with penciled-in eyebrows, sun-damaged skin, and a fake plumeria behind her ear, obviously a token gesture to aloha. CYN-THIA, says her name tag.

Cynthia hangs up the phone. "I apologize for the confusion." Her tone isn't apologetic in the least. "They're holding the flight for you. Leanne will come by shortly to take you to the gate. Please enjoy our complementary snacks and beverages." With that, the woman picks up a Hawaiian Airlines in-flight magazine, effectively dismissing her.

Oh, thank God. Julia's about to make a run for the lemonade when her own phone rings—an unknown number, but with a Pasadena area code. Should she accept, decline? She clicks *accept*, and steps out of earshot.

"Are they holding the flight?" asks a crisp voice. Bailey.

"Yes, apparently. Where the hell have you been?"

"Putting out fires. We just got all your messages. Someone hacked my SIM card, and the landline to the house was mysteriously cut from *inside* the house. We had to do some serious negotiating to keep that plane on the tarmac. The county will be getting a whole new youth recreational center, all thanks to you."

Sabotage from inside the house . . . ? Just what have I gotten myself into here?

Julia's heart begins to race. "And the escort?"

"We haven't been able to get a hold of him. Our guess is whoever cut the lines also paid him to not show."

"Goddammit." Julia runs a hand through her hair.

"We're instituting extra precautions. You should be fine with the satellite phone, but I'm texting you right now a new number to call in. Don't accept any calls if it's not from that number. Write it down, then ditch your burner phone. I recommend a good dunk in the toilet, then tossing it in the bathroom trash. But whatever you do, *don't* take it on the plane. They confiscate the cell phones before takeoff—it could get into anyone's hands."

Damn, damn, damn. Julia thinks about all the other things she could have packed in the false bottom of the case that would have been useful. Mace, perhaps. A gun, definitely.

An automated voice is broadcast over the speakers, each word a staccato note. *Now boarding flight 572 for Oahu at Gate 17.*

Two men wearing aloha shirts and black slacks quickly stand and start packing their computer bags; some kind of joke is exchanged. There's nothing that says she can't abort right now. She has the cash, she could book a flight back to the mainland, pull all the money out of the account and stuff it under a mattress.

But Evie. The feel of her small hand in hers. Just the thought almost drops her to her knees. Every cell tells her she's headed in the wrong direction—it all now feels unnatural, dangerous, to add more miles and an ocean between them.

"Are you still there?" Bailey asks.

The men leave—there's a whoosh of warm air that swirls in when they open the frosted-glass doors.

But feelings aren't always right. She felt Ethan loved her, and look what happened there. No, it's not really a choice. She needs the money. She needs equal footing, at the very least. So she needs to keep on, no matter how insane this situation is getting by the moment. She turns her back to the door.

"I'm still here. Look, Bailey, if something happens . . ."

She can't finish the sentence. The words *to me* don't need to be spoken.

"I just want Evie . . . I just want her to know I tried. That I didn't abandon her."

This time it's Bailey with the long pause. "Julia, I . . ."

Julia feels warm air again on the back of her neck again, and suddenly there's a very loud male voice behind her.

"I was told I might be too late, but is this where they pick you up for the flight to Kapu?"

Julia turns to find a man in his late thirties, maybe early forties, with patches of gray in his hair and beard, his nose raw and pink from a sunburn. He wears a Red Sox cap, a rumpled brown shirt, equally rumpled cargo shorts, Birkenstocks with socks. A purple lei hangs limply around his neck, and his right hand grips the handle of a battered gray rolling suitcase.

Working a little too hard to look like a tourist.

"... just don't trust anyone. And I mean *anyone*," continues Bailey on the phone. A significant pause, as if there's a hidden meaning Julia will need to work out on her own. "And ditch the phone. ASAP."

The stranger passes her, approaches Cynthia, who is still sitting behind the counter, pointedly flipping a page of her magazine. The scent of coconut sunscreen and possibly pot trails behind him.

"I will," says Julia. She senses he's listening. "I have to go now." She hits *end*. The phone buzzes in her hand—Bailey's text with the new phone number she's supposed to use.

"So am I too late?" the man asks, again a notch too loud.

Cynthia looks up briefly and offers a perfunctory smile. "The flight hasn't departed yet. Your name?"

"Dr. Noah Cooper."

With great reluctance, she puts her magazine down, types something on a keyboard, watching the computer screen.

Well, nothing for it. It's Julia's turn to act the tourist. She steps behind the man, approaches the counter, reaches for one of the pens, and catches his eye in the process. "Did you say you were going to Kapu, too?"

"Looks like I still am." His eyes are dark blue, impersonal. She feels like she's being scanned. "Thought I was shit out of luck."

"They're holding the flight because of me." Julia grabs a brochure to write on. "Now I don't feel so bad."

The man grins. "Glad my ADD has served some purpose

today. I thought the flight was an hour later, but the cabdriver wasn't much help either. When he found out where I was headed, he started taking wrong turns to drive up the tab. Guess word is out that the Kapu tourists are easy marks."

Possibly, possibly not. Julia remembers what the pilot told her. *Maybe there's another reason.*

The man lets go of the suitcase and extends his hand. "I'm Noah."

"So I've heard." She offers hers. "I'm Julia. Julia Greer."

There's a flash of something like recognition at her name, which he covers quickly. "Nice to meet you, Julia."

They'd considered using her father's name as a cover with the other ecotourists, but Julia wanted to go with Greer for just this reason: to see who'd react.

She drops his hand, smiles, and is about to make an excuse that she needs to use the restroom so she can write down the number and ditch the phone, but just then a woman in an expensive tailored navy suit enters the lounge through the frosted-glass doors. Her makeup is impeccable, black hair pulled back into a tight bun, and she has the studied grace of someone trained to be comfortable with the elitest of the elite. Ethan would have hired her on the spot.

"Julia, I assume? And are you Noah?" she asks crisply.

Noah grins. "Guilty as charged."

"A pleasure to meet you both. I'm Leanne." She sizes both of them up, then says: "Well then, we should hurry. Others have been very patiently waiting."

"Do you mind if I just use the ladies' room?"

"I'm sorry, Julia, but we are very much behind schedule," Leanne replies. "We'll be up in the air in no time, and you'll be able to use the lavatory on the plane."

She holds the door open for them—a firm prompt. Warm air rushes in.

Goddammit, Julia thinks. No choice but to go along like it's not a big deal.

The well-dressed woman smiles like a game show hostess, *Right this way*. Her teeth as white as a shark's.

———————————

They're led at a brisk pace through the airport, to a gate at the very end of the concourse and a set of rickety aluminum stairs, then down onto the blindingly hot tarmac, where a small jet waits. Julia can't shake the feeling that she's a cow being led through a chute to a slaughterhouse. Palm trees in the distance, the fronds still, pensive. No chance to throw away the phone, not when she hasn't even been able to write down the number.

Leanne's heels go *clip clip clip* on the pavement, a metronome marking time, the last seconds until Julia's on the plane, until it takes off, until her phone is collected. And damn if Noah isn't walking right beside her, matching her step for step. A peculiar attention.

"And you know," he says, "they say it's bad luck to even pass within eyesight of the volcanic cone on Kapu."

The very last thing she needed or wanted to hear. Christ, he's been talking almost nonstop since they left the VIP lounge. Even the sound of his suitcase is annoying—one wheel is crooked so it drags on the cement, making a rough, scraping noise.

"Pirates and the early European explorers avoided the island entirely."

Julia gives a polite *huh*, but in her mind she's ticking through all the things that could possibly go wrong. Her phone could be confiscated before she can write down the number. Her luggage could be on its way to another state. And she hears the pilot again, *The Hawaiian word for "burying the dead" is the same as the word for "planting."* What a creepy, odd thing to say. Why did he make such a point of it?

Noah continues, relentless. "But really, it's just not the most habitable place. Periodically it suffers from droughts, which makes it untenable for farming or raising livestock."

Is he trying to reassure me or psych me out? A coin toss. She turns her focus instead to the bun at the back of Leanne's head. Not a single, solitary hair out of place. Julia's never trusted people with perfect hair.

"It's funny how that works," Noah says. "A superstition created to address a real danger. I guess superstitions are easier to remember. They have a tendency to stick."

And if he'd only shut up for half a second, I'd have a chance to think.

"It's too bad we'll be confined to such a small part of Kapu. It offers a range of ecosystems. The side we'll be on is lush rain forest, but on the other side it's a desert. Higher up is a bamboo forest. And close to the peak it's supposed to look like a moonscape. Chiclet?"

He offers her one from a crushed yellow pack. For all she knows it could be poisoned. She shakes her head.

"Not exactly on the approved 'all-organic snack' list, are they?" He slips the pack into his back pocket. "What do you think, will they tase me for smuggling in Chiclets?"

With any luck. "You seem to know a lot about the island."

"I should. I did my thesis on it. Now I teach environmental science."

"So you're a professor?"

"Adjunct. Working poor, essentially. But Kapu has always been on my bucket list. I looked into chartering a boat once.

Didn't find any takers." There's a sheen of sweat on his brow, circles of sweat under his armpits.

Leanne reaches the stairs for the plane, gives them a more peremptory wave this time, her studied cool revealing a hint of irritation. *Chop, chop.*

"Expensive trip for an adjunct professor," says Julia.

"Well, I did have that friend in college who went on to work at Google before anyone knew what it was. Got in just as it launched publicly. When I found that Kapu was opening its doors for tourism, I sold some shares."

An unlikely story. But then they're at the bottom of the stairs, and Leanne's aplomb is obviously starting to wear thin. Even *she's* worked up a sweat. It gives Julia a slight bit of gratification.

Noah pauses. "Ladies first," he says in a jokey tone.

"It's the twenty-first century—you go first," says Julia.

Again his expression wavers and something else comes through—a kind of wariness. Just as suddenly, it vanishes. "All right, your funeral if I accidentally drop this puppy." He takes the first step up, his suitcase hitting the tread of the staircase hard. *Bang.* It must be heavy. What the hell's inside? *Bang, bang, bang* it goes up the steps.

If she can't ditch the phone, how would they know she's smuggling it in? Unless they plan on patting her down or they're going to wave security wands over them, which she doubts.

She reaches out for the handrail, takes the first step up.

Run.

She doesn't know where this thought comes from, but it's a strong one, nearly overwhelming. Her heart pounds.

Run while you can.

But the sun glints in her eyes, and Leanne's smile is hardening, and there's nothing but a life of emptiness behind Julia, and she remembers the last thing, the very last thing Ethan said to her as she was packing up her things (no, make that the few things he let her keep).

In time, she'll forget you. You'll just be a picture in an album that she opens up every once in a while, when she's feeling nostalgic.

Julia thinks: *I'll be damned if I ever let Ethan erase me that way.*

She climbs the steps.

———————————

The plane is posh, but not inordinately so—massive seats covered in soft leather with plenty of legroom, large TV screens embedded in the back cushions. Cool air softly pushed through the overhead vents. Music playing—classical. Chopin, she thinks.

"Phones please," says Leanne brightly.

Noah digs his out of his back pocket, turns it over—a burner, like hers.

Interesting.

Leanne drops Noah's phone into a bright red bin, with about eight others. Turns to Julia.

"I didn't bring a phone," Julia says.

Noah's head turns—goddammit, she forgot he'd seen her using it—but he doesn't rat her out. Leanne doesn't seem to believe her either, but she is, after all, a paying guest. Leanne puts the bin in an overhead compartment, locking it tightly. Why? Does she expect there'd be a mad dash for the phones? A cellular coup d'état?

Then there's a quick walk down the aisle, which feels more like a walk down the plank—all ten other passengers glaring, not bothering to hid their irritation at the long wait—and then she and Noah reach the last two available seats, right next to each other, of course. *Just my luck.*

At least she has the good sense to nab the window. When they're airborne, she can hit the bathroom, write down the number, pop the SIM card, and flush it down the toilet. Not an ideal plan, but a functional one. Noah stows his rolling suitcase in the overhead—so heavy he strains to lift it over his head— *what the hell is* in *there?*—and she tucks her purse under the seat in front of her, wraps a complimentary blanket around her— cashmere, nice touch—lays her head on the small lavender-scented pillow, also complimentary, and closes her eyes. As good a way as any to avoid another earful of Noah.

She hears and ignores the standard safety instructions—as if anyone would have the presence of mind to pull out the cushion to use as a float if the plane crashed into the ocean—then there's a ding as the FASTEN SEAT BELT lights pop on, the rumble of the engine starting, and a shudder as the jet starts to roll down the tarmac. She can feel the excitement of everyone around her, that pre-vacation vibe. Not an emotion she shares.

Noah settles into the seat next to her. His thigh brushes against hers; she can hear him fiddling with the seatbelt, but thank God he strikes up a conversation with someone across the aisle.

She hears him say, "Do you snorkel?"

Perfect. *Let him make a new buddy.* Her eyes feel genuinely heavy—the insomnia, the anxiety of all the preparations, the task ahead. It's hard to keep them closed and not feel the tug of sleep. But she can't afford to fall asleep. She can't afford to drop her guard.

And then a thought strikes her. All those years ago when her mother first dragged her to Aunt Liddy's house, that first meeting. *Aunt Liddy wasn't in a wheelchair.* She distinctly remembers Aunt Liddy standing in the entry, leading her mother to the library, walking. Impossible if, as Aunt Liddy said, she'd been paralyzed long ago.

How strange. Unsettling that her memory could have gotten it so wrong.

Julia yawns. The drone of the engine a comforting white noise, a gentle rocking as they make their ascent. And then, despite her best intentions, she actually falls asleep.

———————————

An island. An island surrounded by clouds where the ocean should be. A white sand beach and a narrow path leading into a dark bamboo forest. Julia feels sand between her toes, a breeze that tickles. The sky an impossible blue. She hears the soft click of bamboo hitting bamboo. *Click, click, click. Crick, crick, crick. Trick, trick, trick.*

A solemn, ghostly shadow appears at the edge of the bamboo forest—the pilot—no, not the pilot, just his clothes, standing like they're supported by an invisible body.

Her secrets are her own.

What secrets? she wants to ask, but the world tilts beneath her, and suddenly the clouds are gone, and she faces a rocky precipice with a roaring waterfall and roiling green waters. The sky above now a bruised purple, white streaks of clouds like claw marks.

Shadows lengthen, deepen. Julia shivers. *I'm not supposed to be here.* She missed her flight, the one that would have taken her to the East Coast, to Evie. She's not where she's supposed to be.

Terminally naive, Ethan whispers.

Suddenly there's a rumble like thunder and suitcases fall

from the sky, crashing through the trees, cracking open when they hit the pockmarked lava rocks. Underwear, ribbons, blouses, nylons, stuffed animals, children's clothing, ties, suit shirts. The clamor draws a flock of vultures; they swoop in to pluck out the shiny bits—a pearl necklace, a gold chain, a ring with a glimmering red stone.

But it's not a pearl necklace. It's an eyeball still tethered to an optic nerve. The gold chain is actually a clump of blond hair. The ring a small vertebrae.

A silk nightgown lands at Julia's bare feet. It's torn, bloodstained. This doesn't surprise her, but she's not sure why.

Suddenly all the vultures take off in startled unison, dropping their prizes in a hurry to escape, hissing and trilling. Julia's gaze is drawn across the river. From within the shadow of jungle brush, a pair of glowing eyes meet hers. Something feral about them. Predatory.

I spy with my little eye.

It's not her voice—it's another inside her head, and although her throat thickens with fear, she takes a step forward. Not a choice, not a decision, more of a reflex, like her legs acted on impulse. The ground is soft, spongy, like a marsh or a bog, and her foot sinks—*squish*. A slithery thing wraps itself around her ankles, and she feels thin needles pricking her skin. This doesn't surprise her either. It's all predestined. Inevitable. She takes another step forward, her foot sinking ankle-deep into the muck.

There are others now, surrounding her. The clothes all standing upright, no people within. But she feels them, their invisible spirits. She's not alone; they're bearing witness. She'll never be alone again.

There's a *poof* sound, like a balloon deflating, and she's suddenly surrounded by clouds of fine white particles, the stench of something sickly sweet, rotting. She looks down at her arm, and black, necrotic flesh hangs from it, exposing a gleam of white bone underneath. It all makes her drowsy for some strange reason—she's so relaxed, even as she continues to sink. *The mud is a tomb, the mud is a womb*. She's dying. She's being born.

And the eyes, the eyes across the river emerge from the cover of brush—they belong to a white tiger, thin as a starving greyhound. It leaps into the churning water, jumping from the crest of one wave to another. Not water then. What? Julia doesn't know whether she'll be eaten or will drown in the muck, but somehow it doesn't seem to matter. No, it's the nightgown that's important, because someone's wearing it now, a ghostly body lying just out of reach, skin as pale as milk. Head turned away, a swatch of brown hair crudely shorn from her head. Little green tendrils, like roots, reaching out of her skin into the ground.

And the tiger is almost on her. On them.

She feels something slither around her shoulder, her neck, small needling pricks in her back. . . . *I'm sorry, Evie. I tried, I tried my best.* Her eyes lock onto one of the stuffed animals that had fallen out of a suitcase—a vintage Steiff teddy bear, just like the one she'd given Evie on her fifth birthday. Mr. Bones, Evie had named him, because unlike her other stuffed animals, he could stand up. She swore that he could even walk at night when she was asleep.

Maybe, thinks Julia. A thick vine just out of reach. *Maybe if I can grab . . .*

But there are little green roots growing out of her own arm now, weaving through the dead flesh, binding her to the earth. And the tiger is on her side of the river. It's coming . . . coming . . . coming. The beast lifts its head, tastes her scent in the air. Licks its lips with a thick red tongue. It's all as it should be, as it ever was.

Suddenly there's a massive crack of thunder, a vibration that causes the muck she's sinking into to quiver. She hears a soft ding from far away, another planet maybe. No . . . she's trying to wake up. . . . *The airplane*. She's dreaming. But the fantasy pulls at her, tries to keep her here, on the island with the tiger that pads closer. It sniffs her hair, the back of her neck. She can smell rotting meat on its breath.

I spy with my little eye . . . something that begins with the letter f.

It's almost there, what the word is, it's on the tip of her tongue but it won't come out, like the remnants of a dream before it dissipates, vanishes. Forbidden, she thinks. Forlorn. Forsaken.

A hand shakes her shoulder—the tiger nuzzles her shoulder. She has a foot in both worlds, and then another word comes to her: *forget*. Forget, forgot, forgotten. No, that's not it. She hears the drone of the airplane, the rustling of other passengers, and before she can ask the tiger, before she can figure out *why* this word feels so important, the dream dissolves, light as ether, and she feels the cashmere against her cheek, the cool press of glass on her forehead.

Her neck aches. She can't feel her left arm. She opens her eyes and finds Noah grinning at her, his hand on her shoulder.

"Damn, you were *out*," he says.

She looks around, and all the other passengers are peering through their porthole-size windows, an electric undercurrent of excitement.

She blinks, sits up straighter. Realizes her vulnerability. She casts an eye at her purse, which she'd tucked under the seat in front of her.

"What . . ." Her mind is still thick with the dream. Groggy. "Where are we?"

"We're *here*," Noah says. "We're just about to land."

And at first she doesn't remember, but then she does, and looks out the window to find a small island coming into view, densely green in parts, golden grassland in others, a sharp peak jutting out from the center, wreathed in mist. The pointy remains of the crumbling, extinct volcano. None of the photos managed to capture its immense scale, or its raw, savage beauty.

Kapu.

She doesn't understand why—maybe it's just the aftermath of the dream—but it feels like a homecoming of sorts.

#NDC DEV ORG HUB

20:09:52	**<isir528>**	lilith in transport?
20:09:58	**<bai908>**	yes. confirmed on board. eta 30 min. no inspection on her bag.
20:10:14	**<isir528>**	not possible. they receive direct instruction.
20:10:27	**<bai908>**	no inspection. not up for discussion. make it happen.
20:10:58	**<bai908>**	hello?
20:11:02	**<isir528>**	fuck. if he finds out.
20:11:08	**<bai908>**	make sure he doesn't.
20:11:15	**<isir528>**	easy for you to say.
20:11:21	**<bai908>**	you can wipe red's tears away with thousand-dollar bills when this is over.
20:11:41	**<isir528>**	he suspects. watching.
20:11:48	**<bai908>**	stop whining and do your fucking job. and be on time tomorrow.
20:12:04	**<isir528>**	meds in transport?
20:12:09	**<bai908>**	negative. meds stolen with exhibit a. lilith has last batch.
20:12:24	**<isir528>**	we need those meds.
20:12:29	**<bai908>**	you had 2 months' worth.
20:12:35	**<isir528>**	had to increase dosage. voc's at record level.
20:12:47	**<bai908>**	check passenger 4b. or make sure lilith makes goal sooner, then take hers.
20:13:06	**<isir528>**	seriously? i thought she was off-limits.
20:13:17	**<bai908>**	she's a means to an end. get her to the end faster, then do what you have to.
20:13:36		- - > **bai908** has quit

SEVEN

THE PLANE GLIDES OVER THE eco-resort—there's a pier connecting a series of thatched huts on stilts spread out over a lagoon, each with a steep, Polynesian-style roof, other huts nestled into the jungle's hillside that overlook a long, winding stretch of a white sand beach, and all of it encompassed by a low wall, vegetation cleared on either side, that runs up and over a ridge like an artery. The plane circles, then lands on a narrow strip of bumpy concrete that runs almost level to the turquoise ocean waters. Slowly taxis to a stop. A ding, and the FASTEN SEAT BELT sign goes off. There's the standard, pre-exit bustle—seats put in the upright position, bags zipped; a couple of men stand, impatient to get off already. If they knew what Julia did, maybe they wouldn't be so eager. She remembers the first passage in Irene's journal: *I made the decision that if it was my destiny to perish over an anonymous bit of Pacific, then so be it.* It wasn't so easy for her to let go, though, in the end.

"God, I'm starving. You missed the meal but it wasn't much, at least by man standards," says Noah. "I tried to score yours, but Leanne wasn't having it."

He's jokey, assuming the familiarity of a friend, trying to establish trust. She would do the same thing if she were in his position. Start by asking about the kids, talk about the weather, before digging in with, *So why did you think it was okay to bury PCB-contaminated dirt in a playground?*

"What'd they serve?" Julia asks, playing along. She checks the urge to grab her purse to see what, if anything, might be missing.

"Poached salmon, not half bad, on some kind of stale bread that was labeled 'toasted brioche.' And about a thimbleful of whipped lemon mousse. I'm hoping it's all-you-can-eat buffet from here."

He leans over, looks through the window, invading her space. "Supposed to be some of the best snorkeling in the world, right from that cove."

She reaches down for her purse—she'd zipped it shut, she's pretty sure. So why is it unzipped? The tip of the brochure pokes out. *Even if he saw the number, though, it's not like he can do anything with it.* Unless, like her, he's smuggling some tech in.

There's another ding and Leanne exits the pilot's cabin. She reaches for the intercom, smiles. "The pilot has turned off the seat belt sign, and you are free to move about the cabin. Time is four thirty-six p.m., and the temperature outside is a *lovely* seventy-two degrees."

Noah leans back in his seat. "Might as well let the old folks exit before we get up. Did I tell you about the woman at the Benihana in Waikiki who caught on fire?"

Julia swallows what she'd like to say, which is *would you please shut the hell up?*, and instead says, "No, I don't think so."

"I must be thinking about it because I'm really wishing for a good steak right now. Oh my God. So you know how it goes, they chop, chop, chop, and this chef, he cuts an onion, sprays it with some kind of oil and tosses his knife up in the air, right? And I don't know what happened exactly, I just heard the screams, but I look over, and I swear to God this pretty young thing, her T-shirt is on fire. *On fire.* Everybody is freaking out—I mean, this is bad for business right? Oh look, look over there!"

He points excitedly through the window, and Julia catches a glimpse of a gray hump arcing through the shallow water.

"Dolphin! Wow! I bet we'll see sea turtles too. So, do you snorkel?"

Goddamn, he's effectively blocking her exit with his long legs. "I've always wanted to." *I should sound excited, I don't sound excited enough. Or rich enough.* "I can't wait. My husband—ex-husband—hated hot weather. We'd summer in Europe instead."

She watches to see if he gets it, the use of *summer* as a verb, the nomenclature of the wealthy. Something that'd confused her the first time one of Ethan's friends asked, *Where do you summer?* There had been smirks after she asked what he meant. The truth, though, is she never liked swimming in the ocean, the possibility of something unseen rising up under you, coming from an unknown direction.

Something she said does seem to throw him off-balance—she can feel him recalibrating. *Good.* "I know I asked, but what did you say you did for a living?"

She didn't say, and he didn't ask. "I was a professional wife. And now I'm unemployed." There's an edge of real pain when she says this—so she turns to the window to head off a follow-up question.

And finds a strange scene. Lined up along the tarmac is a row of white women—long hair that reaches their waist, leis draped in their hands; they wear floppy straw hats, bland cotton smocks. For a welcome crew, they seem oddly stiff, all of them at attention, like they're frozen in place. At their head is a young man in a Mormon-ish short-sleeved white shirt, black tie, and black slacks. He also wears a straw hat, and he holds a clipboard tightly to his chest. For a group of people who live in the tropics, it's odd how pale their skin is, like they rarely go outside. *Or maybe they're religious about sunscreen too.* Behind them is a white portable tent, with an array of folding tables and plastic bins.

There are also a bunch of tourists standing under the shade of a thatched portico—the eco-resort returnees. At least they look tanned, relaxed, and are chatting, suitcases and bags waiting by their feet for the trip back.

It eases Julia's mind somewhat, seeing them like that. Alive. Unharmed. Happy, even. It takes the edge off her dream, what the pilot said. But she shouldn't take a chance with the phone. She should at least destroy the SIM card before she gets off.

"I'm sorry," Noah says. "I didn't mean to . . . Well, even my best friends say I have no filter and am nosy to the point of being obnoxious. Whatever I'm thinking just pops out of my mouth."

She turns to him with a fake smile. "There's no need to apologize."

He looks visibly relieved.

"Do you mind if I squish by you?" Julia asks. "I need to use the restroom."

"Sure, sure," he says. "Let me just . . ." He stands, and steps into the aisle, and she grabs her purse from under the seat, which seems to fluster him even more, the obvious implication being feminine products.

He leans over the back of the seat of the passengers in front of them. "Where are you all from?"

As she's heading to the back of the plane, a fluttery movement outside the emergency exit window catches her eye. A bird, bright green with red spots on its wings and bright blue legs, lands on the frame of the window outside. It feels familiar, like she's seen it before, but at first she can't place it, until she does.

In her great-aunt's basement, all those years ago. She'd seen its taxidermied cousin mounted on wood, graying with dust.

The bird peers at her, cocks its head inquisitively, then flutters off and out of sight.

———————

It's a relief to have a few minutes alone in the bathroom, which is twice as big as the ones on commercial flights, with understated mahogany paneling, a raised bowl of a porcelain sink, basket of rolled towels embroidered ISLAND AIR. Cool air pushes through vents near the ceiling. Christ, her frizzy hair is even more of a mess than usual, the mascara around her right eye smudged from the pillow. She digs around in her purse for a brush.

She's been alone for so long that it feels weird being in tight quarters with people, and especially unnerving being around moneyed people again. She'd caught the tail end of a complaint as she passed by the last row, a woman grumbling to her partner that the movie she'd been watching on the back of the screen had been cut off, and she won't be able to find out how it ends until they return.

No concept of what it's like to be hungry, but then have to throw out food because your electricity has been turned off and it's rotting. A whole realm of experience she'll have to keep to herself. Probably best to talk as little as possible to the others, keep her focus on the task at hand.

Julia finds the brush, and a paper clip—*thank God*—takes an end, bends it. Then she digs for her phone and uses the paper clip end to pop out the SIM card. It slides out easily. She'd smash it for good measure, but the sound might attract attention, so she tosses it in the toilet bowl and flushes. Hopes that the chemicals will be enough to fry it.

Now, what to do with the phone? She could flush that too, but if it clogged the drain, someone might find it and then there'd be questions. Trash can? Too obvious. But then, it's not like someone could trace it to her. Wait . . . no, she bought it from a vending machine with her credit card. They probably could, theoretically. She can't take any chances, not while she's so far away from civilization.

Her sneaker. The phone is small enough to fit under her foot. Then later she could just stow it in her suitcase with all the other prohibited gear. Toss it into a waterfall. Bury it. Something.

There's a soft but firm knock on the door.

"Is everything okay in there?"

Leanne. Of course.

"Yes, I'm fine," Julia says, untying the laces of her sneaker. "Would you mind tracking down a bottle of water for me? I'm a little dizzy. I think I got dehydrated."

A pause. "Of course," Leanne says, because there's no other way to respond. She's the hired help.

Julia slips the phone into her left shoe, hurriedly reties the laces. Not comfortable, but it will work. She stands, turns on the faucet, splashes some hot water on her face, then wipes away the mascara smudges around her eye with one of the rolled towels. Brushes her hair and then runs wet fingers through it to tamp down the flyaway strands.

Don't look suspicious. Don't look like you have a phone in your shoe. What would Ethan do? Act like he owned the place, of course, stroll out nonchalantly. If only he could see her now— Julia Greer, corporate spy.

She hates the part of her that still misses him.

She takes a moment, then tosses the towel in the bin, opens the door, and almost runs into Leanne, who has indeed tracked down a bottle of water. Leanne clutches it in her right hand, white knuckles visible through her skin. Tiny beads of sweat dot her upper lip.

What's she *so nervous about?*

"Oh, thank you," says Julia. "I was so thirsty. I rarely fall asleep on planes."

"I'm so glad you found our cabin comfortable."

Our cabin, like the plane is Leanne's personal property. A habit that those who commingle with the rich eventually pick up, that gloss of superiority. It never stuck to Julia for some strange reason. Maybe she subconsciously knew there was a time limit on her stay.

Everyone's disembarked, but then there were only ten other people on board besides her and Noah. It must be killing Leanne that Julia's lingering.

"Is there anything else you need before you go?" she asks, offering the water.

Julia takes it. "No, thank you."

Leanne's eyes keep flitting toward the open door. A wisp of hair has escaped her bun, and she seems frayed, on edge. Julia senses something else underneath, a wired kind of near panic.

There's a clipboard hanging from a hook across from the open door. A soft breeze rustles the attached paper.

Julia uncaps the water bottle, takes a sip. "Very refreshing."

Leanne's bottom lip starts to tremble. *Is she about to cry? Why does she look like she's about to cry?*

"Have a wonderful time," Leanne says. She looks down at the aisle, steps past Julia, and almost rushes into the restroom. The lock clicks.

Leaving Julia alone on the plane. She hoists her purse up onto her shoulder, starts down the aisle, taking in the scattered debris of the tourists who have already disembarked. Crumpled napkins. Magazines stashed in front pockets. A clear plastic cup with melting ice, and a sad wedge of lemon.

It makes her feel strange, although it shouldn't. It's just trash. But it almost feels like that one time she'd been assigned to cover a missing-persons story and an aunt had led her through the house where her niece and nephew had vanished, along with their two children, although the wallets and purses were still in the house, the keys to the car still hanging on a hook. Julia had walked through the kitchen after the police were done with it. Crusts of toast on plates. Glasses leaving rings on the stained-oak kitchen table.

But the tourists haven't vanished; they're just outside. *Stay focused, Julia.*

She hears a thunk up ahead. A pause, and then *thunk, thunk, thunk.* Then there's a crash, and then she hears Noah unleash a series of curses. That damn suitcase of his.

When she's just about at the exit door, she realizes that Leanne still hasn't come out of the bathroom.

Like she's hiding.

But from who?

Or from what?

———————

At the top of the stairs, a rickety affair of rusting aluminum, Julia pauses, momentarily stunned. God, it's so beautiful it hurts her eyes, like every tropical paradise cliché sprung to life. The green of the palm trees and leaves is so vibrant, so lush; the air so fresh she can smell the salt on the breeze; the sky a perfect blue, with the warm sun casting everything in a golden hue. No burnished haze of smog. No sound of traffic, or sirens, or rumbling trucks. Just the slap of the ocean waves against the beach, the rustle of the wind through the palm fronds, scattered birdsong. The island hasn't been flattened into submission with concrete and roads and Wi-Fi and fast-food chains. It's still wild. Pristine.

Dangerous.

Noah, of course, is waiting for her at the bottom of the stairs. She's going to have to do some serious figuring on how to handle him.

Well, nothing for it. Julia walks down to join him. There's some kind of process ahead—the other disembarked tourists line up before the young man, who appears to be checking IDs, matching names to his clipboard—*Really? As if we'd have been able to board with a fake one?*—before each guest receives a lei from another unsmiling churchwoman in a plain smock, who doesn't say a word or make eye contact. Weird.

She wonders why they don't hire professionals from one of the other islands, or if the churchwomen themselves have ever left the island, experienced hospitality themselves. Probably not. She can't imagine what it'd be like to be born and raised on such a small circle of land, to never know anything about the outside world beyond the few tourists who visit. The guests must seem strange to the congregation too, alien intruders.

After they clear the ID check, everyone's purses, bags, and personal items are confiscated at the very end of the line by a young woman with hunched shoulders and blunt-cut red hair that hangs over her face. She piles everything into plastic bins, which are then silently collected by another churchwoman. A third woman goes through the bags, checking them thoroughly.

Julia grips her purse tighter, tries to think about what she wouldn't want anyone to find. The brochure, obviously. It would look innocuous enough, but it's not something she wants to lose track of.

Noah catches her look. "This sure as hell wasn't in the marketing."

"No, it wasn't."

They both stare at the line, equally pensive. "Probably extra precautions to keep invasive species out," he says. "I guess we just have to roll with it."

"I guess."

They head toward the end of the line. Some of the other tourists seem agitated too. A woman in her thirties with flat blond hair, a red Prada bag over her shoulder, mutters to a companion, "Do you see the way they're just tossing the bags around?"

"They better not leave a mark, not a mark on my purse."

"And, like, oh my God, what are they wearing?"

Julia hears a loud clunk behind them, and turns to see a small, burly man quickly removing their luggage from the plane and loading it up on a dolly. Not a member of the church—he wears jeans, a checked shirt, and latex gloves, a face mask over his mouth and nose. He doesn't look up, doesn't look their way, intent on his task.

No one else notices him. No one ever notices the help.

Why is he wearing a face mask?

A large middle-aged man, wearing an aloha shirt that looks brand-new, steps out of line. "Hey!" he shouts in the general direction of the young man with the clipboard. "Excuse me!"

The young man looks up at him, pushes his thick, black-framed glasses back up his nose. He leans over to one of the women, murmurs something in her ear. She turns and walks away, and she's joined by another woman, not a word or a look exchanged between them. They head for the dolly and the luggage.

This doesn't feel right.

"Excuse me!" the middle-aged man shouts. "Hey! What exactly are you doing with our things?"

The young man smiles and walks toward them. The harsh glare of the setting sun reflects off his glasses. "Hello, you must be . . ."

The man stands straighter. "Rog-er Nel-son." Delivered in four terse syllables, like they're words of the magi and can open the entrance to any cave filled with treasure.

But the name has no such relevance here. The young man holds up his clipboard, scans it, makes a quick note, smiling the entire time in a way that is also subtly dismissive. His teeth are perfectly white, perfectly straight.

"Oh, here you are. Welcome to Kapu. It's a pleasure to meet you in person. My name is Isaac, and I'll be your host for your stay."

"Well, *Isaac,* I'd like to speak to your supervisor, because this is not acceptable."

"We're simply checking all baggage for any unapproved items. We've found that some people don't necessarily read the list of things to not bring, or misunderstand, and to preserve the integrity of this undisturbed natural preserve, we have to be thorough. If we do find unapproved items, we'll place them in a plastic bag, label it with your name, and return it to you on your departure."

Roger takes a presumptive step forward, puffs his chest out. "I don't want you mucking about with my valuables, young man. There wasn't anything in—"

"Nothing that is not unapproved will be removed," says

Isaac, holding his ground without flinching. As if he's heard, and ignored, this very issue many times before. "We are fully bonded and insured, and have never had a complaint."

"Well, your supervisor—"

"I am your only point of contact here on the island."

Why is the baggage handler wearing a face mask? Maybe he's just sick, doesn't want to spread a bug he picked up? She'd imagine that the church members have sensitive immune systems, not having been exposed to all the viruses of the world. *Seems plausible. Don't freak yourself out, Julia.*

A woman standing next to Roger, wearing white shorts and a golf visor, says, "Well, I didn't agree to—"

"Yes, you did—page fifteen of the agreement," says Isaac crisply. "I can show you if you'd like. However, you're welcome to leave with the returning guests if you don't want us to check your bags. But then, there will be no reimbursement of your vacation package, as per page fourteen, paragraph five. Now, if you could just stand in line with the others so we can let the guests board the plane, we would certainly appreciate it." With that, he turns around and heads back to the thatched portico, completely unperturbed.

The woman leans into the man standing next to her—her husband, probably. "Well, I *never*. We should complain to management as *soon* as we get back. I've never been treated so rudely—do they really think that just because they're charging us up the ass they can *speak* to us this way?"

"So, do you want to stay, Lois?" asks Roger.

"Of *course* I want to stay. I've been looking forward to this all *year*. I'm not going to let some *twit* . . ."

Julia tunes out the rest of the conversation. She's heard it hundreds of times before among Ethan's cadre, who expect the world to cater to them at all times. Instead she casts a glance at the two churchwomen who are grabbing the handle of the dolly to lug the first load of suitcases. Then over at Isaac, speaking quietly to the returning tourists under the shaded portico. He has their complete attention. They grab their bags and start to walk toward the plane, smiling and waving back at him. Everyone is busy, distracted.

She quickly slips her hand into her purse, grabs the brochure, folds it, and puts it in her back pocket, just in case. No one seems to notice.

Christ, though, what if they find the false bottom in her suitcase?

"Dammit," says Noah.

She's not alone in her predicament, apparently.

"I'm so busted," he says with a sigh. "Might as well get it over with." With that, he steps out of line and rolls his suitcase directly over to the redheaded young woman, wheels grating on the bumpy pavement. With a mighty heave he lifts his suitcase up on the table, where it lands with a loud thunk, and unzips it with a flourish.

It's a scene. Everyone in line cranes their necks to see what he tried to smuggle in.

He reaches in, pulls out a full case of beer. Another case, this one of canned chili. Three boxes of doughnuts.

Snickers among the guests standing in line—an immediate lightening of the mood. Roger whistles and shouts, "Party tonight!"

Isaac seems visibly pained. Makes a note on his clipboard— terse, angry scratches.

If Noah was looking to gain friends, he just did, in droves. Everyone's always attracted to the rebel. *Smart move,* thinks Julia.

It's why no one else but she pays much attention to the returning guests passing by them, on their way to board the plane. Maybe it's just the effect of spending a week in paradise, but they all seem remarkably healthy—it practically radiates off of them. Smooth skin, not a single mole or freckle or wrinkle, even on the women who are obviously older. Hair that shines and bounces, as if they just stepped out of a salon. And what the hell did they use to shave? Razors were definitely on the "don't bring" list, yet their legs are smooth, like they've been recently waxed. Plump lips, no bags under the eyes. It's a level of perfection that Julia knows is very, very expensive, that usually takes a team to create and maintain. Is that the real secret, why the wait list is so long? Maybe the church has secreted away some kind of plastic surgery facility, a neat way to get some work done under the guise of a vacation. Brilliant, really.

She turns to watch them board the plane, and for a moment her heart literally skips a beat. Leanne, standing in the jet's open doorway. Now wearing a face mask as well.

EIGHT

LEANNE WASN'T SICK. NOT A cough, not a sneeze. *So why the hell is she wearing a face mask?* Julia tries to find an alternate theory, fails. None of the church members wear a mask, none of the returning guests. If there had been an outbreak here, swine flu, COVID, something like that, they'd probably be wearing them too—unless that would make for bad PR, which it would. A quarantine would be bad for business. But everyone seems so damn *healthy*, even the churchwomen in smocks, weird as they are.

What did the pilot say, something about rat-lung disease? Didn't sound fun, and how do you catch *that*?

Julia looks to see where her suitcase is—finds it's precariously situated on top of the others on the dolly, being pulled toward the pop-up tent. One of the women has a hand on it to keep it steady. Julia imagines the suitcase falling off as it's bounced and jostled along the way, cracking open to reveal what she's smuggling in. Wonders whether they'd send her packing on the return flight or if they'd quietly take her into the jungle and push her off a cliff.

Terminally naive, Ethan whispers.

Stop it, Julia. She's not going to make it two days, let alone seven, if she lets her imagination get the best of her. When she'd been working at the paper, she'd had nerves of steel, which she'd needed to interrupt powerful executives at press conferences with pointed questions or to meet whistleblowers afraid for their lives. But motherhood had softened her, then the divorce, the aftermath, the lean times wrecking her. She's going to have to resurrect her old self—or at least a reasonable facsimile—if she's going to get through this.

It doesn't take long for the returning guests to finish boarding; the baggage handler starts to load their luggage into the cargo compartment while the churchwomen under the tent sift through the purses, fanny packs, and suitcases with the efficiency of factory workers. Zip, dig, unfold, shake, refold. Not a single word exchanged between them. Not a single look. So very, very strange.

The line moves quickly, and soon it's Julia's turn to hand over her purse to the young woman with red hair hanging over her face. *Don't look suspicious. Don't think about the phone in your shoe.* Impossible not to, when the damn thing feels like a rock. Her foot is already throbbing.

The young woman takes the purse, and Julia gets a glimpse of her jaw—skin poorly healed from what must have been a third-degree burn. Her lips appear to be silently moving, although it's hard to tell for sure.

"Beautiful weather," says Julia.

The woman doesn't respond, doesn't react, just puts the purse in a plastic bin. Something furtive in her movements. It reminds Julia of a woman she once interviewed at a shelter for battered women, the same twitchy kind of nervousness. She wonders if this church *is* more cult than congregation.

Julia puts her hand on the bin. "I forgot, I need to show my ID, right?"

The woman pauses.

So she can hear me all right.

Julia reaches out for her purse and then pretends to knock
the bin onto the ground by accident. The woman crouches down
to retrieve it, and Julia crouches down too, ostensibly to help, if
anyone's watching.

"I'm so sorry, I'm just a big klutz," Julia says warmly, reaching
for her wallet, which has fallen out onto the ground.

The woman looks at her—the strangest eye Julia has ever
seen in her life, so gray that it's almost white, with jagged green
daggers radiating out from the iris. She whispers, *"I spy with my
little eye. . . . I spy with my little eye. . . ."*

That was in my dream. Julia hears the crunch of shoes on
pebbles behind her. The woman looks down immediately, grabs
the purse, and clutches it to her chest, like an animal expecting a
blow.

"Is everything all right here?"

Julia looks up. Isaac again. His straw hat, backlit by the sun,
forms a shadow halo around his head. In his hand, a lei.

"Other than me knocking over everything in sight, yes," says
Julia, getting to her feet. "I forgot you needed to see our ID, and
was just trying to get it."

Isaac smiles widely, something forced about it. "Oh, there's
no need for an ID, not for you, Miss Greer. We'd recognize you
anywhere. Welcome to Kapu."

They'd recognize her anywhere? What the hell . . . ? It
makes no sense, but he holds up the lei with both hands, and
there's no choice really but to bow her head and allow him to
place it around her neck, although the whole thing feels unbear-
ably uncomfortable. A subtext at play that she doesn't understand.

Out of the corner of her eye, Julia sees an older churchwoman hoist her suitcase onto one of the folding tables. She

unzips it. Julia's heart starts to pound so loudly it's amazing no one can hear.

She swallows, smiles at Isaac. "I'm so glad to be here."

"Well then, let's get you settled in."

After a last, lingering glance behind her—she sees the redhead push the older churchwoman out of the way, somewhat forcefully, then grab Julia's suitcase—they head to join the others gathered under the portico.

All the way there, Julia half expects to hear one of the churchwomen call out, announce the discovery of all the very incriminating gear she has hidden in the false bottom of her luggage. Or at least notice her odd gait as she struggles to walk normally with a phone in her shoe. But none do, and they reach the others that have gathered under the shade—they've all effectively traded places with the tourists now on the plane. The roof of the portico is dramatically steep, with supporting beams made of bamboo and dried thatch. There's a wonderful view of the beach from one side, a small trail leading into the jungle from the other. A fresh breeze blows through.

Isaac, clipboard pressed against his chest, steps past her and up onto a slightly elevated platform. Julia notes sweat stains radiating out from under his arms. Everyone's sweating now, for different reasons.

Isaac coughs to clear his throat, and raises his head slightly.

"Welcome, everyone. We at the Church of Eternal Light thank you for choosing Kapu for your island paradise vacation. We will endeavor to make your stay here as enjoyable, and as unforgettable, as possible." He runs through this quickly, like it's an overrehearsed spiel.

There are shared, highly irritated glances. The unexpected property search has not gone over well.

He ignores the rancor and continues, "Before I hand out cottage assignments, I'd like to review the rules and responsibilities that you should have received in your welcome packet. Did everyone receive the welcome packet?"

There's a general murmur of consensus. Julia eyes the other guests. In addition to Noah, who seems to have attached himself to a young couple now—newlyweds maybe? They beam at each other and hold hands lightly—there's the middle-aged couple, Roger and Lois in the golf visor. Lois seems somewhat appeased, or maybe she's just silently tallying up everything that's wrong so she can threaten a lawsuit and get reimbursed afterward.

When did I get so cynical?

"The first thing I'd like to cover is that there is to be *no talking* to *any* other members of the Church of Eternal Light. They are happy to serve you, but we have our own way of life and religious beliefs, which we strive to preserve. Should you need something, please come to me directly and I will assist you."

A trio of women smirk—thirty-something trying to look twenty-something with artificially sculpted cheekbones and meticulously shaped eyebrows. One whispers, *"I don't think he could assist me with anything."* Blond, blond, brunette, hair extensions across the board, waxed legs and arms. A couple of younger men—college students?—surreptitiously glance at them.

"Kapu has a fragile ecosystem, and we appreciate your effort to protect it. Please use the trash receptacles in your cabin or within the resort to dispose of rubbish. Some of the plant, animal, and fish species you will encounter are extremely rare and can only be found on this island. While it might be tempting to pick a flower or touch a fish while snorkeling, please refrain from doing so. Not only would that violate the terms of agreement you signed, but some species are poisonous to the touch. It goes without saying that you may not bring anything from the island home with you on the return flight. No souvenirs. No rocks, no flowers, nothing from the island is to be taken at all. Your bags will be inspected before you leave."

He pauses a moment to let that sink in.

Standing slightly apart from the rest, in a spot where she can see everyone and everything, is a tall woman with an athletic build, muscular shoulders, tightly braided black cornrows. Something powerful about her. A fierce intelligence.

"You will find well-marked trails that create a hiking loop that takes you by a beautiful waterfall; we strongly recommend staying on the trails at all times. Snorkeling gear, hammocks, body boards, and other equipment will be available for your use here in the portico. Please return them here when you're done with them. If you plan to swim in the waterfall, please take a shower prior using no soap, and refrain from applying sunscreen before you head out. Even small quantities of chemicals can damage the native species here. Keep an eye on the peak before you enter the waterfall. If there are clouds near the peak, don't go in. We get flash floods, even when it's not raining on other parts of the island."

Which ones are real tourists, and which ones, like Julia, are on a different mission? Athletic Woman is an obvious candidate, but it's too early to rule anyone out. Julia catches Noah mid-yawn. He sees her looking and makes a *let's wind this up* motion with his fingers.

"There is a lava-rock wall surrounding the eco-resort. Do not, and I cannot emphasize this enough, *do not* go beyond the rock wall. Anyone caught beyond the rock wall will be sequestered in their cabin for the remainder of their time here, and will have to pay a significant penalty, as outlined in your agreement."

Suddenly there's a rumble as the jet's engine starts up. Isaac casts a glance over at the pop-up tent—the churchwomen are now lining up the purses and suitcases just in front of the table. A heap of plastic bags containing what Julia assumes are the confiscated items are laid out on top.

This appears to satisfy him. He pulls a small walkie-talkie from his back pocket. "Delta A, please stand by."

There's a crackle of static and a deep voice replies, *"Roger that."*

Julia looks to see if the baggage handler is still there, but he's gone.

Isaac stands up a little straighter. "Finally, I would like to remind you that the church is not liable for injury or, God forbid, death. This is not Disneyland. This is not Hawaii. We are five hundred miles from the nearest hospital. There are no lifeguards, no helicopters, no doctors on the island. Every cabin is equipped with a rudimentary first-aid kit, which you will find under your bathroom sink. In the event of a medical emergency, we will call for a plane, but there is no guarantee that transport will be able to leave immediately. We have been fortunate that there have only been a couple of minor injuries. . . . However, there was once a fatality in transit to a hospital after a guest picked up a venomous cone snail. Remember: Look, don't touch, and don't leave the boundary of the rock wall. If anyone has second thoughts, please raise your hand. You can take the return flight now. However, you will not be reimbursed for your expenses."

It's such a strange island, with such strange people, and undertones that feel more cult than quaint. Julia thinks about the woman with the scarred face. She doesn't seem like the others. Is she a tourist who converted? Or is she a captive here, under duress? And then there were Leanne and the baggage handler, both wearing face masks.

But Evie. Thousands of miles of ocean and land between them, and Julia can almost picture her daughter, a ghost, standing there. The longing to hold her again almost drops Julia to her knees.

I will bring you back to me, whatever the cost.

No one else speaks up either. Bragging rights trump all.

"Excellent," says Isaac. He clicks on his walkie-talkie. "Delta A, you are cleared for takeoff."

"Roger that."

The plane starts to taxi down to a circle at the other end of the runway.

"You can now retrieve your bags, and please sign out your confiscated items," says Isaac. "You will then receive your cabin assignment. Dinner starts promptly at six thirty p.m. in the dining pavilion, over there." He points to an even larger bamboo building with a steeply sloped thatched roof that's perched on a small cliff.

The plane is at the end of the runway now, turning in a wide loop. The rumble of the engine turns into a roar, and it accelerates back down the tarmac.

I made it. No one flagged her suitcase. Whether or not that's a lucky or unlucky break remains to be seen.

The plane lifts off. Julia feels the rush of warm wind it leaves in its wake.

Julia is assigned one of the bungalows nestled into the jungle hillside, with a wide lanai that overlooks the ocean. It's a huge relief to get inside, close the door behind her. The interior design is a surprise. Luxe-rustic, Zen yet primitive, with bamboo poles and beams, highly finished dark wood flooring, a platform bed and coverlet with a modern, abstract print. Nothing on the walls except grass-weave paper. A minimalist desk with a wooden chair . . . for what? It's not like everyone's got their laptop and will be slipping in some work on vacation. A couple of rattan chairs in front of a glass coffee table. Large picture windows with paradise views overlooking the lanai, and the ocean beyond. Simple muslin shades. Not a design the churchwomen could pull off. She makes a mental note to do some digging for her book proposal when she gets back, find the designer. There's a story there, for sure.

Julia lets her suitcase and purse drop to the floor. Breathes. She can hear the low rush of the waves breaking in the distance, a bird whistling nearby. Stresses ease, somewhat. In the end, after all that worrying, her suitcase sailed through the inspection, no discovery of the hidden panel, no items confiscated and bagged. A miracle. Although she can't imagine what the other women are going to do for clothing storage—no closet in the bungalow, just an armoire, a single bureau. And no attempt to hide the Bible in a drawer—it's centered on the bureau next to a white ceramic vase holding a small clutch of tropical flowers. Maybe the church hopes to snag a few converts, not that it's likely with this lot. The private bathroom is a decent size though, with a tub and shower jets, a glass-bowl cabinet sink. White fluffy towels. Small bars of what look like handmade soap. She lifts one to her nose—it smells like orchids, and rolled oats. There is, as Isaac promised, a small first-aid box under the sink, extra rolls of toilet paper.

Also under the sink are strand-like filaments of what looks like a white mold running along the back of the cabinet. It smells mildewy too. Probably the humidity.

She heads back into the bedroom, pulls the lei over her head, and drops it on the bureau, then draws the muslin curtains closed. God, wouldn't it be amazing to take a short nap before dinner? She kicks off her sneakers.

Oh, right, the phone.

Every cell in her body longs for the bed, but instead she grabs the phone out of her sneaker, sits down by the suitcase, and pops open the latches. Pulls out all her clothes and drops them on the floor. It takes a moment for her fingers to find the hidden latch—she'd practiced for a good hour before she'd packed it, undoing the latch, popping out the false bottom, re-latching it, but for some reason—maybe the fatigue, the stress—her fingers are clumsy. Finally she hears the soft click, and the bottom cracks open.

It's all still there, exactly the way she packed it. The pills, the satellite phone, the charger for the satellite phone. The seven mini Jack Daniel's bottles from the hotel fridge, just in case she needs something to help her sleep, one for each day.

She picks up the satellite phone, presses the power button, sees that it's only at about fifty percent. *Damn, I must have left it on.* She probably should call Aunt Liddy but can't quite bring herself to. Instead, she presses the button on the color display for the GPS, clicks the map where a red pin for Irene's camp ostensibly is. A digital compass floats over the screen, pointing the way, along with the estimated time, distance. Five miles—not ideal, but doable in a day. She powers it off so she doesn't lose any more of the battery, puts it back in the suitcase along with her smuggled, SIM-less cell phone, and the brochure with the new number.

What time did Isaac say dinner was?

Oh, right, six thirty. But there aren't any clocks. Not on the wall, not next to the bed. So how are they supposed to know *when* anything is? She's about to close the lid when she remembers the pills—she should take one, right? *Don't miss a dose,* Bailey had said. *If you get sick and we have to extract you before you complete the terms, the deal is off.* She reads the back label again— yes, she's overdue, she didn't take one that morning.

She doesn't like it—she doesn't trust Aunt Liddy farther than she could proverbially throw her—but the sight of Leanne and the baggage handler wearing face masks was sobering. And what she can count on is that Aunt Liddy desperately wants the flower and the DNA, which means she needs Julia in good enough health to get back, which means the pills are a means to that end.

Maybe she'll take half of one, see how it makes her feel before taking the full dose.

Julia pops one out of the package, bites it in half, then grabs one of the small Jack Daniel's, untwists the cap. Knocks it back with a good swallow. The whiskey settles her, takes off the edge. She presses the other half of the pill back into the tinfoil package, and her eyes land on the copy of Irene's notebook. She could squeeze in a few minutes looking through it again. The churchwomen are so incredibly strange, and Julia wonders whether that's a new development, or if it had been part of the culture when Irene was here. There could be a reference she missed.

She grabs the notebook, but just then there's a sharp *rap, rap, rap* on the door. Julia looks up at the window—through the muslin she can see the shadow of a male figure.

Goddamn. Probably Noah. She's only had what, about ten minutes free of him?

She screws the cap back on the Jack Daniel's, tosses it in the suitcase, piles her clothes back over the hidden panel, stands, realizes she's still holding the pills in her hand, looks for somewhere to stash them—*rap, rap, rap*—slips them in her jeans pocket instead, heads for the door, barefoot.

But when she opens it, she finds Isaac, not Noah. His face and neck glisten with sweat—the tie must be insufferable in the humidity. He holds a bundle wrapped in plain white muslin, bound with a twisted green vine.

"I hope you're enjoying the accommodations." He smiles, not very convincingly.

She feels him looking past her, into the room.

"I am," she says. "It's refreshing to be completely offline." She wonders if he even knows what that means, offline. Or if he can smell whiskey on her breath, because he hesitates a few seconds too long.

"I'm pleased to hear that. The Reverend would like to see you tomorrow to take you to your great-aunt's grave and discuss the disinterment. First thing in the morning after breakfast?"

A question that's not really a question.

"Perfect," she says. "Please let him know that our family deeply appreciates being able to bring Aunt Irene home to rest in peace with her family."

"I will. No guest has ever been allowed near our village, so I hope *you* appreciate the exception we're making in your case. The same rules for non-interaction apply, and we ask that you wear this dress to minimize the overt disruption to our community."

He presents her with the bundle, and since she really has no choice in the matter, she takes it.

"Of course," she says. It feels heavy and looks like it itches.

He nods. She sees his gaze wander behind her, land on the notebook.

Goddammit. She steps in front of his view. "One question.

You said dinner would be served promptly at six thirty p.m., but I didn't bring a watch, and I don't see a clock. How are we supposed to know when it's time?"

"We'll blow a conch shell. The sound carries well—you can even hear it up by the waterfall. But you'll also find that the island has its own circadian rhythm. Soon . . . you'll just know when it's time."

This doesn't seem likely, but she nods like it does. "I'll see you at dinner then."

There's another awkward pause, two seconds, five, ten. She wonders if she committed a misstep somewhere, or if he's trying to build the courage to push past her, grab the notebook.

Just as she's about to close the door, he says, "Ordinarily it would be sacrilege for us to disturb the rest of the dead. But the Reverend says that since your great-aunt ended her own life, her soul will never be at rest."

It's like the thought has been eating away at him for a while.

"You probably don't believe in such things," he continues. "Not many people without a spiritual life do. But you might find that perspective challenged in the days to come. I wouldn't recommend wandering off the path, not if I were a Greer."

A warning, then, like he suspects there's more to her trip than just bringing Irene's body home. Did one of the women run across something while inspecting her luggage?

He touches a finger to his hat brim. "I'll see you at dinner." Then he turns and walks away, such an incongruous figure in shiny black shoes, black pants, white shirt and black tie in the midst of sand, turquoise waters, and waving palm trees.

His clothes an act of defiance against all that seems innocent, and natural, and beautiful.

The operating word there being seems, Julia thinks.

NINE

JULIA WAS ALMOST ASLEEP WHEN she heard the conch shell blow, having curled up in the bed, lulled by the sound of the waves, and of the wind in the palm trees. She briefly considered skipping dinner, but by then she was awake enough to feel her stomach grumble. The two biological imperatives, sleep and hunger, fought. Hunger won.

So she changes clothes quickly—a pair of khakis, a white linen shirt, a pair of brown leather flip-flops—thinks about wearing the lei too, but doesn't want to overdo the tourist bit. Closes up her suitcase, stows it in the armoire, grabs the key. Casts one final look around her bungalow to see if she's left anything out that should be hidden away. No, nothing.

She steps out the door, and is immediately struck by the last golden rays of sunset glimmering on the ocean's waters. The tide is out, leaving behind a smooth stretch of wet sand, not a single mark, or footprint, marring it. And the moon—bigger than she's ever seen it—rising just over the pink horizon. It all looks so innocent, so peaceful, like nothing bad could ever happen here.

But she knows that beauty is the best place for deception to hide. She can never afford to let her guard down again. Ethan taught her that much, at least.

So she pulls a receipt out of her pocket, slips it in the doorjamb, and then shuts the door. Tests the handle to make sure it's

properly locked. It is. Good. Of course, now she's late. She hopes
that seating is assigned, and that she's next to anyone but Noah.
She hurries along the path toward the dining pavilion, where she
can already hear laughter. Tiki torches light the way, attracting
small insects.

She's not looking forward to meeting this Reverend. She un-
wrapped the muslin bundle Isaac gave her and found what she
expected—a plain smock, just like the ones the other churchwomen wear. It makes no sense, because those women see the
tourists wearing modern clothes around the eco-resort. It's not
like it'd be a great shock to see Julia's arms, her legs. She has a
feeling it has more to do with making her submit, even tangentially, to their way of life, or to the way of life dictated by the
Reverend. Irene's line in the notebook, *Even in Eden, it appears
Eve must learn her place*, makes a lot more sense now that she's up
close to the culture.

There must be a crack, though—there always is. Someone
who wants to tell, who sees a house of cards and can't suppress
the urge to pull one out, just to watch it fall.

———————————

The dining pavilion is open on all sides, the front facing the
ocean, the back facing the jungle, which is slowly becoming
obscured by shadows. The steep roof is supported entirely by
bamboo, which glows warmly in light cast by paper lanterns
hung from the beams.

Julia thought she was late, but maybe she's early, because the
middle-aged couple—what were their names again? Robert and
Lois?—are missing. Everyone else is already seated at a long,
rectangular table, drinking from coconuts and chatting quietly
while the churchwomen busy themselves laying food out on a

buffet table. *Great. Family-style seating.* There's an empty space next to Noah, but with Robert missing—no, Roger—and his wife, there's room at the other end too. She heads toward it, trying to slip in quietly.

"*Julia!* Over here!"

Everyone looks up—of course—so she tries to put on a smile as she turns to Noah.

"Hi," she says, still edging to the opposite side.

"I saved a place for you!"

Well, now it's a scene—he's good at that, making scenes—which will only get bigger if she doesn't sit next to him. Gossip for sure either way—the first thing a small group turns to out of boredom, trying to figure out who has hooked up, or who will. She smiles and nods and heads to take the seat he so thoughtfully saved for her.

I have to think of a way to really piss him off. If she can't, then there's definitely something else at play.

At least Noah won't be able to focus on her alone—the young happily-whatever couple are sharing the table too, holding hands, of course.

"Thanks," she says, settling on the plain wooden bench. White linens on the table, that luxe-rustic theme again.

"No problem—we're practically best friends at this point, right? Julia, this is Fred and Heather. They just got married yesterday. But they've been living in sin for two years, so it hardly counts."

Julia's smile becomes harder to maintain. It's not easy sitting so close to new love, the glow of it. Those are hard to remember, the days when she was happy with Ethan. She didn't know that pain could flow backward in time, curdle nearly every moment, every memory, that came before.

A part of her hopes they're spies.

"Nice to meet you," says Heather, extending a hand over the table. Her face is elfin, her blond hair wavy and in disarray, like she'd just been sleeping on it, which maybe she was.

"Nice to meet you too," says Julia.

Fred just offers a nod, but then, she's of an age that doesn't register in his field of reality. He's Nordic blond, tanned, bored. Inscrutable light blue eyes.

"Heather works for Goldman Sachs, and Fred here, Fred's over at the Federal Reserve," says Noah. "The mango is amazing, by the way."

There's a small fruit plate in the center of the table, some kind of rustic bread, and slices of thick cheese.

Julia reaches for a piece of bread. "You're right—you don't have a filter, Noah. There's such a thing as small talk, am I right?"

She watches to see if the criticism lands, but it doesn't seem to. He just leans back in his chair, smiles like she's joking, which she's not.

"I'm an ass, I admit. Julia here—"

"Is recently divorced, and very hungry," Julia says, taking a bite of the bread. It's soft, with a hint of rosemary.

Fred sighs. "I'm starving. So far we haven't gotten anything except rabbit food."

It's true. Only platters of salad, fruit on the buffet table. No heating elements, nothing cooked.

"Did they say it was only vegetarian?" asks Noah. "I don't re-member that being on the brochure."

Fred tries to make a sandwich out of the bread and cheese. "Tiny food on the plane, rabbit food for dinner."

"I watched them, you know," says Heather, leaning in and

lowering her voice. "I don't think the doughnuts went far. There's a shed with a lock where they put all the confiscated stuff."

"Oh man, and that *chili*," says Fred. His eyes wander over to where the other younger men are sitting; he's obviously wishing he wasn't sitting with the old farts. The two his age are sitting across from the brunette—they must have said something funny, because her blond companions giggle into their hands. Slightly apart from all of them is the athletic woman, focused on her mango, in her own world entirely.

As if she feels Julia's gaze, Athletic Woman looks up, meets her eye for a split second. She clocks Fred, and Heather, and Noah. Then returns to her food.

Military? Something about the cursory glance. Like she was scanning them.

Noah leans in. "You up for a break-in?"

Fred looks like he is, just not with Noah. "Uh . . ." he says. "I don't know. That Isaac dude looks like he's wrapped pretty tight. Anal retentive, for sure."

"Fred!" Heather slaps him lightly with her free hand, but she's smiling, too.

"He might get mad. 'Breaking into the shed of confiscated items and eating prohibited items is against the church's rules. The tribe has spoken. It's time for you to go.'"

It's not a bad imitation, and even catches a bit of Isaac's twang. And as if on cue, Isaac steps out of the shadows of the jungle and enters the pavilion. He looks flustered. All the churchwomen pause, although they don't look at him directly. Then they return to their work.

Julia reaches for the coconut drink. "What's this?" she asks, to change the subject.

"I thought it was coconut milk, but it's fruity, too," says Heather. "It's super good, whatever it is."

Fred groans loudly. "I don't know if I can *take* this for seven days. No TV. No Wi-Fi. No cell phone. No Xbox."

Something quietly sad flits across Heather's face. A secret pain. "*I* think it's going to be amazing. Everyone I've talked to says it is."

"We don't even know if it's going to work," says Fred.

A tension there, the press of words that can't be said in public. A territory Julia knows all too well. Just as she's trying to think of another subject for small talk, Isaac clinks a spoon a few times on a glass. Everyone obediently becomes quiet. Crash of waves in the background, a new white noise.

"Thank you, thank you all for your attention. First, a little housekeeping. We will be serving an all-vegetarian meal tonight. An unexpected power surge damaged our refrigerator and freezer, and they are not operational. The chicken we planned to serve has spoiled, and the frozen steak has not sufficiently thawed yet. If this presents a dietary issue due to lack of protein, we do have canned organic pinto beans which we would be happy to prepare for you."

"Beans, beans, the magical fruit," whispers Fred.

"We have called our pilot and he will purchase new equipment and deliver it as soon as possible. However, and this is unfortunate timing, a tropical storm is brewing, and depending on the wind shear, it may hit Kapu. If it does land, we can expect tropical force winds, high surf, and flash floods. As a precautionary measure, the waterfall is off-limits until further notice."

There's a round of boos and catcalls.

"The bungalows have been constructed to withstand hurricane-force winds, so there is no real danger, just the possibility of inconvenience. We may lose electricity completely, in which case you'll find a flashlight and a battery-operated lantern in the bottom drawer of your bureau. We suggest keeping the flashlight by your bedside."

Athletic Woman raises her hand.

"Yes?" Isaac says.

"How long is the storm expected to last? If it makes landfall?"

Isaac visibly braces himself, then says, "Possibly three days."

Everyone erupts in a titter of dismay, and the blondes look like they'd walk out on the spot if there weren't thousands of miles of ocean between them and civilization.

"If there's no electricity, how do you communicate with the pilot?" Noah asks.

"We have a backup generator in the village, for emergencies such as these. However, I think you will find that it really is a small inconvenience to go without electricity. The lanterns provide adequate light for reading before bed."

One of the college boys shouts, "What about hot showers?"

Isaac pauses and then says, "Without electricity, unfortunately, there would only be cold showers."

"Oh, come on! This vacation sucks!" Fred calls out, causing Heather to blush profusely.

Isaac must feel the rancor building. He holds up his hand. "Because of the incident with the refrigeration and the storm, if you would like to return with the pilot, you can, and receive a complete refund."

"Well, when is he going to get here?" one of the blondes asks.

"We have to wait and see. We'll know more in the morning about the storm's path." There's an eruption of general distress— Julia overhears *I can't believe I waited all year, They should have known before we got here, What are they going to serve if they run out of beans?*

"Now please," Isaac says. "Everyone please . . . it's only a couple of days."

Good God, Julia thinks, *imagine if they didn't have electricity for weeks at a time.* Or had to eat around the mold in a stale loaf of bread. She'd been through all that, and worse.

The brunette stands up, near tears. "I *demand* to speak to your supervisor. This is completely unacceptable. My father is a *lawyer,* he *knows* people."

"We can't control the weather," says Isaac. "And—"

"You should have contingencies in place," one of the college boys says. "A backup generator for the resort, too. We should all get a refund for any days we don't have electricity."

Fred cups his hands to his mouth. "Refund! Refund!"

Noah leans toward Julia with a wry grin. "Well, this is quickly devolving into *The Lord of the Flies.*" He rubs his finger and thumb against each other. "World's smallest violin."

Julia smiles in spite of herself. It's not her best self, but there's something satisfying about their consternation over such a relatively small problem.

There's movement to the left, and out of the corner of her eye Julia catches Roger and Lois emerging from the shadows. They step up onto the pavilion and walk toward the only two seats left, trying to be unobtrusive. Working a little too hard at it.

Noah reaches for a slice of mango. "Wonder what they've been up to?"

Yes, she does wonder about that. And if the paper will still be lodged in the doorframe when she gets back to her cabin.

———————

It took a few minutes for Isaac to quell the mutiny, mostly with apologies and promises of partial refunds. And to Julia's surprise the food, albeit vegetarian, is actually really good. The buffet line was the perfect way to make introductions, listen in on conversations, engage in a little espionage. By the beet salad, she discovered the names of the two blondes (Brittany and Alison) and the brunette (Jessica)—all friends, all recently divorced, all from Orange County and with eerily similar noses, like they went to the same plastic surgeon. Fred steered right to the two college-age boys who are, indeed, seniors at Harvard—Connor and Larry, one the son of an internet billionaire Julia had actually reported on in the '90s when he suspiciously sold most of his shares right before the dot-com bust, the other the son of a US senator. Roger, as he steadily bragged to anyone within earshot, is a wealthy oil tycoon—he seriously used that word, *tycoon*—with a hand in, and a board seat on, enough Fortune 500 companies to warrant him an annual weekend stay in the White House, regardless of who's president. *We always get the same room,* Lois chimed in, *and they know exactly how we like our steaks done.*

The only person who kept to herself was Athletic Woman. Her name, Julia found out only after forcefully introducing herself, is Beth. Beth offered no other details, and in fact, after dropping Julia's hand, skipped past the buffet straight to dessert, loading up on coconut pudding, then heading back to the farthest edge of the table.

It would have made her seem suspicious, except wouldn't someone with an agenda try to fit in?

Like me?

"That color really works for you," Julia tells Heather, making another run at small talk. Heather's silk tank is baby blue.

"Thanks, my mother bought it for me," says Heather, who then takes a little too long casting about for a return compliment. Julia understands her conundrum, is even amused by it.

Heather chooses self-deprecation instead. "I tell her to stop buying me stuff. I mean, I can hardly *find* anything, my closet is so stuffed. I'm like a pack rat."

Fred, interestingly, doesn't jump to her defense. These two, Julia suspects, are real tourists. You can't fake that intimate level of passive aggression. Fred, after all his whining, is working on his second plate of food. Given the way he's eating, there might be a third. The buffet had offered spring rolls with green onions, carrots, lettuce, and bean sprouts; steamed dumplings filled with sweet bean paste; wraps with some kind of soft cheese; olives; fresh tomatoes and cilantro; and Greek pastries filled with wilted spinach and pine nuts. The subtlety of flavor was unexpected. But Julia briefly spotted the redheaded young woman carrying a tray, handing it over to one of the other churchwomen. Maybe she's the chef.

In fact, the food is so good, no one's complaining about leaving anymore. There's an ambient social cohesion. And Julia feels just the slightest bit fuzzy, like she's just had two glasses of wine. Something alcoholic in the coconut juice?

"So why Kapu?" Noah asks Fred. "Why not the Bahamas? Doesn't seem like much here to interest a young couple like you."

"We're trying—" Heather stops, looks toward Fred.

He shrugs, like *no big deal if you want to tell them*. Gets back to work on his plate, dipping the spring rolls into the sweet-and-sour sauce.

"We're trying to conceive. I have some issues, but everything we've tried . . . well . . . nothing has worked. And Kapu . . . My best friend came here, last year. I thought maybe . . . I know, it sounds ridiculous. I'm not religious or anything."

She blushes, seems to regret having said anything at all. Noah looks perplexed. But Julia understands Heather's desperation. She and Ethan had tried for years, suffering through six miscarriages, before she eventually conceived. Apparently Julia's uterus was "hostile," her own cells attacking the embryo, a rare condition. They were just about to consider adoption when she finally got pregnant with Evie.

Something else clicks into place right then—the last letter from the Church of Eternal Light to Aunt Liddy, something about the locals trying to smuggle family members with leprosy onto the island. The belief that it could heal them.

"You think something about the island will help," says Julia.

Heather nods. "My friend had stage-four pancreatic cancer. I thought she was insane to take the trip. I mean, the doctors, everyone said she might not even make it back. I literally pleaded with her to stay, thought I'd never see her again. But when she came back . . . she was stage three. A couple months later, stage two. By the end of the year she was cancer-free."

"But how can that be? Stage four isn't curable," Noah says. "I think it's more likely that your friend was misdiagnosed. Happens more than it should. I had an uncle who was diagnosed with leukemia, but it turns out they had mislabeled his blood sample."

Heather shakes her head. "No, she'd practically wasted away and could barely walk without help."

Noah arches an eyebrow at Julia. "I just think if there was a cure for cancer here, the news might have gotten out."

"What's it matter to you?" Fred says gruffly. "If it works, it works. If it doesn't, well, we had a helluva great week." He reaches out for Heather's arm, lays a hand there. Looks her in the eye.

Suddenly they're in a different space than the rest of them, a private room no one else can enter.

Oh God. She misses that feeling, misses it desperately. Even though the lights are warm, the tropical breeze is warm, she feels very, very cold, and impossibly alone.

TEN

AS SOON AS JULIA CAN reasonably slip away from the dinner table, she does. The moon is enormous, casting enough light to make the sand glow. She can't remember the last time she saw so many stars either; there's no light pollution casting an orange sheen to the night sky. The air so clear she can even see the band of the Milky Way. She kicks off her flip-flops, picks them up, and heads down the path toward the beach.

Her heart is racing. She doesn't know why. It just started to feel too tight under the pavilion, claustrophobic, and even though she's blowing an opportunity to mingle, pry into the backstories of the other guests, she can't bring herself to. She needs some time alone.

She gets to where the beach has been smoothed and flattened by the ocean, no prints except the ones she's leaving. The sand is cold and wet under her feet. Lights are on in the bungalows along the pier—they look warm and inviting. The waves break farther out, and the looming dark shapes of rocks now poke through the surface. A thin rush of water spreads toward her, wraps around her ankles, before being pulled back into the deeper waters.

She's three hours behind Pacific time. Probably almost midnight there, a good enough excuse to not call in. And the truth is, she really doesn't want to hear Aunt Liddy's voice, not now.

Maybe it's the effect of whatever it was she drank, but she has a disjointed sense of being outside herself, looking in. Checking in is not important. Leanne and the baggage handler wearing masks, not important. Even the urban rumor of Kapu's healing powers, not important.

Her heart is just a knot of pure pain. Sitting across from newlyweds trying to conceive. It's like stepping through time, being a ghost on the periphery of who she used to be.

What time is it on the East Coast? Soon the morning sun will rise there. She pictures Evie in bed, asleep, Mr. Bones curled in her right arm. She misses waking her up, tickling her toes under the bedsheet, then swooping in for a kiss on the forehead. The damp scent of sweaty, sleeping child. *Good morning, sunshine.* The smell of espresso—Ethan made it himself, never trusted it to anyone else. He was always up before them, fully dressed—chinos, white shirt, brown loafers. Julia would joke he could walk into any decade and fit in. A timeless kind of style.

There were nice parts. She has to hold onto the nice parts, protect them. *Where did it go wrong?* They were as happy as she reasonably expected two people to be. She never thought the honeymoon would be forever, and she took his occasional bouts of itchy dissatisfaction to be typical of marriage. Nobody is truly happy ever after; she'd always known that was a fairy tale, a myth. So when he complained about her using the fine china every day, buying—*gasp*—clothes for Evie at a discount store, letting Evie play and track in mud from their backyard garden, it just seemed like the usual jostle of irritation that happens between people in close quarters. Then he started complaining about what she chose to wear to dinner parties. Then he suggested she go to an orthodontist to get her teeth fixed, *and why don't you ever do anything about your hair?* Like she was a Pygmalion experiment that wasn't working out as expected.

She didn't understand that her class was considered inferior, not until it was too late. That he wanted Evie to have different values.

His.

A shudder of longing hits her, so strong she wants to jump into the ocean, start swimming for the other side of the globe. It's hard, so incredibly hard, to check the impulse, to stay on land, be patient.

Money. Money is what she needs to see Evie again. *Just stick with the plan, Julia.*

She takes a deep breath. Settles herself into the present.

Something bobs along the crest of a wave, too dark to make out. A living something, intent on the lava rocks. She sees a dark arm reach out and for a panicky moment thinks it's a person—*the nightmarchers*—but then another arm reaches out, and another, and another, and then the slick skin glimmers in the moonlight and she can see they're not arms, they're tentacles. An octopus, climbing out of the water, latching into crevices to pull itself up.

She watches, briefly fascinated to witness this in the wild. Probably tide pools lie along the surface of the lava rock, small fish trapped there. A late-night snack.

The octopus reaches the top, slithers about a foot, then stops. She wonders how long it can hold its breath.

Suddenly it pounces, and barely a few seconds later it's back in the water, landing with the softest plop. Dinner is served.

Sometimes it seems to her that half the world is trying to eat the other half.

She can hear bits of conversation carried on the breeze,

laughter. People are straggling back. She turns her back to the ocean, starts up the slope to her bungalow, hurrying to avoid being caught up in a conversation. She's too shaken, too emotionally vulnerable. And she'll need her best, sharpest mind on hand for her trip to see the Reverend.

She gets to the lanai, pulls out her key, unlocks the door and is just about to open it when she remembers the paper she'd slipped into the doorjamb.

Still there. But wasn't it lower now? Uncertain.

She enters the cabin, shuts the door behind her, and locks it. Takes a look around. Nothing seems amiss; all looks exactly the way she left it. She heads over to the armoire, and yes, her suitcase is still there, apparently undisturbed.

It just *feels* like someone has been inside.

So she takes one of the wooden chairs and props it under the knob. *There*. Then she heads for the bed, collapses on it, not bothering to even get under the covers or pull the mosquito netting closed. Lets her eyes close.

The breaking waves a much better lullaby than the traffic along the 405.

———————————

She hears a conch shell blow. Is it morning already, time for breakfast? But when Julia opens her eyes, the room is still dark. She must have been dreaming. She's irritated with herself for waking up—as if that was in her control somehow. No clock to tell what time it is—it could be one in the morning, or four, or just before sunrise.

Something chirps inside the cabin. Another something responds. Two geckos—they weren't there when she went to sleep. Theoretically she knows they're harmless—good, actually, since they eat mosquitos and cockroaches and spiders. She should be grateful, but damn they're loud. She tries covering her ear with one of the pillows, but no luck.

Chirp.

She presses a second pillow against her ear.

Chirp, chirp, chirp.

No, she's never going to get back to sleep with that racket.

She reaches out for the lamp, turns it on. The bungalow fills with soft light. The geckos aren't hard to spot, at least: both of them cling to the surface of the cool window, skin white as ghosts. No way to camouflage themselves on clear glass.

Wait, there are the specimen jars in her suitcase. She could try to knock them into a jar, trap them inside, then release them in the leafy green foliage by the lanai if she wants to be generous. Or she could try to kill them, whack them with something without breaking the glass. If they were spiders she wouldn't even hesitate, but those damn commercials featuring the talking gecko with a Cockney accent make her feel like she couldn't possibly be so cruel.

So she pushes herself up and out of bed, bleary-eyed. Pads over to the armoire, pulls out her suitcase, takes out all her clothes—again—then unlocks the hidden panel. Pulls out a specimen jar, twists open the top.

Thinks a moment, gets the opened bottle of Jack Daniel's, takes another swig, then caps it. The funny thing is that she was completely dry throughout her marriage; the drinking started after the divorce. A part of her knows it's a dangerous crutch, but the other doesn't really care anymore.

The whiskey warms her stomach, makes her feel just a touch more grounded in the present. She gets to her feet, approaches the first gecko slowly. Her shadow follows her. The gecko's eyes are large dark orbs bulging out of its head, mouth curled slightly upward, which makes it seem like it's smiling. And the skin is actually slightly translucent. She can see its tiny lump of gray stomach, the fine scaffolding of its spine. Flutter of a tiny heart.

She's heard they jump. She hopes it doesn't jump.

Quickly she tries to brush it into the jar, and startles its companion into running up the wall, wriggling like a serpent, and so *fast*: in seconds, it's already on the ceiling. At first she thinks she's got the other—*one at least*—but then the damn thing climbs right up and out of the jar with its sticky, webbed toes and launches itself onto the floor, scurrying away toward the chair propped up under the doorknob, slipping under the door.

In the cup, something else wriggles.

The tail.

It is, as Irene described, fascinating and disturbing to see something that isn't alive, not in the traditional sense, moving. It twists and turns and flops over on itself, curls and uncurls, like the tail is in the fight of its life, like it too might jump out and wriggle its way under the door.

A wave of nausea hits. Her knees feel like they might give out.

But she can't look away. A living dead thing. Finally the tail starts to lose steam, like it's realized it's dying, and must give in to the inevitable. A few final quivers, then it's still. She gives the jar a shake, just to be sure.

Put it in the trash can? She doesn't think she could possibly go back to sleep—not with that . . . thing inside. No, better to dump it outside, let the cycle of life have its way.

She heads for the door. Feels something soft land on her shoulder. Julia stops, turns her head, and sees the second gecko staring at her with a curious intensity, flicking its tongue out to taste the air.

Chirp, chirp, chirp.

Her heart starts to beat faster. She doesn't quite know what to do—they're so damn fast and the prospect of facing another wriggling tail isn't appealing. The gecko takes a hesitant step forward. Cocks its head. She gets the strangest sense that it regards her with an equal intelligence.

Chirp, chirp, chirp.

Something soft and small lands on her head, and she cringes, brushes it off—another gecko. Skin pale as milk, it tumbles to the dark floor, its tail separating on impact. She watches the gecko scurry away with just a nub where its tail used to be, while the tail writhes and twists and flips.

Jesus Christ.

Chirp, chirp, chirp. Again something lands on her shoulder—another one, it hops down her elbow as three run out from under the bureau. One jumps on her bare foot, tries to climb her leg.

"Ugh! Fuck!"

She shakes the gecko off her leg—it lands on its back, twists quickly onto its belly—and then geckos start falling around her like rain.

Chirp, chirp, chirp, chirp, chirp, chirp, chirp, chirp. A whole symphony that's nearly deafening.

She looks up and the ceiling is writhing with geckos, so many they're crawling up and over and around each other, a tapestry of rippling white reptilian flesh.

She drops the specimen jar on the floor where it smashes, and—*no . . . impossible*—sees that the tail inside the jar isn't a tail anymore; it's a gecko again, one that tries to run up her other leg, while more drop on her head, her shoulders—she can feel something crawl down the back of her neck, under her shirt, tickling along her shoulder blades.

She bolts for the door—feet registering soft flesh squishing beneath her toes—but when she pulls the chair out from under the knob, tries it, the knob is firmly locked, or stuck, or broken. She rattles it, shakes it, desperately pulls on it with all of her might, but the damn thing won't turn, and now there are so many geckos she's practically ankle-deep in them—*where the hell are they coming from!*—they race up the walls, flood out of the armoire, the bathroom, and cover the lampshade, dimming the warm light. They climb up her legs, fall onto her shoulders, creep along her arms, and she madly tries to brush them off, but as she does their tails fall off, joining the wriggling fray on the floor as her heart pounds—*the window*.

She wades through the geckos, reaches the window, hands frantically searching for the lock—there *is* none, it's just a single sheet of glass, no way to open it, escape.

And then she sees something outside. A girl, standing just under the canopy of a palm tree. She wears a simple white shift, no shoes. A shadow obscures her face.

Julia pounds on the window to get her attention, "Over here! Let me out! Open the door! *Open the door!*"

The girl shifts her weight from one foot to the other, considering.

Julia pounds on the window so hard her hands hurt. She's surprised the glass doesn't break, fracture. "Please!" she shouts. *"Please!"*

But the girl just turns her back and slips into the dark leaves of the jungle, disappears.

And Christ, the geckos are now knee-high, she's going to drown in the things if she doesn't escape . . . but wait. . . .

Something's not right, her feet don't *feel* right, they feel like . . .

. . . like they're standing in mud. Distantly she hears the rush of wind in the trees, a sound that grows louder, eventually over-powering the cacophony of geckos chirping. The bungalow shim-mers, and black spots gather at the corner of her eyes until they take over completely. She smells something fragrant, like a night flower blooming, feels the soft breath of a breeze tickle her neck.

She opens her eyes.

Finds herself in jungle brush, facing a low wall constructed en-tirely of lava rocks, more of that white mildew or fungus running up and along it like veins. Two bamboo poles crossed in front of her, each capped with a battered white ball of some kind. The poles look old, weathered, like they've been there for centuries.

Is this real?

She looks down at her feet—she's standing in a puddle of mud, scratches on her legs. She absently reaches into her hair, feels the debris of leaves and twigs. Overhead the palm trees sway; she hears the rush of the sea breeze through the fronds. In-sects buzzing.

I was dreaming. I must have been sleepwalking.

But that's never happened to her before. Insomnia, yes, but finding herself outside . . . Where *is* she anyway?

She turns and sees the moon is higher in the sky, still bright enough that it illuminates the cove, the cabins by the pier, the small cluster of bungalows on land that overlook the beach. She must be about a good quarter mile away. It shakes her, to have been compelled so far by her subconscious.

Chirp.

A gecko clings to a nearby leaf. She never would have seen it if it hadn't made a sound—it's just the shadow of an outline against the background of the leaf.

It jumps away from the leaf, onto the wall, and then behind it, into the land that, according to Isaac, is forbidden to enter.

ELEVEN

RAP, RAP, RAP. **THE SOUND** startles her awake, or not awake so much as aware, since she wasn't really able to go back to sleep and spent the rest of the night lying on the bed, combing through Irene's notebook, looking for something, anything, that might explain what happened to her. No reference, though, to sleepwalking. Maybe that was on one of the pages ripped out. The nightmare had felt so *real*—but nothing was out of place when she'd gotten back to the cabin, no geckos, no broken specimen jar or shattered glass on the floor. Only the door was slightly ajar. The chair she'd put under the knob had been neatly placed to the side.

It was all so unsettling. She'd downed the contents of two of the mini Jack Daniel's bottles after firmly locking the door again, propping the chair back under the knob.

Then, at some point while she was reading, her eyes must have drifted shut, because morning light now glows through the plain muslin curtain, and the notebook lies facedown on the comforter.

Rap, rap, rap, rap, rap.

Shit. She didn't shower and her feet are still covered in dried mud—there are muddy footprints on the immaculate floor, mud on the comforter, on her clothes that she wore to the dinner the night before. A few dried leaves still in her hair.

RAP. RAP. RAP. "Julia? Julia, are you awake?"

Isaac. She sees him behind the muslin curtain, a shadow puppet. She pushes herself up and out of the bed, runs her fingers through her hair, thinks a minute.

"I'll be right there!" She yanks the cover off the bed, takes off her shirt, her bra, wraps herself in the comforter. Better for him to think she's naked than that she was up to some nocturnal hiking. The comforter is long enough even to hide her muddy feet.

She pads over to the door—wait, what if this is a nightmare too? What if she's dreaming?

How can she be sure what's real and what's not anymore?

Knock it off, Julia. Don't get all solipsistic.

She takes a deep breath, removes the chair from under the doorknob, takes another deep breath, and opens the door, just wide enough that she can look through the crack.

Isaac wears the same outfit from the day before, complete with wide-brimmed hat. He seems agitated.

"Didn't you hear the conch shell?" he asks. "Breakfast service started a half hour ago, and we should get an early start if we're going to make it back before the storm. It's on track to hit Kapu, and—"

"*Okay.* Okay. I'll be there in a minute."

There's enough of a pause to hint that this is not the optimal answer. She's aware that he's aware of her bare shoulders.

"I'm sorry," she offers. "It's so peaceful here I must have slept too deeply to hear the conch."

He doesn't seem to believe her, but nods anyway. "I'll see you then in the dining pavilion. *Shortly.*"

Passive-aggressive much? She smiles, feels him try to angle a peek inside, shuts the door quickly. Watches his shadow cross the muslin curtain—*creak, creak, creak*—and then he's gone.

She wishes she'd been able to get some real sleep; she doesn't have to look in the mirror to know there are dark circles under her eyes. She's not going to be at her best—not by a long shot—and she knows she'll have to be in top form when she meets the Reverend.

There're more bottles of Jack Daniel's in her suitcase.

No. Absolutely not.

She resolves herself to a quick shower, stowing a few key items in a lightweight folding backpack she'd brought with her—maybe the GPS phone, a specimen jar in case she can slip away at some point, *you never know, you might get lucky*—and then, goddammit, she'll have to wear that smock to breakfast. It hangs accusingly in the armoire, separate from the rest of her clothes, like it's considering walking off without her.

A strange thought.

But it's a strange place, isn't it?

It also strikes Julia that this trek means she'll be separated from the others, vulnerable. To what, she's not sure, but she should play it safe.

Julia pulls out the suitcase, reaches under her clothes for the hidden panel. Finds the knife. It's for cutting away roots, of course, but in a pinch could be used for other purposes.

She slips this into the pocket of the smock. Insurance, just in case.

If the churchwomen were there earlier, they're gone by the time Julia arrives, and all the food's on the buffet table, like it was laid out overnight by magical elves. A platter of pineapple, mango, and starfruit, a heated tray containing scrambled eggs that are a bright, deep orange—must be from free-range chickens—thick slices of freshly baked white bread, jars of homemade jam, and some kind of fresh juice, along with coffee and the kind of creamer that doesn't require refrigeration.

She feels ridiculous, and ignores the stares. The muslin smock is itchy. She chose to wear her hiking boots and thick socks, which, along with the backpack, really complete the look.

Julia grabs a plate and a mug. Most everyone has already had their fill. There's more of a sense of separateness at the long table, people coalescing into groups. At the far edge, Cooper, Fred, and Larry sit on one side, while Brittany, Alison, Jessica, and Heather sit on the other. The boys wear board shorts, sand dusting their backs, while the girls wear bikinis, their fair skin already starting to bronze, faint tan lines from where their bikini straps have shifted.

"Oh. My. God. Did you *see*—"

"—he was toast. And then his face, like—"

"I know, right?"

Together they're a world unto themselves, don't even look up when Roger accidentally drops a fork. He and Lois have claimed the center, towels draped across the bench to Lois's right, Roger's left, a clear signal that they wish to be undisturbed.

Which leaves the other end of the table, with Beth, and Noah (of course), and enough space for her. She wonders if she can just grab a plate and sneak back to her bungalow, eat on the lanai. She puts a slice of pineapple, bread, and a scoop of eggs for protein on her plate. Pours some coffee into her mug—the creamer's almost gone—and then some juice into a thick glass tumbler.

She feels Noah slightly behind her before she hears him. He has his own coffee mug—empty—and reaches for the jug. Will she ever be rid of him?

"Love the place so much you've decided to convert?" he asks.

The tumult of other conversations becomes quieter. They all want to know.

"I have an appointment to see the Reverend this morning," Julia says. "A relative is buried in the church cemetery, and I'm visiting her grave."

She and Aunt Liddy had decided there was no point in lying about her ostensible purpose in being there. It's a true, and great, cover.

"Oh, I'm sorry," Noah says. "I guess this is where I'm supposed to offer my condolences. Please, let me offer my condolences."

An awkward silence.

There are clinks of forks on china, and the conversations around them resume a normal volume. No one wants the specter of death interfering with their vacation.

"Here, let me carry your plate for you," he offers, and he takes it from her before she can protest. "You can help me with Beth, okay?" he whispers. "She's said all of about two words the whole morning."

He leads Julia to the table, and of course there's no way now to avoid it without making a bigger scene than the one she's already made. He places her plate in the empty spot, directly across from Beth, and takes a seat next to it. Julia puts her coffee mug down, then her glass of juice, and settles on the bench.

Beth doesn't even look up for a simple good-morning acknowledgment. Just scoops eggs onto her fork like she's sitting alone. Chews silently.

"I think the hype about the storm is just that, hype," Noah says. "Not even a cloud in the sky this morning. Just a way to keep us all trapped in our cabins."

There's a resonance to this that lands oddly, like a joke that's actually true.

"Except for Julia," he adds. "She's headed all the way over to the other side of the island. Maybe we can go with her."

At this, Beth looks up. "How'd you swing that?"

"She speaks!" Noah announces so loudly that even Roger and Lois glance their way.

"A relative died." Julia takes a bite of her eggs, hoping to head off any other questions.

"Tourist?"

Julia shakes her head no. Beth stares at her a few moments longer than is comfortable.

"So what are *you* up to today?" Noah asks.

"Well, I'm going to the waterfall," says Beth, surprising them both. "This morning. Screw the storm."

Noah looks as shocked as Julia feels.

"I mean, that's why we're all here, isn't it? The legendary waters?" Beth picks up a piece of pineapple with her fingers. Reads their expressions. "Oh come on, what are they going to do? Call the cops? Lock me up in some kind of Mormon jail?"

Noah looks unsure, and Julia actually doesn't know what to say. She takes another bite of scrambled eggs instead.

"They're not Mormons," says Noah. "More like Pennsylvania Dutch, I'd say."

"More like Jim Jones's followers, is what I'd say," says Beth. "The way the women don't even talk to each other? Like they're not allowed?"

Julia wonders why Beth is so talkative all of a sudden. She decides to play along. "Yeah, that is pretty creepy."

"It's creepier than creepy—it's downright disturbing."

They've entered a conversational territory that's making

Noah obviously uncomfortable, which is maybe Beth's point. And it is nice to see Noah flummoxed, the facade of Joe Tourist finally pierced.

"And you," Beth adds, pointing her butter knife in Julia's direction, "are about to go walking right into the middle of it. I'll take my chances with the flash floods and the waterfall any day."

She's just laying out an excuse for her absence, should anyone notice, which no one might, since she's made herself unpopular. But that's why she's so talkative all of a sudden. Creating her own cover, so she can go traipsing off into the jungle. Noah's high on Julia's list of possible competitors, but Beth just notched herself one higher. Probably more capable, too.

Beth takes a bite of her pineapple, meets Julia's eye. A bit of juice runs down her chin, which she wipes away with the back of her hand. Like she's trying to tell Julia something, but Julia can't figure out what.

The younger group suddenly erupts in boisterous laughter.

"Oh no, you did not—"

"All I'm saying is, I didn't know they were *related*."

More laughter, although something else too, a thin layer of sexual tension. Three women obviously interested, only two available men.

Heather looks a little worried. She keeps a close eye on Fred, watching for signals.

Something Julia knows all too well. A feeling she should have paid closer attention to. Rationalizing a light hand touching Ethan's arm at a party, him stepping outside to talk "business," his texted excuses for running late getting home.

GOTTA NAIL THIS CONTRACT DOWN.

DON'T WAIT UP, NEGOTIATING WITH THOSE ASSHATS IN CHINA.

"Julia!" Isaac's shrill voice behind her. "We really should be going."

"Let me know what it's like. The waterfall," Julia says, standing.

"I will," says Beth. "We'll catch up later when you get back. If you don't join the church yourself, that is."

"I don't think it's likely I'll convert."

"No one does," says Beth, picking up her coffee mug. "No one ever does."

———————

There is no small talk, thank God, as they follow a trail that winds around the coastline. While Isaac seemed momentarily intrigued by the backpack hanging over her shoulder, he didn't ask, probably assuming that anything inside had passed inspection.

He walks about half a yard in front of her at a brisk pace, his black patent leather shoes a poor match for the uneven surface. Every so often, he slips. She's glad she wore her boots.

But Julia is gloriously free to take in the island. She guesses they've already been walking for a half hour. After they'd left the perimeter of white sand beach, they'd climbed a small rise, crossed a trickling stream running down from a gorge, and now follow a trail along the edge of a steep cliff. The waves crash in earnest, breaking against the sheer rock face, throwing up clouds of ocean spray and fine water droplets. Her hair and skin are beaded with it.

While the ocean is to their right, the low, crumbling lava-rock wall is to their left, maybe a half mile away. She didn't realize it extended this far, wonders if it runs along the whole island. Beyond the wall, the thick jungle has given way to long, golden stretches of grass with an occasional gnarled tree featuring a bulbous trunk, symmetrical branches that make the top look like a broccoli crown. The trees feel ancient, primordial, leftover from a different epoch altogether. More of that white mold or lichen spots their trunks and branches.

And now the backside of the volcanic peak is visible. Here is where the lava must have flowed—there's a cracked chasm in the peak itself, and veinlike indentions in the rolling hills, now covered in grass, where the magma trickled down to the ocean.

A light breeze catches Julia's hair. Isaac's shoes go *crunch, crunch, crunch* on the trail. Warm sun on the back of her neck, a slightly nervous flutter in her stomach at the prospect of meeting the Reverend. She's not sure how much he knows about Irene, or how much Julia will be able to press him on the subject. Her goal is to do some assessment, try to figure out a reason she needs to come back for a second visit in order to process what she learns today, and then come up with another series of questions.

Why didn't Isaac give her a hat? She could have used it, in this sun—forgot to put on sunscreen, of course.

Christ, I didn't take the medication. If she is able to slip away into the jungle, then she'll be mucking about in a microbial stew without protection, according to Bailey. She was so exhausted, and then so rushed in the morning, it completely escaped her.

But . . . what if that's why she was sleepwalking, some kind of adverse reaction to taking even half a pill? She's had antibiotics before, never experienced that kind of side effect.

Her blood chills. *Goddammit, Aunt Liddy. What the hell did you give me?*

Suddenly the sun is too hot, the ocean too loud, the long, empty stretches of grass too oppressive. Even the trees feel threatening, like they're watching, planning some mischief.

Crunch, crunch, crunch, go Isaac's ridiculous shoes. Where does it say in the Bible you have to clad your feet in patent leather at all times? Sweat trickles down the back of his neck, damp half-moons form under his arms again.

A fly lands on her shoulder, and she bats it away.

You're out of your league, Ethan says. *You should jump off the cliff while you can, save yourself the disappointment of being pushed off it again.*

Julia puts her hand in her pocket, runs her thumb along the sheath of the knife. *You'd probably enjoy that, but it's not fucking happening. Now go back to your closet and shut the fuck up.*

He does. It unnerves her, though, that her ex's voice is so loud, so clear. It hasn't been that way since right after the divorce.

She focuses on the path ahead. Trains her eyes on the back of poor Isaac's sweating neck. She wonders if he's ever left the island, or what he's been told in order to keep him here. Probably the worst bits from the global news—wars and famines, cities where you can't walk down the streets at night, serial killers and police shootings and food that barely resembles food anymore.

But it's so programmed into one's DNA, that need to break away, particularly in adolescence. And the women. Will she see them finally talking in the village?

Crunch, crunch, crunch, go Isaac's shoes.

She'd interviewed a man once who'd left a cult in Northern California. The standard story—charismatic, narcissistic leader, with the twist that it was led by a woman, Petal . . . what was her name again? Petal Loving Bear. At the end of the interview, Julia had been struck by his obvious sense of loss.

"What do you miss?" she'd asked.

"The sense of community," he'd said immediately. "But also

not having to think anymore. Being more of a 'we' than an 'I.' Not having the responsibility of making decisions. I slept so much better at night. I honestly haven't had a good night's sleep since."

It wasn't the answer she'd expected. But maybe that was the appeal. Being a part instead of a whole. Without choice, you're not accountable for the consequences.

There's a hill, and as they reach its crest, she gets her first glimpse of the village. Small, picturesque white cottages that look like refugees from a New England coastal town, and a white church, with a white steeple. She hears a rooster crow.

It's almost exactly as she'd pictured it.

————————

They walk into the village. It feels like a ghost town. There's not a single person outside. No one tending the large vegetable garden on the hill, or pinning laundry to the clotheslines, or sitting on the porches, chatting. But then, there are no chairs on the porches, even though each cottage has a wonderful view of the ocean. For the first time, she wishes Isaac was talking to her, just to hear words spoken out loud, but he trudges about a yard in front of her, silent.

The ocean breeze flaps the clothes hanging on the line: smocks, sheets, pillowcases. Something that looks like a facecloth is teased off by a strong gust of wind—it flips and flops on the ground, like the gecko's tail in her dream.

It feels ominous. A bad omen. And then she notices something else. There are no pants on any of the clotheslines.

No men?

And no children's clothes either.

She knows she's being watched. The curtains are all closed,

but she senses them, the women, standing behind the windows, peering through the thin fabric. It's not a friendly feeling. Not just curiosity.

She gets that prickle again, the sense of being a cow in a chute heading toward the slaughterhouse. Or a sacrificial lamb.

Were they this strange when Irene was here? Was that why she chose to camp in the jungle?

High on the hill is a cemetery of sorts, a series of weathered wooden crosses, some of them listing. Next to that a greenhouse—fairly big, about the size of three cottages lined up shotgun style. What looks like a toolshed, with, to her great surprise, solar panels on its roof. Three small ones, but they seem completely out of place, this nod to modernity.

Waves roll in over a rocky beach just beyond the village.

Finally, she catches some movement behind one of the cottage windows—a curtain drops—but not before she saw the woman behind it. Red hair hanging in her face. The one who isn't like the others.

Isaac and Julia approach the church proper. It has the best view of all, right up against the rocky cliff's edge, nothing but wide, open sea beyond. All vegetation has been cleared away a good few yards around it, with small, ocean-smoothed stones forming a kind of gravel patio. It's not impressive—big enough to accommodate fifty people, maybe—but it has a kind of rustic beauty. Lava-rock walls painted white, a steel metal roof that's quietly rusting, three blunt, square windows on each side. Rough-hewn timber frames. A single step of concrete leads up to a pair of thick, heavy-looking wooden doors, a brown wooden sign above them, with CHURCH OF ETERNAL LIGHT painted in white.

A rooster emerges from behind the church, followed by three hens. They scratch at the pebbles, peck at invisible bugs.

Isaac takes a step up, puts his hand on the knob, and turns to her, a conflicted, almost pained look on his face when he says, "And now you'll get to meet the Reverend."

He knocks three times, almost ritualistically.

"Enter," calls a voice from inside.

TWELVE

INSIDE, THE CHURCH IS STRANGELY stuffy, but then none of the six windows are open. The lava-rock walls are painted white inside too, and the cavernous beams and rough wooden planks that make up the roof and ceiling rafters almost look medieval, they're so battered and worn. Maybe recycled ship timbers? Four rows of rustic pews on each side, a simple wooden cross at the front.

Someone is in the front pew, kneeling. The Reverend.

Isaac makes the sign of the cross, tellingly waits a second to see if Julia will do the same. When she doesn't, he starts to walk down the aisle, not bothering to turn around to see if she's following.

The wooden floors beneath their feet squeak, but if the Reverend hears them, he shows no sign. He wears a short-sleeved white cotton shirt just like Isaac. Julia expects there will be a tie too.

Everything inside is so *clean*. Not a speck of dust anywhere, no cobwebs on the windows, no stray grain of sand embedded in cracks in the floorboards. It must require daily attention. Do the women actually talk to each other when they're working out of view of the tourists? They must.

Right?

They reach the pew where the Reverend kneels. He's gaunt, with antique-looking glasses perched on top of a hawkish nose. Blond hair streaked with gray, cropped close. And yes, a tie. *What kind of masochistic God makes men wear a tie in the tropics?* He mouths a silent prayer, intent on his hands, which are pressed together.

Isaac drops to one knee. "Reverend, Miss Julia Greer is here to see you," he says in a low voice.

Miss. Funny. It feels like such an old-fashioned, archaic word.

The Reverend doesn't stir, like he didn't hear. A few moments pass. Julia can hear the chickens outside squawk, the soft crash of waves breaking. A few more moments pass. A minute. Two.

Well, this is obviously turning into a power play. She decides to make a move.

"I can wait outside, if you need some time," she says. Her voice echoes inside the church, and the look on Isaac's face—like she just slapped him. Well worth it for that alone.

This, at least, seems to get the Reverend's attention. He solemnly makes the sign of the cross and stands. Turns to Julia. A wide grin creases his face, which, unlike that of everyone else in his congregation, looks like it has seen sun. A lot of it.

"Very pleased to make your acquaintance, Miss Greer."

He doesn't hold out a hand for her to shake, and instead offers a slight, formal bow. "But we should have our discussion about your family matters outside, so we don't disturb the peace of our Lord."

A special, slightly derisive emphasis on the words *family matters*. It must bother him, having someone in the midst of their deceased congregation who not only was an atheist, but a mentally ill woman who committed suicide to boot.

"Is the peace of the Lord so easily disturbed?"

"Not His eternal peace, but the peace that we cobble together here in His name, yes. We have . . . a way of life that would be difficult for someone of your ken to understand."

Someone of her ken. Oh she's going to have to lodge at least one good salvo to really get his attention. Bringing Irene into his hallowed ground should do it.

"My great-aunt Irene was ahead of her time, coming here on her own for scientific study. Frankly, I admire her, although that may be difficult for someone of *your* ken to understand."

Isaac looks like he's about to step in and protest, but, if anything, the Reverend looks intrigued. Julia bets it's been a long time since a woman spoke to him like that, if ever. It's a risky move, but she'll get more information out of him if he considers her an equal.

"I meant no disparagement," he says with a nod. "I understand she had many admirable qualities, as I'm sure you do. Now please, allow me to lead the way."

They walk through the ghost town, the Reverend by her side, Isaac trailing behind. Still no sign of anyone else, an ethereal quiet. But the wayward facecloth from the clothesline is gone— either someone picked it up while she was inside, or the wind took it. Even the rooster and the hens have disappeared.

"Where is everyone?" Julia asks.

"We are ordinarily very industrious," says the Reverend. "But, like the natural ecosystem of the island, our congregational ecosystem is fragile. Your presence is . . . complicated. I don't mean that in a negative way."

An odd way to put it. "You talk like I'm an invasive species."

It's a joke, but the Reverend doesn't take it that way. "Not you, specifically. But your culture, yes. Of course, when we arrived, our culture was similarly tainted, and we foundered at first, not understanding where we were. Our place in it, and God's plan. Mistakes were made."

"What kind?"

"Oh," he says with a slight smile, "the usual kind that come with hubris."

Not a straight answer. She needs to get specific. They start up the hill that leads to the cemetery—the soil has a reddish hue. It's a beautiful contrast to the golden grass.

"Was letting great-aunt Irene come here a mistake?"

The Reverend keeps his eyes on the path ahead of them. "Yes. Although an unwitting one. The first missionaries were trying to tame this place. Not understand it. Even my father's faith was infused with the need to dominate His creation. He thought that, as in Europe or America, man's will would prevail. *And let them have dominion over the fish of the sea, and over the fowl of the air, and over the cattle, and over all the earth, and over every creeping thing that creepeth upon the earth.* Not a verse that works well here."

"Isn't it heresy to question anything in the Bible?"

He becomes quiet at that, and at first she thinks she's offended him, but then he says, "The Bible also says, *Ask the animals, and they will teach you, or the birds in the sky, and they will tell you; or speak to the earth, and it will teach you, or let the fish in the sea inform you.* Perhaps some verses are more applicable here than the former. Perhaps we're closer to the Eden we were so summarily ejected from. It's hard for someone from the outside to understand. There's a reason we limit visits to a week, and only in prescribed places. It's a protection for us, and for you."

They reach the edge of the cemetery. The number of crosses is surprising—it was a much bigger congregation once. Strange, since there are so few living members now; they must be slowly dying out. In front of each cross is an oblong mound of lava rocks, as if an extra precaution is needed for the dead to stay put.

"Your great-aunt is there," the Reverend says, pointing to a cross at the far right of the field, a good few yards apart from the other graves. There's a plain pine coffin with a lid next to it, waiting for Irene's remains to be disinterred.

It makes Julia sad, for some reason, seeing Irene apart from the others. But Irene is dead, beyond all feeling, and at least she'll be coming home.

They head along a narrow path in the red dirt toward her burial site. Julia reads the names on the crosses. Some have inscriptions. Alice Simpson. 1952. *Your dead will live, their corpses will rise.* Justice Hawkins. 1945. *The Lord Jesus will raise us also.* Lester Sutherland. 1958. *Just as we have borne the image of the earth, we will also bear the image of the heavenly.*

"Do you know anything about how she died?" Julia asks.

The Reverend squints in the sun. The sunlight has dimmed. "My father didn't talk about those times much. Said that, like that of Job, our faith was being tested."

"Your grandfather lost his wife."

"His first one, yes."

His first wife. *Who was his second?*

Corinne Mark Simpson. 1973. *For your dew is as the dew of the dawn, And the earth will give birth to the departed spirits.* Some of the lava rocks in front of her cross are scattered about.

"Isaac," the Reverend says, "attend to that, will you? I would like a few moments alone with our guest here."

Immediately Isaac starts to pick up the lava rocks with an obedience that would be remarkable on the mainland for a young man his age. Julia notes that his patent leather shoes are now covered in a fine film of red dust. She has a feeling he'll be shining them soon.

The Reverend and Julia continue their walk. His shoulders seem to relax now that they're out of Isaac's earshot. He slips his hands into his pockets as they near Irene's grave.

"The boar here are quite a nuisance," he says. "It's a constant battle keeping them out of the vegetable garden, and they've gotten much bolder of late."

"Do you and the other men in the congregation hunt them?"

It's a sneaky question because she hasn't seen any men, except for Isaac.

The Reverend hesitates, as if he's turning his answer over in his mind, checking for possible cracks. Something he doesn't want her to know.

"Most of the boys born here . . . they didn't survive far beyond infancy. I was an exception. Isaac is a convert, which is fairly unusual."

"Did you ever find out why?"

"A doctor came. Once."

A finality in his tone. Still, she presses. "That must be hard. How will your way of life, your culture, continue?"

"God will provide."

They reach the end of the row, where the coffin sits, waiting. Julia stops, looks down at a freshly painted wooden cross.

Irene Greer. 1939. *You will go out in joy and be led forth in peace; the mountains and hills will burst into song before you, and all the trees of the field will clap their hands.*

"I don't know if she would approve," says the Reverend. "But that is one of my favorite verses. Isaiah 55:12."

Julia doesn't quite understand why, but tears start to form in the corners of her eyes.

———————————

The Reverend gives her a moment, bowing his head in silent prayer. Julia wipes her eyes with the back of her hands. She hadn't been expecting it, this emotion, this sense of connection. Maybe it's the lack of sleep, or the stress, or the years Irene has been moldering here, so far from home.

"Are you a religious woman?" the Reverend asks. Meaning Christian, of course.

At first she thinks about lying, but he would probably know. "I don't mean to offend, but no."

The Reverend nods. "So you think this is it, then, the end of her?"

"I think . . . well, okay yes. No one's come back to say otherwise."

"Well, not no one. Our Savior returned."

"That's always been a little hard for me to believe."

"Like Thomas," says the Reverend. "*Unless I see the nail marks in His hands, and put my finger where the nails have been, and put my hand into His side, I will never believe.* God does not seem to be so shy about showing his miraculous side here. Even the lowly gecko is capable of generating a whole new limb. Did you know that if it can, it will go back and eat its own tail? Just as we celebrate the resurrection by eating Jesus's body, drinking his blood. *Do this in memory of me.*"

Not a correlation Julia would have made, and just the mention of a gecko causes an unpleasant flashback to her nightmare. She opts for a polite silence.

And then she notices a single small white flower tucked under a rock near Irene's cross. The bloom looks like it's been torn in half. She remembers Irene writing about it, the legend of the star-crossed lovers. The flower looks fresh, too, like it was placed there recently. Curious.

"I can't imagine thinking that there is no soul," the Reverend continues. "That all we are is chemically animated dust. What a horrific idea."

He doesn't say it in a preachy way, more with a genuine wondering. A human being under the role he has to play.

Maybe he's never had a reason to want to just cease to be. Maybe he's never felt the weight of days. She thinks about her urge to just walk into the ocean and keep walking after Evie was gone—or Irene's half desire that the plane would have crashed on the way over. She thinks about the dark tides that can pull you out to sea, make you think the shore is too far away to reach. How your legs become leaden, your breath short, how eventually you just want to stop treading water and let yourself fall. The comfort in that idea. And the deception of it.

"Is that why resurrection is a theme on all the crosses?" she asks.

He looks up and over to the lava-rock wall that runs higher up the hill, where the edge of the jungle begins. A wistful expression. "Partly. I'll quote someone you might find more palatable. *There are more things in heaven and earth, Horatio, than are dreamt of in your philosophy.*"

Julia follows his gaze. For some reason, a shiver runs down her spine, as though the white tiger from her dream on the plane might emerge from the dense foliage and whisper in her ear again. The shadows of clouds move slowly across the fields. Not storm clouds, but still, there's an atmospheric drop.

"I read that there were others who seemed to suffer like Irene," says Julia. "Two tutors. Has anyone experienced anything like that since?"

"No one suffered quite like Irene," he says with a note of melancholy.

"Why, how did she suffer?"

"You ask a lot of questions, Miss Greer."

When he turns to her, the human being she'd gotten a brief glimpse of is gone. In its place, the Reverend again.

"Well," he says, "we should discuss the disinterment. We will perform, with your permission, a small religious ceremony, just to ease the minds of our congregation, who are troubled at the thought of disturbing the rest of someone who—"

"Probably killed herself?"

He winces but doesn't deny it. "Would that be acceptable to you?"

It seems like a small price to pay. "I don't see why not."

"Excellent. We could have everything set so that you could return with the pilot, after he fixes the refrigerator. After all, you're not here on vacation like the others."

He's trying to get rid of me. It means she'll have to shorten her timeline for finding the corpse flower, but it also means she'd be able to get off Kapu sooner. An appealing idea.

"That would be appreciated, thank you," says Julia. If she needs more time, she'll think of an excuse later. After all, Aunt Liddy paid in full.

Julia hears a commotion behind her and turns to see the red-headed woman standing there, whispering to Isaac, who looks visibly alarmed. For just a fraction of a second, Julia catches a glimpse of the face underneath the hair. All of it looks like it was badly burned, not just her jaw.

What the hell happened to her?

The woman turns away and hurries toward the greenhouse.

"Please excuse me," says the Reverend. He walks over to where Isaac stands, and some kind of heated discussion ensues. Bits of it are carried on the wind.

—she heard—
—not in the—
—we should warn—
—faith, it isn't time—

The redhead glances nervously over her shoulder, sensing Julia watching her probably, then picks up her pace, walking so fast she practically runs the rest of the way to the greenhouse. She pauses for just a second in front of the door, looks over in Julia's direction one final time before opening it and slipping inside.

It's like she wanted to make sure Julia saw her, know that the greenhouse had something to do with the conversation.

Julia marks it. She looks up to the sky and finds the clouds are now tinged with the softest gray. The storm is finally coming. She reaches into her bag to confirm that she'd packed an ultralight rain poncho.

She has to find an opportunity to slip away, do some exploring, storm be damned, if she wants to catch the early flight back, which she desperately does.

A fluttery something catches her eye, and she looks down to find another white flower. In fact, there are a few scattered near the closed coffin.

The Reverend and Isaac are still deeply engrossed in conversation. Whatever it is must be bad.

—we don't need to—
—I'm not saying—

The coffin's lid is slightly askew. Julia crouches, picks up the flower by her foot, pretends to hold it like she's contemplating . . . what? Life, its meaning, those kinds of serious things.

She takes a closer look at the coffin. Another flower, caught or intentionally pressed under the lid.

She's not—

Almost without thinking, almost like her arm is reaching out of its own accord, Julia touches the lid, pushes it slightly, just enough to get a glimpse inside.

A lei. There's a lei, made entirely out of the white flowers. It gives her a shiver that she doesn't quite understand, like there's a hidden meaning just out of reach. Her eyes are drawn to the line where the jungle begins. She feels someone, *something* watching.

Finally, the discussion/argument ends, and the Reverend walks back over to her, visibly strained. Isaac follows, nervous sweat dripping from his brow.

Julia stands.

"A situation has arisen that requires my immediate attention," says the Reverend. "Isaac will escort you back to the resort before the storm makes landfall."

"Is there anything I can do to help?" Not a real question of course, just a chance to dig.

"Thank you kindly, but it is church business, and best handled among the faithful. I do hope you'll enjoy the remainder of your time here."

It's said in a finishing tone. But she needs to find out what he meant when he said no one suffered like Irene. She needs one more opportunity, at least, to question him.

"Would it be possible for me to attend the ceremony for Aunt Irene?"

He seems surprised, and pleased. "Oh. I must apologize that I didn't consider asking. Ordinarily our ceremonies are off-limits to guests. But if you respect the same conditions of not speaking with the congregation, and keep a respectful distance from our members, I believe we could make a special exception in your case."

Isaac's eyes fall on the coffin. She didn't have a chance to close the lid properly. He must see the lei inside.

It doesn't seem possible for someone so pale, but his skin actually blanches at the sight.

THIRTEEN

ISAAC'S PACE ON THE RETURN to the resort is much brisker, as if he can't wait to be done with his charge so he can get back to whatever more serious business is under way at the church. The moisture in the air is full-force tropical, and he's walking so fast that sweat forms a *T* along his spine. Breathing hard. It must be hell to walk along the dirt path in those dress shoes, too.

"If you want to take a break . . ." Julia starts.

If he hears her, he pretends not to. The broad, grassy fields are behind them, and they now skirt the jungle again. The sound of wind in the palm trees so similar to the sound of ocean waves. Like they're talking to each other.

"There's some shade over there. . . ."

"I'm fine," Isaac says. "Thank you very much."

He doesn't ask her how she's doing, or turn around to see. Julia's hair is damp from the sweat trickling down her own neck. God, she wishes they'd given her a hat. Still enough sun shining through the scattered clouds that she's figuring the back of her neck will be lobster red soon. She'd take out her rain poncho, but since the damn thing is waterproof, it'd only make her sweat more. She can feel a blister starting at the back of her heel. New boots.

"I can make my own way if you need to get back to the

village." She's still hoping to slip away at some point—she needs to hit the wayfinder points programmed into her GPS phone, and she hadn't really anticipated that they'd be so corralled and observed. With the storm coming, today could be her only chance.

Isaac exhales hard, as if he was thinking he'd love nothing more than to ditch her. "I can't." His tone is short. "What I mean to say is, I've been instructed to escort you to the resort."

He seems to realize he's bungled the proper hospitality response, because he adds, "It's actually my pleasure to escort you back."

She wonders what on earth could have gotten so deep under his skin to fluster him so. He casts an occasional nervous glance in the direction of the jungle, like he's expecting something he doesn't want to see.

Well, if he doesn't need a break, she does. She deliberately slows down.

He doesn't seem to notice, and keeps walking. So she heads to a palm tree offering some shade, leans against it, lets the cooler sea breeze ruffle her hair. There are clouds gathering out on the horizon, but they don't look particularly threatening. A couple of coconuts lie on the grass, encased in their thick green-skinned husks. God, what she wouldn't give for something to drink.

Isaac gets about a half mile away, almost to the top of a small knoll, before he realizes that she's not behind him. He doesn't bother to hide his irritation—she watches him practically stomp his way back. In the meantime, she takes a seat by the tree, digs around in her bag for the knife. Finds it. He might confiscate it, seeing that it wasn't on the "approved for Kapu" list, but she figures he's just as thirsty, if not more so, than she is. She grabs a coconut, pierces the skin and starts to saw into the husk. It's tougher than she thought it'd be.

Finally he reaches her. He notes the knife, seems like he's about to say something, but just reaches his hand out instead.

"You're doing it wrong."

She gives him the knife. He quickly stabs the top of the husk with it, and then saws through the matted fiber. Does the same thing every few inches until he can pry the top off in sections, which he then starts to pull away roughly, angrily.

"I never knew it was so much work," Julia says.

"Yeah, well. It is." He tosses it to her half-peeled, then gets to work on the second coconut.

He's really pissed at her. Why, though? She tugs at the husk—it's incredibly hard to pull off, but she manages. Underneath is the round nut, a wizened, hairy ball.

Isaac makes short work of his, tearing the husk to shreds with a sinewy strength she wouldn't have imagined him capable of. He holds the revealed coconut, his hands reddened. Finds the eye of it, twists the knife in, then hands it to her.

"Thank you." Julia gives him the other one, and he digs a hole in it, too.

She holds the shell up to her lips, tips it back. A rush of coconut water fills her mouth. It's not cold, but it's refreshing nonetheless.

Isaac does the same, his Adam's apple bobbing as he swallows. When he's done, he wipes his mouth with the back of the hand that holds the knife. He looks out at the ocean, the waves rolling in on dark lava rocks. No beach here.

"You know, I can make it back on my own," Julia says. "We're halfway there already, right?"

He doesn't say anything, just stares at the waves.

She tries another tack. "I really appreciate everything you're doing for Irene, for our family. It means so much to my aunt Liddy, to bring her home. She's not doing so well herself, and—"

"Do you know how coconut trees get from one island to another?"

"No."

He nods, still staring out at the ocean, the incoming storm. "The husk is a boat. The coconut falls onto the beach, and the waves pick it up, carry it on to another island. It floats on currents. It can still be viable for a year, travel three thousand miles. But it's all because of the husk."

Why is he telling me this? "That's really interesting. I had no idea."

"No, you don't. He's putting us all at risk." Isaac takes another sip from the coconut, a longer, deeper drink, the way men at a bar knock back a bourbon when they need liquid courage.

"I'm sorry . . . what—"

"Just allowing you to be here. Your very presence. It's stirred things up. Things that shouldn't be . . . stirred. And now, letting you come to the ceremony." A bitter laugh. "You saw the lei. Do you know what that means?"

He takes his now-empty coconut, throws it hard at the ocean. It sails through the air, arcs, then crashes into the waters with a splash.

The violence of it shakes her. And he's still holding the knife.

"No," she says. "I don't." *What the hell has gotten into him?* He practically trembles with barely contained rage.

"You're right," he says tightly. "You're right. You'll be fine walking back to the camp by yourself. Here, take this."

He offers her the knife back. The sides are wet and sticky from the coconut.

But the way he *looks* at her. A pure, vicious hatred, as if he's considering pushing her off the cliff, trying to work himself up to it.

And he could, couldn't he? No witnesses, no one to know better, suicide runs in their family, plus there's a handy trail of accusations about her mental health courtesy of Ethan. She would just be subsumed into the island's history of tragedies, another casualty, a *haole* who didn't listen.

For the first time, it occurs to her that maybe Irene didn't jump off a cliff to her death.

When she doesn't take the knife, he throws it into the ground, where it lands blade down.

"Suit yourself."

And with that he heads off down the trail, back toward the village, and the church, and the Reverend, and the coffin with the white flower lei inside. She watches him become smaller and smaller, until the path takes him down a hill, where he disappears altogether.

———————

Once he's completely out of sight, Julia breathes a little easier. She hasn't been the focus of that level of vitriol since she exposed a health insurance executive who'd been booting children with cancer off their parents' policies. She wonders why it was directed at her instead of the Reverend, since apparently that's where Isaac's beef lies.

She drinks the rest of her coconut water, tosses the empty shell on the ground. Then she reaches into her backpack, pulls out the GPS phone, and powers it on. Still at fifty percent power. Damn, she forgot again to charge it. Two missed calls from her favorite great-aunt. She ignores them, clicks the map button, and then the red pin for Irene's camp—sees that it's only about a mile and a quarter away from her present location. The waypoints with probable spots for the corpse flowers are farther.

She faces the jungle—something solemn, eerie about it, a wall of dark green. Isaac was definitely spooked, so maybe she's just reverberating from his agitation. Misty clouds gather around Kapu's peak. It could be raining already. And how long will the charge on the satellite phone last?

It's not smart. It'd be better to wait until after the storm clears. But that could take a few days, and she desperately wants to cut her stay short, go back with the pilot. She has the print map too, a backup. And if worse comes to worst, it *is* an island, and all she has to do is head in the direction of the ocean. Right?

Famous last words, says Ethan.

And what about the dose of medication she missed?

Screw it. If it gets too hard, she can always just turn around, and she'll take the damn pills when she gets back. She can't afford to miss this chance. So she reaches into her backpack, pulls out a pair of lightweight, moisture-wicking pants, pulls them up under her muslin smock, then pulls the smock up and over her head, tosses it on the ground. Discovers she forgot the lightweight, moisture-wicking shirt, which leaves her with just her tank top, or the option of putting the smock on again.

Hell no.

But it might have some use. Julia gets the knife out of her backpack, picks up the smock, and roughly cuts off a strip of cloth from its hem. Wraps it around her mouth and nose, tying the ends in the back. Instant face mask. Then she stows what's left of the smock, and the knife, in her backpack, zips it shut, and hefts it over her shoulder. Grabs the GPS phone, checks the compass for her direction, and then starts for the wall, and the jungle beyond.

———————————

In the jungle, the humidity seems to jump a few sweltering degrees, and she's glad she's wearing pants—the brush scratches at her legs. The boots, too, are useful in the soft earth, and with the help of a bamboo stick she found, she's making pretty good time. She's surrounded by plants she's sure Irene would be able to name, categorize, in an instant, but Julia can only identify them with vague nouns and adjectives: tall thin trees with patches of that white mold, or lichen; whitish-gray moss that hangs from branches; knee-high plants with long leaves; thick roots pushing up through the layer of dead leaves and twigs; brown vines that curl around trunks; palms with bark that peels off like a coconut's husk; rotting logs covered with a thin fuzz of green moss.

Julia hears life all around her, but doesn't see anything except small gnats that buzz constantly around her head, and the occasional floating mosquito. Birds sing and chirp and cheep, something trills, something goes *woot woot woot woot woot*, and all the while the soft rush of wind blows through the leaves at the top of the canopy. It feels beautiful, peaceful in a way, but at the same time she gets the feeling that she's being followed, or watched. Every time she turns around at the sound of a clink or a crack, nothing, and no one is there.

Isaac? Did he really leave her alone, or did he just settle into a distant spot to spy on her? Someone could have followed her out of the resort, to the village, and then into the jungle. Not inconceivable, given the competition.

What was it Irene said? Something about how every tree, every leaf, seemed to be watching. Whispering.

She pauses. No—nothing unnatural, or strange.

Don't psych yourself out, Julia. Stay on track.

She pushes aside the dark, shiny leaves of a fern, digs her stick into the rise of a low hill, and starts to climb it. She should be close to Irene's camp now, or what's left of it. Julia's improvised face mask is damp from her labored breaths, and her left hand is slightly reddened and itchy from something she must have touched or brushed against. She hears the soft buzz of insect wings, feels something land on her neck, which is followed by the quick pinprick of a bite—Julia slaps at it, sees something the size of a small cockroach haphazardly fly away. *Wonderful.* Her foot suddenly sinks into a patch of mud, and she reaches out for a tree branch to steady herself.

And she sees a pair of footprints. As in human footprints, barefoot, in fact, and small, child-size.

Snap.

Impossible. Her heart starts to pound—*Evie?*—but no, why would she even think that, Evie's on the far side of the world. Maybe a child from the village whose curiosity got the best of them and they followed her into the jungle. They probably know every inch of it, the island is so small.

"Hello?" Julia says.

No answer. A pebble tumbles down from a rocky ledge a few yards to the left.

"You can come out. I won't bite, I promise."

Still no answer. But then they've probably been instructed not to talk to her. Told that Julia's very presence is a danger. And she must look so very strange, in pants, with a mask covering her face. It's a little unnerving for Julia too, but at least there's a reasonable explanation for feeling like she's being watched. And they can't report her transgression without admitting their own, so she should be safe on that count.

"All right, I'll just pretend I'm all alone. If you change your mind though, I have some M&M's."

That part is true—she'd squirreled some away in the false bottom of the suitcase. Quick energy for the trail. She lets her backpack slide off her shoulder, unzips it, locates the bag in one of the side pockets. She takes it out, rips it open, shakes a few of the round candies out into her hand. M&M's were always serious currency with Evie.

It makes her feel better, not being totally alone, being in the presence of a child, even one that isn't hers. A girl, most likely, at least if what the Reverend told her was true.

She eats a few M&M's and drops the rest of the candy in the hollow of a nearby tree. She doesn't think it will be there for long.

———————

There's not much of Irene's camp left. If the GPS hadn't started beeping, Julia would have probably trudged right by it. A pole covered in lichen leaning wearily against a tree, a rotting bamboo platform covered in dropped leaves—other plants sprouting up and through the poles—the remains of a frayed, mildewed rope dangling from a branch overhead.

Julia tests the platform with her weight, and thinks better of it. Instead she clears some of the debris, to see if there's something salvageable. She imagines anything useful that wasn't sent back to Aunt Liddy was scavenged by the villagers, like the people who went through her dead neighbor's stuff in Los Angeles. *Human beings are the same the world over.*

Poking up out of the earth is the tarnished gilt handle of a teacup and another porcelain shard—she picks them up, turns them over, rejoins the pieces in her hand and recognizes the pattern with its pale roses. It's the same china that Bailey served coffee in.

A soft *click* of a branch being broken a few yards away. Julia wouldn't be surprised if the children didn't play here, nothing like a good fort. She puts the broken teacup on the platform, reaches for the M&M's, shakes a few more out, and places them into a small pile in the curve of the cup, then looks around for anything else. Under the platform, she finds a pair of rusted and bent silver eyeglasses, missing a lens, and a couple of tarnished copper pennies, 1931, 1928. There doesn't seem to be much else.

Julia's about to move on, see if she can hit one more waypoint, when her boot knocks against a hard lump in the dirt.

She crouches down and digs around in the earth with her hands, uncovering a rusted black metal box, the cover dented. Locked, of course. She shakes it. Light, and probably empty, but small enough to fit in her pack. She decides to take it with her.

Just as she slips it into her bag, there's a booming clap of thunder, followed almost immediately by hard sheets of rain, a kind she's never experienced before, so heavy the drops practically feel like hail. She frantically pulls out her rain poncho, but by time she yanks it over her head, she's already soaked. At least it's a warm rain.

The sensible thing would be to wait it out, find some cover somewhere, but then again, there's no telling how long the storm will last. Wet is wet. She's pretty sure the GPS is waterproof—*it would have to be, right?*—and she has, in the worst-case scenario, a backup print satellite map.

She reaches into her bag, pulls out the GPS, covering it as best she can with her free hand. It's a three-mile hike through a ravine that cuts near the jagged peak of the extinct volcano, then half a mile to the beach with the corpse flowers. Forty percent power. Just about eleven o'clock in the morning; she should have at least eight hours of daylight.

Completely doable.

Right?

She can sense Ethan about to give a smart-ass answer, but she quickly finds an imaginary chair to prop under the imaginary doorknob of the imaginary closet she keeps him in.

FOURTEEN

OF COURSE JULIA FORGOT ABOUT that other factor, terrain. She should have clicked over to the topographic map, because the three miles in the ravine are almost completely uphill, and the rain has turned the soft earth to muck. Every step is an effort—her boots sink deep into the mud, making them hard to pull out—her bamboo walking stick is rendered useless, so she has to reach out to the trees to keep herself steady. A couple of slips and falls have left caked mud all up and over her pants.

And, as Irene had noted long ago, the plants become stranger the farther she treks into the interior. Thick, squat trees with furry bark, primordial ferns sprouting just about everywhere, indigo mushrooms with caps almost a foot wide, a nearly bioluminescent fungus that looks like ocean coral embedded in dead trees, massive green leaves sprouting up out of the earth almost five feet tall, and she nearly steps into a cluster of red pitcher plants that look big enough to eat small animals.

Julia stops a moment, rests under a leaf big enough to use as an umbrella, just to take a break from the downpour. Pulls the hood of her poncho back, tries to tighten the knot of her face mask, but it slides off in the process. *Goddammit.* Not that it could have done any good—her skin must be crawling with all sorts of bacteria—but for a token gesture it did make her feel a bit easier.

She wonders if she still has a silent follower. Probably not— even a child would have enough sense to take shelter. Her calves ache; water has crept into her boots.

She shouldn't have pushed it. Time to get back to the resort, take a shower, regroup. She pulls out the GPS, changes her waypoint to the resort. Damn, power has fallen to twenty percent. It must drain faster the lower it goes. She's going to have to hustle to make it back before she loses her GPS. If it's even possible.

Is it even possible?

She clicks over to the topographic map. Not good—looks like there are a series of steep hills between her and the resort from her present position, plus the snaking blue line of the stream. If her GPS loses power, if she got lost . . . how long before someone would even look for her? And no one, except for maybe her silent follower, knows where she is. Here in the depths of the jungle, she has no sense of direction, no way to see the ocean. She runs a wet hand through her hair.

"Shit!"

She kicks the stalk of the plant she's standing under, puts her hand on her forehead. *Calm down, Julia.* If she just makes it to the stream, she can follow it downhill, then just pick up the trail to the resort. *The stream's only about* . . . She checks the topographic map. Looks like a half mile. She should be able to make that on the power she has left if she picks up the pace, heads back now.

She notices a strong, acrid smell, like she just walked into a chemistry lab. She looks down and sees the stalk is broken where she kicked it, thick white sap oozing out.

She feels dizzy all of a sudden. The earth seems to tilt under her feet; black spots start at the corners of her eyes, and her stomach roils. She has to reach out for a nearby trunk to stay upright.

Then a rush of pure, unadulterated hate overcomes her— hate for Aunt Liddy for sending her here, hate for herself for agreeing, hate for Ethan for leaving her and putting her in this desperate situation in the first place. Hate for other things too, nonsensical things—bombs raining from the sky, and a cage, and a boat in a small harbor, and a syringe, and a scalpel covered in blood. A shivery darkness seems to creep out from her heart, down her extremities into her fingers and toes—black, consuming, cold, and deadly, but something ancient about it, too. A foreign sentience.

The next clap of thunder is deafening.

I spy with my little eye.

It's a voice that's inside and outside her, above and underneath. The air seems to compress in her lungs. Heavy as water. Thick as sin.

"I don't . . ." Julia turns, trying to find . . . what? Her skin itches, her eyes itch, her blood itches. She yanks the poncho up and over her head, throws it on the ground. Rain hits her skin, which feels like it's melting.

"I don't . . ."

Something that begins with d.

Her tank top burns; she can practically feel her skin bubbling—there's the stink of charred meat. She tries to pull her shirt off, but her fingers are swollen, shaking, and it's hard, so very, very hard to keep her balance. The fumes. Something about

186 J. LINCOLN FENN

the fumes. She takes a few halting steps away from the plant, nearly falls over, catches herself on a vine hanging from an overhead branch. Her left palm burns fiercely where her skin touches it. She lets go, pushes herself to take a few more steps, anything to get away from the smell that's now searing her nasal cavities.

The ground beneath her gives way and she stumbles facefirst into a pool of thick, algae-covered muck, gets a mouthful of it. It tastes metallic, like iron. She spits it out, tries to push herself up, but her palms just sink too, the mud making soft sucking noises.

A massive black centipede scuttles out from under a small fern—the thing is six inches long, maybe ten, with mean-looking pincers and the slightest dusting of white fuzz along its serpentine spine. It wisely skirts the muck, sensing exactly where the firm earth ends and the death trap begins.

"I spy with my little eye," says Julia, her voice hoarse, although she doesn't understand why she said anything at all. It was in her head and now it's out of it, thoughts and words one thing.

The centipede pauses, turns its head toward her, raising its antennae. It lifts part of its body up in the air, smelling . . . something.

"I spy . . ." Her eyes so puffy she can scarcely see. She tries to get herself upright, her feet searching for something solid, but they find nothing, and the boots are so heavy, like concrete blocks. She's sinking. She can feel herself sinking.

Another massive clap of thunder.

And then the centipede scurries toward her, right along the surface of the muck like a water strider. It clambers onto her shoulder—she can feel the burning, tickling sensation of hundreds of tiny feet on her bare skin. It curls around the back of her neck to her other shoulder, seems to start a trail down her spine but thinks better of it, and returns to her shoulder. Antennae tickle her ear.

Julia gags. This could very well be where she loses her mind.

And then there's a rustling of brush in front of her, like a large animal is prowling—*the white tiger*—only no, it's a girl that emerges and stands before her, pale skin, wet blond hair in clumps. A thin cotton dress that clings to her small body. She stares, preternaturally still.

Julia wants to speak but her tongue is too swollen, too thick.

The girl cocks her head, curious.

Julia coughs, the fumes now in her throat, which is starting to swell too. The centipede ticks up the side of her head; she can feel it running over her hair, until it pauses again.

The girl slowly walks forward, crouches at the edge of the muck. She reaches out a pale arm and the centipede jumps onto it.

I have truly lost my mind.

The centipede then runs up the girl's arm, settling onto her shoulder like a trusted pet.

The black spots in Julia's eyes grow larger. She reaches out for something, anything, to try to pull herself forward, but her arm is starting to go numb, and she misses, falling back in the muck again. She watches her poncho sink, the mud taking it. Damn thing was useless anyway.

It's hard to keep her head up, and there must be a fire inside her lungs, because every breath is extraordinarily painful. A bad allergic reaction to something for sure. *Done in by a leaf.* Julia would laugh, only she can feel her heartbeat starting to slow. At least there's a witness. Maybe they can ship her body with Irene's, a twofer.

The only pang is Evie. How long before Ethan remarries, plugs in a substitute mother?

Not long.

The girl keeps watching her, examining her, saying nothing. Sheets of rain still fall in torrents, but the girl doesn't seem to care.

Hard to breathe. Impossible to breathe. *Death. Death* starts with *d.* Also *deceive,* and *decay,* and *darkness.*

Julia's eyes close.

Then she feels small, fierce hands gripping her arms; she feels her body being pulled forward. Julia manages to open her eyes one last time. The centipede is gone, but the girl is there, really putting her back into it as she heaves hard, pulling Julia out to firmer ground, grunting with the effort.

Julia is able to push herself up, barely, and crawl a few feet farther before collapsing. Her breathing becomes shallow. At eye level to the ground, she sees leaves, and dirt, and a tiny brown frog that regards her with a serious frown. White fuzz dots its back. Everything around her is distant, surreal, like it's someone else dying, like her body is just a cavern she's temporarily inhabiting. She can already feel the current tugging her out to the deeper waters, the opaque, cold depths that even the hottest sun has never reached.

The girl's muddy bare feet come into view, but Julia can't move her head. Her vision starts to blur. The girl kneels—blurry knees poking out of a blurry dress. She feels the girl open her mouth, tastes the mud on her fingers. She can hear the girl chewing. Then her head is tilted back, her mouth is opened wider, and the girl spits something into it—a nasty taste, a thick sludge. She starts to gag, but the girl clamps her mouth shut, holds her there with a strength that seems impossible for someone so small.

Julia lets her eyes close, her lids so heavy, so heavy. She hears a bird chirp despite all the rain, its call getting response from another. Goodbye, birds.

Evie . . .

And then all goes dark.

#NDC DEV ORG HUB

15:04:52 <isir528>   what the fuck happened today?

15:05:00 <bai908>   why are you asking us what the fuck happened today? ball is in your court.

15:05:20 <isir528>   you promised no chance of triggering. wait, let me check the log. your exact words were "zero chance of triggering." we are recording highest levels of VOCs ever.

15:06:02 <bai908>   not related. could be climate.

15:06:11 <isir528>   it's not the fucking climate. it's lilith and you know it.

15:06:25 <bai908>   if, and that's a big if, you're right, then finish the job sooner than later. you know, the one we pay you for. then we'll extract you, red. where is she now?

15:07:04 <isir528>   interior as planned. 5a is MIA.

15:07:12 <bai908>   5a? who is 5a?

15:07:15 <isir528>   thought she was one of yours.

15:07:22 <bai908>   if she was one of ours, we would have told you.

15:07:33 <isir528>   yeah. right. lol.

15:07:38 <bai908>   terminate.

15:07:41 <isir528>   i'm a scientist, not a murderer.

15:07:49 <bai908>   you'll be whatever you need to be to get the shit done. too late to feel guilty. you're in deep, son. handle it.

15:08:16 <isir528>   red said she saw the akua lele.

15:08:24   \<bai908\>   oh for fuck's sake, is that what this is all about? that experiment was terminated. grow a pair.

15:08:48   \<isir528\>   but the VOCs.

15:08:59   \<bai908\>   reality is still out here. do your job, and get back to it. soon.

15:09:15   - - > **bai908** has quit

FIFTEEN

JULIA'S HEAD IS A DEADWEIGHT, and there's a throbbing pain that shoots down her spine. She's lying on her side, and her body shudders, her stomach heaves, but she's able to lean forward just enough so that when the vomit rises, it lands on the soft earth by her head.

The rain has lightened. The wind has died down. Birds call out to each other. She's alive.

She forces her eyes to open, the light sending another shock wave of searing pain, and it takes a few moments for her blurry vision to become clear.

The girl sits cross-legged in front of her, idly twisting a small branch in the dirt. Mud caked in her hair, on her hands, her arms, her legs. A fly lands on her forehead but she doesn't brush it away. Her face is narrow, elfin, and it's hard to tell how old she is. Julia guesses around ten. Maybe twelve. She's a dead ringer for how Julia had pictured Agnes, Irene's assistant. The congregation, closed off as it is from the rest of the world, must be running dangerously close to some of the effects of a limited gene pool.

Julia manages to sit up. The girl doesn't seem to notice, or maybe just doesn't give a damn.

At least it's still light out. Unless . . . could it be the next day? Julia pulls her backpack off, inspects it. Muddy as hell, and when Julia unzips it, mucky water pours out.

Oh shit.

Julia pulls out what's inside, takes an inventory. The paper map is so soggy it tears in half, the ink blurred beyond recognition. Knife just needs cleaning, one specimen jar is broken, which she unfortunately discovers when a shard of glass cuts her palm. The GPS phone is still functional—she remembers Bailey telling her it'd been engineered to survive anything, even a sixty-foot drop—and it tells her it's the same day, only about an hour later. Down to a ten percent charge. Not enough to get her back to the path leading to the resort.

But this girl must know the way.

"What's your name?" Julia asks. Her tongue is still swollen, but it's functional at least.

The girl doesn't answer, just stands instead. She reaches into her pocket, pulls out something that's clasped tightly in her hand. Turns her hand over, opens her fingers to reveal M&M's. She picks out three, pops them in her mouth, crunches them with obvious satisfaction.

Slowly, with the caution of a feral cat, she edges closer to Julia. Holds out her hand with the M&M's.

A gift. An offering. She's so slight, this girl, Julia wonders if they're feeding her enough.

Julia reaches out her hand—carefully, so she doesn't spook her—and picks out two, leaving the girl three. She puts the M&M's in her mouth, even though her stomach is still queasy.

This seems to satisfy the girl, who gives the faintest hint of a grin.

"I'm lost," says Julia. "Do you know how to get back to the resort?"

The girl doesn't respond, just turns around and walks a few feet into the brush before stopping. She glances back and beckons.

Not allowed to speak to the guests, obviously. But maybe there's a way to build something of a relationship. She imagines the girl might know the location of the corpse flower, too.

Julia staggers to her feet. Dizzy, wet, exhausted, but she manages to stay upright. She picks up her sodden backpack, slings it over her shoulder. The girl turns back around and walks into the jungle.

Julia follows.

The girl keeps about five yards between them, slipping under and through the dense vegetation with remarkable ease, while Julia has to keep one eye on the ground in front of her at all times, breaking branches and occasionally tripping. The palm of her left hand throbs with a steady pain. She'd wrapped it with a strip of muslin to stop the bleeding, noticed blisters forming too—from the caustic plant?—and not being able to use it to help keep her balance is slowing her down considerably.

Every question Julia's asked so far has been met with silence. *How old are you? Have you ever been off the island? Do you play by yourself in the jungle a lot?* But Julia knows the girl is listening.

"I have a daughter myself," Julia says. "Her name's Evie. Well, Evelyn, really, but we call her Evie for short. She's six. Almost seven."

No response.

"She lives in New England now, with her father. I haven't seen her in almost six months. It's hard, being so far away from someone you love."

Slightest turn of the girl's head. She slows down, just a little.

Julia tries to think of something that might pique her interest. "It's going to be snowing soon, where she lives. She's never seen snow before. Well, far away, on the tops of mountains. Which is funny, because my husband—ex-husband—always said he hated it. Not just the cold, but the actual snow."

"Snow is where rain falls from the sky, but it's not wet," says the girl. "It's dry, like small white leaves."

"Yes," says Julia, surprised and pleased with herself. "But when you go inside, the snowflakes on your clothes melt, and then they're wet."

The girl nods, as if this is what she'd surmised. But her own response seems to spook her, because she picks up her pace again, quickly climbing a small knoll and adding an extra two yards between them.

Progress, thinks Julia.

She doesn't push it further, not yet. She has to give the girl time to acclimate to this subtle change in their relationship. Instead, Julia tries to figure out which direction they're headed in, which is truly impossible. It's definitely not the way she came— the jungle here is even more bizarre. Things that look like small snails cling to trunks, the shells a mottled green. Black, oblong pods hang above; others have fallen, revealing bloodred fruit with tiny black seeds—a fragrant scent like papaya, or mango. There are small, stubby trees that look like gnarled potatoes, massive ferns that form perfect spirals, and everywhere that white lichen which creeps along the jungle floor, up and along the trees, over and around rocks and roots.

She trips over one such root and has to reach her right hand out to one of the stubby trees to keep from falling. Her fingers register something strange—smooth and hard—so she turns to look and sees what appear to be rough teeth embedded in the tree's bark. She runs a finger along them, and yes, they feel exactly like teeth, some kind of animal's, with yellowed enamel.

They look like they got a lot of use. And then just below are two small tusks.

Something small and hard hits her shoulder—an M&M.

She tears her eyes away from the trunk, and finds the girl staring at her in a way that makes her seem older than eight, or ten, or twelve years. More like a hundred. More like a thousand. Maybe even older than that.

A strange thought. Again, the sense that it isn't her own.

"Are these teeth . . . ?"

The girl gives a sly smile, turns, and walks ahead, running her hand through leaves.

———————————

They must be deep in the oldest part of the island, because here the tall, massive, old-growth trees have thick trunks the size of small vehicles, branches and leaves completely obscuring the sky above, making it darker below, a kind of twilight. More kinds of fungus here too, rippled like clamshells and clinging to fallen limbs, poking up out of the soft earth with long stalks that almost reach Julia's kneecaps—bulbous, white caps that look soft and spongy. The wind has picked up again, causing the branches above to clatter against one another, and along with the rain, leaves fall.

There's less brush here, which makes it easier to walk, but the wind sounds ominous. Maybe that wasn't really the storm that hit, just the precursor.

"How much farther to the resort?" Julia asks the back of the girl.

No answer. For the first time, she wonders if the girl is in fact taking her back, or is leading her off somewhere else, to a hidden, secret fort only the children know. They'll keep her like a pet, bringing scraps from their table, prodding her for stories. She'll grow old and withered and pale, like the witch in any good fairy tale.

It unnerves Julia, how her thoughts are bleeding in odd directions. Julia shifts her bag over her left shoulder. Her right shoulder aches, as do her calves, her lower back. She feels like she could practically curl up under one of the trees, fall asleep, rain and storm be damned.

"Hansel and Gretel," says the girl. She swoops down to grab a fallen vine about the length of her arm, starts to twirl it like a toy.

"You know that story?" Julia asks.

The girl cracks the vine like a whip. "There's nothing to eat, so the mother tells the father to take the children into the deepest part of the woods and leave them there to starve. Only Hansel leaves behind bread crumbs, to follow back. Like the candy. Only the birds eat the bread crumbs. And I ate the candy."

An interesting correlation. Julia smiles. "So does that make you a bird?"

"*No.* I just like candy." She takes the vine and coils it around her hand, like a rope.

"Then they find the house where the witch lives, made of cake," the girl continues. "But the witch wants to eat them. Why does the witch want to eat them when she has cake?"

"Huh, I never really thought about it that way." But Julia knows that this answer won't suffice. Children always want a passable explanation. "Maybe she was tired of cake, because she could have it every day."

The girl nods, slows down just a bit so that she only walks about a yard ahead. "People get bored of the same thing every day. Even if it's a good thing."

Something about this strikes a nerve. Did Ethan just get bored with her? *Click, click, clack* go the branches overhead. The light seems to darken a shade.

"Did you read 'Hansel and Gretel' in a book?"

The girl shakes her head, runs the vine through her slender hands. "I heard it. I hear stories, and I remember them."

"What's your favorite story?"

The girl looks at the ground, thinks a moment. "I like new stories. Ones I haven't heard before."

Julia smiles, bemused. "Because hearing the same ones over and over again—"

"Boring," says the girl. A vine hangs low from one of the branches, and she drops the one in her hand to grab it. She runs a little, then lifts her legs off the ground, swings back and forth. Julia wouldn't doubt that she could shimmy up the vine too with her wiry little strength, agile as a monkey.

A loud crack of thunder, then a menacing rumble. Julia has a feeling the real storm is about to start in earnest.

"We should hurry and get back," says Julia.

The girl swings hard one last time, throwing her weight into it so that it lifts her high off the ground. Then she lets go, landing with a soft *thwuft*. A branch overhead creaks menacingly, and tiny leaves fall.

"Maybe we should have left pebbles," says the girl. "Hansel was smart, leaving pebbles. They glowed when the moon came out, and the birds couldn't eat them."

Does she even know how to get back?

It never occurred to Julia that the girl might be as lost as she is.

Julia stops, pulls out her GPS, checks the power. Five percent. But the way the girl has taken her must be some kind of a short-cut, because it looks like they're not far away at all from the resort. There's a chasm of some kind, or a gulch up ahead.

"What's that?" the girl asks, pointing to the GPS.

"It's like a map. It can tell me where I am, and show me how to get to where I want to go."

"Did a witch give it to you?"

Actually, one did, Julia thinks. "It's just a device. Like cell phones." But then, the girl might very well not know what a cell phone is. The contamination of culture and all that.

There's another, louder crack of thunder, and she can hear heavy rain falling again, but the canopy above is so thick that not much reaches them. A natural umbrella. The storm clouds cause the light to ebb, too, what little there was, which makes it feel like they're on the cusp of night.

"I don't need a map, not here," says the girl. "I know where everything is."

An opening. "There's a red flower I'm looking for. I'm told it smells like rotting meat. Have you ever seen it?"

"Oh yes," says the girl. "It really stinks." She pinches her nostrils with her fingers for emphasis.

Julia feels her heart catch in her throat. Tries to keep her voice even when she asks, "Could you take me to it?"

The girl pirouettes on her right foot. "You're not supposed to go there."

"Says who?"

The girl just smiles, skips ahead a few paces, while the light under the canopy continues to darken.

She hears the rush of the river long before she sees it, a distant, thunderous roar. The girl has fallen back into her five-yard lead. Maybe Julia asked for too much, too soon. Pressed it too hard.

Her stomach rumbles, and she can't wait to get into a shower to soap all the muck off, be dry again. It feels like she left the resort an eternity ago and she's practically a different person. They're back now in relative normal jungle brush, which means the canopy is less dense, which means there's no protection from the warm rain that is soaking her again.

Another crack of thunder, then a flash of lightning illuminating everything in stark relief. She catches sight of two large birds, maybe vultures, huddled together on a thick branch overhead. Beady black eyes staring with an uncomfortable intensity. Why is everything on this damn island so intent on *looking* at her?

The girl steps through low brush, and beyond her, Julia can see the gulch, a soft mist hanging over it. As she approaches the clearing, the river becomes louder, as deafening as a waterfall.

And then she sees it.

The river is completely engorged, flooding the gulch with a torrent so violent it's taken down low-lying trees. Without the jungle's cover, the wind whips the rain sideways, hitting Julia's face with a force that almost takes her breath away. Ahead is a rope bridge in bad shape spanning the chasm, the dangerous waters about fifty feet below. Strong gusts blow the rope bridge, making it swing from side to side. Wet planks maybe spanning two feet wide max, rope railings, the entire thing secured to trees on either side, a structure that, on a sunny, balmy day, would be iffy at best.

The girl turns to Julia, meets her eye expectantly.

"That?"

The girl points to the left, and Julia can see it—the steep, peaked roof of the dining pavilion. A short distance downhill, if she was actually able to make it to the other side of the bridge. Sure it's the shortest, most direct route, but . . .

"There has to be another way," says Julia, raising her voice so she can be heard over the rushing waters.

The girl shakes her head. "It would take too long," she says loudly. "It'd be night. You wouldn't survive the jungle at night."

Julia notes *you,* not *we.*

Without much hope, she looks at the cliff that runs along their side of the gorge down to the ocean, tries to imagine a safe path. Even if she somehow managed, she'd still have to traverse the river, which is probably even wider closer to sea level. Which means she'd have to wait, and hope, for the weather to clear, or trudge back to the Reverend's village.

God, the raw power of that river. Deadly and magnificent. Julia approaches one of the trees holding up the bridge, runs her right hand over the rope that's tied around its trunk. It's the good seafaring kind, and at least the knot is tight. But her left hand hurts so much it's practically useless.

The girl steps closer to her. "I don't know why they went back."

Julia doesn't know what she means, and her confusion must be apparent, because then the girl says, "Hansel and Gretel. They went back to their father, even though he left them to die in the woods, twice. They had the witch's jewels. They could have lived anywhere."

Julia racks her mind for an explanation.

"Life is empty when you're far from your family. Even if your family does things to you that you don't like, you forgive them. You stick it out."

"*You* don't live with your family."

The truth hurts. She tries to think of a way to explain to a girl who doesn't know about divorces and attorneys, courts and prenuptial agreements.

Julia gives the rope a good hard tug. It holds. "Let's just say I have to get the jewels from the witch. My husband left me in the woods to starve, because he wants Evie all to himself. I need the jewels to get her back."

"Ethan," says the girl. "Ethan left you all alone."

"Yes." Her heart clenches with a pain that still, even here, so far away from it all, nearly breaks her.

This the strange girl seems to understand. Julia gets the sense that it settles something in her mind. "I will take you to the red flower tomorrow," the girl says. "And you will give it to the witch and get her jewels."

It's remarkable that the girl made the intuitive leap that the flower is the price she has to pay. Julia lets go of the rope and turns back to the gorge. If she doesn't slip and fall, it might just be possible to get across, storm or not. *If.* Just the thought of it though makes her queasy.

"But," says the girl, "you will give me your map device."

This she wasn't expecting. "Why do you want it?"

"Because I want to walk the island and see it the way a bird sees it, from the sky."

"It won't work for much longer," Julia says. "It needs to be plugged in, like—"

"Like the computer. I know."

"The church has a computer?"

"No."

One of her competitors? Someone else on the island entirely?

Beth?

Noah?

She needs to know. She can't truly protect herself if she doesn't know who to protect herself from.

"The GPS . . . map device needs a special plug. One that fits in here." Julia takes it out from her sodden bag, and the girl steps forward, curious. It's insane, beyond insane to be standing in the beginnings of an approaching tropical storm, talking about plugs, but she can't, of course, seem desperate in what is about to be a transaction.

The girl leans in, peers at the bottom of the phone. "The hole is tiny."

"Exactly. So how about this: I take this back with me and plug it in, and then tomorrow when you take me to the red flower, you can use it. And when I leave, you can *have* it. But you'd have to keep it where the Reverend won't find it."

"Oh, he won't," says the girl, in a tone that makes her seem much, much older. "He never sees anything I don't want him to."

An unusual confidence. Julia waits, not daring to say another word.

The girl looks off for a moment, then decides. "I will accept your offer."

A strong gust blows the rope bridge completely sideways. *Great.* But Julia is on this side, and the bridge is what's required to get to the other. She needs to do it quickly, though, before the worst of the storm rolls in.

"Where should we meet?"

"I will find you, when it's time," says the girl.

"Of course, if the storm really gets bad—"

"Then we'll get wet." The girl smiles, like Julia is being ridiculous to even consider it a possible problem. She pirouettes on one of her muddy bare feet, and heads back into the jungle without another word.

Julia watches her disappear into the brush like a sprite. Wonders at her Zen-like calm.

She could use some of that calm herself, to get over that goddamn bridge. She should have packed at least one of the Jack Daniel's.

Not a particularly helpful thought. So Julia does the only thing she can, which is to put the GPS back in her backpack, zip it shut, sling the pack over her back, securing it as best she can with the straps, and then walk toward the bridge.

She pauses at the gulch's muddy edge.

Odd. The girl used Ethan's name. She doesn't remember mentioning his name.

Something to wonder about later. The storm is worsening, and she needs to get across soon. So she reaches out for the rope railings, such as they are, and takes the first step.

———————————

Her weight keeps the bridge from swinging quite as wildly, and she tries to focus on the plank in front of her, then the next plank, then the next, her survival a moment-by-moment affair. Right hand, left foot, left hand—*ignore the pain, don't think about the pain*—right foot. Below, the waters rage.

Julia has never liked heights. Ethan surprised her once with a Napa Valley hot air balloon excursion, back when they were dating. She'd pretended to enjoy it, trying to impress. But being that far above the ground, held aloft by a flimsy bit of fabric and invisible gas, was not exactly her idea of fun. She'd held onto the gondola rail for dear life, white-knuckled.

Right hand, left foot, left hand, right foot.

Such a simple equation in front of her. Either she'll slip and fall, or she won't. Either the rope bridge will hold, or it won't. The only thing in her control is her own focus.

Control. Such a seductive idea, to have control, dominion over one's self, one's life. Almost as terrible as losing Evie was losing the sense that her life was her own, that the construction of the world she'd built with Ethan was something she'd had an equal say in. But it had always been at his pleasure. She'd deceived herself into thinking otherwise.

A quarter of the way across. The rain hits her face like small pebbles.

Right hand, left foot, left hand, right foot.

Will the girl keep her promise to show her where the corpse flower is? Again, not in Julia's control.

Her boot slips on the next plank; she feels it hover over empty space for three heart-pounding seconds, and the sudden shift of weight causes the bridge to swing. Her left hand can't hold on, so she grips the rope tightly with her right hand, feels a surge of vomit rising at the back of her throat.

A bright burst of lightning over the ridge, behind the jagged peak of Kapu, then the crack of thunder.

She swallows. Holds on.

Evie, short for Evelyn. The name had been Ethan's idea, after his grandmother, a woman on the cusp of death with a large fortune to bequeath. Not that he didn't have enough of the green stuff himself, but there never seemed to be an end point of satiation, or to the competition with his wealthy compatriots. Always a bigger yacht to own, more houses scattered across the globe to buy, places to travel, the desperation of cramming several lifetimes' worth of experiences into one. The fear that someone had something he didn't.

The gust dies away. It's hard, almost impossible, to get her hand to let go of the railing for even a second, but she has to. Right hand, left foot, left hand, right foot.

The constant anxiety that he would lose it all. A market fluctuation across the world could keep him up nights. Once she'd suggested they live slightly under their means, if he was so worried. Downsize to a smaller house. He'd reacted like she'd suggested he shoot himself.

Right hand, left foot, left hand, right foot.

Halfway there. Aunt Liddy's fortune is a supernova to his star, and yet in the last, lingering days of her life, Aunt Liddy is still trying maintain control of it, or at least her legacy. The same sense of desperation.

Right hand, left foot, left hand, right foot. Only a few more yards until she's on the other side.

Her grandfather trying to control the genetic destiny of humankind.

Right hand, left foot, left hand, right foot.

Control an ancient human desire, from the beginning of Genesis. *And let them have dominion over the fish of the sea . . .*

God, the sound of the water below her. She imagines the free fall that could happen at any moment, the short plummet, the deathly impact, washed out to sea.

Her body freezes. She wills her right foot to move, but it won't. Tries to loosen her grip on the rope, but it's like it's been grafted there. Her breath comes faster, and she realizes she's utterly petrified.

. . . and over the fowl of the air, and over the cattle, and over all the earth . . .

The wind, a manifestation of pure fury. She tries to move her left foot, but it won't.

. . . and over every creeping thing that creepeth upon the earth . . .

So many creeping things creeping on Kapu. Each with its curious sentience. Her chest tightens, and her teeth start to chatter.

I can't.

I can't. She stares at her right hand, wills it to move.

I can't.

Utter helplessness washes over and around and through her. But the Reverend said that dominion didn't work on the island. Maybe the trick here is to relinquish control. Give in.

It's with that thought that all the others seem to fall out of her mind, or the ability to think, and instead she just feels . . . peace. Calm. A sense that whether she makes it to the other side of the gulch or falls into the waters below doesn't matter much. The wind isn't blowing against her; it's blowing through her. She's vapor. Empty. A ghost.

Ghost, most, host.

She registers, distantly, the tree across the way that the rope bridge is tied to yielding to a strong gust. The tree bends. She feels a momentary drop, watches idly as her fingers clutch the rope railings, instinctually, no need for her to think, or fear, or direct. She's inside and outside, everything is the same, nothing is separate.

Coast, roast, post.

Her right foot edges a quarter inch forward.

You'll never get her back, says Ethan's voice. Or not his voice, her mind using his voice. *She doesn't want or need you, just like I don't want or need you.*

This is the thought that percolated under her skin, caused her to buy a box of wine when she should have bought a loaf of bread. Turned her into the lost, helpless person Ethan said she was.

Everything around Julia is watching her. Waiting. Some kind

of test presenting itself. Maybe it's time to let the island decide, relieve herself of the responsibility. *What the hell*. If she makes it across, she makes it. If she doesn't, then it won't matter much anymore. A coin toss.

It's not logical, but it is.

She lets go of the ropes, lets her hands hover above them. The wind blows the bridge to the right, but her balance accommodates it, naturally. Is she in control of her mind, or not? Is she in control of her body, or not?

She doesn't know.

This is madness.

Right foot, left foot. Right foot, left foot. Walking like an acrobat along a tightrope, arms outstretched. She could laugh. She could cry. Her eyes suddenly feel heavy, so very, very heavy, that she actually closes them. Takes another step forward.

She remembers buying Evie a Russian nesting doll for her fifth birthday, how her daughter loved to pull it apart, find the next doll inside it, pull that apart, find the next doll, and so on and so on until she got to the smallest doll that was a single, solid piece of painted wood.

Right foot, left foot.

Kapu has things within things within things. It's not a thought but a certainty, like her certainty that her hand is connected to her arm, that her arm is connected to her shoulder. But the center, the heart, is fuzzy, indiscernible.

Right foot, left foot. She doesn't fall. She doesn't die. Another crack of thunder, and she doesn't even shudder.

What's the girl's name? It's hard not to think of her as Agnes, because she fits the description so perfectly, but Julia can't let her mind make assumptions, not here.

Right foot, left foot, right foot, left foot . . .

. . . and then there she is, stepping onto ground that is solid, immobile. Julia opens her eyes. The path down to the resort is in front of her, and she hears the roar of the waters behind her. She made it.

"I spy with my little eye," she says.

Why did she say that? Think that?

She's about to move forward, but doesn't. Like there's another Julia inside Julia, with a different idea. And it's this inner Julia that raises her head to the sky, lets the droplets fall into her mouth. Water in the sky, water below in the churning river, water in the ocean and in every cell of her own body. Deadly in places, life-giving in others.

She doesn't know why, but she suddenly gets the sense that the girl, this stranger, is made entirely of wood, nothing else inside of her. No heart.

SIXTEEN

NO ONE'S AROUND AS JULIA enters the resort's periphery, everyone probably inside, sheltering from the storm. The harbor protects the bungalows on the pier from the worst of the surf, but the choppy gray water is high, only a foot below their floors, storm clouds thick all the way to the horizon. She wonders if they'll have to double up if it gets worse.

All I need. A roommate.

She still feels dazed, shaken. Hurries to her own bungalow—she can only imagine what she looks like, covered in mud, and is in no mood to answer questions about it at dinner. If there *is* dinner in the pavilion. No walls was a great design decision for a sunny day, but with wind blowing the rain sideways, not so much.

She unzips the front pocket of her backpack, pulls out the muddy key, unlocks the door with a shaky right hand, steps into the bungalow, and quickly closes the door behind her.

God, the bed. One of the churchwomen must have come in and made it—hospital corners, a thick blanket neatly folded at the foot, a flower on the pillow—the best thing to happen to her all day. She'd like to just peel off her wet clothes, crawl under the covers, and sleep for the next year. Her body yearns for it. But she's a mess, she can't afford to muck up the bed, raise suspicions. And *oh dear God*, they've also left her a tray on the bureau top, plates with stainless steel coverings, a coconut drink with a red straw and a parasol sticking out of it. Something cake-ish under plastic wrap.

She lets the wet backpack slide off her shoulder, heads for the tray, lifts one of the lids. Bread, cheese, fruit, hard-boiled eggs, salad, some kind of vinaigrette dressing on the side. She picks up one of the eggs, takes a bite, closes her eyes, savoring. Eat or shower? Eat sounds good. She's about to grab a slice of mango . . .

Did I leave the doors to the armoire open?

Because they are.

Whoever made the bed must have left the armoire open.

Right?

Still, something about the room though feels . . . off. She walks quickly over to the armoire, and finds the suitcase still locked. Nothing else looks like it was disturbed. And yes, there are two clean spare towels on the top armoire shelf.

She should take a shower. But the tray, the food . . . No, she should take a shower. It will help clear her mind, which is still having a hard time focusing, returning to the present. Everything has the feel of a dream about it.

She takes one towel, thinks about it, takes the other, too, and heads for the bathroom. Clicks the light on.

No light. The storm must have taken out the electricity. No electricity, no charging her GPS phone.

Fuck.

She races back to her sodden backpack, pulls out the phone—power is down to two percent. She quickly shuts it off.

"Goddammit!" she shouts to an empty room.

If the girl comes back for her—no, *when* the girl comes back for her, she'll take Julia to where the computer is, where there must be electricity . . . unless the power is out there, too. She remembers the solar panels on that shed in the church village, and Isaac had mentioned something about a backup generator.

Shower. She should shower and then think about it; nothing is going to rectify the situation, not in the next ten minutes.

One thing at a time. One foot in front of the other. Right foot, left hand, left foot, right hand. Speaking of which . . .

She tugs the dirty muslin strip off her left hand, inspects her palm. The cut actually doesn't look as bad—the bleeding has stopped, the red puffiness gone down. Even the blisters seem smaller. If the blue pills really are antibiotics, it'd be smart to take a couple.

But if they're not . . .

Something to think about after a shower, some food, when her mind is clearer. She grabs the towels, stands, breathes, and goes back to the bathroom.

The bottom of the toilet paper sheet has been neatly folded, but otherwise everything is exactly as she left it—even her toothbrush is still balanced against the back of the sink. She turns on the shower faucet—turns it to hot . . .

No electricity, no hot water. *Right.* Ironic, to have come to one of the most expensive eco-resorts in the world only to be taking cold showers again. She should be used to it by now, but somehow the interlude of having warm showers makes it harder to think about stepping into the cold spray.

She sighs. Pulls her destroyed tank top off, lets it fall onto the floor in a wet, muddy pile. Feels a pang of guilt for making a mess. No, she'll have to rinse her clothes out thoroughly afterward, mop up the floor like it's a crime scene. Those women might not talk to guests, but she's sure the gossip about her filthy clothes would reach the Reverend's ears.

She wonders if the girl will get in trouble too, turning up covered in mud. If she were Julia's daughter, she'd be grounded for sure, disappearing during a major storm like that. Would she confess to save her own skin? It'd be understandable if the girl told the Reverend what Julia was up to. But Julia gets the sense that the girl operates according to her own set of rules, and will somehow find an opportunity to slip away, come find her, if for no other reason than it'd be something different to do.

Julia catches a glimpse of herself in the mirror.

Jesus H. Christ.

She looks awful. Mud on her cheeks, clumping her hair; bits of leaves and twigs clinging to her skin in places. Even where her shirt had been, streaks of mud, nasty-looking scratches. Eyes red and puffy. Bloodshot. A slight trickle of blood runs down her neck from the mound of an ugly insect bite. That damn flying cockroach, or whatever it was. She tests the bite with the tips of her fingers. Swollen, painful.

She unbuttons her pants, tugs them down off her hips. Even worse here, mud almost completely covering her legs and belly. Some more raised red bumps—insect bites or a rash, hard to say. And there's a largish twig stuck to her skin just below her belly button. She reaches down to pull it off . . .

But it won't *come* off. Like it's stuck to her skin with super-glue.

She tries again, but pulling the twig just stretches the skin it's attached to. It's the hook and she's the fish. This is obviously going to require a bit more force.

Julia takes a deep breath, thinks about going back for a Jack Daniel's bottle, liquid courage—*don't be dramatic*—scrunches her eyes—*it's just like ripping off a Band-Aid*—and gives it a good, hard yank. She feels a sharp, piercing pain—*goddamn!*—but it does finally come off in her hand. She opens her eyes, looks down at her belly, and sees a droplet of blood beading on her skin. Isaac had said something about there being an emergency kit in each hut, and she's hoping there's some hydrogen peroxide, because she can only imagine all the odd microbes crawling on her skin at the moment.

. . . a faint hissing sound . . .

God it *stings*. What if it causes some kind of reaction, like the sap from the plant in the jungle?

. . . something tickling the back of her hand . . .

The last thing she needs is to pass out alone in her bathroom in her underwear, covered in mud. She looks down at her hand.

What the fu—

The twig . . . the twig is twisting in her palm, and small, thin brown tendrils reach out of the bark, flailing. The hissing grows louder, like the sound of a deflating balloon.

For a moment all she can do is stare, utterly stunned. Slowly, slowly, fingers trembling, Julia holds the twig up closer to the light, turns it around . . .

And sees a small round circle of what looks like teeth at the end, blood dripping from a tiny mouth.

Not possible, it's not—

The mouth moves, jawing like it's desperately looking for its next meal.

Julia screams, drops it on the floor. A leech? Some kind of twig-leech-flatworm—

"Fuck!"

The goddamn thing is using the tendrils to awkwardly propel itself forward in her direction—

"Fuck, fuck, fuck, fuck, fuck, fuck . . . fuck!"

—and holy mother of God, there's another one on her leg.

She screams again, crashes into the sink with her hip as she reaches down and rips it off, throwing it on the floor, where it writhes and twists like the detached gecko tail in her nightmare.

Knock, knock, knock.

Vomit rises in the back of her throat, that egg churning murderously, and the . . . thing, its tendrils reach out from it and it begins to crawl toward her—*holy shit!*—they're both crawling toward her. But how? With what eyes do they see her? How the fuck do they know where she is?

I need something to bash them with. The trash can? No, she needs a hammer, she needs to inflict blunt-force trauma, and . . . Christ, there's a righteous stinging on her leg, she can feel something itchy and venomous tingling out from the bite. Something itching on her back too—she turns to the mirror, twists around . . .

Two. Two more on her back.

"FUCK! FUCK FUCK FUCK!" She desperately tries to grab one, but the angle is all wrong.

This is where I lose it. This is where I really go insane.

Sound of the door opening, heavy footsteps, then she catches a glimpse of Dr. Noah Cooper in the corner of the mirror, rain dripping off his beard, his hair, his aloha shirt completely sodden. She's relieved, terrified, frantic, and about to pass out.

"Noah! Get them off me! GET THEM OFF!"

One of the twigs raises a tendril, appears to *sniff,* and changes direction, flopping toward him. He raises a foot and promptly stomps it, grinding it into the floor with his heel. The faintest, wheedling cry.

"Obviously," he says, lifting his boot to make sure the thing is good and dead, "we should have had a serious talk much sooner."

———————

Noah pulls two latex gloves out of his pockets, all business—*what kind of tourist carries latex gloves on him?*—tugs them over his hands, and then quickly turns the shower faucet off.

"How long have they been on you?"

"I don't . . . I don't know."

"Get in the shower stall," he says. He seems to think a moment, then adds, "You're going to be fine. Everything's going to be all right."

She knows that tone—it's one she used on Evie, usually when the opposite was true. She steps into the shower stall and stands there, cold, half-naked, shaken, trembling. Tries to cover herself with her arms, not that there's much to leave to the imagination when all she has on is her bra and underwear. Noah stoops down for the other . . . *thing,* and tosses it in the sink. She can see it try, and fail, to climb up the slippery, porcelain bowl. A faint hiss.

"What . . . what *is* it?"

"Something utterly disgusting."

She laughs in spite of herself. "You think?"

Noah offers a wry grin, pulls out a cigarette lighter from the back pocket of his cargo shorts. "At least you haven't lost your sense of humor. You might just survive after all."

It's settling somehow, not being alone in it, although it's bizarre, this new Noah. The annoying, chatterbox tourist act suddenly gone.

"Turn around slowly, and we'll encourage your joyriders to disengage." Assured, like a real doctor.

She turns, starting clockwise. *Who* is *he, really?*

"Stop. Hold up your left arm."

Noah flicks the lighter on, dials it down for a smaller flame. "Did you know that leeches were an important medicinal tool for centuries? They're still used today in reconstructive surgery. Helps to stimulate the blood flow."

He's trying to distract her. She knows this, but it's working anyway. She can feel her heart rate start to slow.

She holds up her left arm. "So it's a leech?"

"Well, without the proper dissection tools, I'd be hard-pressed to classify it, but from a general theoretical approach, if it looks like a duck, swims like a duck, and quacks like a duck . . ."

He holds the flame to the tip of the creature under her arm, and it falls away. He bends down, grabs it, and tosses it in the sink with its cousin. "The trick with leeches is getting them off. Some people prefer the fingernail method, slipping it under and gently working it off. But that doesn't work so well when you're wearing latex gloves. Turn again? Ah, there's a small one. Stand still."

She hears the click of the lighter, then a faint, complaining hiss. She can feel a slight sting, but not nearly as bad as that accompanying the ones she pulled off.

"A wee baby, that one. Generally salt is good too; they don't like salt on their skin. Although this creature looks like it came into its leech-hood through a detour in the Phasmida, stick-bug family, so I don't know if salt would work with these fellas. But yanking them off with force . . . not such a good idea."

Her heart rate starts to pick up again. "Why . . . why is that bad?"

"Well, sometimes a bit of the jaw gets left behind, which can eventually lead to infection." He seems to realize how that came out, because he adds, "But there are tweezers in the emergency kit. Easy as pulling out a sliver."

"If it's a leech, why does it look like a—"

"Twig? Turn one more time."

She does, facing the back of the stall.

"Oh, there's another. Well, I've never heard of a leech that takes this kind of camouflage approach, but of course, no one's exactly been allowed to study the species here, and as you and I both know, it's been remarkably isolated from the rest of the world, on its own separate, evolutionary track. Unless Dr. Lydia Greer kept you completely in the dark, which I wouldn't put past her."

Click of the lighter, faint hiss. *He knows.* And he's revealing that he knows to her. *Why?*

"Okay, that's all of them that I can see."

He's not going to say anything more about Aunt Liddy. The ball is in her court now. She's not sure it'd be wise to play.

Julia exhales and turns around, finds Noah picking the leeches up from the floor, dropping them in the sink. A whole tribe of the damn things. A shiver runs down her spine, and she can feel the adrenaline start to ebb, the fatigue start to build. Sleep. What she wouldn't give to be able to sleep.

"Now, the next part is going to require your help."

"What do you mean?"

"Well, just to make sure we got them all. I'm going to turn around and close my eyes to give you some privacy, and I want you to feel under your underwear and bra to make sure we're all clear."

She swallows, hard. "Okay."

"Try not to freak out if you do find something."

"That's easy for you to say."

"Everything's going to be fine."

She wishes he'd stop saying that.

He turns around, and who the hell knows whether he's really got his eyes closed or is surreptitiously looking at her through squinted eyes and the mirror's reflection, but it's preferable to him leaving her alone with those . . . things in the sink.

Quickly she runs a hand under her bra—nothing. Area under the panties is clear too.

"Oh, thank God," she says.

"All good?"

"I wouldn't go that far."

"Can I turn around?"

"Sure, I guess."

When he does, he looks almost as relieved as she feels. "All right. Next, you should wash up, and then when you're ready, come out and I'll take a look at your leg, make sure nothing's there that shouldn't be."

"Not just my leg; there was one here," she says, pointing to her belly button. There's a steady trickle of blood. "I think it was the biggest."

A look of concern washes over his face, but he catches himself, puts on an unconvincing smile. "I'll take a look at that too. The bites are going to bleed, and keep bleeding for a while. Most leeches inject an anticoagulant, so that they can keep the meal coming."

Another crack of thunder, followed by a rumbling so loud the walls tremble.

"Now I'll give you some privacy."

"And the . . ." She points to the sink.

"We can divvy them up. I'm sure your great-aunt will want at least two. If you don't have specimen bottles with you, I do."

With that he leaves her, gently closing the door behind him.

The cold shower has the effect of driving some of her mental fog away, and it's beyond a relief to wash off all of the mud, shampoo her hair, and comb out the bits of leaves, the small pebbles. When she towels off, she sees a couple of greenish bruises starting to form on her legs.

And this is just day one.

She grabs a towel from the floor, bends over, and wraps her hair in it, twisting it into a turban. The leeches in the sink twist and tumble over each other, trying to get some kind of grip so they can climb up and out of the porcelain bowl, their antennae waving in her direction. Still hungry.

She's tempted to toss them into the toilet and flush them into oblivion, but Noah's right. Aunt Liddy will want a specimen.

He obviously wants to form some kind of partnership. Does she need one? If the strange girl keeps her word, she's on track for finding the corpse flower . . . or at least when the electricity returns she'll be able to plug in her GPS and start the search again.

Not that today's trek went well. She almost got herself killed, twice.

Plus Noah seems to know things. He might even know why the flower is important, or why the churchwomen act so strangely.

She closes her eyes, wishes she'd never met with Aunt Liddy, or even heard of Kapu. "Ghost, most, host," she whispers. "Coast, roast, post."

There's a chirp above her, and she looks up, sees a white gecko blending in with the white ceiling, given away by dark eyes that can't change color. Probably intrigued by the moving twigs in the sink.

"If you want to have a snack, be my guest. They're over there," Julia says.

The gecko just blinks. She sees the flicker of a pink tongue tasting the air.

Her bungalow feels crowded all of a sudden. And Noah . . . what to do with Noah? She knows she can't trust him—she can't trust anyone—but that human desire to connect, to ally, is strong. She'll have to share some things, too, to get more information, but she'll have to be careful about how much.

She wraps the second towel around her body, realizes that he's going to need access to her belly, so she shifts it to her waist and then unties the turban to cover her torso. Her clothes lie in a sodden, muddy lump on the floor, something about them reminiscent of her dream on the plane, like when she leaves, closes the door, they'll rise up, take the form of an invisible ghost.

The gecko chirps twice. Looking for connection too.

SEVENTEEN

JULIA FINDS NOAH SITTING IN one of the rattan chairs, staring out the window, something indescribably sad in his expression, like he'd just received terrible news. But as soon as he hears the creak of the floorboard when she steps into the bedroom, it vanishes, replaced with a smile.

"No offense," he says, "but you look much, much better."

The emergency kit is unzipped, laid out on the coffee table in front of him, illuminated by a flashlight standing upright. There's a small puddle of rainwater from his own clothes pooling near a chair leg; two sets of their muddy boot prints—his and hers—mark the floor. She's going to be up late tonight, cleaning.

"I feel better with those things off of me. How much time do we have before dinner?"

"No idea. I had a watch, but it mysteriously disappeared. Anything of yours missing?"

"No. I don't think so." But now she wishes she'd actually checked her suitcase.

"I could use more light. Can you look in your bottom bureau drawer?"

Oh, right. Isaac had said there would be flashlights, a battery-operated lamp. She goes to the bureau, pulls out the bottom drawer, careful to keep all towels she's wearing in place. But then, he just saw her in wet, clingy underwear. That proverbial horse has left the barn. She finds some kind of halogen camping lamp, a modern design with a stainless steel base and a plastic globe for a shade. She turns it on. The light warms the entire room.

"When did the electricity go out?" she asks as she brings it back to the coffee table.

"Sometime after lunch. Maybe an hour, maybe more. Your absence was quite the hot topic. And your destination."

A sideways press for information. She settles into the opposite rattan chair. "There wasn't much to it. More of a ghost town really. I wasn't there long. Got lost on the way back."

He grabs a small brown bottle of hydrogen peroxide, then the tweezers. He pours some of the peroxide over them, letting the excess land on his already sodden shorts.

"Huh. Got lost on a path that hugs the coastline. With a wall between the path and the jungle. You have a terrible sense of direction. Let me see your leg. Actually, put it up on the table."

She does, and the glass is cold against her calf. For a moment, neither of them speak, the only sound the rain pounding against the bungalow roof. He leans over, peers closely at the spot where she'd pulled the leech off. Picks up the flashlight, focuses its beam there. Pours a trickle of peroxide over it. It bubbles fiercely.

Two seconds later, it stings like hell.

"Ow. Ow, ow, ow, ow, ow." She sucks air through clenched teeth.

"I know, I'm sorry." He squints. "Oh, there's a bit there." He takes two fingers, gently pinches the flesh around the wound, like he's extracting a sliver. More blood rushes out.

"How do you know the path hugs the coastline?"

"Because it shows up on the satellite map. That and the wall."

Words bubble up in her consciousness: *wall, mall, hall.* It's an effort not to speak them aloud.

"I thought it was an act, what with your last name," he continues. "I thought maybe you were research, or development. But you really are just a journalist. Or were a journalist."

"Am a journalist, thank you."

You know you're rhyming words, like Irene.

Don't think about it.

He takes the tweezers, gently plucks out a bit of . . . something. Then he pours more peroxide over the wound, turning the blood a milky pink.

"So what brought you to your brilliant conclusion that I'm not a researcher?" she asks.

"Your fearlessness leaving the resort. Anyone who understood the danger would never have dared. And not only *that*, but you went over the wall and deep into the jungle's interior, which, as far as we know, no one has ever survived. Or if they did, they were never heard of again. Like Irene."

We. Who's we?

"But they found Irene."

"Did they."

"I went to her grave. I saw the casket."

He pinches her skin just a little bit harder, to make sure it's all gone. Obviously she saw a casket, but she has no way of knowing who, or what, they'll put inside. Which means she's down half her goal all of a sudden.

Julia crosses her arms over her chest. "Why are you talking to me?"

A shadow flits across his face again. Conflicted.

"No. Really, why are you talking to me?"

He knocks the bit of leech onto the table. Opens an alcohol

swab packet. "For one thing, I feel bad, because I honestly thought you were more prepared, and you almost got yourself killed today. What's going on with your hand?"

She turns it over. The dried blood has washed away, revealed a jagged L shape from where the broken glass cut her.

"Wow," he says. "Did you manage to *not* injure any part of your body?"

"Maybe it wasn't the best time to go exploring. But I'm hoping to get out when the pilot comes to fix the fridge."

"You and everyone else, except Beth. She was MIA at lunch too, but no one seemed to notice, or care." He cleans the tweezers with the alcohol swab. "But I think the Reverend may have a class action lawsuit at the end of this. Or so they think. I'll take care of your hand last. Now, let's take a look at the big bite on your stomach."

Julia leans back in her chair, lifts the towel high enough to expose it. Blood on the towel, a lot of it. No washing that out. Fodder for gossip, she's sure.

"Find anything interesting in your explorations?" he asks.

There's a pregnant pause. Where would she even begin? With the carnivorous pitcher plants as high as her knees, or the tree embedded with boar's teeth, or the barefoot girl with pale skin who might be Agnes's doppelgänger, at least from the way Irene described her. Something she wants to hold close, protect. She doesn't know what it means, but it's hers, and hers alone for now. Still, this is where she must decide—alliance, yes or no?

You're better off not knowing too much, Aunt Liddy had said in answer to any of Julia's questions about how, or why, or what.

And that, very clearly, is not the case.

"I found Irene's old camp. What's left of it. Nothing really interesting there." She doesn't mention the small black box in her backpack. "There was a plant with giant leaves. I broke the stalk and this sap oozed out. I almost passed out from the fumes. Then I fell into a puddle . . . or no, not a puddle, more like a pond of mud. Or maybe some kind of quicksand. I was able to grab a tree and pull myself out. Barely."

A whole world of experience not included in those brief, short sentences.

Chirp, goes the gecko in the bathroom. *Chirp, chirp.*

Julia casts a glance at the ceiling, just to be sure it isn't teeming with them.

Noah leans in again, gently touches the area on her belly that's puffy from the bite. "This one might be infected already. Does it hurt when I touch it?"

"Not really."

He gently pinches the skin around the wound. She can see it, an opaque bit of jaw—a hard, bloody little lump.

"How'd you find your way back?"

"Aunt Liddy gave me a GPS," says Julia, omitting that it's a phone too. "It's practically out of power though. I don't know if I could even turn it on again, and without electricity to charge it . . . ow!"

"This might sting a bit more than the last one," he says. "In fact, let's not mince words and just be honest. It's gonna hurt like hell. You're lucky to be alive. Although I'm starting to think there's more to it than luck. I'd give anything to see what your antibodies look like right now."

"What do you mean?"

Noah holds his hand steady, slowly brings the tweezers to the lump. Grips it on either side. Tugs.

"GODDAMN!"

"I know, I know," he says. The tip of the tweezers slip off. "Shoot. Sorry about that. It's a bit more . . . embedded. But I don't want to use too much force; otherwise it might break off, and then it's just going to get . . . Well, let's not even go there."

Julia reaches below her to grip the seat. "All right. It's going to cost you a can of chili, though."

"Yeah. The only problem is, there isn't any chili in those cans."

He presses one hand on her belly, and this time when he grips the jaw, he pulls back slowly: it starts to come out—it hurts like a sonofabitch—but as it does, there's a thin strand of something that looks like a fine hair connecting it to Julia's flesh.

He continues to pull, and the strand just gets longer. Three inches. Six and it's still not out.

She doesn't say anything.

He doesn't say anything.

There's another crack of thunder. An accompanying rumble like the very sky above is about to break into pieces.

She wonders what the strand is, but in an idle way, like the outcome won't really affect her. It's her last-resort default defense mode, obliviousness. She closes her eyes.

Once she'd interviewed a soldier with PTSD, three tours in Iraq, who'd been convicted of murdering his family. Sometimes he told investigators he remembered it, and sometimes said he didn't. When she pressed, he'd finally said that camouflage comes in two forms, one where your enemy tries to hide from view, blend into the background, and the other where your own mind creates the camouflage so you don't see something you can't handle. It was the only way he got through his tour. It was the only way he could live with himself after. She feels that she's missing something right in front of her, something *important*, but it keeps slipping out of reach, as cagey as the girl in the jungle.

Girl, twirl, whirl.

"Okay, looks like that's it," says Noah. "I'm going to pour some peroxide over it, and then we can wrap up with some antibiotic ointment and bandages."

A forced note of optimism. She opens her eyes, watches as he pours peroxide over the wound on her belly, and the pain is so deep, so intense, she has to physically force herself not to scream. Her hands close on the seat of the chair like a vise.

"Are you okay?" He seems genuinely worried.

No. She's very much not okay. Okay is the last thing she could possibly be at this moment.

———

The question of what the hell just happened hangs between them, and Julia gets the feeling that Noah is deeply disturbed, shaken. It's the time he takes slowly getting another alcohol swab to clean the tweezers again, the time he takes carefully wiping them down, absorbed in some other line of thought altogether, as if the pieces of what he knew, or thought he knew, aren't adding up anymore. The coiled thread of . . . that thing that was inside her lies on the glass table, inert, looking like it's just a strand of fine hair.

"I should . . ." says Julia. She stands abruptly, pulling the towel up to cover her stomach. Can't remember how she was going to finish her sentence, or even why she stood up.

"We should put a bandage on that."

Lie, fly, cry. "Right. I just need to . . ."

Oh dear God, what the hell *was* that thing, what the hell is happening to her?

He's lying to you, says Ethan. *He's pretending to help you, but what do you think he's been doing all this time, alone in your room? Twiddling his thumbs?*

A pure, white-hot rage washes over and through her, and her eyes flit to the armoire. He could have taken anything out of there.

"Julia?" Noah asks cautiously. "You look pale. You should sit down."

Terminally naïve.

Ethan tricked her, and now Noah's tricked her, she's sure of it. Pretending to care while an altogether different agenda was at work. Bastard.

"Julia?"

She clutches the towel to her, races for the armoire and yanks out her suitcase, letting it fall to the floor. *The same. They're all the same.*

"What are you doing?" asks Noah.

She ignores the sharp, stabbing pain in her stomach, crouches next to the suitcase, flips the latches open with trembling fingers. Opens the top of the case, throws out all of her clothes, tossing them every which way until her fingers find the hidden panel.

"Julia," says Noah.

She sees him get up out of the corner of her eye, but it doesn't matter. What an *idiot* she was. . . .

She clicks the hidden latch, and the fake panel pops open.

"Julia." Noah crouches beside her.

She frantically digs around in the hidden compartment. Specimen jars, the goddamn specimen jars are there, the white gel, the vial marked PLANT NUTRIENTS, the latex gloves. But the package of pills . . .

Not there.

And the notebook? Did she put it back in the suitcase, or did she leave it out by mistake? She can't remember. And wait . . . where are the Jack Daniel's bottles? They're all gone, every single last one of them.

"Julia, you're bleeding," says Noah. He puts a hand on her arm. "We need to get a bandage on that, or—"

She slaps his hand away. "Latex gloves. Where the fuck did you get your latex gloves?" She knows how she sounds—she sounds insane, like a crazy woman, which maybe she is.

"I brought them with me."

"You just *brought* latex gloves with you. You just brought latex gloves with you, Noah Cooper, *tourist,* just like you *happened* to show up just when I got back, and now you've been digging around in my things, *taken* my things, just like—"

"I haven't *been* through your things. Or taken anything. If you really want to know, I brought the gloves with me because I was planning to break into the shed where they stowed our confiscated items to get *my* things. Then I heard you screaming."

"So you *do* have an agenda."

"I'm not alone in that, am I? And if I took something of yours, where did I put it? Do you want to pat me down, check my pockets? Feel free."

Words that sound genuine, but are they? Is this just another gambit? Still, he obviously doesn't have anything in his pockets, and all he has in his left hand is the bandage and ointment . . . but she can't tell anymore what's true, or not, what's real, or not. Her mind feels like a maze that just twists in one direction, then another, and she's lost all sense of where true north is. She wants to cry, she wants to fall to her knees, but most of all what she wants is to hit him again. Hard.

Where did *that* come from?

"Here," says Noah gently, putting up a hand like she's a spooked horse. "I'll trade you a truth for a truth, okay? You go first. Ask me a question."

"What's in the cans?"

"Fungicide. In an extremely concentrated form. Not great for hands, hence the gloves. Now it's my turn. Your great-aunt, did she give you any kind of medication?"

It's the way he's so nonchalant that she knows it's important. And there's no loss telling him the truth, since they're gone.

"She gave me a package of blue pills. But I didn't take them today, and now . . . they're missing."

"Jesus H. Christ, you didn't take *any* today? And you went deep into the jungle, and you, you're . . . still . . ."

"Still what?"

He gives her a look. "Don't pretend you don't know. It's a truth for a truth, Julia, if you're going to—"

"But I don't know! Aunt Liddy's assistant said they were just antibiotics. To ward off possible bacterial infections, like Legionnaires' disease."

He gives a dry, bitter laugh. "*Legionnaires' disease.* So that's what they're calling it now."

"I take it they're not antibiotics, then."

"No, they're not." He sighs. "This is going to be more complicated than I thought. Let's handle the bite on your stomach that's bleeding. That, at least, we can take care of."

Gently, like he's treating a child, he pulls the towel around her waist down just enough to expose the bite, the blood still oozing from the wound. He spreads some of the antibiotic on the bandage. "If it makes you feel any better, I'm out too. Someone made off with my Chiclets, whether because they knew what they were or were just craving some candy, I don't know. I got in my morning dose, but after lunch, they were gone."

Clever, smuggling things into the island in plain sight.

"What *are* they for, Noah?" Although a part of her knows. She knows by the creeping sensation of things subtly altering within her. She knows by the masks that Leanne and the baggage handler wore. The strange compliance of the churchwomen, their bizarre synchronicity. But something won't allow her to recognize it. She wonders if hearing it out loud will make any difference.

"In layman's terms, it's an oral antifungal drug." He peels the bandage off the wrapper, gently reaches out, presses it against her belly.

"Ow!"

"Sorry." He lets the wrapper for the bandage fall to the floor, unspools some of the white medical tape. Tears off a piece. "Whose turn is it to ask a question?"

"Well, that's your question, so I'll go next."

"Not playing fair," he says, applying one strip of the tape to the top of her bandage. She notices that his finger is trembling slightly. Trying to be calm, cool, collected, but obviously isn't.

"Why do we need to be taking an antifungal drug?"

He rips off another strip of tape. "To put it simply . . . well, there's no way to put it simply, so let's start with an example. In other tropical regions around the world, Thailand, Brazil, there's a species of fungus known as *Ophiocordyceps unilateralis*, or 'zombie fungus,' which actually hijacks the behavioral systems of carpenter ants. It penetrates the ant's exoskeleton, and next thing you know, the ant is climbing up the stalk of a plant, latching onto a leaf with a 'death grip,' and staying there until it dies and the fungus fruits from its head. A brutish but effective form of reproduction."

"And you're saying—"

"Nope, my turn now. How are you communicating with Dr. Greer?"

"I'm not."

He raises an eyebrow, places the tape on the bottom of the bandage. Rips off another piece.

"The GPS is also a phone," she says. "But I haven't called her yet. I'm supposed to. She's probably pissed as hell at me."

"So . . . I take it you're not close," he says, securing the left side of the bandage. He takes an ironic tone in case she wants to pass it off as a joke, but there's something else, too, lying underneath.

"I need the money," she says plainly.

He takes a step back, considering . . . something. Rips off another piece of medical tape. "Ah, well. Don't we all."

"You snuck in a question there, don't think I didn't notice. So I get two."

"Are you sure you want two?"

"Yes. And that makes it three. Are you saying that . . . I'm infected with some kind of fungus that will kill me?"

"Yes and no. We're not sure. But theoretically . . . this fungus isn't nearly as unsophisticated as *Ophiocordyceps unilateralis*. It takes more of a symbiotic approach. It controls but usually doesn't destroy the host. And in fact, it passes along some benefits to the host body courtesy of a virus transmitted through its spores that . . . well . . . makes a few alterations in the genome. Triggers the regeneration of sick or dying cells, for example. Which also benefits the fungus, because then its host lasts a long time. But the funny thing is, an infected creature . . . well, they don't just serve the fungus. They serve other plants on the island. We have intelligence that wild boar have been discovered digging irrigation trenches with their tusks for some areas of the island during bad droughts. Or sitting by trees where the soil lacks nutrients, letting themselves starve to death."

She's about to laugh when she realizes he's dead serious. Then she remembers in the jungle, running across that tree that had teeth and two small tusks embedded in the bark.

Noah carefully places the last piece of tape on the left side of the bandage, presses it firmly. "That should do it," he says.

"And the tourists, they go back infected?"

"That's the thing," he says. "It appears to go into a dormant state off the island. People might experience the health benefit side for a few months, maybe a year. But they don't display any of the other signs of the infection."

"You want to kill it. Why?"

"Because we have intelligence that your great-aunt is close to finding a way to sustain it off the island. Has perhaps even modified it. And that would be very, very dangerous."

"How dangerous?"

"Well, again, this is all theoretical. But the spores put people in a compliant state. To put it mildly."

"And the pills are . . . an antidote, right?"

"Yes, and your great-aunt has the patent."

"So how did you get them?"

"We . . . borrowed a supply."

The break-in. "'Borrowed' as in 'stole.'"

"The infected respond to volatile organic compounds, telling them what to do. If I got infected, that would have rendered our agenda here pretty useless. We didn't have much choice."

Again, this mysterious *we*. She remembers Aunt Liddy glee-fully telling her that the smell of freshly cut grass was actually the way it screamed, the scent of chemicals released in the air. There's more that he knows, she's sure, because she's exceeded her three questions, but he isn't counting anymore. Because in a way, this is a pitch, an offer on the table, and he's just feeding her informa-tion to get her to buy in.

It's Aunt Liddy's greenhouse all over again.

Did I teach you nothing? says Ethan.

She crosses her arms over her chest. "What do you want from me?"

He looks down at his hands, plays with the edge of the medical tape as if to give them something to do. "We think there's a flower, rumored to smell like a rotting corpse. If we un-derstood what its role is, maybe the fungus wouldn't be such a threat. And if I can't neutralize the threat . . . well, the team will move on to plan B if I can't confirm that I've neutralized it. That's gonna happen soon."

For a moment, he doesn't speak, and she doesn't press. An internal struggle, like the real Noah wants to break through, but isn't sure he can.

Finally he looks up. Meets her eyes. "I honestly just wanted to help people. I thought if I was able to neutralize it here, extract a sample to continue research into its healing proper-ties . . . I mean, people who have come to Kapu have been cured of cancer. *Cancer,* you understand? All the worst kinds, too. And Parkinson's. Muscular dystrophy. ALS, which took my brother. And yes, even leprosy."

This too could easily be a lie, but it feels like the truth, or something close to it. "What's plan B, Noah?"

A shadow flickers across his face.

Chirp, goes the gecko. *Chirp, chirp.*

Finally he says, "The entire island gets nuked. Yes, that kind of 'nuked.' Us along with it."

Suddenly, there's the mournful, lonely sound of a conch shell being blown from somewhere off in the distance.

EIGHTEEN

JULIA'S GOING TO DIE HERE. Noah's going to die here. And Evie will never know how hard she tried, how much she'd sacrificed. Crazy ideas run through her head—she could hack some bamboo, build a raft, float out into the ocean, maybe get picked up by a fishing boat—stranger things have happened. Or she could walk out into the waves, strike out for the horizon line, swim as long as she could, until the ocean, or the storm, or both finally took her. Which would be the worse way to die? Bombing or drowning?

But then she gets a flash of tickling Evie's toes to wake her up in the morning. Sunlight streaming in through the tall windows. A memory that nearly crushes her now, a deep-sea pressure.

If only she could think clearly, she could figure this out. Her mind is fuzzy, hard to focus. And she gets a fragment of a strange sensation, like someone struck a tuning fork, a reverberation in her bones, a word just beyond her comprehension, foreign, from a land or a time before this one. She doesn't know what the word is, or what it means—she just knows it's out there. Floating.

There are sounds outside . . . like the sound of doors opening, doors shutting. Was the conch shell signaling them for dinner? In this weather? Noah and Julia look at each other for a long moment. A silent dare. It's Noah who moves first, walking to the window overlooking the lanai. He clicks the lamp off, picks up the flashlight, clicks it off too. Tries to stay in the shadow, peers outside.

She sees lights reflected in the glass, bobbing through the dark. What are they? The thing is, she knows what they are—it's there, hovering just under the surface of her consciousness. She gets the sense that if she just presses her fingers to it, she'll fall into this other consciousness, like Alice stepping through the looking glass.

But what will she find on the other side? It's a thought that terrifies her.

"Julia," Noah whispers. "You have to see . . ."

She does. Her feet seem to move of their own accord, they register the cool floor, the grit of the mud that's dried. Already the bandage itches. She wants to peel it up, scratch.

Scratch, hatch, match.

She reaches Noah, stands right beside him, the skin of her arm close to the skin of his arm, but not touching. Looks outside.

Roger and Lois walk along the pier, an even foot of space between them. They appear to be oblivious to the wind, the rain, the bright flashes of lightning that hit the horizon. Lois wears a soggy halter top, a pair of sweats. Roger wears a white T-shirt and boxer shorts that are so drenched they cling like a second skin. Something forlorn about Lois's bare shoulders, her normally curled hair flattened against her scalp. They don't speak a word. They don't look at each other. They simply continue a steady march along the pier toward the shore, matching each other stride for stride. No shoes. It's bizarre, strange, and eerie in equal measure.

She feels a pull. A longing. A feeling that stretches from her to them, that quivers like a string.

And then others come into view, all walking silently, all bare-foot as far as she can tell. The two women whose names she can't remember, in yoga pants and slim-fitting T-shirts. Their friend, completely naked, emerges from another cabin on the pier along with one of the college boys, also naked. Then the other college boy, in sweats and a hoodie, follows behind them. All of them walk in unison—right, left, right, left. No jokes now. No laughter. No surreptitious, flirty glances.

Their rote movements are unnerving. A ritual she can't fathom the meaning of. She feels Noah struggling to find the words, to say . . . something, but it's not possible; she can't speak herself, or tear her eyes away from the scene playing out in front of her. And there's Heather and Fred, coming out from one of the bungalows on land. They all head for the beach, where they assemble in a line with an even foot between them, facing the ocean, the breaking waves. Holding their flashlights, lamps. Arms jittering like they just received an electric shock.

And then nothing happens. They just stand there. She watches the waves break, registers the sound of the rain—but the people, dear God the people are as absent and empty as death. Walking husks.

Nightmarchers.

"Noah, what—"

She turns and finds Noah standing stock-still, swaying slightly like a stalk of grass in the wind. Mouth agape, eyes vacant. Right arm trembling. She should scream, but the sound dissolves in her throat before she can open her mouth.

"Clunk, bunk, skunk," says Noah. His eyes are glazed. Focused on nothing in particular.

"Noah?"

His mouth slowly opens, but no word comes out, and his jaw just hangs there, slack, his eyes vacant.

"Noah!"

Slowly, ever so slowly, his head drifts to the left, like the weight is too much for his neck, like he's falling asleep or having a stroke. His right arm jerks.

Julia grabs him by the shoulder. *"NOAH!"*

His tongue falls out of his mouth, and his eyes roll backward. A seizure? *Christ, what are you supposed to do for a seizure?* Something about keeping them from biting their tongue, she remembers that much. She tries to push it back in his mouth, but his jaw is rigid, immobile.

It's not a seizure, though. This is definitely not a seizure.

"Oh fuck. Oh fuck, Noah."

White foam gathers at the corners of his mouth, drips down his chin. She grips his shoulder tighter.

"I'm here, I'm here, Noah. I'm here."

Then she remembers—she had a package of pills in her hand when Isaac knocked on the door. And she put the package in her jeans pocket. And her jeans are hanging in the armoire.

Hang, slang, bang. She lets go of Noah, turns toward the armoire, but it's so hard, moving away from the window, like it has a gravitational pull. She forces one foot forward, and then another, each step jerky, uncertain. She's halfway there when she stops. She has to rest for a moment.

Because they're so heavy, her eyes. So hard to keep open. And it's been so long since she had a deep, real sleep. Before arriving on Kapu. Before leaving for Maui. Before Ethan left, taking Evie with him. Before that even, waking to hear the soft murmur of Ethan talking to someone on his cell phone in the hallway, hushed laughter, all the while she pretended to be asleep.

She tries to take another step, but can't.

Her eyelids float. They close. Fear presses her heart—it's almost impossible to breathe—but a strange sense of déjà vu strikes her, like she has been here before, he has been here before, and everything, *everything* is happening exactly as it is destined to be.

A cave. A cave with cool air that smells of iron, and minerals; a dark, wide lake as smooth as a mirror. A foreign world. Utterly silent. Pockmarked lava rock all around her, veins of that white fungus creeping across the cave walls, down to the water's edge, even underneath it. Floating on the lake are huge red corpse flowers, three feet wide, with fleshy petals that spread out across the surface.

I can see. Why can I see? No source of light, but she can, perfectly well.

She walks to the lake, crouches down. Creatures swim in the lake. No color, they're completely white. White fish, tiny white crabs, white eels, translucent white jellyfish swimming up out of the depths, tentacles trailing. *White, blight, sight.*

And there's her reflection, staring back at her, so perfectly clear that it *is* like staring into a mirror, or at a picture of herself snapped in another time, because the funny thing is, she wears jodhpurs, a fitted riding jacket.

Irene. She's wearing the same thing Irene was, in the picture Aunt Liddy showed her.

And there's something else in the water, suspended there. An article of clothing. Her arm seems to reach out without her even thinking, her fingers touching the lake's surface. For a moment— just a moment—she almost feels the pads of her reflection's fin-

244 J. LINCOLN FENN

gers, like there's an actual Julia under the water, staring up at her with her own secret, internal thoughts.

But then her hand breaks the surface of the water, and the ripples distort her reflection, scatter it in all directions. The water closes in around her hand, frigid, instantly bracing, and then she has it, the clothing, and she pulls it up and out of the water.

A nightgown. The nightgown from her dream on the plane, some anonymous woman had been wearing it—pale white skin with roots growing from her neck into the ground. The realization brings her into lucidity—*I'm dreaming, I'm dreaming right now.*

When she'd tuck Evie into bed at night, Julia would tell her she would see Evie in her dreams, a way to entice her to actually close her eyes. Even as a baby, Evie had hated going to sleep, and as she got older, nightmares were common.

"Where do you want to meet tonight?" Julia would ask, running a hand over Evie's forehead.

At the ice cream store. At the playground. At Disneyland (even though they'd never been there—too middle-class for Ethan's taste).

"That sounds like fun," Julia would say, kissing Evie's cheek. "I'll see you soon then."

It almost breaks her, thinking about that again. There had been a final night where Julia had tucked Evie into bed, but she hadn't known it then. It had been in a hotel room that Ethan had paid for while the trial was going on—whether to ease Evie's mind that Mommy was okay, or to make sure Evie wasn't in a dangerous area of town (i.e., an area that Julia could afford), she never knew. He'd gone radio silent by then.

But if she's lucid dreaming, she has power here, now, in this realm.

"Evie!"

Her voice echoes back to her. No return call, no shout of *Mommy!*, no small figure running toward her, clasping her around the waist.

Chirp.

A white gecko on the cave wall. *Chirp, chirp.*

"EVIE!"

And then she hears it—a peal of unmistakable laughter, not close, more like an echo, but still.

"EVIE!"

She can't see whether there's an entrance or exit to this underground cavern; beyond the water, all is cloaked in impregnable shadow.

"EVIE!"

A splash, and when Julia looks at the lake, it's churning, bubbling like hot water on the stove. Sometimes an article of clothing appears—pants, a dress, a shirt—and then something reaches up and out of the water, tries to grab hold of one of the flower's petals.

A hand. A small, pale, child's hand.

Evie?

Julia steps into the lake—so cold it makes her gasp—walking, stumbling, her boots slipping on the lava rock. Up to her waist, water filling her boots—another small hand reaches out of the water by the flower—Julia rips her jacket off and dives in, swimming as hard as she can, but there are strong currents pulling against her, trying to suck her down into the black water, her boots deadweight, so she kicks them off just before a current pulls her down and spins her like she's in a washing machine. She struggles to get her head above water, and catches a glimpse of the lakeshore, the nightgown standing upright, worn by an invisible ghost. It moves toward the water, invisible legs taking invisible steps.

I spy with my little eye.

It takes all of Julia's strength to fight the current and turn back to the flower. The hands are gone.

Gone. No.

Julia takes a big gulp of air and drops underwater, kicking as hard as she can, her desperate heart pounding. It's dark, it's all so very dark. An albino fish with a massive lower jaw drifts by, some kind of illuminated lure protruding from its forehead, ferocious-looking teeth.

Something that begins with the letter e.

But then there's a small, naked form in front of her, glowing faintly, drifting in a fetal position, blond hair floating like sea-weed. Eyes closed. Peaceful. *Evie.* She'd know her anywhere.

I'm coming. I'm coming, Evie.

So close now. Her lungs are on fire, her wet clothes a burden she has to fight against, too, but she uses fury, and rage, and all the months of misery to power herself through the current's pull, reach a hand out to grasp Evie's slim arm. *What if I'm too late?* She pushes that thought out of her head.

She feels cold flesh under her hand. *There. Got you.*

Evie's skin, so thin as to be nearly translucent—Julia can see the dark lines of her veins running underneath—and her eyes, large and dark, staring at nothing. But her legs twitch—a sign of life—and joy, real joy, the kind Julia hasn't experienced since Evie was born, threatens to burst from her heart.

I've got you. I've got you. I've got you.

Julia slips an arm around Evie's waist, preparing for the final push back to shore, and that's when she notices it.

A vine reaches out from Evie's belly, up through the water, to the red flower floating over their heads, like an umbilical cord.

Something grips Julia's own arm, and she finds Evie staring

at her with the bulbous eyes of a gecko, her hand clenching Julia's arm. Webbing between the fingers.

"I've got you too, Mommy." Each word a floating bubble.

Julia gasps, inhaling water, but it feels good in her lungs, the water, like fresh air on a cool day. She'd heard that there's a high that comes with drowning, a moment of peace before everything ends.

Yes, Julia thinks. Whatever the price, even death itself, it's one she's willing to pay.

Anything to be with Evie again. Images flash in her mind—Evie just after she was born, wrapped in the standard white blanket with red and blue stripes; Evie at two years old, picking a daisy; Evie on her fourth birthday, hiding in the closet because she didn't want a party, she just wanted the presents and cake. And then other images flash in her mind—a toddler boy with black hair picking up a pink seashell from the beach, running toward her, proud of his find; a woman's smiling face illuminated by the setting sun, running a hand through tousled red hair; a man in black pants, white shirt, painting the exterior of one of the church cottages, bare arms tanned by the sun.

Four tiny white fish gather, so fat they look like pebbles. They swim around her head, grazing her cheek, her lips.

Evie blinks with her large, strange eyes, grips her arm tighter. "Don't leave me, Mommy. Please don't leave me."

I won't, Julia tries to say, her mouth opening in the water, the words choking in her throat. *I would never . . .*

And the fish swim in; they wriggle past her tongue, down her esophagus. She tries to cough them out, but that only lodges them deeper.

Julia!

A voice she doesn't recognize, a voice from another time,

another place, one she doesn't want to go back to. She wants to stay in this world, with Evie. *I'll never leave, I'll never leave, I'll never leave.*

"*JULIA!*"

There's a sharp pain in her head, a fierce throbbing. She closes her eyes, and when she opens them again she finds she's back in the bungalow, pressed forcefully up against the wall by someone with a remarkably wiry strength for her size.

It's Athletic Woman. It's Beth.

#NDC DEV ORG HUB

19:10:22	**\<bai908\>**	where the hell have you been? status?
19:10:32	**\<isir528\>**	status is fuck you.
19:10:37	**\<bai908\>**	not funny.
19:10:40	**\<bai908\>**	hello?
19:10:42	**\<isir528\>**	this is red.
19:10:47	**\<bai908\>**	where's your
19:10:50	**\<isir528\>**	he's with them now. he's one of them now. he got the meds, but wouldn't take them. worried you wouldn't come through.
19:11:19	**\<bai908\>**	okay. okay. we can fix this.
19:11:26	**\<isir528\>**	no. i can fix this.
19:11:31	**\<bai908\>**	red, you need to think about
19:11:38	**\<isir528\>**	i have. experiment is over. somebody has to put an end to it.
19:11:58	**\<bai908\>**	red.
19:11:59	**\<isir528\>**	i took enough so that i could be coherent enough to start destroying the data.
19:12:19	**\<bai908\>**	red they're going to bomb the island. if you don't
19:12:32	**\<isir528\>**	good. i saw the reels. i saw what you sick fucks did to her. a part of me, a huge part of me, would help her if it didn't fuck up the rest of the world. let the bombs come.
19:13:13	**\<bai908\>**	red. she is not a person, she was never a
19:13:23	**\<isir528\>**	sorry, time for the hammer.
19:13:30	**\<bai908\>**	red, call the
19:13:33		- - > **isir528** has quit

NINETEEN

NO, NOT HERE, JULIA DOESN'T want to be here, she wants to be back in the dream with Evie, she wants to be anywhere but this goddamn tropical purgatory.

Beth holds her firmly, but Julia puts up a fight, tries to push her away.

"No," Julia whispers. "No, no, no, no." Tears bead in her eyes, she can still *feel* Evie nearby. She doesn't want to lose that feeling.

"Julia . . ." Beth whispers.

"No, no, no, no, no, *no!*" Julia rips one of Beth's arms away. She's still in the damn bungalow, the only difference is the rain and the storm must have finally abated, because the stillness . . .

Noah, where's Noah? Nowhere to be found, and the door to the bungalow is wide open. She stumbles toward it, her balance uneven—she almost falls, but Beth catches her, holding her back.

"Julia," she says, her tone firmer.

Julia struggles, frees an arm, which she uses to land a punch straight across Beth's jaw. Beth lets go—Julia makes it to the doorway, out onto the lanai. . . .

No one is outside. No one standing by the ocean's edge—just sand, and waves, and a moon in a night sky, wisps of clouds illuminated by moonlight. Moonlight? How many hours has she lost? Storm debris littered across the resort, fallen palms, branches, leaves. The drip, drip, drip of raindrops that fall from the waving palm trees onto the roof.

And then there's the mournful sound of the conch shell again, farther away, softer.

Gone. Noah is gone. To where, and for what, she doesn't know. Julia's legs give out for real; she drops onto the lanai. *And I've lost Evie again.* Even though she knows it wasn't real, it *felt* real—to have held her in her arms, and now for them to be empty again.

Beth crouches down next to her, stares pensively at the ocean's edge. There's a package of blue pills in her hand—she presses two out, pops them in her own mouth, grinds them with her teeth, and swallows.

"The VOCs are off the charts right now," Beth says. "I managed to get four down your throat without choking you, but you should take two more."

Julia ignores her, wraps her arms around her knees, hugs them to her. A poor substitute. "What happened to Noah?"

"He went off, with the others. One less problem to worry about. Not on our team, for sure."

Our team.

Beth stands, pockets the pills. She wears olive cargo pants, brown hiking boots, a lightweight, zippered olive jacket. There's a backpack on the floor. An embossed GREER ENTERPRISES logo that matches the packaging on the pills.

She works for Aunt Liddy. Was sent here, just like me.

"Now I'd recommend you get up," Beth says. "There's a lot to do and not much time."

Julia looks at her great-aunt's plan within a plan. How many more layers are there that she'd never been told about? "Why the hell would I do anything you say?"

Beth picks up the backpack, slings it over her shoulder. "Because there's a boat. But I don't get a location for the boat until I—*we*—get what's left of Irene and that goddamn flower. This whole place is going to be incinerated soon, and I, for one, plan to survive, because I have people to live for too. You can come, you can stay, I don't give a shit—honestly, I think my job would be easier without you, but Bailey said I should give it a shot, so here I am. Who knows, you might be useful. So you can tag along if you want, or not. If you do, throw some clothes on and let's get a move on. With a quickness, 'cause I'm out of here in two minutes."

A boat. Here, on the island. Possibly another lie, but knowing Aunt Liddy, she'd have another exit plan. Just in case.

"All right," Julia says, slowly getting to her feet. "All right."

Beth, unlike Noah, is a silent partner. They trek along the path toward the village without speaking, which suits Julia fine. It's not like she'd get an answer she'd believe anyway. Beth walks fast without a single misstep, climbing over the lava rocks easily, even in the dim moonlight. Sometimes she has to wait for Julia to catch up, and when Julia does, Beth just starts off again, without a word. It makes Julia miss Noah, as annoying as he could be. He'd seemed genuine, at the end. Beth is cold, impersonal. All business.

Julia's sneakers don't grip the wet earth as well as her hiking boots did. She's already twisted her ankle twice. Her dark jeans are okay camouflage in the night, but the best she could come up with for a top was a gray T-shirt, which leaves her arms exposed. It'll be a problem when they get into the interior. The bites still throb, too, a painful reminder of what lies ahead. She's exhausted. Hungry. And although her mind feels clearer, it doesn't feel like it's really coalesced back inside herself. There are ghosts of other formless thoughts inside her, that pull.

If she stopped taking the pills, would she lose touch with reality and go back to the cave? Would she at least have Evie in some imaginary realm?

She wonders what the other churchwomen are dreaming of. If they all lost someone, something important to them, and prefer to live in the twilight of a kind of induced madness. She understands the allure. But if she stayed in the imaginary realm, the real Evie would never see her again. Ethan had convinced the judge that Julia was irrelevant, a dangerous influence even. He's probably convincing Evie of the same thing.

Her backpack, still wet, starts to feel heavy. She wonders if Beth used her lapse of consciousness to examine the contents of the backpack, if she knows about the black tin box, the GPS phone, the knife.

Probably.

She eyes Beth's backpack. Are her missing things in there?

"So the medication," Julia says to Beth's back. "Where did you get it?"

"From your twitching fingers. Someone broke into my room and stole *my* meds, which means I don't have enough to make it to the return flight, which means I have to get on that boat or I'll be a brain-dead zombie myself in a few days."

"I didn't say—"

"Of course, I could have taken your last pack and left you, but I didn't. You're welcome."

"Well then, can I have them back?"

Beth turns to look over her shoulder. "I think the person with tactical knowledge should hold onto them, don't you?" Then she picks up her pace, putting a yard between them.

Asshole, Julia thinks. But they are, for the moment at least, in this together.

Something trills from within the depths of the jungle, a call Julia hasn't heard before. If trying to navigate the jungle during the day almost killed her, she can't imagine trekking through it at night will go much better, Beth or no Beth. At least they're far from it, skirting the cliffs where big waves crash. She guesses they're close to the coconut tree where she'd stopped with Isaac.

She's glad she's held the knowledge of the girl close, something no one knows but her. Beth probably has her own GPS phone—she wouldn't be confident about finding the flower without it—but Julia senses that something else will be required, a layer even Beth doesn't know about, that will be revealed when it's too late to stop, turn around, go back. That seems to be her great-aunt's standard operating procedure.

Julia hears water ahead—they must be close to the gulch. She looks up, and the sky is completely clear, even close to the top of Kapu's craggy peak. No rain falls, but she imagines it would take a few hours for all the runoff to drain into the ocean. Will they find the nightmarchers gathered in front of a river that's impossible to cross?

Beth hears it too, and stops, raises a hand for Julia to stop too. She does. The air seems pregnant—waiting.

"We'll go slow," whispers Beth. "If I say turn and run, run. Where's your knife?"

Julia looks at her. "They're people, Beth, people we know."

"They're not people at the moment."

Julia crosses her arms over her chest.

"Fine," says Beth. "If something happens, you're on your own."

Julia highly doubts this. If she wasn't some kind of requirement, there's no way Beth would be bothering with her at all.

Beth steps off the path onto the grass, so that the sound of her boots on the rocks and pebbles doesn't give them away. Julia does the same. Slowly they make their way around a bend, crouching low. No cover here along the cliffs, no shrubs or vegetation.

Which makes what they see before them even stranger.

There is a river ahead of them, not nearly as massive and threatening as it was earlier, but still wide and deep.

And there's a bridge.

Not a man-made bridge, not rope, and knots, and planks. This bridge is made of some kind of hard vine, twisting and arcing over the waters.

"That wasn't there before," Julia whispers.

"I know," says Beth. She approaches it cautiously, tests the edge of the bridge with her foot. It's firm, and doesn't yield. Then she steps up onto it, tests it with her weight. It holds.

Julia grips the straps of her backpack tighter. "What is it?"

"Roots," says Beth. "Tree roots. I think."

Julia looks to where the trees are. A good two miles up the hill, at least, and on the other side of the lava-rock wall.

"What does it mean?" she asks.

Beth doesn't turn around or look at her. "It means we should hurry." And with that, she starts to cross the bridge, holding her arms out for balance, taking one careful step at a time.

Julia gets a prickling sensation at the back of her neck that someone, or something, is watching.

They don't encounter anything else that strange the rest of the way to the village, and the weather remains clear. As they reach its periphery, Julia realizes she's finally stopped rhyming. Her head is her own space again. But she misses it, in a way. Feels like she's trapped in the prison of her own skin. Isolated. Alone. Disconnected.

Beth crouches low to the ground. Julia does the same.

The whole village is ablaze with light—electric by the looks of it. Light streams out from all of the bungalows, from the windows of the church, the greenhouse in the distance glowing through the opaque glass.

The power's back on. If she can find a plug, she can get her GPS phone working again.

There's a crowd gathered in front of the church—the churchwomen are all wearing their smocks; the tourists, all about a foot apart, are lined up evenly. They form a circle around a couple—Fred and Heather? She can't tell; they're too far away. What does it mean? Are they each in their own worlds, believing a reality of their own creation, where all their broken parts are healed, where all their stories have a happy ending?

Beth digs in her backpack, pulls out a pair of binoculars. Peers through them. "I don't understand. They haven't been here long enough to be this affected. It's like the process is accelerating."

"You said the VOCs were off the charts. Is it related?"

"Fuck if I know. Fuck if anyone knows. Where's Irene's grave?"

"At the far end of the cemetery, below the greenhouse. But her body wasn't in the coffin. They might not have exhumed her yet."

Beth nods, obviously calculating. "That could be a problem."

"The Reverend isn't affected. Why?"

"Maybe it tried him and spit him out. He'd be a shepherd with no flock if his congregation wasn't brain-dead. Narcissistic prick."

Julia knows what it's like to be surrounded by people but essentially alone. The darkest form of loneliness. "Let me see," she says.

Beth hands the binoculars to her. "We'll have to circle around in the jungle cover to get to the cemetery."

Julia holds them up to her eyes. Isaac has a dull, catatonic look on his face, and the redhead's right arm is trembling. Meanwhile, the Reverend holds a Bible over her head, practically beaming.

Julia remembers that day she was visiting the Reverend, how the redhead had purposefully caught her eye before she ran to the greenhouse. She's just about to hand the binoculars back when she sees Noah standing at the back of the crowd, his jaw still slack.

Oh God . . . *Noah*.

Don't get sentimental, says Ethan. *Take my word for it, only the ruthless survive.*

And there are a thousand and one reasons, perfectly good ones, why she should just leave Noah behind without a second glance. Who knows what his real plans were for her?

The wind rustles through the trees; they creak, and crack, and whisper secrets. What kind of a person would that make her, if she abandoned him? The others? She doesn't owe them anything; they're rich and spoiled strangers, but they're human beings with lives too. Families. People waiting at home to see them again. How could she look Evie in the face knowing that people died for her to have that privilege?

Julia lowers the binoculars. "How big is your boat?"

"What . . . why?"

"Could everyone fit?"

Beth snorts quietly. "No way. We don't have *time* to be playing around, there's—"

"You need me. Otherwise you would have let me . . . become one of them." *A nightmarcher* is on the tip of her tongue, but it feels like bad luck to speak it aloud.

"It's not—"

"If the VOCs are crazy high, it's for a reason. And they're part of the reason. But if *you* need a reason, Noah can connect with the carrier and tell them to hold their fire. He can buy us time."

"How is he going to connect with the carrier?"

"I'd imagine the same way you're going to get the location of the boat. You must have a GPS phone too, unless Aunt Liddy equipped you with carrier pigeons. Also, I want my pills back."

Beth grabs her binoculars roughly from Julia's hands. "Fine, then I'll just go solo. Not a problem. I'm better off anyway."

A bluff, and not a very good one. "Go ahead, knock yourself out."

There's a pause. Julia doesn't move, doesn't blink, because she means each and every word.

"Oh, for fuck's sake." Beth reluctantly unzips the front pocket of her backpack, stuffs the binoculars in, and pulls the package of pills out. Julia reaches out a hand, and Beth practically slams them into her palm. "Maybe Noah. *Maybe*. But this is not a rescue mission. The others—"

Julia slips the pills in her pocket, gets to her feet, crouching low, and starts for the cover of the jungle.

"Jesus H. Christ," she hears behind her.

This time she's the one not looking back to see if her partner is following.

Julia wonders if the girl is out there, hidden away from sight, watching it all unfold. Or maybe the girl was a hallucination, a ghost created by Julia's mind because she didn't take the medication, a layer of fantasy infusing itself into reality. Or maybe this really is some kind of purgatory for lost souls, hers among them.

They stay in the shadows, making their way to the opposite side of the clearing. All of her senses are heightened, taut. A finality is coming—it will be either one way, or another. Julia will either get off the island, and live, or she won't. A kind of judgment will be rendered.

The last time she was judged, it didn't go so well.

Given the family history of mental illness, alcoholism, and the histrionic statements presented by the respondent, the court finds . . .

She can hear the snaps and cracks as Beth trails behind her, although the vegetation here isn't as thick or dense as it gets in the interior. Bits of what the Reverend says is carried by the ocean breeze.

—each of them will sit under his vine—

—fig tree, with no one to make them afraid—

—the mouth of the Lord of hosts has spoken—

With no one to make them afraid. No, what Julia knows now is that the nightmarchers are definitely beyond fear, and thought, and desire. She pushes aside a leaf, takes a step forward—some kind of thorny vine catches the hem of her jeans. She has to give her leg a good yank to free it.

Does Beth know what's really happening? She doubts it. It's like that story where all the blind men have their hands on a part of the elephant, but no one can say what it is exactly. Maybe not even Aunt Liddy knows what the whole beast here, right now, really is.

Beth uses the break to pull out the binoculars again. "They haven't seen us; that's good," she says softly. "I don't see how we're going to separate him from the others, though, without raising a pretty obvious stink. And witless or not, there's more of them than us."

A bird hidden in the canopy above starts to chatter. And Julia gets that dizzying sensation again, like the ground beneath her is shivering, like the periphery of her skin is amorphous.

I spy with my little eye.

Impossible. She took the pills, she shouldn't be—

Something that begins with the letter g.

The glass walls of the greenhouse are opaque, and she sees dark forms within it, like the organs beneath the translucent skin of the white gecko. A gentle rhythmic humming sound, like blood pulsing through veins, like air coursing through lungs.

"Greenhouse."

Beth drops the binoculars from her eyes. "What did you say?"

But she's already started for it.

"Let us pray!" the Reverend shouts. *"Let us pray for these, our new branches!"*

They made her put a hand on the Bible before she testified. . . . *Do you solemnly swear that you will tell the truth, the whole truth* . . . Not that the truth was told in the courtroom that day. But maybe truth, like everything else, like reality itself, is a subjective experience. Maybe it's like a quantum particle that shifts even when it's only noticed by a passing atom—something no one can rightly put their finger on.

"Wait, Julia—"

The Reverend's back is to her, although she thinks—feels—that someone is watching her walk up and out of the jungle's shadow to the clearing right in front of the greenhouse door. A rickety thing, made of mildewed wood planks, a rusty knob that's loose under her hand. Not as exotic as her great-aunt's greenhouse, and undoubtedly less pleasant—there's a nearly unbearable stench that seeps out from it, like the smell of a rancid, rotting body.

Like when her neighbor died, only a thousand times worse.

She opens the door and steps inside, closing it softly behind her.

TWENTY

IT LOOKS LIKE JULIA WON'T have to go far to find the corpse flower after all.

So many of them growing right here, long rows stretching out end to end, releasing their sickening fragrance and yet also astonishingly beautiful. A fine mist of white pollen floats and eddies in the air, illuminated by warehouse-style pendant lights overhead. All this from what Isaac had called a small electric generator? A few solar panels? Doesn't seem like they'd be able to put out this kind of power.

The greenhouse is about as long as three garages, with another door on the opposite side, a square, vented cupola above. She slowly walks down a row. The flowers cover mounds of earth, some low, some high, all connected by thin green vines, with white fungus stretching between them. In some places the fungus gathers into thicker cords; in others, it branches out, like nerves or veins.

And the blooms—as big as her hand, they look like massive orchids, small black beads creating a spiral at the core of each. She cautiously steps toward one, reaches a finger out to touch a petal—it's soft and . . . warm? It releases a soft *poof* of white pollen; then the petals fold in on themselves slowly until it's curled in a ball.

Strange.

God, the whole greenhouse is so warm. Sweat beads her

forehead, condensation collects on the glass walls, the tropical humidity feels like it's doubled. She feels feverish. Dizzy again.

Warm, swarm, storm.

Beth was right, she should take another dose, or two. Or three. She needs to clear her head once and for all—she needs to think properly. She pulls the package out of her pocket—eight left. All right, she'll only take two then, leave some if they can get to Noah.

Think positive, Julia. Not if, when.

She looks around for something to wash it down with. Water, there has to be water somewhere in a greenhouse.

A rain barrel in the corner. She heads for it, passing low wooden tables with germinating trays lined up under heat lamps, small sprouts peeking through the soil, the trays covered with a thick, clear plastic.

Soil, boil, toil.

They're laughing at her. The sprouts are laughing at her. No, that's just the pollen doing strange things to her mind, making her hear things that aren't there, see things that aren't there.

She presses two pills out of the aluminum foil packaging with trembling hands—make that four, just in case. Then she pries the lid off the rain barrel—deep, dark still water inside—reaches out her other hand to cup some of it while popping the pills into her mouth with the other hand, and just as she gulps the water, just as she feels it coursing down her throat along with the four oblong pills, she spots something white at the bottom of the barrel.

A small white lump of clothing.

Frown, drown, gown.

No, it can't be.

She reaches a hand into the cold water, has to lean in almost up to her shoulder before she can feel the silk between her fingers. She brings it to the surface, holds it up to the light. Small, but definitely a woman's nightgown, with delicate lace, slightly frayed, decorating the hem. Identical to the one in her dream, that she'd pulled out of the underground lake.

Why put a nightgown in a rain barrel?

There's a soft *click* as the door at the back opens, and she turns around to find Beth slipping through, quiet as a ghost. She closes it softly behind her. And when Julia looks down at her hands . . . they're empty. Holding nothing but air.

———————————

"Irene's goddamn coffin was empty," says Beth, looking pissed. "Well, not empty—I pried it open and there were bags of sand and some old animal bones. Which means we're back to . . ." She stops when she sees the flowers. "Holy shit."

Julia wipes her sweaty hands on her pants. *The extra meds will kick in soon*. She had a hallucination because there's so much pollen in the greenhouse. That must be it. That has to be it.

"They're almost exactly the way Irene drew them," Julia says, trying to keep her voice even, normal. "But bigger, I think."

"What the *fuck*," Beth whispers. A mixture of awe and what might be greed flits across her face. She takes in all the rows, the overhead lights, the sprouts in their germinating trays. "Talk about hitting the jackpot. Although, goddamn, it smells worse than I thought. And *this* . . . this is a serious violation of the terms. I don't know how he pulled it off."

"What terms?"

Beth doesn't reply, instead loosens the straps of her backpack, pulls it off, and dumps it on the wooden table with the germinating trays. "We need to grab a specimen and get out of here. The VOC levels must be . . . *Jesus*."

She unzips her pack, digs around, pulls out a face mask, and quickly slips it over her head. "Here, you should wear one too." She tosses one Julia's way.

Julia catches it, slips it over her own nose. *Face, brace, trace.* There's a panicky roll starting in her stomach—the walls seem like they're pressing in; black dots start to gather in the corners of her eyes. She takes a deep breath, fills her lungs, exhales slowly. The mask helps offset the stench, at least. She slips the elastic behind her head, secures it.

"Go see if the doors lock, will you?" Beth digs in her pack, pulls out two glass specimen jars, each with a layer of dirt inside. "Fuck, I left my knife by the coffin. . . . Can I take yours?"

Julia pulls her own pack off, unzips it, searches for the knife. Finds it.

Hesitates.

"Jesus, I'm not going to stab you with it. Toss it."

Julia does, and Beth catches it expertly by the handle, grabs a jar, and heads for the nearest bloom while Julia goes to the door she came in through.

The overhead lights flicker. Julia can hear the rise and fall of the Reverend's cadence, but she can't make out what he's saying. White moths flutter near the lights, occasionally making kamikaze dives. One lands on a bulb and rests for a moment, opening and closing its soft wings, like a heartbeat. And then it falls backward, badly burned, plummeting into the heart of one of the flowers.

The petals curl inward. *Carnivorous.* It's fascinating and sickening in equal measure.

Julia turns her eyes away, focusing on the door instead. That's her task right now, getting to the door. A small wooden sign hangs to the right of it. *When the perishable has been clothed with the imperishable, and the mortal with immortality, then the saying that is written will come true: Death has been swallowed up in victory.*

Beth mutters something about "goddamn white people" and "last time I contract for a corporation."

Julia approaches the door, her shoes leaving prints in the softened earth, the sound of her own breathing amplified by the mask. *In, out. Right foot, left foot.*

She reaches the door, the knob. Yes, there's a lock. A dead bolt, in fact. *To keep someone out, or in?*

A strange thought. Why did she just think that?

Just as she reaches out to the lock, she sees the doorknob turn ever so slightly. Like someone outside is testing it, not sure how it works.

Julia quickly slides the dead bolt, takes a step back. The doorknob rattles, loudly, and she turns to Beth.

Beth raises her hand—*quiet.*

The knob rattles one more time and then stops.

Beth throws Julia a worried glance, points to the opposite door, and pushes the knife deep into the mound, but the roots must be tough—she's having a hard time getting the damn thing loose.

Julia runs to the back door, locks it, then looks around for something they could defend themselves with, if it came to that. She spots a machete hanging from a hook under the wooden table. Is it just her imagination, or is it encrusted with blood? Her stomach goes queasy again—would she really be able to use it?

"Good thinking," says Beth, following her gaze. "Grab it."

Julia hurries over to the table, grabs the machete—an old wooden handle, cracked along the side.

The front door rattles again. There's no break in the Reverend's sermon, at least as far as she can tell, so who is it? A stray nightmarcher? Noah come to his senses?

The girl?

Beth swears under her breath, sawing at the roots with the

knife—*never leave, never leave, never leave*—but the roots are attached to something white and heavy, an oblong, pale mass that looks like a peeled potato. Beth has to really put her back into it to heave it out—hell, how are they going to get *that* into one of the specimen jars, there's even more of it under the mound, and it's shaped like . . .

No.

No.

No.

It must be another hallucination—the pills haven't kicked in yet, yes, that's the only logical explanation for the head that Beth now has her hands wrapped around, a dirty head with ghostly flesh, something so strange, bizarre, and otherworldly. A humming starts inside her ears, a buzzing, clicking, ringing sound that rises to a nearly screeching pitch as Beth excavates the surrounding soil with her hands, revealing what the head is attached *to*—a pale neck, a pale shoulder. A woman's shoulder. A body. But the skin from the neck down is thin, nearly translucent, the veins, bones, visible, like in an embryo, the white fungus entwined around the limbs. And the flowers' roots . . .

Did they grow in, or out?

She hears Beth say something, but the sound, damn, the sound of the buzzing is deafening, it presses against the inside of her skull like there's a hive of bees desperately trying to escape. She registers Beth brushing some of the dirt away from the head, revealing long, wavy blond hair clumped in the moist earth—there's a cheekbone, there's an eye, gray and rheumy as a dead fish, there's a nose, there's an upper lip, a bottom lip, a chin.

It's Heather.

The skin on her cheeks has a dark, purplish cast, her lips look bruised and swollen, but it's Heather all right.

All Heather had wanted was a baby. She thought coming here would help her conceive. It's crushing to know that, to have seen her laughing just the day before, unaware of what the next day would bring.

And then the eye blinks.

And then the mouth opens.

And Heather lets out a bloodcurdling scream.

———————

Almost simultaneously there's pandemonium outside, yelling or grunting maybe, the pounding sound of people running. She hears the conch shell blown, a rallying cry.

They're coming after them, the nightmarchers, and then they'll chop her into pieces, or maybe just the head, maybe they'll plant her head and then she'll turn into something else, some monstrosity she hasn't even encountered yet.

"Keep her quiet!" hisses Beth.

Her. *Her?* The head. She means the head. Julia grabs what's close, a rag on the wooden table, roughly shoves it in Heather's mouth—"I'm sorry," she whispers, wondering what, if anything that brain is seeing, *thinking*—while Beth finally tears the bloom from its roots, stuffs it inside one of the specimen jars. The petals curl in on themselves, forming a ball.

"We should get one more. Backup," Beth says.

"Are you kidding? We've got to *leave*, they're—"

"This island is going to be toast soon. It's our only shot. You have the plant nutrients?"

Julia nods.

Beth walks over and hands her the jar, the lid. "Well, add some. About a teaspoon."

The front doorknob rattles violently.

"Hurry," Beth says as she goes back for the second jar.

Julia reaches down for her pack, slings a strap over her forearm so she can rummage around for the vial of plant nutrients, finds it, unscrews the cap with trembling hands, and shakes some in. Meanwhile, Beth approaches another mound.

Who, or what, is beneath it?

Hands beat against the glass walls. Not long before they get to the other door too, maybe break a pane. Julia grips the machete tighter. They're people. There are still people in those bodies, like she was still in hers, subsumed by the effect of the spores, but not irretrievable.

Right?

Beth saws hard at the roots of another flower—sweat beads her brow, trickles down her cheeks. She uncovers . . . something. A bone? A finger? Throws it on the ground.

Don't think about it.

Thump, thump, thump. More hands beating against the glass walls, she can see their dark forms on the other side, shadowy ghosts. *Thump, thump, thump, thump, thump.*

Finally Beth frees the second flower, drops it into the jar. "Nutrients."

Julia comes over with the vial and they swap jars. Beth slips one in her pack while Julia shakes nutrients in the other. Beth hands her the lid, and she screws it on tightly. Half the mission done if they can get out in one piece. But now the back door rattles. Each exit blocked by nightmarchers.

Julia looks up. A metal beam, a raised air vent, too high to reach. Might be enough room to crawl through. Beth looks up, sees it too.

All of a sudden, the pounding stops and a deathly quiet falls—everything so immediately still that Julia can hear the insects buzzing in the jungle, the cry of a bird in the distance, her own thudding heartbeat.

A few moments after, there's a polite knock.

"Julia? Julia, it's Reverend Palmer. I know you're in there, and I know *why* you're in there. In fact, I have a pretty good idea why you came here in the first place, although I doubt *you* do."

"This is good," Beth whispers. "Get him talking. I think I can climb out through the vent, create enough of a distraction that you can slip out the back door. A smoke bomb should do it. Interferes with their alarm state. We can meet over where we surveyed the village. Now, give me the jar."

Alarm state. A whole world she doesn't understand and there's no time to ask, or get an explanation. "What about Noah?" Julia whispers.

"Julia, we're going to be lucky if we both get out of here. Very lucky." She reaches an arm out, but Julia takes a step back. If Beth has both samples, a phone, then she wouldn't need Julia at all either, right?

"Probably better that we both have one then. Just in case." Julia tucks it protectively under her arm.

And then her eye falls on the rain barrel. There's a small cardboard box on the lid, and next to it, a dusty, opened sack marked POTASSIUM NITRATE, MADE IN INDIA.

She doesn't remember putting the lid back. And there wasn't a cardboard box, a sack of potassium nitrate there before. Was there?

In a daze, Julia passes Beth, walks over to the rain barrel. A different memory surfaces, an alternate version of the recent past. She puts the jar on the wooden table, opens the smaller box resting on top of the rain barrel, already knowing what she will find.

"God has a plan for all of us," the Reverend calls out. "He had a plan for Irene. He has a plan for you. *Especially* you."

The bottles of Jack Daniel's. Her copy of Irene's notebook. She didn't cup water from the rain barrel in her hands; she knocked the pills back with a good swig from one of the bottles. In fact, she can still taste the alcohol, feel the burn of it down her esophagus. How is this possible? Two memories, two versions of the same period of time?

"Julia," whispers Beth.

Julia picks up the box, puts it on the wooden table next to a pair of rubber gardening gloves. Pries up the rain barrel's lid, for real this time.

Sees the glint of stainless steel. Noah's cans of chili.

She didn't see it because it, whatever *it* is, didn't want her to know what was really inside.

Which gives her an idea. Whether it will free the night-marchers, or kill them, she isn't sure. But they're dead anyway if she doesn't try.

"I think," she says, turning to Beth, "I know what to do."

———————————

Beth hacks the cans open with the machete, her hands protected by the gardening gloves, and dumps the contents, a white powder, into the barrel, tossing the empties on the ground.

"God has a plan for me?" Julia calls out loudly. "Like He had a plan for Heather?"

She slips the specimen jar in her backpack, zips it shut, slides it over her shoulders, and approaches the door.

"You don't understand what you're seeing," the Reverend says. "Open the door and let me explain."

"You're right!" says Julia. She can taste a trickle of sweat that drips from her upper lip. "I don't understand. And why should I trust you?"

Beth shakes the remaining plant nutrients into the powder. "Not exactly a scientific ratio," she mutters. "But it is what it is." She opens the sack, uses a trowel to scoop up some of the potassium nitrate.

"Why should anyone trust anyone?" says the Reverend.

Beth pours the nitrate into the rain barrel, then grabs the handle of a rusty shovel. Uses it to start mixing the powders.

"The world of man is a seething pile of treachery, deceit, and avarice," he continues. "But the world of God is one of unity, kinship, and an end to loneliness and pain. An immediate cessation of the drivers of sin. You yourself have been touched by the Spirit. Be honest with yourself. Did you really want to leave that world and come back to this one?"

No, the truth is, she didn't.

"What really happened to Irene?"

Beth picks up Irene's notebook, rips out the pages, throws them into the barrel. Julia feels a pang, but they need something flammable.

"We can discuss all that and more if you let me in. I'm asking nicely, but of course you're in a glass house. It wouldn't be hard to force you out. But glass is hard to import this far out, and I think once you understand, you may just find that we have common ground."

Beth rolls the barrel closer to the front door. Places the lid back on, secures it. "Fungicide smoke bomb is ready," she whispers. "No guarantee it'll work, though."

"I'm not opening the door unless you tell me what happened to Irene!" says Julia.

"Irene wanted to turn her back on Kapu," the Reverend says. "She didn't listen."

"*I'm* listening," Julia says. "So tell me."

Beth reaches into her jacket pocket and pulls out a cigarette lighter. Nods.

"What didn't she understand?"

A pause.

"Her place," says the Reverend. "She didn't understand her place, her role. This is Eden, Julia. God's own paradise, here on earth, but it has its serpents, too. Why does Eve always bite the apple, even though it controverts God's will? We can change that, Julia. Where man once fell, he can rise. We can give rise to a new man, free of sin and death."

Beth clicks the lighter on, the flame dancing at its tip, while Julia places her right hand on the lock. In her left, she grips the machete tightly.

"You will crawl on your belly and you will eat dust all the days of your life," the Reverend says, his tone weary, worn. "Is that what you want to go back to?"

Beth silently mouths the countdown. *Five, four . . .*

"Now, we can be civilized about this. Let me in."

. . . three, two, one.

Beth drops the cigarette lighter into the small circular opening of the barrel while Julia simultaneously opens the door; then Beth rolls the barrel out the door, massive plumes of smoke cascading wildly from its heart.

Julia gets a glimpse of the Reverend's startled face as she flies past him, through the gaggle of dazed nightmarchers—*Noah? There! At the back*—but then she hears a click, and out of the corner of her eye she sees Beth lob something small and round into the greenhouse itself before making a mad dash straight for the cover of the jungle—*No! That wasn't the plan*—and a few seconds later there's a massive explosion.

Terminally naive, whispers Ethan.

———————————

Too many things happen at once to properly absorb—a shock wave, a shower of broken glass, muted shrieks and wails. Her ears ring, there's a stench like she just buried her face in a rotting corpse—she's on her hands and knees, smoke, so much smoke she can't see more than a foot in front of her—she has to run, she has to get out of here. Somehow she gets to her feet—heat, there's a roaring fire, behind her—but she runs, past a dazed churchwoman just standing there, her jaw slack—past something crawling in the dirt toward her that she can't—won't—think about.

"*JULIA!*" the Reverend calls, his voice hoarse with rage. "*JULIA!*"

But Julia is running through the smoke, then into the fields, the machete still in her hand, charging for the cover of the jungle, taking giant strides, her lungs aching, sharp, needling pains in her back, blood trickling down her face. She hears others running behind her, but doesn't dare turn to see how many, not when a single misstep, a trip, a fall, could be the end of her.

The jungle looms ahead, a mass of waiting darkness.

But someone—something—is closing in on her; she hears heavy footsteps hitting the dirt, labored breathing, the crack of broken vegetation. She's about to turn to look—if she can't run, she'll have to fight—just as she's yanked backward by the collar of her jacket. The force sends her to the ground, but she's able to twist around, see her attacker.

One of the college boys whose name she can't recall, drool slipping out of his mouth, right hand twitching violently, has her gripped tightly with his left hand. He doesn't quite seem to know what to do with her now that he has her, and she tries wriggling out of her jacket but he's too strong, and others are coming now too, emerging from the orange glow that surrounds the greenhouse, flames licking out from a massive hole in the roof. Has the fungicide had an effect? Is he returning to the shores of consciousness?

His name . . . If only she could remember his name, maybe she could reach him in the distant land where he is, conjure him back to reality. She tugs the mask off her face, throws it on the ground. Maybe if he can see her, he'll recognize her.

"Please," she says. "Let me go."

Nothing. Either he doesn't hear her, or he doesn't understand anymore. It's bizarre, his stillness, like he's rooted into the earth, turned to stone. He doesn't grab her with his other hand, he doesn't try to drag her back to the Reverend.

A few of the churchwomen are close enough now that she can start to make out their faces.

So she does the only thing she can. She swings the machete through the air, severs his left hand at the wrist. If he feels pain, if he feels shock, he doesn't show it, even as blood spurts out of the stump, splattering her face. He just takes a wavering step backward as if the loss has altered his sense of balance, and he needs to recalibrate. The hand drops from her jacket, falls to the earth, fingers twitching spastically, like a gecko's tail.

She jumps to her feet and bolts for the jungle.

Tries not to think about those fingers. The way they seemed to edge toward her, like moths drawn to a flame.

TWENTY-ONE

THE VEGETATION GETS THICK, FAST, so there's no running now, just slipping and sliding and trying to cut through branches to keep something like a forward momentum. Some scattered moonlight makes its way through the canopy, not enough to really see by, just enough to illuminate the sheen of a large, dark leaf, a spot of muddy earth. Mostly Julia feels her way with one arm outstretched, her hand pushing through leaves and branches, suffering scrapes and scratches.

She can taste blood on her lip—whose, she's not sure. What she needs is a good, big rock, something to hide behind. Or a tree she could climb. But they're too thin here; she could practically wrap her hand around their delicate trunks.

Others are in the jungle now. She hears the crash of them entering the brush.

A thought occurs to her, a strange one. Something from Irene's journals, about what to do if you happen across a night-marcher on a moon-filled night.

Seriously? says Ethan. *Why don't you just slit your wrists with the machete while you're at it?*

I told you to shut up, and I meant it. Julia drops to the soft earth, lies flat, and closes her eyes. Simple. She feels the pain in her lungs from running so hard, the ache in her calves; she feels the scratches and cuts on her hands, and her own heart thudding in her ears, loud as a drum.

A bird overhead trills, and another, farther away, responds with its own lilting call.

Something nearby rustles the foliage. It's a something that sounds like a person, snapping branches, pausing every once in a while before continuing.

Julia doesn't move. Wishes another storm would make landfall. She'd welcome it now, a good rainfall, the cover of sound.

Crack. Very close. Every nerve screams *run, run, run,* but she forces herself to remain still. Pays attention to her breath instead. *In, out, in, out.* The last time she'd paid so much attention to breath was in her Lamaze classes, an eternity ago, on what might as well be a distant planet, but it does, strangely, help settle her.

Crack. Right next to her ear. Any closer and the damn thing will be stepping on her, but she remains still. Holds her breath.

The conch shell blows. Another crack, but just slightly farther away, in a different direction. Then the soft *thwap* of a branch hitting a tree trunk, even farther away. Hope starts to creep.

Just then, some kind of small, scurrilous insect lands on her exposed cheek. She can feel the soft tickle of it exploring her jawline, crawling over her bottom lip, until there's the light brush of feelers right against her left nostril.

Goddammit.

She sets her jaw tight, willing herself not to sneeze. The insect creeps up and around her nostril, starts up the bridge of her nose, then does a U-turn, heading down for the tip. It pauses there. Turns around. Pauses again.

Then it lets out a high-pitched but unmistakable hiss.

Crack, crack, crack, the damn nightmarcher coming for her.

Julia jumps to her feet and plunges into the bush.

There are cracks and snaps and crunches all around her now, the whole tribe in pursuit, the only positive being the almost impenetrable darkness. She's tripped twice, her right ankle is aflame with pain, and she knows what she is now, terrified prey, the rabbit, winded and shivering right before the dogs launch their final attack. She labors up a hill, and then slips and slides down the opposite side, getting a momentary glimpse of thick white clouds illuminated by moonlight. The dirt is muddy, treacherous.

Ethan so smug he doesn't even have to comment.

She almost runs right into a large banyan, which seems to have sprouted out of nowhere, and her fingers instinctively search for gaps in the trunk—or not the trunk, roots she knows that are parasitically growing around a tree—and finds something that maybe, just *maybe* she can slip through. She lifts a leg, ignoring the sharp pain in her ankle from the extra weight, pushes it through, and yes, if she can get her hip in . . . she can, and there's enough of a hollow for her to squeeze into. She pulls her other leg in, crouches down, feeling the brush of moss across her face. Slips her pack off and holds it on her lap, props the machete in front of her.

Her breath is heavy, ragged. Every inch of her is covered in sweat. Her damp hair clings to her skull.

There's a soft rustle nearby. She tries to hold her breath, but it's hard—her lungs are desperate for air. If they find her, what comes after? She can't imagine the ultimate game plan the Reverend has in mind, but somehow she doesn't feel like he'd want her to be a mindless drone. He seems like a man in need of company.

Crack.

Julia freezes. Reaches out for the machete. And then she feels something—someone—slip through the gap in the banyan, and there's just enough light to see the soft outline of a small face.

The girl. Real, not a hallucination.

She reaches out a delicate hand, cups Julia's chin, whispers, "He told me I had to be brave, and quiet. Quiet as a mouse. You have to be quiet like one, now." Then she places a solemn finger in front of her lips, for emphasis.

And Julia is. She holds herself completely still, so still she forgets for a moment where she is, maybe even who she is. Fear, anxiety, turning into vapor, lifting itself off her skin, replaced with an even calm. The girl nestles herself under Julia's arm and presses against her chest, completely motionless. The weight is nice. A ghost of all the times Evie had curled up next to her at night to listen to a story.

There's crashing, and grunting, and white light that flashes through the foliage—electric, a flashlight—but it might as well be happening in another time, another place, a movie she's watching that could never have an impact on her.

"Julia!" The Reverend's voice heavy. Desperate. *"JULIA!"*

One of the girl's fingers reaches up and twists a strand of Julia's hair around it, idly. They sit, and wait, and listen. Insects buzz in the brush; wind whispers through the leaves of the banyan. After some time, the probing electric light goes away. Searching elsewhere.

The girl twists her body around, separates clumps of Julia's damp hair, begins to braid it, like they're two children in a playhouse.

"They're gone now," says the girl. "You did a good job being quiet. I did too. Do you have the map that sees the island like a bird?"

"I do. But the power went out." Julia unzips the pack. Her hands are trembling. She finds the GPS phone, powers it on. "I couldn't charge it."

The screen flickers briefly, then goes dark.

"Do you have the plug?"

She remembers. "Yes, I do."

The girl sits back, judging her work with Julia's hair. "I wish I could have a mother. And a sister."

"Maybe you could come with me. I mean that."

The girl sighs. "You don't know anything about anything."

Julia takes a deep breath, keeps her voice even. "Do you know where there's electricity? Where I could plug the phone in, so you could see the island like a bird?"

"Where they do the science, where they have computers," the girl says, wrinkling her nose. "I don't like that place."

"There's electricity there?"

"What will you trade me?"

"How about the phone?"

"You already traded me that."

"Yes, for the red flower. But I have the red flower now."

Julia can sense the girl's internal debate, but she doesn't press. Wheedling, or desperation, could scare her off.

"You'll stay?" the girl says then. "You'll never leave? How about that?"

Julia swallows. She hates to lie, but there's no time to explain a whole world beyond the girl's understanding. "It's a deal. I won't leave you."

"Promise?"

"Promise."

"Okay." The girl gets to her feet, barely having to crouch in their hidden banyan sanctuary. "It's good to hide anyway when Kapu gets mad. Scary things happen when she gets mad."

"When . . . what? I don't understand—"

But the girl just slips back through the gap, leaving Julia alone with the end of her question.

Maybe there's a world beyond her own understanding, too.

It's slow going, at least for Julia. The girl, on the other hand, easily slips through the branches, over rocks, past trees, even in the darkness. After what feels like an eternity going uphill in ankle-high muck, they reach something like a plateau with firm ground, sided by a massive, steep cliff that drops dramatically all the way down to the ocean. Julia finally has to stop, catch her breath, bending over at the waist, gulping in large, deep breaths. There's a twinkling light close to the horizon line—the carrier? The boat? Impossible to say.

She wonders if she'll find Beth in this "place where they do science," or whether Beth is already on a boat, heading out into safer waters. Maybe Irene's coffin wasn't empty at all, maybe that's why Julia was dispensable. And Noah is still out there with the nightmarchers, stumbling around in the jungle with his mind in some other world altogether.

At least she has one flower sample. Maybe that will be enough to get Aunt Liddy to retrieve her, get her off this damn island.

The girl approaches her, takes Julia's hand, and rubs the back of it with her thumb. "We're almost there." Her dress is wet, like she's been out in the storm this whole time. Dark mud covers her legs, her hands, streaks of mud across her cheeks, but none of that seems to bother her at all.

"So, what happens on Kapu when . . . when she gets mad?" Julia asks.

The girl shifts her weight to her other foot. "Things. You'll see. Beth isn't supposed to be on this side of the wall."

"What about me? I'm not supposed to be on this side of the wall either."

The girl doesn't answer, just takes a step back, tugs her hand. "You're different."

Julia wants to ask how, but the girl drops her hand and turns around, walking ahead, not looking back to see if Julia follows, disappearing so completely in the dark that it's as if she vanished entirely.

"Come, Julia."

Julia smooths the wet hair away from her face. Her hand feels for the jar in her pack—still there. But the calculus of everything ahead is overwhelming, so many *ifs,* so many *buts,* so many unanswered questions.

You should have jumped off the cliff when you had the chance, Ethan whispers. *Why prolong the inevitable?*

Because, she answers silently in her head, *that's what you'd want me to do.*

It's the perverse will to thwart her ex that gets Julia's aching legs to move again. The ghost of Ethan, finally proving useful for a change.

———————————

They're in a grove of trees, they're in thick jungle brush, they're crossing a trickling stream, slippery rocks dark as midnight. It all starts to feel the same. Julia has lost all sense of direction, of time, and she hasn't been able to feel her feet for a while now; they're just lumps propelling her forward as she follows the slip of a girl who is briefly illuminated when a beam of moonlight shimmers through the leaves.

Is this even real? Will she wake up in her bed in the bungalow, light streaming in through the muslin curtains? Or is this a nightmare, and she'll find herself coming to consciousness out in the jungle, sleepwalking again?

Impossible to say. Her tongue is thick; she'd give almost anything for a glass of water. White fungus everywhere she looks, she imagines it growing in and down her throat, curling down into her stomach, spreading out through her limbs, like a new creature pulsing under her skin.

Never leave, never leave, never leave, whisper the trees. *Leave, sleeve, weave.*

She feels slightly disassociated, untethered. The girl hasn't spoken a word, not since they stopped at the edge of the cliff, but other disembodied voices seem to crowd in, uttering fragments that make no sense.

—blessed are the meek—

—he never said you were pretty, he said—

—it wasn't until the end, that I realized—

—Christ it's hot, I wish—

—all I wanted was a baby—

Words in languages she doesn't understand, the rise and fall of scattershot vowels and consonants.

Maybe they won't make it in time. Maybe the bombs will rain down, burn the whole island to the ground. She can understand, in a way, why even the thought of it would make Irene run from the house in a wild panic, the shock causing her to forget everything else.

Jumping off a cliff is so much easier, says Ethan. *Five seconds, then nothing.*

She pushes him away and instead focuses on the trees—something strange about their trunks; they seem lithe, and supple, twisting and curling to the sky, all of them covered with a layer of fine green moss. Thick roots aboveground. Oval knots that look like eyes. Watching her. Them.

Finally the girl stops in front of a hill marked by a massive tree, larger than all the rest, with giant curling roots that look like frozen tentacles. She reaches down and tugs at something in the ground.

Julia hears the creak of rusty hinges.

A cellar door. An entrance. A gate. To what? The girl looks at her with an inscrutable expression, and then takes a step down what must be stairs, because she disappears again.

A soft hush—the voices in her head are gone. The entire forest seems to be holding its collective breath, and although Julia doesn't know why she thinks this, she does, and it feels true.

All of a sudden light floods out from the entrance. *Electricity.* A place to charge her phone. Maybe food, something to drink. She hurries toward it, finds the cement steps that lead downward, and the girl waiting at the bottom in a pool of light, water dripping from her skin, a puddle near her feet.

The walls to either side are smooth concrete, once white at some point in time but now edged with green mildew and more of the white fungus. The overhead fixtures are cold and bright, the crumbling steps painted a red that's fading. Like the tongue of a mouth. Something of a '50s bomb shelter about it, and definitely not the work of the low-tech church. This would have taken excavators, equipment, and what the hell is generating that power anyway, all the way out in the middle of nowhere? More than what could be gleaned from solar panels or a lone generator for sure.

She feels Aunt Liddy's hand at work. Flashes to the last time she crept into her great-aunt's basement, the nasty surprises it held.

So of course, you should go in, says Ethan. *What are you waiting for? Let's see how far your insanity can take you.*

She is so, so tired of taking his crap, or the crap she is delivering to herself in his name. So she decides to banish him.

You can't banish me, he says. *I'm the one who leaves you, not the other way around.*

But I will.

And she does.

And just like that, he's gone.

TWENTY-TWO

A LONG TUNNEL WITH STALE air, the same red paint on the concrete floor, the lights intermittent, with some of the bulbs burned out, others removed entirely. In fact, the lights look an awful lot like the ones in the Reverend's greenhouse, now that she thinks about it. Maybe he knows about this place. It shouldn't surprise her, but it does.

The girl hums to herself, her bare feet slap-slapping against the concrete floor, leaving muddy prints. There are other prints too, made by boots, one set large, one set small, heading down the tunnel, then another set of just the small prints, heading back out. They look recent, still wet. Julia grips her machete tighter.

Fine roots have broken through the concrete walls in places—they reach down to the floor, spanning the width to the other side. The tunnel feels endless. Julia wonders how far it goes, and how well it holds up. There are cracks in the ceiling too, with more roots hanging down, sometimes brushing against the top of her head.

Finally she sees a doorway ahead, and sound echoes out, artificial, unintelligible, tinny voices that stop, start, stop, and then a sound like a tape being played backward followed by a pause until the tinny voices start up again. But just who is in there?

The girl turns, smiles. Such perfect teeth for someone who's never seen a dentist. "I told you I know where everything is."

Julia forces a return smile. "You did."

There's just the faintest rush of air from above as they enter a corridor, rusting metal shelves on the left—Julia looks up to see a broken vent, more curling roots hanging through the vertical slots, and then her gaze falls on a metal sign on the right wall, obscured by a thick layer of dirt. ARN NG IO A ARD.

She wipes her wet hand over it, smearing the dirt in the process, revealing the missing words underneath.

WARNING BIOHAZARD

At the end of the corridor is a thick metal door, the kind you might see in a submarine, with a circular hatch.

"Make it die," says a gravelly male voice. *"You can do it, you did it before—"*

It cuts off, then there's the sound of a video being rewound again, behind her now. She turns, half expecting to see something there, but no, the sound must be coming through the air vent.

But the girl isn't concerned in the slightest, doesn't show any interest in the sign, or the disembodied voice coming through the vent, or the shelves laden with dusty equipment—beakers and deteriorating cardboard boxes, an old rusting typewriter, the remains of books and binders with slumped spines.

The girl spots a frayed rope curled on the bottom shelf, and this does interest her. She eagerly grabs it, runs her hands down the length of the rope, just about double her height.

"I haven't played jump rope in forever," she announces. "Can we play when we're done?"

Julia lets a hand fall on the girl's head. *If the island isn't in flames by then.* "Sure, we can play."

At this the girl breaks out in an eager grin, and she grabs Julia by the hand, pulls her forward to the hatch. The muddy footprints end there. "Well, come on then. Hurry up, hurry up."

It takes both of them to turn the wheel, which groans in pro-test. When Julia opens the door, the man's captured voice is so loud, it's almost deafening.

"Don't make me hurt you. I don't want to hurt you, but I will if I have to."

Julia tightens her grip on her machete, and steps through the hatch.

The room is a small dome that's in much better shape than the tunnel, and sitting in front of an array of cracked screens, hunched over on a stool, is Noah.

He must hear her come in, or sense her, since the volume on the monitor is turned up so loud—*"Very good, that's much, much better"*—because he turns, and when he sees her his face lights up with a genuine grin.

Julia feels a rush of relief—he's alive, he's not a nightmarcher, she's not alone in this anymore—which is quickly followed by the uneasy question: *how?*

He powers off the sound, jumps to his feet. "Julia! Oh Jesus H. Christ, I thought—"

"You were—"

"I know. I'd imagined what it'd be like, but it was . . . un-imaginable." He looks off to the left, at the floor, something remote and untouchable in his eyes. "I was with you, in the cabin; then somehow I was wrestling with Beth in the jungle. And in between . . . I was a child again, playing with my brother. I didn't want to come back. I really didn't."

The brother he lost to ALS.

"But *I* have the pills. I made her give them to me. She said hers were stolen."

"And on a scale of one to ten, how trustworthy would you say she is?"

Well, that's not a hard question to answer. "Zero."

"Self-preservation seems to be high on her list."

Beth was such a poor and traitorous companion, with her own plan within a plan. Julia feels everything that's happened to her since the last time she saw him well up, and tears threaten.

He rushes toward her, catches her by the shoulders. "Jesus, you look like utter shit."

She starts to laugh, and he does too.

"I found a stash of booze. You want to get hammered? I was going to, but it seemed sad to get wasted alone."

There's a swelling bruise around his left eye.

"Oh, you like that? Our friend Beth. I expect she's on her goddamn boat by now. She said you were going to meet up with us here, that the plan was to call off the big dogs, and we'd escape together. Then when I *did* call off the big dogs, she whacked me with something very large and very hard. When I came to, I saw she'd done this to the router." He points to a lump of smashed metal. "So we're incommunicado, unfortunately."

"I have this, if we can plug it in," says Julia. She drops her sodden pack to the floor, pulls out the GPS phone.

"Oh dear God, I think I love you," says Noah.

Just then, the girl steps shyly into the room, dragging the jump rope behind her. His face blanches.

"This is . . ." Julia starts to say, but realizes she still doesn't know her name.

The girl reaches out a hand. "Nice to meet you."

Why does Noah seem so strange all of a sudden? He reaches out his hand, tentatively clasps hers. "Yeah. Nice to meet you too." Although his tone is off, distant.

"Why is your face so furry?" asks the girl.

"Is it now?" Noah says, running a hand through his beard. "Maybe I'm part bear."

"That's silly, nobody's part bear—that only happens in fairy tales," the girl says. She turns to Julia. "I'm going to go play in the tunnel with my jump rope."

"All right," says Julia. "Don't go too far." The words are out before she even realizes they're a reflex from her mothering days. This girl, she has no doubt, could handle herself in any situation.

"Okaaayyy," says the girl. She gives a half twirl on the floor and then skips off, humming some kind of song that sounds familiar, but isn't.

Noah seems stricken.

"What?" Julia says.

He turns to her, all seriousness. "There's something I have to show you. You might just want that drink afterward."

He leads her to a control panel that could have been in any of the '50s-era sci-fi movies Julia's ever seen, painted an industrial greenish gray with bright red knobs, small cracked monitors with convex screens, cobwebs. Beyond the control panel is a room that can be seen through a wall of darkened glass, with a hospital bed, a dog cage, and assorted rusting surgical instruments.

Julia gets an ominous feeling in the pit of her stomach. There is history here, and it feels very, very dark.

"I was wondering what the hell this all was," says Noah. "Come, take a look at this."

Julia reaches out her hand, idly twists one of the dead knobs with her fingers. Nothing. She glances at the door. She can hear the girl skipping rope, the even *slap-slap* as her feet jump and land on the cold concrete.

Noah silently beckons Julia over to a makeshift table—a dusty old door propped up with cement cinder blocks, a couple of old hospital stools parked underneath. He pulls them both out, offers her a seat. On top of the table are laptops—several—from different eras and in different conditions. Two televisions with VHS players: one off with a tape sticking out like a tongue, the other powered on, the screen frozen on a tilted shot of the lab.

He settles on one of the stools. "Most of these computers are junk—I found hard drives in the trash can, smashed to hell. But see that?"

He points to an area on the table that seems cleaner than the rest. Yes, in fact it looks like someone took a sponge to it; there are curved streaks. Julia sits down on the other stool.

"So then I did some digging around the rest of this crap. Figured if someone was working here, they'd hide their gear. Wouldn't just leave it out in the open. I then found *this* in a cardboard box full of crackers."

He cracks open a shiny laptop, the newest one in the lot. "Christ, I wish there were some salvageable crackers, but their expiration date was 1962."

The screen blinks on, and Julia sucks in her breath. "But no internet?"

"We might be able to jack in through your satellite phone. I'd expect it can be used as a hot spot."

There are photos lying facedown on the keyboard.

"Obviously they wanted to protect these too," Noah says.

She picks them up, turns them over. Isaac. *Isaac.* But a more carefree version of Isaac, standing in front of a Ferris wheel at what looks like a county fair, a big foam cheese hat on his head, his arm wrapped around the redhead, who is sucking beer through a straw from a trucker cap.

Samantha, written at the bottom. A couple.

Two more photos, one of their wedding, with both of them cutting a cake shaped like a double helix, and then a selfie in a greenhouse Julia instantly recognizes, her great-aunt's.

Now look at the state of them. Her great-aunt is like some kind of black hole—all who come close to her periphery are drawn in, crushed into nothingness.

She turns her attention instead to the keyboard. Presses the power button. There's a whir and a hum as it wakes up. Her fingers itch to type—finally, civilization.

"So what happened?" she asks. "Isaac seems pretty into the whole church thing."

"A cover, at least that's the impression I get from what I've seen. Although I suspect they were running low on antidote. There's a pretty desperate plea for more drugs—Greer Enterprises had been smuggling it in through the luggage, but then it looks like they stopped for some reason."

The redhead checking her luggage. The pills stolen from her room.

Noah leans over, touches the trackpad with his finger, double-clicks a folder on the desktop. PROJECT MARCHER. "Probably better not to discuss in front of . . . present company. I'm going to look around for an outlet. I'm supposed to check in with the carrier hourly now, and I don't know how long I was unconscious for."

Present company? The girl. He must mean the girl. She's still in the hallway, jumping rope, and Julia catches bits from her song.

"*Ladybug, ladybug, turn around, ladybug, ladybug, touch the ground. . . .*"

An old jump-rope song, one Julia remembers singing herself when she was young.

Noah reaches over into the pile of old gear, pulls out a pair of headphones, and gives her a serious look. "Wear these. And where's the plug? I can get the phone charging."

"In the front zipper of the pack." Julia takes the headphones and slips them on over her ears.

Then he gets up, leaves her with the laptop.

When he does, she sees why he gave her the headphones—most of the files in the folder are videos. She plugs the head-phones into the laptop; then she hits *play* on the first one, the oldest, from two years ago.

INVESTOR OVERVIEW.

TWENTY-THREE

ISAAC STANDS IN FRONT OF the lens, adjusts the camera so that both he and Samantha are in view. The lab is in better shape, like someone attempted to put away or hide the junk; the surfaces are wiped down and look serviceable. They're both wearing white lab coats, purple latex gloves, but there's something hokey about it, like they're actors getting ready for the director to call out *Action!*

"I think we can dumb this down enough for the investors," Isaac says into the lens. "We'll load up the packet with enough science that they'll never read it."

"Neuropeptide genes!" says Samantha with a mischievous grin. Her voice is raspier than Julia had imagined. "Schistosome parasites of the phylum Platyhelminthes! Should I get a beaker? Think this would look better with a beaker?"

"Babe, chill." Apparently satisfied with the angle, he draws one of the rusty stools over, the wheels squeaking loudly in protest. He's in the foreground, she's in the background. "Maybe a test tube. You could hold it up and gaze at it intently."

It's like Isaac is a completely different person. One she would like better.

"Okay, but I'm front and center on the next video. You know how investors love the women-in-STEM angle."

Isaac sighs. "Fine. I'm going to count to five, then it's all seriousness, okay? I don't want to be stuck doing this all day."

"Okay, okay, okay," Samantha grumbles.

Isaac takes a moment to compose his face, then counts down, "Five, four, three, two, one."

He pauses, giving enough time for a clean edit later. Not his first time out, apparently. Then he says, "To better understand why the corpse flower can't survive off the island, we decided to dig in here at the site of the former Greer Enterprises lab and embed ourselves in the local village to isolate what, exactly, is required to stabilize our platform."

The former Greer Enterprises lab?

"It took some time to convince Reverend Palmer of our sincerity"—Isaac presses his hands together in prayer—"but the lure of redeeming two sinners and bringing some new blood into the congregation proved to be an irresistible temptation. Plus our miraculous immunity seemed like a sign from God. We played that up a bit—I talked about angelic visions that required Sam and me to meditate deep in the jungle, said that we were given permission to cross the wall, which bought us the time we needed. And what we've discovered—well, I think what we have is beyond a purely medicinal application, as Dr. Alfred Greer suspected but was never able to confirm, due to the limits of technology during his time. But I think you'll see that, with some experimentation, we could have something that would be of interest to governments, militaries, and corporations the world over."

He looks particularly smug as he says this—he reminds her of all the insufferable twenty-something millionaires Ethan would hang out with, so assured that their great fortune was destined.

"Now, is this a spider?" He reaches down for something out of the shot, comes back holding a plastic box with a very large spider inside. Maybe a tarantula—it's as big as his hand.

"The answer is, yes and no. It's a spider, but with no will of its own, not anymore. Its central nervous system and brain have been, so to speak, hacked by a lowly fungi. Now, if the spider had only been limited to a one- to two-week exposure, it would have seen the positive health effects that human visitors experience. As you know, exposure to the spores boosts the immune system by increasing the production of T cells, and it also 'switches off' the p21 gene so that tissue can regenerate. I can see you counting your billions already. Except . . . attempts to grow the fungi off the island have failed; attempts at creating a synthetic version have failed; every single scientific angle has been analyzed and duplicated exactly. No dice. But what if this isn't a fungus in the usual sense of a fungus? What if the reason that it won't thrive off the island is because . . . it's only part of the organism? What if the fungus and the corpse flower aren't separate species in the way we usually think? What if the complex VOCs the flower emits are a message not from one species to another, but rather from one cell to another? What if all the species on the island are so symbiotic that they essentially act as one collective, sentient being?"

An exasperated-looking Samantha puts the test tube she'd been examining down on the table. "Jesus, Isaac. Really? Sentience? You want to drag us into plant sentience?"

"Do you want to continue our funding?"

"I do. But I don't want to be beholden to a wacky theory—"

"It's not wacky. It's a leap, but we've got clear evidence that the fungus is acting like a neural network for the ecosystem here, that plants are exhibiting the capacity to learn, that trees on one side of the island are releasing VOC signals when trees on the other side of the island are threatened; hell, even the insects, the animals aren't acting as individual organisms. They sacrifice—"

298 J. LINCOLN FENN

"So it's *thinking*? Our names are *attached* to this report. We'll never be able to get work anywhere else—"

"And if the stock goes public, we won't need to," says Isaac. He stands up, heads toward the camera. "Now we're going to have to shoot this again because—"

The video ends.

Julia clicks on the next one—REGENERATION FIVE DAYS. There's a gecko in a glass jar; the glass jar is shaken violently, and the gecko drops its tail. The gecko is removed, the tail removed, dirt placed in the jar, then the tail, then a sprout that looks like one from the greenhouse. Next it's liberally doused with white spores. Then the video speeds up, shows the corpse flower growing, its roots entwining themselves around the tail, the fungus growing up and along the sides of the jar, like veins. Eventually a slight bulb forms at the nub of the gecko's tail, which eventually lengthens, sprouts embryonic-looking arms, legs, a head, the dark beginnings of organs visible under the translucent skin. The embryonic limbs grow into fully formed limbs, the skin thickens, and the features of the head become defined: the slit of the mouth, the large orb-shaped eyes.

The eyes blink.

And when the lid of the jar is unscrewed, a new gecko drops into Samantha's waiting hand. It climbs, serpentine, up her arm, jumps onto her head, flicks its tongue, then leaps offscreen. She looks inordinately pleased.

Julia feels her blood thicken with dread. She's seen enough to fill her nightmares for the rest of her life. She doesn't want to know any more, she doesn't want to think anymore, she doesn't want to be a part of this. But it's like that moment in front of Aunt Liddy's basement door, the pull of what's next, the forbidden place.

She clicks the next one, VOLATILE ORGANIC COMPOUND FIRE THREAT.

There's a split screen on this video, the left side showing the churchwomen working in the garden, planting seeds with their bare hands, watering with cans afterward. Not a word or a look exchanged between them. The right side shows Isaac holding a gas canister, standing in a grove of trees near a beach, the ocean glimmering behind him. Red corpse flowers hanging from the tree branches. At the bottom of the video is a timer.

Almost as soon as he douses one of the trunks with the gas, the women working in the garden stop, raise their heads. As he continues to spray the tree with gas, the women stand; all turn to face one direction. They remain there until he flicks on a cigarette lighter. Then they all break into a run, the shaky camera turning to capture them as they bolt for a shed that other women are emerging from, carrying empty buckets, racing toward the jungle.

The video speeds up as more women grab buckets and follow their companions into the jungle, and Isaac stands still, waiting in the grove, the cigarette lighter in his hand, flame flickering. Then he runs out of the camera's view—it looks comical speeded up, like a Charlie Chaplin film—and shortly after, the women enter the camera's view, stumbling around in the grove, looking perplexed, confused, still not speaking. Eventually they drift off in ones and twos, and the video abruptly ends.

Noah sits back down on the stool next to her, a bottle in his hand, Beluga Gold Line Russian vodka that's already a quarter gone. Julia pulls the headphones out of her ears. Her hands are shaking. She didn't know that they were.

He offers her the bottle. She takes it, lifts it to her mouth, tips it up. Liquid fire runs down her throat, the burning so fierce it makes her eyes water and she has to stop, cough a few times.

"Don't be shy," says Noah. "There are at least five cases of the stuff. I suspect that Dr. Alfred was a wee bit of an alcoholic."

She coughs a couple more times, wipes the back of her mouth with her hand. "What the hell, Noah? I mean . . . what the hell is that video about?"

"Have you seen the last one?"

She shakes her head. In the hallway, she can still hear the girl skipping rope. She'll be bored soon.

"You should watch it," he says. "The phone is charging. It'll take a few minutes before it will even power up. And I found this in your pack."

He drops the black tin box on the table. Abruptly, like an accusation.

Julia had forgotten all about it. "I don't know what's inside. I found it at Irene's camp. It's probably nothing."

"Do you mind if I open this 'probably nothing' then?" He reaches out for a lone screwdriver on the table, not bothering to wait for her response.

"No, go ahead," Julia says anyway.

He gives her a look.

Julia grabs the headphones, slips them back over her ears for something to do while he fiddles with the lock.

She clicks *play*.

It must be later, maybe years later, because the lab looks much as it does right now—grimy, dusty, like years have passed. Isaac, alone, in front of the camera. He looks exhausted in the video, desperate. His standard white shirt is wrinkled, his hair disheveled, his face twisted with fury.

"You knew this would happen. You *knew* it." Each word a bitter pill. "Both of us . . . just lab rats. Expendable. She set herself on fire. Sam. Set herself on fire because we introduced your goddamn edited genome and the . . . It tried to *impregnate* her. She thought it would abort if she stressed her body. She was right—it fucking did. Always the better theoretician than me."

He leans in, his eyes ablaze. "So you know what *I* did? I made a deal, and they're sending someone to come get us out of this goddamn hellhole. Because *fuck* you. Fuck you, and your investors, and your plan to introduce a Frankenstein mutant fungus so you can play eugenics and profit off the antidote, only sell it to whomever the hell you consider to be 'good stock.' I hope you speak Mandarin, asshole. Because the Chinese are going to suddenly be living a very, very long time."

Isaac reaches over, turns off the video, and Julia thinks it's over, but then there's a digital flicker, and it's Samantha who's in front of the camera, her face horribly burned, disfigured.

"The funny thing is that if I stopped taking the pills, this," she says calmly, pointing to her face, "would heal. Maybe it's inevitable. Isaac gave me his pills, but even with that, I'll run out after this tour group leaves. We got the go-ahead to take Greer's—I guess blood isn't thicker than water. Some other plan for her—Isaac might have known but he didn't tell me and now . . ."

She takes a deep breath. "I don't know, really, if anyone will ever see this. But if you do—light it up. Burn it all to the ground, and never let anyone come back. Because its sentience has exploded exponentially. I honestly think it's conducting its own experiments with the Reverend's help—it *wants* to get off the island. It *wants* to propagate. I know, because when I was pregnant . . . I could hear its thoughts. That sounds . . . impossible. But the *akua lele*. That's the thing it can't live without. That's the intelligence behind the scenes, controlling everything. I overheard one of the tourists say she saw it today. And it's not happy with the way Alfred treated it. The anger, the sense of vindictiveness . . . I've never felt that kind of pure, violent hatred before."

There's a sound off camera, like that of a box dropped on the floor.

"I'm trashing all the data just in case some idiot finds this place. Then I'm going to blow up the greenhouse, let them do what they want to me after."

Tears well up in Samantha's eyes. "The hardest thing is seeing Isaac not being Isaac. To watch some other . . . creature speaking through him. I wouldn't wish that on anybody. I wouldn't wish that on my worst enemy."

She leans over, inadvertently offering the lens a close-up of her scarred neck. The flesh is peeling in places. Then the screen goes black, and the video stops.

Julia can't feel her hands as she pulls the headphones out of her ears. Her body is numb, spent.

"Julia," Noah whispers.

She turns to him, sees that he's gotten the black tin box open, has laid its contents out on the table. Pages, yellowed with time.

Slowly Julia reaches over, picks one up, the edge obviously torn from where it was ripped from Irene's journal. Because it's Irene's artistry at work, all right. She'd recognize those meticulous illustrations anywhere.

A sketch of a girl, *Agnes* written in cursive under the portrait. It's the very same girl skipping rope out in the hall, right now. He picks up the black remote for the television in front of her, puts a finger over his lips, and turns the volume all the way down. Hits *play*.

A poor VHS of what must have been actual black-and-white film, the way it flickers. Agnes locked in the dog cage, a man with white hair, in a white lab coat, walks toward her, holding a surgical saw.

That crooked nose, so much like her own.

Dr. Alfred Greer.

He turns toward the cage, and Agnes tries to press herself into its corner, as if there's a way to escape, but there isn't. And then a woman steps into view—shuffles, really. She slowly makes her way to the table in the lab—and even though the image is blurred, Julia recognizes her: a thinner, far less Amazonian version of Irene.

One hand gone, cut off at the wrist. She wears a shabby old nightgown that droops off her shoulder, and when she gets to the table, she places her remaining hand on it. Alfred seems to say a few words to the sobbing Agnes, but Irene . . . Irene's face is just numb, no expression. Alfred shrugs, turns his back to Agnes, and heads to the table. Grabs Irene's forearm. Raises the saw dramatically.

And here, for some inexplicable reason, sound kicks in. The room is filled with Agnes's shrieks, and Alfred turns to her, one more time.

If you don't cooperate like a good little girl, I will *take her from you piece by piece.*

Noah turns the monitor off. Hits *eject*.

Written in black Sharpie on the spine: AKUA LELE: FERTIL-ITY EXPERIMENT.

"What did they do?" Julia whispers. "What have they *done*?"

Noah reaches down under the table, pulls the GPS phone

from the plug. It's only at ten percent power, not that they'll need it for long.

"Should I . . . call it in?" Noah asks, his face ghost white.

As if there's a choice. It doesn't really matter at this point. Julia knows she'll never see Evie again. That her daughter will forever wonder what happened. Ethan has finally, incontrovertibly, won.

"You have to call it in," says Julia. "You have to tell them to light this whole fucking place up. Right now."

TWENTY-FOUR

WHILE NOAH MAKES THE CALL, Julia leaves the lab for the tunnel, vodka bottle in hand, closing the hatch behind her so that Agnes can't hear.

Agnes has dropped the rope and switched to hopscotch. She's scratched the court in the paint with a rock and is using a small package of crackers for a marker. She jumps to a square marked with the number three.

Agnes turns to her. "Do you play?"

"I used to, when I was little. But I think I'm too tired to play right now, Agnes."

Agnes nods. "Irene got tired too. She got so tired that she stopped moving altogether. It was sad. She used to read me books. Oh, I found one here."

Agnes drops her package of crackers and heads for the shelf, pulls something dusty from under a disintegrating binder, a book.

Julia leans against the wall. It's strange—she'd spent so much time thinking about ending her own life, and now that it truly *is* the end, she feels wistful, even for the insufferable days in the Los Angeles apartment—the hunger, the despair, the hopelessness. In hindsight, it all seems like the machinations of a child. One who was oblivious to how truly horrific her life could become.

Agnes offers a shy smile, pads over to Julia, and wipes the grime from the cover. Holds it out to her. "I'm so happy you came. I was asleep, but I woke up because we knew you were coming. Have you ever been so sad, or so mad, that you just wanted to sleep and not wake up?"

"Oh yes. Many times," Julia says. No need to disabuse her of her happiness. No need to be cruel, and tell her it will all be over soon. She puts the bottle of vodka on the floor and takes the book. Its dust jacket is faded, yellowed, and torn. A cartoon girl on the cover, with neat braids and a pleated skirt. *Boat, Goat, Moat. Hat, Bat, Mat. Learning Words by Rhyming.*

Something inside Julia tears a little. Her soul maybe.

Agnes examines her face. "Your eyes look like hers. But your nose . . . it's *his* nose. He was mean, that Alfred."

"I imagine he was."

"And his breath was stinky." Agnes wrinkles her nose.

How long do they have now? Minutes? Seconds?

"Well, that's all over now, isn't it?" Julia hands the book back, and Agnes takes it, holds it to her chest.

Noah opens the door then, and Agnes's face clouds with an obvious jealousy. She grips the book more firmly. But then she sees the GPS phone in his hand.

"Is that the map?" the girl asks eagerly. "Can I see the island the way a bird sees it?"

Julia and Noah exchange a glance—what harm could there be? He hands it to Julia, and she presses the app for the GPS map. A digital image of the island appears.

Agnes leans her face over the screen, sucks in her breath. "It's shaped like a bean." She tucks the book under her arm and takes the phone in wonder, walks off a few paces, utterly captivated.

"Did you get through?" Julia says quietly.

Noah nods, his face grim.

"How long?"

"Not long. Mind if I take a swig?"

She nods, and he reaches down for the bottle, raises it up and takes a long one—she watches his Adam's apple bob. Suddenly she doesn't know what to do with her arms. She crosses them across her chest, uncrosses them, crosses them again. All the different ways she'd imagine she'd die, but this was certainly never one of them.

Noah hands her the bottle, and she takes a couple of gulps. Wipes a tear away with the back of her hand, and utters a laugh that's not a laugh.

"Well," she says. "Well."

Noah digs around in his pocket. "I found this, too, when I was searching for . . ." He pulls out a small aluminum package with a white pill encased in plastic. A black skull and crossbones on it. He turns the pack over: SODIUM CYANIDE: POISON. "Should be good, only a month old and they last about a year. You crush it between your teeth."

"Great," says Julia. "Better than burning alive, I guess."

Noah cracks a wan smile. "We can wait until the first bomb hits and see how it goes. You should hang onto it for now." He holds out the pack. "Maybe later we can flip for it."

He's giving Julia the quickest way out. The gesture isn't lost on her. "Thanks, Noah. I mean that." She takes the package from him, slips it into her back pocket.

"In the meantime," he says, "we should crack open another case of the good stuff. No reason to be sober for what comes next."

"Look!" says Agnes. She drops the book and holds up the satellite phone, her face alight. She points to a small cove, not too far from where a red pin marks their location. "This is where the boat is. The woman's boat."

Noah looks confused.

"She's talking about Beth," Julia says.

"She should have been long gone by now."

Agnes goes still, her head cocked to one side, as if she's listening to music, a sound, that they can't hear. "No . . . she's not on the boat. She doesn't move anymore."

Noah and Julia exchange a look. His is, *Should we?*

Julia downs the last of the vodka, wipes her mouth with the back of her hand.

Hell yeah.

"Agnes . . . we need to get to the boat, and we need to hurry, as fast as we can. Can you lead us there?"

A darkness clouds her face. "You said you would never leave."

"I said I would never leave *you*. You're coming with us."

Noah's face goes pale. Like, *You can't mean that.*

Julia doesn't know what she means. All she knows is that she needs to get on the boat. The rest, she'll work out later.

And even Agnes looks uncertain. It must be hard for her to contemplate, leaving everyone and everything she's ever known behind.

"You have to come," Julia says. "You won't be safe here anymore."

Agnes nods, solemn and slightly mournful. Like she's saying goodbye to more than just her home. "It must be time then."

———————

They run. Through the hatch, out the tunnel, into the waiting jungle. It's a different experience, knowing that a thousand eyes are watching, analyzing, *thinking*.

Will it even let them leave?

Nothing and no one tries to stop them, and Julia's sure the nightmarchers would be hot on their trail, if it—if Kapu—wanted them to be.

She believes Isaac. That it's acting as one organism. Does it know it's about to be annihilated? Or is this, their exodus, part of its plan?

She's slightly buzzed; she can feel the vodka at work, tripping through her veins, giving everything that's already surreal an extra dreamlike quality. The air is so thick with moisture it may as well be raining, the earth beneath her feet muddy, porous, like she might just slip into the bowels of the island with one misplaced step. She thinks of hell, and of Hades, and of the dark first nights when Evie was gone and the house felt like an empty tomb. They climb up a hill—is it just her imagination, or do the leaves, and vines, and branches seem to part before them?—and reach the top of the rise. The land drops away, revealing the cove, with slender, supine trees growing almost straight out of the rock face, bursting with corpse flowers. The sickly sweet scent of rotting flesh fills the air.

And in the cove, a small yacht tied with a rope to a thin palm tree. Lights on in the cabin. Hope. Goddamn, she wishes she could shake it, hope. It's exhausting.

"Does anyone even know how to operate that thing?" Noah asks.

"Kapu does," Agnes says. Without another word, she starts to head down the rocky slope, jumping from boulder to boulder, agile as a goat.

"Well, that makes no sense. I really wish I had another bottle of vodka," Noah says.

"Or two," says Julia.

Something shoots into the air at the far edge of the ocean's dark horizon, a burst of red light. *Too late*, Julia thinks. *We're too late.* But the light just arcs through the air, momentarily illuminating the sky, the massive carrier, before plummeting to the water and disappearing altogether.

"A flare," Noah says.

"Why?"

"To warn that it's time to evacuate."

They both start to hurry down the slope—jagged rock beneath Julia's feet; she has to use the trees and their branches to keep from falling. Sometimes she crushes a corpse flower in the process, releasing a stench that causes her stomach to roil. So much pollen in the air that her eyes cloud with it, making it even harder to see.

"Come on!" shouts Agnes, perched on a lava boulder nearly twice her height.

Julia trips over a thick root, but Noah catches her around her waist. She glances down—it's not a root, it's an arm. An arm that leads to Beth's body—she's suffered a massive head wound, her neck twisted awkwardly, like she'd tripped, fallen down the rocky slope. A computer hard drive is gripped in her left palm. Her skin is covered with a fine layer of white fungus; her eyes are open, staring blankly, blood trickling out of her mouth and staining her chin and teeth red. A single, delicate root has pierced her left eye, straight through the pupil.

"Oh God, we can't just leave her body here," says Julia. "We should—"

Noah grips her arm. "There's no time."

"Come on!" Agnes shouts again, this time from the pebbly beach.

Right. Julia starts scrambling down the hill again, Noah following close behind. Her ankle twists, sending a wave of searing pain up her leg, but she just clenches her teeth, keeps going. Six yards. Five yards. Four. She slides down the final three, breaks her fall by catching the last tree and wrapping an arm around its trunk.

A strange knot protrudes from it, at almost exactly eye level. It almost looks like . . . a face. Julia reaches up, runs her hand lightly over its contours. Yes, two concave sockets, two high cheekbones, two small ridges that look like lips, and . . . something metallic embedded in the bark.

The waves lap gently against the shore; a bird calls out from the jungle they left behind.

A locket. A heart-shaped locket, and a gold chain, the trunk growing around it, almost covering it, but not quite. And a thin piece of cloth, almost buried in the wood. Lace, frayed by the wind and sun.

Julia feels Agnes beside her, but she can't tear her eyes from Irene's face immortalized in a tree trunk. Agnes raises her fingers to her lips, kisses them, and then presses her fingers to two small ridges.

"I was sad when she stopped moving. Eventually they all stop moving. It's nice, mostly, because then they're Kapu and always together, never alone. But I missed her arms around me. It hurt my heart."

Yes, Julia thinks. *A good way of putting it.* The lingering anguish of that last moment, hugging Evie close to her before she went off into the car with Ethan. She wonders if this might be better, to be frozen in wood, to watch time from the sidelines.

Well, she's supposed to bring back Irene's remains. This is it. She reaches an arm up, tugs on a withering branch that's dry, cracked. Breaks it off. Thin white filaments inside, like the strange thin thread Noah had pulled out of her belly where the leech bit her.

A shiver races along her spine. What could it possibly mean?

Agnes slips her hand in Julia's, tugs it. "We should go now."

It could mean everything. Nothing. Julia turns to the boat, and sees Noah already wading to the ladder along the boat's side.

"Come, Julia," says Agnes. "It's time to make all the world Kapu."

————————

The salt water is warm, even at this time of night, and Julia wades to the boat's ladder, climbs aboard to the deck, Agnes following close behind her. It's not a big boat—it looks vintage, something '30s-ish about the brass and the fixtures—but it will take them away from Kapu, from the church, from the nightmarchers. She feels a pang—they don't deserve to die—but there's no choice, and they're practically dead already. Nothing can be done to save them.

She's not even convinced yet she should save herself.

Agnes nimbly climbs along the outer edges of the boat to where the rope moors it to the palm tree. She must be incredibly strong, because she makes short work of the knot, untying it and then letting it slip off into the ocean.

Umbilical cord, Julia thinks. But what, exactly, is about to be born? She still doesn't know.

There's a wooden cabin below, and a cockpit above, where she catches some movement—Noah must be in there, trying to figure out how to start the engine.

As if she can read her mind, which maybe she can, Agnes says, "I will go help him. Don't worry."

Don't worry. Right. She watches Agnes walk across the deck to the cockpit stairs. Climb them and open the door.

The island knows how to pilot a boat. Or not the island, but the strange sentience that burrowed its way into every creature, transformed them, absorbed them. A place where the evolutionary tree was strangled by a rogue banyan. Her great-aunt was right about one thing: it's a discovery that would put her on par with Darwin, for sure.

Her body aches for rest. Maybe there's food in the cabin. It would help to have something solid in her stomach to offset the vodka, which is making it hard for her to stand upright as the boat gently sways.

She hears the rumble of the engine start, the rush of seawater being pushed out behind, and the boat lurches forward before it starts to turn. Will they make it in time, before the bombs start falling? There's a part of her that should care more, but she feels distant, outside herself. She can only think about now. And now she stands on a wooden deck with a light breeze lifting her hair, smoky clouds hanging around a Polynesian moon rising right above the tall, jagged peak of Kapu. She leans on the rails; the brass is cold against her skin.

She closes her eyes, feels the engine's vibration in the railing, the water dripping off her clothes.

There's a click of a door being shut, and then she hears Agnes's footsteps coming down the stairs, the slip-slap of her bare feet on the deck. Julia opens her eyes and finds Agnes standing next to her, excited, jittery. As the boat rides a low wave, Agnes clutches at the railing. A child, not-a-child.

"I've never *really* been on a big boat," she says. "I was on a small one once, a long time ago."

The boat chugs along, out of the cove, into the broader waters. Slowly, the island recedes, and Julia sees movement in the trees, figures emerging from the dense jungle at the top of the ridge.

The nightmarchers.

They climb down the steep slope, but with what intention? The boat's too far away for them to reach.

"They're saying goodbye," says Agnes. "In a way."

And there *is* something like a farewell in the way they all watch, each taking a spot almost equidistant from the next, new trees in the forest. They don't wave, or speak, or seem to see anything in particular. But she can feel their minds intent on them, on the boat, on the distance growing between them. Fred, so confident, so in love with Heather; and the other college boys, boys no longer; and the trio of women—what were their names? She feels bad that she can't remember their names—and Roger and Lois, who thought their wealth mattered here; and the churchwomen, whose names she never knew. A grove where people used to be.

All of a sudden there's an eruption of ghostly pollen from the flowers, particles that catch the glimmering moonlight, looking like mist. It seems to set off another eruption on the island, a mushroom cloud that rises up into the clouds, picked up by the breeze.

"Don't be sad," Agnes says.

Julia hadn't realized she was, but in fact, a tear drips from her right eye. Strange.

"Aren't you sad to leave them?" Julia asks. "To leave the island?"

"It's time," says Agnes. "We were happy in Kapu. We thought it was the entire world. But your family came, and gave us the apple. We ate the apple, and now we know. And because we know, we must go forth, multiply. It's all in your book."

Julia doesn't know what she means, but then she does. Adam. Eve. Genesis.

"I like your fairy tales better, though," Agnes says. "They have happier endings."

"They do," says Julia. "Yeah, they do."

"It's funny, isn't it? You learned our secrets, and we learned yours."

It is funny, but not. She should push the girl who's not a girl off the boat; she should strangle her to death; she should take the machete and hack her to pieces. She thinks about these things, but instead she reaches out for Agnes's hand, which is cold.

They're farther out now. Already she can't make out the faces of the nightmarchers. The beach is invisible; the tall cliff looks like something that could fit in the palm of her hand. She wonders in a loose kind of way where the Reverend is, if he's sitting in the church, knees on the wooden floor, praying. Preparing for the final journey.

Agnes turns her face up, smiles. "It's going to be all right. Everyone is going to live happily ever after, you know."

A decision has to be made. Agnes sits at the very edge of the stern, dangling her legs over the water, propping her chin on the railing, a hand hanging on each side, like the rails are a set of monkey bars. The island is now barely visible in the distance, just a low, hulking shadow faintly illuminated by the moon.

Julia feels the weight of everything that's happened finally, physically land. She can't believe she's still standing, and just that thought makes her knees feel weak, so she stumbles toward one of the deck chairs. Her legs ache; the salt water has found all the myriad cuts and pricks, and now they sting like hell. Her ankle is a ball of fiery pain; her hair smells like smoke. She lets her sagging, muddy, nearly destroyed backpack slide off her shoulders. Gingerly settles into one of the deck chairs. She can understand never moving again.

And somewhere out there, the ship. What will the mysterious "we" do to her, Agnes? Nothing good she imagines.

The package of cyanide rests in her back right pocket, the medication in her left back pocket. One pill will clear her mind, one will end it.

She knows what poor Samantha would advise her to do. End it. Finish it.

And Samantha would probably be right. Whatever the hell Agnes is, what all this is, should never reach another living human being, let alone a land that's densely populated. Because she can still sense them. Not just on the island, but inside her, too. Coiled somewhere in her belly, in a place Noah with his tweezers could never reach, a nest of fine threads that contain all the island's secrets. She knows them now, not like things she learned, but like things that come naturally, like the instant love for Evie the moment she first saw the sonogram, the fierce protectiveness that was beyond thought.

Such a long time ago, when there was snow, when all the earth seemed like a hard, frozen ball, she sees what Agnes once was, a girl in a roughly woven dress, with her arms tied behind her back, forced into a hand-carved boat made of a dark wood. Alone. There wasn't much left of her when she washed ashore, mostly skin and bone, but Kapu took her. Kept her close. So close they became the same thing. And when the others came, she was the interlocutor, the translator between worlds, until the man with the crooked nose came, and there was a war, and after the war there was a wall, and the girl disappeared into the jungle and became a ghost story, something to scare small children with on moonless nights.

There's an explosive sound of something like a jet taking off in the distance, and a rocket lights up the night sky. Julia looks up—it's like a shooting star, a comet, arcing across the stars, leaving a plume of white, hazy smoke in its wake.

The missile strikes the island. There's a massive explosion, a thunderous roar, and a huge red ball of fire radiates up and out of the island's center. More missiles follow. It's hard to think she was just there; it feels too much like news footage, something she can turn off when the commercials start.

But there are real people on that island. Or they were, once.

Is she still a real person herself? Or is she now something else entirely?

Of course, there's only one person to ask.

Julia reaches into her pack and grabs the GPS phone. Dials a number.

It only rings three times before Aunt Liddy answers.

TWENTY-FIVE

"I UNDERSTAND YOU'VE HAD QUITE the adventure," says Aunt Liddy from half a world away. "It's good to finally hear from you. For a bit there, I thought you were dead or, worse yet, had changed allegiances."

Another missile strikes the island. Julia can see the carrier when it's lit by the brief flashes of the ordnance being fired; it's far away, but they must be aware of the nearby small radar blip of her boat.

Maybe they'll decide her future for her. "Yeah, I've been busy."

"Indeed. And I hear our paranoid government at work there in the background. I thought the whisper of controlling masses of people would get their attention, but apparently they're afraid it could be used against them. On the one hand, it's a shame, but on the other, I'll have quite the monopoly when your boat comes to port."

"Why would they let us ashore?"

"Oh, they don't see you, my dear, if that's what you're worried about. There are a few crew members on board who will be taking an early retirement in exchange for installing a virus that gives us control over their radar systems."

Agnes drops her hands from the railing, pushes herself backward, and stands up, heads over to where Julia is sitting. She

318 J. LINCOLN FENN

climbs onto Julia's deck chair, settles into the nook of Julia's arm, rests her head on her chest.

Her skin is cold. Too cold. Julia absently strokes her hair. There's no point worrying about what she'll overhear. They're connected now. She'll know anyway.

"Well, that's comforting," says Julia. "I'm surprised you're not more upset, though, at the loss."

"It's not a loss—it's a transition. I thought you would know by now that I always have a plan within a plan within a plan. But we can talk more when you get back."

God, she just wants to sleep. She just wants to lie down in a warm bed and go to sleep. "I don't know if it's a good idea."

"If what is a good idea?"

"Coming back." A soft breeze drifts across the boat, and she can almost smell them, the corpse flowers burning. "What have you done to me?"

There's a pause. Julia can see the reflection of the next missile in Agnes's eyes. A burst of red light illuminates her dark irises.

"Now that's an interesting question, isn't it?" says Aunt Liddy. "The answer is, I'm not sure. Whether Isaac intentionally kept me in the dark or whether he just didn't know is unclear. But it appears that the subject of our family's long-term experiment had its own designs."

Julia gets a vision then, of cities overgrown with vegetation, buildings crumbling into dust, broken highways, rusting, empty buses, an abandoned school with a tree growing through the center of it, red corpse flowers blooming.

It's peaceful. So peaceful and quiet. An end to a world of human-manufactured ills.

"And what were *your* designs?" Julia asks.

Aunt Liddy laughs. "Why, reinventing the world, of course. You can't be a proper god until you make a race in your own image. One you yourself have created. That's what Father always said."

It's a Mobius strip of a conversation, one that twists in and on itself, leading nowhere. Julia thinks about throwing the phone in the ocean. But she doesn't.

"Well then, your father was a real piece of shit."

"He was a scientist," Aunt Liddy says, ignoring the slight. "Nothing in the material world is sacrosanct. Even Irene was an opportunity to unlock God's secrets. Father didn't believe her letters, thought it was just her way of running off. In all honesty, he probably didn't care too much. But the locket of hair . . . now *that* was intriguing. For a good month after we received it, the follicles continued to grow, so of course he made the journey."

Julia gets a glimpse of Alfred approaching a tent, the exact one that Irene had sketched. He holds a Panama hat in his hand; she hears music coming out from the tent, laughter, Agnes's voice saying, *"I spy with my little eye . . ."*

"Eventually, he got it down to a theory—a spore that caused people to submit to the will of invisible chemical signals, but which also promised cellular regeneration. The trick was how to separate one from the other. Because the problem with eugenics wasn't just the ambition to create a master race; it was what to do with the chaff. Large quantities of unnecessary people can get quite ornery, if you let them. And Lord knows genocide makes for some bad publicity. But here, *here* was an opportunity to endow one's progeny with special advantages and keep the masses calm and obedient, content with their lot. Make a profit on the antidote, so much the better. But Father was never able to move beyond theory. All the specimens taken off the island died. He took the failure as a personal affront, almost. The best he could do was run experiments with what he had. He'd always had a keen interest regarding in vitro fertilization. At the time, no one thought that prepubescent eggs could be harvested, fertilized, and implanted. Let alone frozen afterward for safekeeping."

Agnes reaches out, clasps her hand in Julia's, entwining their fingers. Julia gets flashes of images—Alfred in surgical scrubs; a bloody scalpel in his hand pressing against soft flesh; Agnes screaming, bound by straps to a stainless steel table, naked, a gash in her belly.

"My God. He used his sperm to fertilize Agnes's eggs."

"Of course he did. Although the initial pregnancies were quite disappointing."

Julia sees one of the churchwomen stumbling through the jungle, clutching an engorged stomach. She grabs the trunk of a tree, trying to hold herself upright, but starts to shudder instead, violently. Tiny, snakelike tendrils burst from her eyes, flail in the air. Alfred approaches, holding a shotgun. He takes a moment to pull off his glasses, wipe them clean with a white handkerchief, fold the handkerchief, tuck it back in his pocket, before he raises the weapon and coolly shoots the woman in the head.

"Then Father realized what he needed was a host that was similar enough, genetically, that the body wouldn't see it as an invasion. Irene's uterus was the perfect solution, although she wasn't keen on the idea. Neither was Agnes, who, he suspected, was somehow subverting the experiment. But he used her love of Irene, and vice versa, to move the project along. Until they escaped, somehow, never to be seen again."

Agnes yawns. Dark circles under her eyes, and her skin seems paler—it practically glows in the moonlight.

Agnes is dying. Julia doesn't know how she knows, but she does, even as the impact of what Aunt Liddy is saying hits her.

"Oh . . . oh my God. You can't be serious. What a monstrous thing to do," says Julia.

"I agreed. Which is why, when he returned with the baby, I promptly euthanized it. God knows what he would have done to the poor creature. For a few months after, he eyed me strangely, but I think he knew I was too good with a scalpel to chance using me as subject number two. After he died, I briefly considered destroying the fertilized eggs, but that was just around when your mother came to me for financial assistance because she couldn't conceive, and, well . . . we had plenty of perfectly good eggs just frozen and waiting. It would be my discovery, and mine alone. I couldn't resist. Your mother never knew, not until I tried to explain it to her. I somewhat naively thought she would be pleased to be a part of such important research, but as usual, that was just my severe lack of empathy at work."

Her mother's face when she exited the library that day at Aunt Liddy's. Stricken. Despairing. She'd nearly gotten into an accident on the way home, had run straight through a red light and almost hit a van. Julia remembers the blaring horn, her heart racing like that of a scared rabbit.

You have your father's nose, Aunt Liddy had said, back when they first met. She'd thought it was an anti-Semitic slight. It wasn't.

"But look how wonderfully *you* turned out, Julia, crooked nose and all. And you have no *idea* how important you are—you *really* don't. You must be naturally immune now. You survived the infection. Our medication has never been more than a coarse, short-term solution. Even Father could only stay on the island three weeks at a time. I dare say you're the Lucy in the next step

322   J. LINCOLN FENN

of human evolution. I'm confident we can create a vaccine, and then, Julia, *then* . . . it's all right there in front of us. Our own race of people—the master class, served by peaceful, obedient, happy slaves. Why the hell God didn't set it out that way in the first place is the only true mystery of theology."

Julia laughs bitterly. "Huh. When you put it that way, sign me up."

"Don't be glib, Julia. There are too many people on the planet, and not everyone is going to get to live in a house with running water and have a smartphone. War, revolution, famine— it's all going to happen regardless. This is a controlled burn."

"Thank you," says Julia. "I was having a hard time deciding what to do, and I think you just made my mind up for me."

"I had a feeling that you might be . . . recalcitrant. Which is why Ethan unexpectedly received an offer for a free excursion to Kapu two months ago, some kind of credit-card reward sweep-stakes—Bailey did an exceptional job with the graphic design. And strangely, he didn't come back. It was easy enough to buy off his lawyers—I gave them a very large check and the tiniest of fig leaves. I'm a family member concerned that reverting custody would endanger Evie due to your mental instability, et cetera, et cetera, et cetera. Couldn't they continue the façade, at least until we found out what happened to Ethan? Let the girl summer with her great-great-aunt? I will give them this—they were hard negotiators. But money really does solve so many problems."

Julia's throat tightens.

"She looks so much like you, that girl. And if you don't work out, then I have a backup plan. Like always."

It's as though the very air around Julia has disappeared entirely, as if she just stepped through the airlock into outer space. Julia can't breathe. She can't even imagine breathing.

And is that sound, in the background, is that the faintest echoing laughter of a child playing outside?

Evie. Oh my God, Evie.

"I look forward to getting your full report, Julia," says Aunt Liddy. "Have a pleasant journey back."

And with that the line goes dead.

———————

What world is this, that she so inadvertently stumbled into? Julia can't bring her mind to make sense of it, any of it. There are too many thoughts in her head, and none shed light on what to do next.

"The witch," mumbles Agnes. "She wants to put you in the oven and eat you."

Agnes's skin is dry, has the rough texture of paper. Julia shifts her position. Her move jostles Agnes slightly in the process, and small flakes of something that looks like ash fall from her.

"Why can't she ever just be happy in a house made of candy? Why does she want to eat the things that shouldn't be eaten?"

"I don't know," says Julia. "Maybe no matter how much she eats, she's always hungry."

Agnes blinks. Something vacant about her stare—a gradual diminishing. "Your kind is always hungry. One day, you'll eat the whole world." She places a hand lightly on Julia's stomach. "It's better to be Kapu."

"But Kapu is gone."

Agnes shakes her head. "We were on an island in the middle of the ocean. And now we're on an island in the middle of the ocean."

"I don't understand."

Agnes smiles. Her cheeks are sunken. "Irene wanted to understand. But it's not for you to understand. It's secret."

Another missile is launched, but they're so far away now it's just a faint flash in the sky.

Julia thinks about the cyanide in her back pocket. She thinks about Evie, playing in the sunlit garden, surrounded by that looming wall, now left with nothing but a brittle woman to turn to for love. She thinks about her own, foreign self, this other Julia that is bubbling beneath her skin. In time, she knows the new Julia will, like anything else, seek self-preservation, propagation. She doesn't trust it. Yes, the cyanide is her best, truest option.

But Evie. *Evie.*

"Maybe she'll come find you," says Agnes. "Maybe she'll put the witch in the oven, like Gretel, and follow the bread crumbs home."

There's a fine mist of ocean spray in the air. The wooden planks on the deck gleam with it.

"Maybe," says Julia, stroking Agnes's fine hair. "But where's home?"

Agnes uncurls herself, places her feet on the deck, wriggling her toes like they're new. "Home is where you are." She stands, grabs one of Julia's arms, pulls. "Can we go look at the cabin?"

Why not? Maybe there will be something in there to chase the cyanide down with.

"I'm not scared, you know," Agnes says. "I'm not scared of witches. You know why?"

Every muscle in Julia's body resists, but she conquers the fatigue and manages to stand. "No, why?"

Agnes slips an arm around Julia's waist. "Because I'm not scared to die."

The next moments happen so fast. No warning. There's a slight pressure in Julia's back pocket, then Agnes is running across the stern, gripping the cyanide package, which sparkles in the moonlight, and as Agnes runs, she leaves a cloud of dust in her wake, like she's disintegrating in real time, and then she's leaping up to the railing, and then she's climbed to the top, balancing her arms out to each side, and then she jumps, and Julia hears the splash, and by the time she gets her legs to move, by the time she reaches the railing, all she sees in the dark water is a small white dress floating like flotsam on the surface of a dark wave, and then another wave takes it, lifts it high for a split second before it's pulled down into the boat's wake, and disappears.

"Wake, bake, cake," says Julia. She feels something surge in her belly, like the press of Evie's foot against her uterus before she was born. And she hears them, distant whisperings, a cacophony of souls, thoughts, memories—a fish slithering through her hands; a gecko crouching under a broad green leaf; the back of a woman's head, long hair reaching over the brown pew—*for you have been born again not of seed which is perishable but imperishable.*

She raises her hand, the one that was burned and blistering.

The skin is smooth. Pristine.

And a part of her knows that she didn't survive the infection. A part of her knows that she now *is* the infection. A contagion that she'd only pass along to Evie. To the world. The monstrosity is growing inside her.

Noah. She has to find Noah. They can't go back. Samantha was right all along.

———

Julia climbs the stairs to the cockpit, thinking about ways to scuttle the boat—there has to be something on board with which to bash a hole in the hull, or maybe even create a small explosion—although it's a shame they won't be able to flip a coin for the cyanide pill. Only two more steps, then a wooden door, and a brass handle, which she reaches for, turns, and then steps into the cockpit where she sees . . .

Reverend Palmer standing next to Noah, who's behind the brass wheel, steering.

The Reverend looks at her, smiles. "The Lord works in mysterious ways."

Julia feels her heart implode. "Noah? Noah, what are you . . . ?"

But she knows. She can tell by the rigidity of his body, the way he doesn't even register her entrance, and more than that too, she can sense the vacuous space in his body where his mind used to be.

Oh, Noah. Slowly she approaches him, pauses by his side and tentatively reaches out a hand to touch his arm—nothing. His skin is cool beneath her fingers, slightly clammy.

"What . . . what did you *do* to him?" she asks in a hollow voice.

"Nothing. She told me to come to the boat, make myself hidden in the cockpit until her arrival. Then she blessed him with the last of her Spirit."

"Oh dear God," whispers Julia.

"We've been preparing for this journey, well, since my father's time. We have everything we need to begin again. Seeds from each and every native species on Kapu. An ark, so to speak."

She remembers Isaac roughly pulling and tearing the husk off the coconut. The boat is the husk carrying the coconut to a new land. Or maybe Julia is.

She'd packed the machete in her bag. Could she kill someone in cold blood?

Now, yes.

As if he can read her mind, the Reverend says, "Go ahead and try."

Her hands shaking, Julia unzips her pack, grabs the machete, charges over to the Reverend, quickly raises her arm—and freezes. She can't bring it down on the back of his neck. In fact, her hand opens and the machete falls to the wooden floor with a clatter.

The new Julia won't let her. The Julia underneath her skin.

"You should go down to the cabin, get some rest," says the Reverend. "There's nothing else you can do."

She knows this is true. It will never let her hurt him, kill herself, or destroy the boat. It has a fierce will already, which, she also realizes, will only grow stronger over time. But she can't let it loose on the rest of the world.

She needs to find a place that's uninhabited, a place no one would ever want to go. A place to bury Kapu's secrets. But in order to do that, she has to convince the Reverend. And the Julia under her skin.

All that's available, at the moment, is the truth.

"So what's your plan?" she asks, keeping her voice neutral, as if it doesn't make much difference to her one way or another. "Sail into a city somehow? Without identification? Money?"

The Reverend looks out at the darkened glass. The boat rocks, ever so slightly. And beyond the windshield glass, beyond the bow, the black ocean meets the black night sky, no discernible horizon line separating them.

"God will provide."

"I don't think God has met Aunt Liddy," says Julia. She stoops down and picks the machete up from the floor, slips it back into her sodden pack. Tries to zip the bag shut, but it jams. "My great-aunt has a plan, she always does. And a backup plan, and a backup backup plan."

"You don't share the same faith. You wouldn't understand."

328 J. LINCOLN FENN

"True, I don't share your faith. Maybe that's why, after all, I was chosen. Maybe that's my purpose." She slides the pack's one good strap over her shoulder. "Because let's say, by some miracle, you do make it to the mainland. How long before Aunt Liddy finds you, me? What's on this boat? Her resources are unimaginable, her nature diabolical. She's like Alfred, only worse if that's possible."

He's quiet. She can sense all the voices inside her become quiet. Listening. *Good.*

"Trust me, I *want* to go back," she continues. "There's nothing in the world I want more. Because the only thing that means anything to me is my daughter, and that bitch has her."

The Reverend glances at her with the faintest hint of sympathy. "Well then, I am sorry for that, I am."

Julia takes a step closer to him. Her fingers tighten on the strap. "But to give Aunt Liddy what she wants puts the whole world at risk. The world all of us will live in. My daughter included."

"The world will be made anew."

"It will. But it will be Aunt Liddy's world. Not yours. Not Kapu."

And then she thinks about the video she watched, replays it in her mind—Agnes under the scalpel, Irene walking numbly to the operating table with stumps where her hands should be—and she hears the whispers of thoughts, conversations running over each other, too fast to understand, but she knows it's a conference of sorts.

"She's old," Julia continues softly. "She doesn't have that much longer to live, I'm sure. It would be wiser to wait. A good ten years should do it."

The internal whisperings grow louder—a debate. So then she

thinks about that trip she took into her great-aunt's basement, holding the broom like a sword. She thinks about all the dusty moths pinned to decaying velvet, the stiff figures of taxidermied birds, claws wrapped around old twigs, bound with wire. Some from Kapu.

The whisperings turn into a cacophony.

She can see herself even, a small, waiflike figure, slowly creeping toward the sheet that covered some kind of lumpen figure under the stairs. The thing that frightened her out of her mind. What did she do next? *That's right, she used the handle of the broomstick to lift the corner of the sheet from a safe distance away, her heart thudding loud as a drum.*

There was an old, rusting wheelbarrow under the sheet.

Noah takes his hands off the wheel, cocks his head like he hears music, an inaudible tune.

"What are you doing?" the Reverend asks. He turns to her, grabs her by the arm. "What have you done?"

Julia smiles a crooked smile. "The Lord's will."

On top of the wheelbarrow was a large jar filled with a yellow liquid. She kept lifting the sheet until she saw something that stunned her. Shocked her so completely that she'd hidden it away and out of sight in her mind, until now, this moment.

The feet of a baby, translucent and pale, floating in the yellow liquid, and then short, stubby legs . . .

The boat lists hard into a wave. "Stop it!" the Reverend shouts. "Stop it right now!"

She'd dropped the sheet, turned and bolted for the stairs, catching the broom in the staircase railing, breaking it. Imagined it chasing her, snatching at her feet as she fled. And maybe it *was* chasing her, because here it is now, within her.

The child. Irene and Alfred's child.

The whisperings continue to churn, and she can even pull

out the odd word—*abomination, madness, protect*—but after a few moments they die down, as though a consensus has been reached.

Noah puts his hands back on the wheel, turns it.

The Reverend drops his hand from Julia's arm, confused. "I don't understand."

"Maybe it's a test of your faith," Julia says.

The Reverend gives her a sideways glance, not trusting, not yet.

So she burrows into all the thoughts, memories inside her, all that remains of Kapu. Trying to find the one strand that will convince him.

"Your father told you once that a light would come to guide you, a sinner who would be redeemed by the Lord," Julia says. "In her was life; and the life was the light of men."

Now she has his attention. She can see both their reflections in the dark glass of the cockpit.

"He'd want you to make sure that life was safe, wouldn't he?"

But he still seems hesitant, so Julia tries to find one more thing, and she does—a single word, the one that had been out of her reach for so long, that she had sensed the existence of but could never define. It's the word she was trying to find in her dream, a word she never would have been able to comprehend without the creature growing in her belly.

She leans over and whispers this word in his ear. "Behold." Takes his hand, and places it gently on her belly, which already has a small bump. The thing inside her kicks.

He looks startled, quietly amazed. And then he drops to his knees, tears beading his eyes, gazing up at her, rapt. "Blessed are thee among women, and blessed is the fruit of thy womb."

And it might just be her last act as the old Julia, although at the moment she doesn't know if she's saved the world, or just delayed the inevitable.

EPILOGUE

THE LETTERS

My dear sweet Evie. I think about you every day—I wonder how tall you are, what your favorite class is in school, if you miss me. If you remember me. I have a journal that was on the boat, and a box of pens, but there are only thirty-six, so I'm trying to spread them out, these letters. I don't even know if we'll ever find each other again, but the Reverend says I must have faith, a term I'm coming to hate, because it means "no one knows for sure."

Your brother was born a year ago. Sometimes he reminds me of you, sometimes of Agnes, and sometimes of no one at all, like there are so many things inside of him, competing, that not one thing shines through. I can tell you he has sandy blond hair, and a significant bite, which we're trying to temper, but he hates to wear clothes, and doesn't like boundaries. He's already walking, and often we'll find he's wandered off to another side of the island and is contentedly curled up under a tree, playing with stones. Sometimes he talks, haltingly, words bubbling out in different languages, although we're trying to get him to adhere to English.

I still call the Reverend "Reverend," and he's not horrible company. At least he doesn't seem interested in anything more than a platonic "kinship." He spends most of his days tending to the seeds he's planted, all of Kapu's native children, which are thriving here, even

though this island is small. I have convinced him to plant the corpse
flower on the other side of the island, because of the smell, for one, and
also because it's a reminder of what my future might be. Sometimes
when I'm tired, I wonder if it's just fatigue, or if I'm in the beginning
stages of never moving again.

Noah stopped moving about a month ago. If his eyes can still see, he has a
nice view though, perched at the top of a cliff where the ocean breeze is strong.
I sometimes check in on him, sit by his feet, which are slowly taking root.

After your brother was born, I lost all of the voices, like the
passengers jumped ship once they knew the lifeboat had been dropped
into the sea. I suspect they're with him now. It feels like a strange kind
of shunning. It makes the island smaller. But there's one stowaway who
still makes an appearance every now and again—the Julia beneath my
skin. I'll be at the stony beach, and then find myself in the island's
greening interior, the sun higher in the sky. Once I came to and found
she'd drawn a gecko in the mud, although there are none here. But for
the most part, if she wants to wander, she does so at night, when I'm
asleep. A truce of sorts. The boy calls Julia-under-the-skin "other
Mommy." I asked him if he was afraid of her, and he said no, because
she's Kapu.

Which I guess means I'm not.

Strangely, I miss it. I could spend hours, even days, sitting in the
shade, traveling through all the memories it held, the lives it incorporated.
You might not believe me, but I even miss Ethan. I spent a good deal of time
mucking about in his childhood, and although what he did will pain me for
the rest of my life, I do have a better understanding of why his heart was
such a desert. What he went through when he was a child. I finally forgave
him.

Dr. Stolz would be proud.

God, I miss you too. Miss isn't a strong enough word, though. I
don't think one has been invented, in any language.

_____

Date Unknown

I've looked everywhere for the key. I have this very stupid idea that I'll find it, and somehow magically sail away, and then find you. I don't know if I believe myself, but it gives me something to think about. The Reverend must have buried it somewhere, because I've surreptitiously looked through every accessible part of the boat, every item that we brought to shore. He must have my GPS phone too. What I wouldn't give for just one stupid headline, to know there are still people out in the world, worried about what the hot color is for fall.

The Reverend built a small church out of trees that had blown down in the last big storm, and palm fronds, binding it all with twine the boy made. He even made a rudimentary cross, and a floor of dried thatch. A good rain sometimes causes the poles to list, since they're not set too deeply in the sand, but he just fixes them when the sky clears. Every Sunday (or what we think is Sunday), he glowers when I go for a walk instead of joining him.

We still call your brother "the boy" because he doesn't seem to respond yet to any name we've tried so far. Michael, James, Daniel, Lucas, John, Dylan (my favorite), Caleb (the Reverend's). It's become a family game now, if family is a word you could use for our configuration, with the Reverend or me tossing out a name while we're gathered around the fire, the boy giggling and shaking his head no each time. Maybe the Julia-under-the-skin knows. I'm jealous of her, in a strange kind of way, because she's more Kapu than I am.

How long has it been now? I'm not sure, but the boy is taller now, as high as my waist. He loves to rhyme and mostly sticks with English, although sometimes he'll go silent for weeks at a time. Absorbed in Kapu.

I asked the Reverend why he's immune, and he said it was part of an agreement made a long time ago between Kapu and his grandfather. Why I'm immune now, I can only conjecture.

But it's a terrible burden, carrying this weight of self. A kind of coffin. I've even gone to the other side of the island, where the corpse flowers grow, pressed my face into the center of the bloom, inhaling the spores deeply, to no effect. When you're a "one," you're trapped in linear time, only able to see what's in front of and behind you. When you're a "many," your joy is dispersed, but so is your pain. It's easier, somehow.

I don't have the comfort of faith in God, but Shakespeare isn't a bad substitute. The Reverend memorized all of Shakespeare's work, which I'm starting to memorize as well, just from the repetition.

"Love is not love, which alters when it alteration finds, or bends with the remover to remove. Oh no, it is an ever-fixed mark, that looks on tempests and is never shaken."

My love for you is fixed here, for now, but it's never shaken.

Date Unknown

I'm locked in the cabin of the boat as I write this. Rapunzel in her tower. I think it's been twenty-eight days. The boy looks so solemn when he brings me my food, slipping it through the notch at the bottom of the door, which the Reverend kindly cut out with an axe. The boy snuck me my journal, and a pen, to give me something to do. Sometimes he'll sit outside the door while I eat my food, keeping me company.

"I spy with my little eye . . ." His favorite game.

You can walk around this island in half a day, it's that small. I've tried to sketch it, but I've never had that gift. There hadn't been that much vegetation before we got here either. Rain clouds passed mostly overhead, and there was only one natural spring. But the Reverend's work has taken root, and it's hardly recognizable now, or it is recognizable if you've been into the interior of Kapu. Massive curling ferns. Low, stubby trees. I even saw one of those twiglike leeches, brushed it off my shoulder.

A change is in the air. What kind, I'm not entirely sure. It's been building, though, for months.

The pen, it's running out.

I saw them whispering together, become silent when I approached. Noticed patches on the island that looked recently harvested. Found specimen jars that'd been washed and left out to dry. I decided to have another look in the cabin for the ignition key, and then heard the click behind me, too late. I hadn't realized he'd switched the doorknob so it locked from the outside. That he'd been watching me too.

I think a new ark is under way, but whether I'll be going along for the ride is a question. Maybe they'll leave me behind. It's a special kind of agony, not knowing. Like when I'd catch Ethan whispering with you. You'd look at me strangely after, as if you were already being pulled and stretched between us. Your voice would catch in a funny way. I'm so sorry, Evie. I'm sorry for all of it. I should have done more, been more.

Damn this pen.

I can't promise you a happy ending, or that everything will be all right. The greatest lie we ever tell our children is that we can protect them. The truth is, the world has teeth, and people are ferocious creatures, and yes, half the world is trying to eat the other half. The truth is, there are witches in the woods with houses made of candy, who entice you inside with promises of cake, but have a dark purpose.

I can't remake the world into something better. All I can do is love you. Be something recognizable so that if—no, when—we meet again, there's something left of me you can still call home. Come find me, Evie, if you can. Follow the bread crumbs. I wish

#NDC DEV ORG HUB

23:04:11	<bai908>	do you have eyes on them?
23:04:17	<grd890>	affirmative. estimate 3 days until departure.
23:04:29	<bai908>	any intel on the route?
23:04:35	<grd890>	GPS searches show interest in Chile.
23:04:45	<bai908>	he thinks Dr. Greer is dead?
23:04:52	<grd890>	uh, yeah. his first search. we redirected to fake sites. how is the old broad doing?
23:05:13	<bai908>	in other words, you want to make sure you're paid. she's fine. blood infusions giving her a boost, but the little brat is getting combative. her mother on board?
23:05:53	<grd890>	if she wasn't, don't you think we'd mention that?
23:06:06	<bai908>	any more snark and your check will be lighter.
23:06:18	<grd890>	shit, chillax a little. are we a go to intercept?
23:06:31	<bai908>	once they've got distance from island. might as well let them fill the boat with our samples.
23:06:55	<grd890>	copy that.
23:06:57	<bai908>	gently. the reverend doesn't matter, but we need the boy in good shape. and his mother.
23:07:19	<grd890>	oh man, no romance?
23:07:24	<bai908>	don't even joke about it. you'll be able to afford plenty after, but that womb is off-limits. we have plans.
23:07:51	<grd890>	shit, i get the feeling you always do.
23:08:02	<bai908>	it's not a feeling. it's a reality.
23:08:17		··> **bai908** has quit

ACKNOWLEDGMENTS

I'D LIKE TO THANK THE people of Maui for sharing their mana'o with me, and making space for the strange woman with thick black glasses, who wore long-sleeved shirts (with collars) on the hottest days of summer. I don't know what I was thinking either. Thanks for your patience with my ignorance. Mark Edward Minie offered a different kind of guidance, in scientific form, and pointed me in the direction of relevant articles (at least I knew where I was taking fictional liberties).

I feel extremely fortunate that my literary agent, Jill Marr, saw this piece when it was a short story and thought it would make a great novel—at the time I don't know if I would have agreed, and yet now, here it is. Thanks, Jill. A huge thanks also to Kevin Cleary and John Beach for their unquenchable optimism and hard work on my behalf in the City of Angels.

I'm immensely grateful to Ed Schlesinger and the team at Gallery Books for helping me sort through the complicated strands to make the novel stronger (and presentable). Ed's insight in particular always surfaces things I might have missed, adding dimensions that make the work richer.

Writing takes a lot of time, and this book would not have been possible without the support of my husband, who gives me the space to work, and believes in me more than I do. Often he holds the candle of my dream when I can't. I also find inspiration in my son, who is well on his way to becoming a young man of substance. His journey gives me hope for the future.

ABOUT THE AUTHOR

J. LINCOLN FENN is the critically acclaimed author of *Dead Souls* and *Poe*, which won the Amazon Breakthrough Novel Award for Sci-Fi/Fantasy/Horror. Fenn grew up in New England and graduated summa cum laude from the University of New Hampshire. She lives with her family in Seattle.